PRAI

"*Trident Code* is scary good. The science and technology are as convincing as they are chilling, with an original trifecta of cyber, nuclear, and environmental terrorism all worked into one wild ride of a plot. And hoo boy, you'll love to hate Oleg the Russian mastermind, who is cleverly creepy and unforgettable. Thomas Waite has big ambitions—and delivers on them."

—Dale Dauten, *King Features* syndicated columnist

"*Trident Code* is a powerful and nerve-tingling tale, and its authenticity is right up there with Tom Clancy. Waite gives us brilliant storytelling and a real winner of a book."

—Vice Admiral N.R. Thunman, U.S. Navy (retired) and former Deputy Chief of Naval Operations for Submarine Warfare

"Nobody can accuse Thomas Waite of thinking small, so if you're looking for a fast, awe-inspiring thriller brimming with cybercrime, environmental disaster, and human dilemmas, the only question about *Trident Code* is—can you think big enough?"

—Clare O'Beara, *Fresh Fiction*

Lethal Code

"Taut, tense, and provocative, this frighteningly knowing cyberthriller will keep you turning pages—not only to devour the fast-paced fiction, but to worry about how much is terrifyingly true."

—Hank Phillippi Ryan, Agatha, Anthony, and Mary Higgins Clark award-winning author of *Truth Be Told*

"*Lethal Code* is a compelling and well-researched thriller about a major cyberattack against America. Waite's characters bring to life the very real cyber vulnerabilities we face every day and demonstrate that America's cyber insecurity is a serious national security issue."

—MELISSA HATHAWAY, former cyber advisor to Presidents George W. Bush and Barack H. Obama, now President of Hathaway Global Strategies

"No matter what you do or where you live, a massive cyberattack against the United States will impact your life. That's what Waite demonstrates so convincingly in *Lethal Code*. He shows us the effect a hit to the country's solar plexus would have with a tale that will leave you gasping for days, whether you're a business person or a private citizen concerned about our nation's defense vulnerabilities."

—DAVID DEWALT, Chairman and CEO of network security company FireEye

Terminal Value

"I believe with time he will be called the John Grisham of the murderous technology novels. This is an excellent beginning to what I hope is a long writing career for Mr. Waite."

—*Literary R & R*

"Thomas Waite opens a window into the world of technology that even a technophobe can appreciate. Filled with tension, romance, humor, mystery and avarice, *Terminal Value* is a captivating tale that holds your interest right through to its surprising conclusion."

—DAVID UPDIKE, author of *Old Girlfriends: Stories* and *Out on the Marsh*

"*Terminal Value* is a sizzling thriller convincingly set in the world of emerging technologies that even industry insiders will appreciate. Thomas Waite has earned the right to belly up to the bar with the likes of Brad Meltzer, Scott Turow, and David Baldacci. A great read!"

—PAUL CARROLL, author and Pulitzer Prize-nominated *Wall Street Journal* editor and journalist

UNHOLY CODE

BY THOMAS WAITE

Lana Elkins Thrillers
Lethal Code
Trident Code
Unholy Code

Terminal Value

UNHOLY CODE

THOMAS WAITE

MP
MARLBOROUGH
PRESS

This is a work of fiction. Names, characters, organizations, places, events, and incidents are either products of the author's imagination or are used fictitiously.

Copyright © 2016 Thomas Waite
All rights reserved.

www.thomaswaite.com

No part of this book may be reproduced, or stored in a retrieval system, or transmitted in any form or by any means, electronic, mechanical, photocopying, recording, or otherwise, without express written permission of the author.

Published by Marlborough Press

ISBN-13: 978-1532871122
ISBN-10: 1532871120

Cover design by Stewart A. Williams

Printed in the United States of America

PROLOGUE

JIMMY MCMASTERS DIDN'T MIND working the Labor Day weekend, not when it left him at the helm of a fifty-foot carbon-fiber speedboat racing at 170 mph across the Gulf. The scorching pace thrilled him but scarcely strained the twin turbine engines, which rocketed him past oil platforms that loomed ghostly in the Louisiana mist like prehistoric creatures marching toward land on mighty steel legs.

The honey-haired twenty-two-year-old throttled up to 180, but kept his eyes peeled for debris. At that speed a single ding to the hull could mean death. He was giving the factory-fresh showpiece named *Sexy Streak* a vigorous shakedown for its new owner, who was heading down from Kentucky for the rest of the holiday weekend.

Fully pumped with the raw wonders of speed—and the engines' sharply tuned performance—Jimmy slowed long enough to notice a coastal cruiser on his starboard side. The small open vessel was steaming toward shore, its single engine straining as if overloaded. A moment later Jimmy saw why: the little boat looked as jam-packed as a clown car at the circus.

He assumed its occupants were tourists who'd chartered the twenty-footer for the weekend without having any notion of water safety. His first impulse was to keep a healthy distance between them and *Sexy Streak* to avoid having his beauty rammed by drunken revelers. But the U.S. Coast Guard had been calling on sailors everywhere to keep an eye on any behavior that appeared the least bit suspicious. The nation's defenders needed all the help they could get. ISIS suicide bombers had been penetrating the country's flooded coastlines since the nuclear bombing of an Antarctic ice shelf by Russian hackers four months ago. The strike had dislodged a massive glacier and raised global sea levels by four feet. ISIS invaders hadn't wasted any time exploiting America's newly porous borders and blowing themselves up on arrival. Hundreds of innocents had been slaughtered in malls, baseball stadiums, and on crowded beaches since the terrorist group had announced on the Fourth of July that it was launching a "Summer of Blood."

Jimmy doubted the little boat was any sort of problem. It appeared to pose a threat primarily to itself. Still, he throttled *Sexy Streak* down and raised his binoculars for a closer look.

Holy shit.

Seven fully bearded men were staring at him, the one at the wheel using his own pair of binocs.

Jimmy felt an icy tingle shoot down his spine. He pulled out his phone and punched in a new three-digit emergency code set up by the Coast Guard for shoreline alerts. No connection. No signal this far out. It wouldn't be the first time in recent weeks that a cellular network had been cybersabotaged.

He was preparing to peel away and race for the Port of Oysterton and a land line when he saw more than eyes bearing down on him from the cruiser: two men had raised automatic rifles, and were making no mystery of their target.

Jimmy ducked as bullets ripped into *Sexy Streak*'s starboard hull. He turned the boat sharply away from the gunfire, fleeing as fast as he could, trying hopelessly to outrun the bullets that whizzed by his head.

In seconds, he'd put a half-mile between himself and his assailants. He risked a glance back and saw that the little boat had adjusted its course. It was heading straight for Oysterton's waterfront park, which was already packed for the big Labor Day jamboree.

Jimmy groaned and his stomach sank. He was no hero, and knew he should keep his distance. But he couldn't. The bearded men had the cruiser's inboard motor fully revved as they rushed toward the celebration, clearly bent on spilling their Summer of Blood across a bright white beach.

Jimmy swore to himself and hit the throttle hard, barreling back toward them. Staying low, he heard gunfire kick back up. He hoped like hell he wouldn't catch a round ripping through the lightweight hull.

At the last second, racing at 115 mph with his eyes just above the dash, he swerved and sent a sizeable wake into the cruiser, then pulled away.

The heavy wave rolled the smaller craft to starboard, but it didn't capsize or take on water.

Jimmy throttled up for another pass as the terrorists' craft eked more speed out of its straining engine. It was on course for a beachside bandstand in the park less than a quarter-mile away. From this distance, Jimmy could see the high school band and members of the audience raising their heads and looking out across the water.

This time he didn't think about it. He had no choice, not if he wanted to save those kids. He raced *Sexy Streak* toward the cruiser's bow, leaving his upper body wide open so he could see better. Gunfire sounded and bullets punctured fiberglass and pinged off metal. But Jimmy kept on course, intent on sending an even larger wake at the overloaded boat.

This time he'd cut it too close. The speeding race boat clipped the cruiser's bow, sending *Sexy Streak* careening toward the beach and bandstand, which was festooned with red, white, and blue bunting.

No longer in control, Jimmy killed the engine in a desperate attempt to slow his momentum. But it was too late. He was already plowing up the sand at a frightening speed. He glanced back and saw the cruiser following his course, coming in for the kill.

Bombs, he assumed. *Hundreds dead, with me first.*

Screaming band members in purple and white uniforms jumped to the sand and tumbled to the side to avoid the boats, tripping over fallen instruments in their rush to get out of the way. Audience members panicked too, stumbling over lawn chairs and one another in their hasty retreat.

Jimmy struck the bandstand a second before the cruiser followed suit. The impact shattered *Sexy Streak*'s windshield and showered the craft with old boards and rusty nails, patriotic bunting, drums and cymbals, and a dark-haired piccolo player in a short white skirt with purple boots adorned with pom-poms.

Nobody fell into the cruiser, but its occupants looked every bit as battered as Jimmy felt. Most of the men were cut and bleeding. Then Jimmy realized that he was, too.

Jimmy hoisted up the piccolo player and rolled over the port rail with her onto the sand.

"Stay low," he warned, still fearing the gunmen.

For the first time, Jimmy heard sirens. The local police department appeared to have just arrived. Several officers ran through the rubble, guns drawn.

Still expecting a blast, Jimmy instinctively covered the young woman with his body. A moment later, though, he was shocked to hear one of the bearded men shout, "We surrender." He peeked over the gunwale and saw all but one of them had their hands up. The exception was gripping an arm with a bone sticking out of his skin just below the elbow, red as a gutted gator.

Jimmy's eyes darted back and forth between the terrorists, looking in vain for a suicide bomber or a backpack with a bomb, anything that could hide deadly explosives like the ones that had killed seventy-three men, women, and children in Liberty Square in Philly last weekend, and destroyed the cracked bell that had once rung out for liberty.

He saw nothing suspicious, yet everything was . . . even the way the bearded men offered their bloody hands to be cuffed as they shouted their allegiance to ISIS.

Hundreds of celebrants watched the arrested men in mute shock; others were rushing to attend to their children on the beach. A few used their cellphones to shoot video of the aftermath. Jimmy figured he was already on YouTube, or destined to debut in minutes.

In short order the EMTs had patched up the piccolo player and escorted her and other injured band members to an ambulance. Two police officers shook Jimmy's hand. "We got damn lucky 'cause of you," the huskier one said as they led him to their patrol car. "Could have been a massacre. They had enough ammo for a war. Crashing them onto the beach bought us some time. Way to go, Jimmy."

"I got lucky, too," he replied, still feeling a little numb as he climbed into the cruiser's backseat.

The cops whisked Jimmy over to Oysterton General Hospital, where the nurses and doctors made a big fuss over him. At this point he was catching on: he'd become a local hero.

At no great cost, it seemed. He wasn't too beat up. A few contusions, cuts, but that was it. Bandaged, he headed down to the Shady Lady Lounge that very afternoon, pursued by journalists and camera crews, of course.

He danced with half the house over the next few hours, changing partners so fast their faces blurred as much as the derricks in the mist had earlier, while the drinks—courtesy of friends and strangers alike—provided their own special haze.

Jimmy found the attention of a young gal in a sleeveless LSU tee and short red skirt particularly alluring. By closing time they were hee-hawing in the back of the bar.

Stepping out of the men's a few minutes later, he got an "open invitation"—that was how she put it—from an old girlfriend. He figured the invites would last all summer, if his luck held out.

It didn't. Neither did the nation's.

CHAPTER 1

LANA ELKINS WATCHED THE surrender of the ISIS terrorists on a satellite feed. Their meekness scared her more than any of the brutal suicide bombings of the past few weeks. Gruesome as those attacks had been, there had been nothing secret about their murderous results. But this surrender made no sense.

It's too easy.

This was a mystery. Either ISIS's recruiting standards had softened—and there was no intelligence suggesting that—or the captured men had yet to make their real threats known. Islamists, feared for their willingness to die so they could kill others, simply did not allow themselves to be cuffed and hauled off like common criminals.

Not during the Summer of Blood.

Lana wished she were down in Oysterton to witness this firsthand, not in a large windowless room in the heart of her cybersecurity firm in Bethesda, Maryland. The secure space had been constructed with special metal cladding inside the walls and doors to prevent cyberattacks and signal snooping from others. With proprietary encryption and other cutting-edge information security for their own work—and the U.S. under siege—it had become their war room. All her senior staff were pulling eighteen-hour days at hastily assembled workstations, their mission clear: intercept jihadi communications and provide them immediately to the National Security Agency, which had contracted with Lana, once again, for the special services of CyberFortress.

Lana had also told her staff to "hack to pieces" specific targets promulgating hatred both against westerners and the moderate Muslims who formed the great majority of the faith's followers worldwide. Islamic moderates in the U.S. and elsewhere were now in the crosshairs of the crazies as much as anyone else, if not more so.

And no country was being targeted by the most radical elements of Islam more than the U.S. The intelligence community was coordinating a wide spectrum of strategies to try to thwart the first real invasion of the States since the War of 1812.

The footage showed the bearded men in Oysterton shouting as they were led to a police van. "Can you tell what they're saying?" she asked Jeff Jensen, her VP for security. He'd already called upon one of his former navy colleagues, who was talking to the Oysterton police chief.

"Pretty standard stuff," Jensen replied. "Proclaiming their devotion to the caliphate. At least one of them is speaking in English. He just yelled that thousands of them are already in the U.S. Thousands more are coming."

Bullshit, Lana thought. *Maybe hundreds*. Which was frightening enough.

The consensus of the intelligence community was that mid-size pleasure boats packed with ruthless Islamists had stolen past the hundreds of thousands of government and private vessels trying to escape flooded marinas and ports from Miami to Boston, San Diego to Seattle.

In short, America's vast coastlines had devolved into chaos as owners tried to save their investments from the ravages of rising seas by fleeing to open waters, only to find shifting tides and underwater hazards setting off collisions and sinking countless ships. That created only more hazards, and thus more accidents, leaving the country with the most vulnerable coastlines in the world—and a slow-motion invasion of suicide bombers.

The U.S. Navy and Coast Guard were doing their best, but no federal agency, including the military, had ever drilled for this kind of catastrophe, and the results were apparent every time Lana linked to satellite views of the nation's principal ports. She clicked onto a video feed of the mess in Boston Harbor, where an ocean liner had run aground on a sunken container ship late yesterday, rolling onto its port side. A submarine was cruising past it, along with four fishing trawlers, six luxury cabin cruisers, a three-masted sailboat, and what appeared to be dozens of lookie-loo kayakers, paddle boarders, and canoers. All were squeezing around the half-sunken wreck while a phalanx of tugboats ran thick chains to the fully exposed starboard side of the liner's massive black hull. There had been numerous injuries in the grounding, but no deaths—yet.

In contrast, in the less populated Gulf of Mexico, the biggest concern had been the possibility of attacks on offshore oil platforms, not invasions. But the territory had proved too vast to cover properly. The navy hadn't even had one of its new, heavily armed and fast-moving Mark VI patrol boats anywhere in the vicinity of Oysterton.

Despite all this, shore-dwellers around the country were making do, even managing to party during the holiday weekend. Down on the Gulf, other than in the Big Easy, which had flooded as badly as any city in the world, some folks had been so far removed from the madness that they could still plan on a fun-filled Labor Day.

Lana felt a light tap on her shoulder. Galina Bortnik handed her the phone, whispering, "Mr. Holmes."

Galina was a brilliant young Muscovite hacker whom Lana had helped save from the man who'd been behind the nuclear attack on the Antarctic ice shelf.

"Yes, Mr. Holmes?" Lana was always formal with Bob in the presence of others.

"What do you think?" The deputy director of the NSA rarely minced words with her, especially with the country under fire.

"I'm not buying it," she replied. "How soon is Homeland Security going to get down there and take over?"

"Forty-five minutes. Not soon enough."

She imagined her weary, septuagenarian friend raking his steel-gray hair back, a recently acquired habit when exasperated.

"So far," he said, "we're just lucky there isn't a shoe bomber in that bunch."

"That we know of." Lana glanced at the screen showing the police van driving toward downtown Oysterton. It did not take a hyperactive imagination to envision the vehicle exploding at any second.

"Don't those locals know we have protocols for this sort of apprehension?" Lana asked.

"Evidently not," Holmes replied.

"Send me down," she said.

"We can't do that. I was calling to let you know that they're happy about this in Congress."

"They must really be hungry for heroes."

"Or money. I think they'll be using this capture to push for more local control of our national defense. Anyway, you've been warned about the mountebanks on the Hill."

Lana knew that even small shifts toward decentralizing defense would mean additional federal funding for the locals, which in turn would mean more political support for incumbents who were bringing the pork home. All at a time when the nation desperately needed follow-through on existing *national* directives. Just look at the shoddy police procedures in Oysterton. The cops had run up like they were rushing to an open bar at a barbecue, instead of keeping a safe distance from men who had already fired weapons and might well have bombs.

She took another glance at the monitor, shaking her head at what could still prove to be a debacle down there.

Or a victory. Don't rule that out completely, she told herself.

Galina caught Lana's attention with a slight Slavic nod, pushing black bangs that needed trimming away from her eyes. She was cute as a cocker spaniel, but had a vicious cyber bite, which was why Lana had brought her back to the United States and a job at CyberFortress.

"These close-ups?" she began.

Lana nodded.

"I think they're just enough for screen shots. We could use facial recognition."

"Make it happen," Lana replied.

The video improved measurably when the first television news crew in Oysterton showed a ground-level shot of the local police putting the seven banged-up, bloody men through a perp walk. They were so unprotected a Jack Ruby could have jumped out and killed them all. Instead, they were jostled by freelance news crews and a throng of tourists with cameras.

Jensen had been by Lana's side long enough to read her frustration. "It's a mess. I keep waiting for a bomb to go off."

"They did a quick pat-down before you came in," said a woman with red hair and a swan-like neck from the end of the table. "That's all," she added, shaking her head.

Lana nodded at Maureen, her most recent hire. MIT. Jensen had been her first. He was a navy veteran, a cryptographer during the two Gulf Wars, and a Mormon with five children and a doting wife carrying number six.

There were lots of Mormons in the spy service, as true now as it had been at the height of the Cold War. Lana hadn't known Jensen's religious affiliation during their first interview, but she'd sensed right away that she could trust him. A panoply of deception-detection tests—polygraph, voice analysis, Facial Action Coding Systems, and pupil-size studies—had reinforced her eerily accurate gut. The man was dependable. No vices.

Not true for her. Lana had a failing that could tank her career if she ever let it get the better of her again, as it had several years ago. Of late, Lana had felt the urge to gamble recrudescing, like a tumor that refused to shrivel up and die. It had been tough enough to fight those impulses when she'd actually had to find a poker table or dealer, but with online gaming, the ability to wager any time of the day or night was never farther away than her phone.

She hadn't been to a Gamblers Anonymous meeting in months. Hadn't thought she needed to. She'd been too busy trying to protect the country from cyberattacks, a high-stakes proposition in and of itself. But thoughts of cards and betting had been insinuating themselves into her awareness every few minutes of late, a desire that was potentially career-ending for her. The intelligence community couldn't afford to have operatives falling deep into debt gambling.

You can bet on that.

Gambling lingo, even when she was chastising herself. Although a look at her financial assets—which she forced herself to endure once a month—was sufficient to bring back the wincing memory of her last betting binge. That was when she'd gambled away enough money to have paid for her daughter Emma's college education.

Lana had found professional help, but the sad truth for her was the lure of gambling wasn't only about money. The lure was the thrill that came in the teeming titillating pause that lay between hope and outcome. Not unlike the rush that came from hunting—and finding—cyberterrorists.

Which brought her back to the men claiming to be ISIS: *Who are they, really?* "Any facial recognition yet?"

Galina nodded. "Got it," she said in her Russian accent. "The one who was speaking in English has been identified by NSA as Fahad Kassab. Till two years ago he was studying electrical engineering at Cal Tech. Then he disappeared after traveling to Turkey. NSA thinks he crossed into Syria at some point along the five hundred mile frontier between them. The CIA says he fought in Mosul and Saladin, Iraq."

"So he's a veteran," Lana said, "which means this inept display down there *really* makes no sense."

"What did Holmes say about Homeland Security?" Jeff asked Lana, who glanced at her watch.

"They're flying in from Camp Blanding," she answered. "North Florida," she added for Galina's benefit. Galina hadn't been in the States long enough to know the location of hundreds of military bases and installations in the U.S., many now threatened by the extensive flooding. "They should be there in half an hour."

But Lana strongly suspected that every minute the self-proclaimed ISIS crew remained in the hands of those local yokels made the country that much more vulnerable to whatever their controllers had set in motion. She didn't like mysteries—not in books, movies, and definitely not when she was dealing with murderers who planned to die with their secrets. And in combating horrific terrorist attacks, thirty minutes could be an eternity. A lot could go wrong—*no, everything could go wrong*—in a half-hour. In a world that had made a mockery of geologic time by raising seas in weeks to levels that should have taken eons, days and months— even years—had been wrenched free of real meaning. Now terrorism not only killed people, it also murdered the notion that time itself could be measured on a rational human scale.

When the monitor finally showed the dark-suited men from Blanding racing up to the police station, she took a break and walked down the hall to the bathroom.

She didn't need the facilities. She needed to look herself in the eye and say, *No, don't do it.* She needed the forcefulness of those words to really register. They did not.

Reaching into her pocket, she stepped past the door and pulled out a private phone on which she'd created an encrypted connection to a private server. Then she hit the app for *Texas Hold 'em.*

So far all Lana was holding was her cell and her breath.

Don't. Don't. Don't.

She slipped into a stall, hiding herself much as she kept her addiction from everyone but those in her Gamblers Anonymous group. Nobody in the intelligence community knew about it.

Stop it, she told herself.

She'd have fired anyone, even Jeff Jensen, if she ever found such a weakness in them.

Lana drew a deep breath, assuring herself that she was okay, that she'd avoided the only pitfall that could sink her family, career, and financial well-being.

She reached for the door handle to leave. It felt cold, almost icy, a testament to how gambling could turn up her body's thermostat. She stepped out and looked in the mirror. Several strands of wiry gray hair poked from her scalp, unruly as her addiction. She plucked each one, as if she were exorcising more than the telltales of age, but when she looked back at her face she saw blatant excitement in her eyes: exuberant expression, shaky hands—the glitter of gambling sprinkled over the whole of her. Then she felt a familiar itch in her fingers—as she had many times before—and a shock to her system as startling as adrenaline.

Lana was so well practiced at using her phone that she was back in the gambling app without having to think about her motions.

She drew a jack.

She drew another jack.

She won.

But it felt like the fear she'd known with the arrest of those terrorists, a keen sense that winning the first round was the worst thing that could possibly happen.

Get out of here. Quit while you're ahead. You've got a kid up to her neck in trouble.

Which was the unerring truth. Her seventeen-year-old daughter's life had taken an edgy turn, and Lana's ex-husband, so recently reunited with his family, was hopeless in dealing with his daughter's recent decisions.

You're not doing much better with her. Or yourself.

Seconds ago Lana's life hadn't simply veered off course. She'd taken a dive, like a bribed boxer, and had hit the mat so hard she was still shaking as she dragged herself back to the conference room.

Jeff caught her eye immediately and waved her over. "Take a look at this. Hey, you okay?"

"I'm fine," Lana replied, pressing her hands to her sides to steady them.

Jeff nodded at a large screen. Steel Fist, the online identity of a notorious neo-Nazi and hacker, was operational once again on his website, *For the Homeland—Ready!*

Steel Fist was not only back but he'd also managed to intercept the satellite video of the arrests at the Oysterton beach. Less than an hour ago, Jensen had exploited the neo-Nazi's server and encrypted all of his data, per Lana's instructions, but Steel Fist had resurrected *For the Homeland—Ready!* from the Dark Web so swiftly that the speed of recovery itself was frightening.

These hidden realms of the Internet remained a cyber netherworld whose denizens included gun runners, drug dealers, despots, sex slavers, and all manner of hackers and haters—along with whistleblowers and others with high-minded ambitions. Almost all the mayhem for money was conducted anonymously with encrypted currencies that caused huge headaches for intelligence communities around the world.

The Dark Web was also the redoubt of Steel Fist. Whoever he was, wherever he was based, the demagogue was a supremely gifted purveyor of hate with a huge following in the U.S. and Europe.

As Lana watched, his home page filled with flashing freeze frames of each terrorist now in the Oysterton jail. Below the photos ran this message:

"Look at the face of America's future. Sharia law is coming to kill you, your wife, your kids, your life. Grab your guns. It's time to turn your targets into corpses. You know who needs to die. Kill them now. Spare none."

The pace of the flashing photos accelerated till they blurred and turned in an instant to grinding surveillance footage of the bombing in Liberty Square, showing only the white victims. "ISIS's brothers and sisters are killing you. More are pouring across our pathetic borders every day. This is their Summer of Blood." Video appeared of the high-school kids with their instruments jumping from the bandstand as the boats crashed into it. "You know who needs to die" rolled across the screen again. "Kill them all."

"Whoever this guy is, he just declared war on America's Muslims," Jeff said. "He's putting the moderates of their faith in the crosshairs."

"Which means he's declaring war on everyone who stands for basic decency." Lana realized that her hands had stopped shaking. She'd dodged the bullet in the bathroom—*maybe*—only to find an arsenal of threats on-screen. Steel Fist wasn't merely another Internet thug with a big mouth. He had more than ten million followers, hundreds of thousands of hits a day. Never had the aggressive tone of that term sounded more ominous to her.

When Steel Fist called for death, body counts rose.

Civil war in America?

She swore softly to herself, respecting Jeff's devoutly held religious beliefs. Lana also left unsaid her rising fear that the nation was about to become as divided as she was—between its best impulses and its worst.

One of the firm's receptionists opened the door to the conference room and motioned to her.

"I'm sorry, but it's an emergency," the young woman said. "Someone from the Senate wants to see you."

The Senate?

A stately woman waited for her by the front desk. "Lana Elkins?"

"Yes?"

She handed Lana an envelope. "You've been summoned by the United States Senate Select Committee on Intelligence."

CHAPTER 2

THERE WAS BLOOD ON the water. You'd swear that was true. Crimson streaks from the northern Idaho sunset. Vinko Horvat stood on the shoreline with his border collie Biko, studying the shifting colors, red as the anger that once defined Hayden Lake, blurred as the region's memory. Two decades ago it had been home to the Aryan Nations until a lawsuit left the white supremacists broke and homeless. They'd lost their compound after their idiot guards shot up a local's car—with locals in it. That was not how you conducted yourself if you were keeping your eyes on the prize.

But Hayden Lake had a proud white heritage, even if many in the mountain town wanted to set it aside once and for all. And Vinko Horvat knew the little town's legacy was more important than ever, now with the country's borders wide open as a beer cooler at a biker picnic. His own heritage was no less vital to him, extending back many decades and three generations of Horvat men to the Nazi-created Independent State of Croatia.

He lifted his eyes from the lake as the sun settled behind a distant mountain, then headed back toward his barn, snapping his fingers to bring Biko to heel. As he approached the large looming structure he heard his goats bleating inside. Gallas from Africa, of all places. "Super goats." That's what the breeders called them. Gallas had tough teeth, produced a ton of milk, and could take African heat. It had been getting plenty hot in Idaho, too.

Horvat threw open a wide barn door. Biko backed up the goats, kids chasing their nannies' teats. Gallas matured twice as fast as other breeds and reproduced as fast as Muslims.

Muslims.

He forced himself to use the proper noun, not the many epithets that came so easily to the tongue. He'd trained himself never to use such words, never to appear as vigorously stupid as his Aryan Nations predecessors. But he wrote about Muslims, posted about them nearly every day. Long ago he'd said hordes of them would be coming, and now they were. Didn't take a prophet to see something that obvious, just a good listener.

Muslims—all of them, no matter what they said—never made a secret of their plans. The only time they'd ever confused him was with their easy surrender, down in Louisiana. Probably had the same effect on anyone with more than half a brain, but that's all those southern cops seemed to have—half a brain and not one cell more. *And those cretins are protecting our borders? People should think about that.*

To Vinko, the biggest wonder of all was that there wasn't a turban in the White House by now, other than the man who'd been in disguise the whole time he'd occupied the presidency. *Hussein? Are you kidding me?* There was no figuring the American people, except to conclude the obvious: half a brain.

But Vinko knew you worked with what you had. And he'd been making significant inroads with his fellow citizens. They were starting to see the truth. It had gotten a lot easier since the bombing of Antarctica and the surging of the seas. Terrible, to be sure, but it might just wake America up, and if it did that, well, a man could argue—*privately*, of course—that the bombing was a good thing, especially if he'd had the foresight to stay inland where there were fish and fresh water and a blood-red sunset to remind you of why you'd never left your family's land.

Biko kept the goats at bay while Vinko drove his tractor into the barn, though the Gallas were smarter than most people when it came to surviving. They did not wander at night. This was cougar country. A big cat could devour one of those floppy-eared creations in a single sitting. Plenty of coyotes around, too, running in packs. Cougars could start doing that as well. Animals adapt, man included. Right now "adapting"—surviving—meant guns and ammunition. On his website, *For the Homeland—Ready!*, he'd been repeating a simple message for years: "Ammo up!"

They're sure listening now.

Trouble was, they weren't the only ones. Some hacker had taken him down exactly at 11:00 a.m. this morning. *The eleventh hour.* Were they sending him a warning? Had they identified him? The hacking had sure shocked the shit out of Vinko. Four years of computer engineering at Boise State, another sixteen studying the Dark Web's deepest secrets, then setting up alternating proxy servers and running the most sophisticated cyberdefenses—only to have some son-of-a-bitch knock him down like he was no more formidable than a bowling pin.

But that wasn't the real shocker. Before he could even begin a digital forensics operation, his website had come back to life. He would have liked to take credit for the quick comeback, but he couldn't. The help had come from elsewhere. A powerful force had put him back in business with a private message that had been haunting his evening walk with Biko:

You have a guardian angel, Steel Fist. I am here to keep your message online. You are doing the Lord's work. Your enemies are crude. They don't know who you are or where you're based. But I do.

Those words still gnawed at him as he closed the barn door and strode back to his big log house and stepped inside.

But I do.

A religious type, a real believer, had identified him, claimed to know where he lived. Not a little ironic because Vinko didn't share any hope for a heavenly presence. But a guardian angel? If some hacker wanted to call himself that and fight back on his behalf, Vinko wasn't going to protest. But an urgency was now upon him. The walk had finally crystallized one major concern about the day's disturbances: if his so-called guardian angel could put him back online, he could also have been the hacker who'd taken him down. Someone who might be toying with him for reasons Vinko could not yet imagine.

He now paused only long enough to drink a cold glass of goat milk before heading back to his office, a room that looked as sleek and pristine as any clean room in Silicon Valley.

He needed the latest and most sophisticated gear. Cyberchaos was taking down America. He'd been spared till eleven o'clock this morning, but for weeks hackers had taken aim at rescue efforts trying to save cities and coastlines from the flooding. Dams, bridges, pumping stations, and large-scale sanitation plants had been caught in the crosshairs of America's most dedicated enemies. But one development Vinko could not accept—and never would—was that almost two months ago the government had "accidentally" released almost a thousand pages of documents online that demonstrated how simple it would be to cyberattack a long list of power and water industrial control systems. They showed that if a cybersaboteur disconnected a generator from the grid, it would immediately speed up because it no longer had any load. Then, if it were reconnected to the grid, tremendous damaging force would be exerted on the generator as it tried to bring it back into sync. A blueprint for all that had quickly followed.

We're supposed to believe that bullshit was a mistake? When it made it easier for terrorists to come in and kill us?

You'd have to be a madman to accept that excuse at face value. Vinko had been called a lot, but never a madman. Possessed by the importance of his mission, yes. But not mad.

With his website back online, he planned to conduct a thorough disk and memory analysis to determine who his guardian angel was. Just one critical task had to take precedence: the prime-time posting of files packed with data he'd obtained from penetrating the NSA—unless he were taken offline again before he could deliver his priceless trove. He'd feared the files had been destroyed by the hacker, but the takedown had been the crudest form of cybersabotage and it left those files fully intact. Every page showing the secretive U.S. agency was *still* mining and amassing private information on millions of Americans.

He started uploading the files in seconds, working his keyboard like a pianist tickling the ivories, the tap-tap-tapping soothing and reassuring—with data that would enrage his followers.

With those files in motion, he began sending out teasers to his faithful: "Are you ready? Tell me you're ready to see your government's latest crimes." Most of his readers had signed up for alerts when he went live.

Vinko sat back and waited, scratching Biko's ear. The dog leaned into his master's ranch-hardened fingers. Even the pinky that wouldn't straighten could exert strong pressure, the sole injury that the six-foot-four-inch Vinko had sustained while quarterbacking the Boise State Broncos for four years.

Thousands, then tens of thousands of encouraging messages started pouring into Hayden Lake. Vinko's entire operation was powered by solar panels that harvested bright mountain sunshine from every square inch of the roofs of his large home and barn. Each kilowatt counted now with power outages afflicting so many other Americans.

He checked to make sure the files were live, then turned serious: "Go ahead, look for yourself," he told his subscribers. "You'll probably find that you've been spied on, too. Ed Snowden was a creep, a criminal leftist and a turncoat, but he was right about government surveillance. That's where the political right and left come together, folks. Not to kiss and make up, but to kick the government's sneaky ass."

He let those words sink in, imagining the NSA files cascading down across the country like the braided sparkling streams that ran into the lake. He felt as if he'd just thrown another touchdown pass to "Bones" Jackson, his tight end his senior year. They'd tolerated each other. Bones, a junior college transfer, had shaken his head when he'd learned the white quarterback hailed from Aryan Nations country. But business was business, and big-time college football was nothing if not business.

Vinko slid his chair forward and resumed his tap-tap-tapping. "If I can access this info, America's enemies can, too. Your government can't protect your borders and they can't protect your most private information. Enemies could target any one of you, and every one of you is important to them. They have your home address, where you work, the schools your children attend. The NSA has it all. Your bank records, data on your phone calls. They've cracked your encryption codes, scooped up your text messages, IP addresses, webcam images, and even your online games. THEY KNOW EVERYTHING ABOUT YOU. And now they're targeting me. The NSA took me down this morning." He hadn't confirmed that yet, but blaming the agency was too easy to pass up. "But they couldn't keep me down, and they can't keep you down, either. Not if we stay strong and fight back. They have plenty to answer for."

He uploaded more video of bombings already familiar to his followers. "Look at Liberty Square. Look at Turner Field in Atlanta, King of Prussia Mall in Pennsylvania. Those surveillance cameras tell the whole sorry story, don't they?

"It's time your friends and family and neighbors opened their eyes just like you. They'll see that the dark-skinned hordes we've been trying to cull for years just keep coming.

"Ammo up, America! Ammo up!"

Three minutes later, just as he was about to begin his forensic study of this morning's cyberattack, his guardian angel hacked into a highly encrypted communications channel that Vinko reserved for a select few and left him a message: "Lana Elkins took you down."

While Vinko had been uploading, the guardian angel must have been finishing his own investigation. Lana Elkins made immediate sense to him. She was an infamous NSA contractor who hadn't been able to keep herself out of the headlines because she'd been so deeply involved in the cyberwars—*and* kinetic battles—of the past two years, though he had to question her effectiveness lately, given the paltry state of the country's defenses.

Vinko had long suspected that the reason the NSA used private contractors was they would be less constrained by government surveillance guidelines, in practice if not in law. From what he'd seen, the contractors were basically given a license to create as much cybermayhem as they wanted, much as America's military snipers and unmanned drones were sanctioned to take out anyone deemed an enemy.

He wondered for fleeting seconds whether Elkins had taken him down *and* put him back up, toggling to torment him.

Or maybe setting him up somehow.

No matter. He'd fire back at her hard and fast by using the most fundamental threat of all, the one that wasn't written into government guidelines for spying and hacking. The lone threat that *always* worked.

His grandfather and great-grandfather had known all about it. They had both been members of the Ustase, an organization of violent extremists who formed the backbone of the Nazi puppet state of Croatia. Both the Ustase and their German backers knew what you had to do to Serbs, Jews, Roma, and communists. You had to exterminate them like so much vermin—upwards of one hundred thousand harvested during those war years. Then they buried them in pits or on the banks of the Sava and Una Rivers, where flooding periodically still unearthed their bones to this day.

Vinko's grandfather had been nostalgic about those years, especially the way he'd played the intelligence game to maximum advantage. Once the Ustase reign had been defeated, he'd provided information on the communists overrunning Yugoslavia to the Americans. In return, the country's fledgling CIA had given his family safe haven in northern Idaho.

Before his grandfather died from lymphoma, he'd told his young grandson that the Muslims were worse than the Jews. "Back during the war we had to put up with those ragheads, but we hated them. We never would have put up with their shit now, not with what they're doing."

An angry man, even while dying, though the seven-year-old Vinko had been more confused than convinced by the old man's words. But he'd noticed his father listening in, nodding the whole time.

Then, when Vinko was nine, his dad had walked him down to the lake, as he had many times for an afternoon of fishing. But that day was different. After casting his line, he'd gestured to the majesty of the mountains and told his son that he deeply loved their home. "The CIA knew what they were doing when they moved Grandpa to the mountains. It's ninety-nine percent pure."

Vinko hadn't known what his father meant, either.

"Look at the water, boy."

Vinko peered at its smooth surface and saw his reflection.

"Your face is white as the clouds, isn't it? Just like everyone else you see around here."

Vinko understood. He'd never known anybody who wasn't white.

They'd fished until sundown. After gathering up their gear, his father told him to look at the water again. The blood-red colors had appeared, darkening the boy's face.

"You're no longer white. That's what's going to happen if we let the sun set on America. The white will disappear, and we'll pay for it with blood."

His father had been right. The men in his family had all known that the most important threat of all wasn't a gun or a knife, or even the mongrel races raging to get everything that belonged to whites. But it *was* all about blood.

Vinko began dishing it out by posting a full-color photo of Lana Elkins. Her bio as well. Then the address for CyberFortress, along with a photo and the address of her home. Next, he offered maps of her possible routes to and from work.

"Know your enemies," he wrote. "She attacked me today."

But he was hardly through. Now for the final stroke. He added a picture of Emma Elkins, Lana's daughter, and another shot, an especially incendiary one of the young woman with her boyfriend. He added their bios, too, and the name of their high school. Their routes to and from school.

Tap-tap-tapping into a mother's greatest fear, which was also Vinko's burning hope: that the photo of the girl and her boyfriend would galvanize his followers, even the ones with half a brain. But in case they had any doubt about his intentions, he posted his two most persuasive words right below the smiling faces of the two high school kids:

"Ammo up!"

CHAPTER 3

LANA LEFT CYBERFORTRESS AT nine-thirty. With summer fading, the sky had finally darkened. Traffic was light, the norm these days, as gasoline shortages still plagued most regions of the country. While supertankers received top priority at the nation's ports, deliveries had been significantly hampered by the flooding and maritime crisis. The Port of Long Beach in southern California was completely shut down, as were ports in Seattle, Oakland, Galveston, and Miami. In fact, most of Florida's harbors remained an unmitigated mess.

As a contractor for the NSA, Lana received priority gas allotments at Fort Meade, where the agency had its headquarters and where she had a meeting scheduled with Deputy Director Holmes in the morning. With an economical subcompact, her fuel needs were light, but she still planned to top off her tank after the meeting.

Her ex-husband Don had texted her just before she left CF to see when she'd be home. "*He's* here," had been his parting words.

Don had abandoned Lana's and Emma's lives for fourteen years, reuniting with his family only after last year's terrifying crisis in which he applied his navigating skills as a Caribbean pot pirate to saving Lana and Emma from horrific deaths. His reappearance after all that time had been a surprising but ultimately pleasing turn of events for all three.

Lana took the turnoff for home knowing that a heavy emphasis on "he" in Don's world referred to Sufyan Hijazi, Emma's first serious boyfriend. Lately, Don hadn't been able to bring himself to say the young man's name.

Lana faced her own challenges with Sufyan, who had emigrated to the U.S. with his family from the Sudan when the boy was nine years old. He'd grown into a strikingly handsome guy, but with the ever-serious mien of a devout Muslim. Emma had met him at school, where he was in the a cappella choir. She'd tried to persuade him to audition for the award-winning Capitol City Baptist Choir, which was more ecumenical than the name might suggest. Emma herself didn't identify as a Baptist, and at this time was trending more toward Sufyan's passionate beliefs in Islam. Which frankly worried her mother. Lana had jettisoned her Catholicism in her first year of college on her initial foray into what she viewed as intellectual freedom. She'd never looked back and would have liked her daughter to relish the same sense of open inquiry.

Sufyan had refused to consider the church choir, and after the two had been seeing each other for six weeks Emma stopped going to Sunday school and began attending services at Sufyan's mosque. She'd also taken up Quran studies. All of this was a sharp departure from the churchy comforts the young woman had clearly enjoyed last year.

Emma still made it to weekly services at Capitol City Baptist, which was mandatory for choir members who, after all, were there to sing. But Lana wondered how long Emma would continue under the spiritual and musical direction of Pastor Barnes. Already Emma's closest friend in the choir, Tanesa, had grown distant from her.

Lana pulled into the garage and watched the double door shut behind her, always conscious of her personal security—she was now licensed to carry a concealed weapon in Maryland and DC—and walked into her gracious home, steeling herself for whatever might follow.

Don was standing by the kitchen island, mixing himself a coconut rum drink, maybe reminding himself of his high life in the Caribbean. Since last year's high-seas adventure, Don had been assessing flood damage in harbors on Chesapeake Bay. Pretty sedate for a man who'd been accustomed to flight-or-fight gigs, first by moving tons of bud from Colombia and Mexico, then, following his arrest, as a DEA informant.

He smiled at her and held up the Bacardi. She shook her head. "Scotch, straight up."

"Oh, one of *them* days, I see."

"Yup, one of them days. You?"

"Don't ask."

Even as he'd settled into domestic life he maintained the pleasantly shaggy appearance and sun-bleached strands of a boatman. Brackish scents of the sea still rose from his skin and collar when she kissed him. She wouldn't mind if he'd shave every day but he did wield a soap brush and razor when it counted, and it counted often enough that she had no cause for complaint in their bedroom.

She set her computer case on a counter and glanced at her phone, trying to put aside the winning pair of jacks that still tugged at her attention. She settled on a stool at the island. "So what's our spawn up to? Or dare I ask?"

"My guess," Don lowered his voice, "is they're rutting like crazed weasels, no matter what his religion thinks they should be doing." He made an unseemly gesture and grimaced.

"She's seventeen. She's responsible about birth control."

Don shook his head.

"Don't be such a dad," Lana said. "You weren't a virgin at that age either."

"But at least I had the decency not to do it with my father twenty feet away."

"You're not twenty feet away. They're upstairs and I don't hear a thing."

"I'd rather Sufi," Don's pointed nickname for Sufyan, "took his sex drive and religion elsewhere."

"The more you push her on that stuff, the more she'll push back."

"It's not me I'm worried about, it's *his* father, or uncle, or whatever he is."

"Uncle." Which Don knew; he was just being difficult. Sufyan's father had been killed in the Sudanese civil war, which spurred the family's emigration to America. Amazing what Don could try to forget, which was just about everything when it came to the Hijazi clan—except that they were Muslims.

Lana lifted the tumbler and let the Scotch warm her chest and belly before going on: "You've got to be careful, Don. You're starting to sound like a bigot. It's not appealing."

"I don't care about his skin color—"

"I know, but it's still—"

"You can't tell me you're happy she's going to a mosque. Studying the Quran."

"I'm working on my attitude, okay? I'd rather have a good relationship with a Muslim daughter, if it comes to that, than no relationship. I want her to have the life she wants, not what you or I might want. And moderate Muslims are getting it from all sides these days. I don't want any part of that. Not from you, not from anyone."

Lana looked him in the eye. No sense dancing around the subject any longer. She'd been warming up to Don. Well, more than warming up, but his attitude toward Sufyan was starting to harden. Don was better than that, or at least she hoped he was. Bigotry was a deal-breaker for Lana. "How long have they been up there?" she asked, changing the subject.

He looked at his watch. "Ninety-four minutes. But who's counting?"

That did ease a smile from her.

"And it's a *school* night," he pleaded playfully.

"I'm sure their hormones noticed." Lana finished her drink with a gulp. "I'll go."

She walked upstairs to Emma's room, listening closely as she approached. She found them quiet as church mice. *Or mosque mice*, she thought. Lana knocked gently. "It's me, Em. It's getting kind of late, don't you think?"

"Yes," Emma squeaked.

Definitely sex. "I think you'd better call it a night."

"Why, Mom?"

More bold than breathy now. Probably the first time Emma had used the breathing exercise Lana had taught her for steadying her nerves. Now if she'd only think about that when her temper flared.

The front doorbell chimed.

"Don, would you get that?" she called down the stairs. A final tap on the bedroom door: "So please finish your homework and come down. Sufyan, I'm sorry but it's time to go."
Homework? What a euphemism.
"Where is he?" Lana heard in a loud, distinctly African cadence downstairs.
"Sufyan, your uncle is here," she said before heading back down.
Tahir Hijazi stood erect as a soldier in the tiled entryway, a tall bald man with skin as perfectly smooth as burnished mahogany. His eyes rose to her, unblinking, intense. Hunter's eyes. This was only their second meeting. The first had been outside the high school. He'd been curt as a bodyguard, which Lana suspected was the role he'd taken with the young man. If possible, he appeared even less pleased now.
"Are they up there in a bedroom?" he demanded.
"They're coming down," she replied evenly, doing her best to avoid his question. Her words quickly proved insufficient to that task.
"Were you supervising them, or was your . . . daughter alone with my nephew?"
Lana bristled as she stepped into the living room, having no difficulty imaging how he'd almost described Emma: *Whore. Kafir.* Which meant infidel.
"I believe they were upstairs doing their homework."
"So Sufyan has been alone in her *bedroom.* How long?"
Lana glanced at Don, who looked ready to explode at Tahir. She tried to warn him with her eyes, but Don's were glaring at the man.
"We're not keeping a clock on them," Lana replied.
The pair started down the staircase. Emma looked flushed, hair unkempt, face moist. *Christ, could she have been a little more obvious?* And Sufyan looked as rumpled as a laundry basket.
"Get in the car," Tahir snapped at the young man, who remained by Emma's side. "And you," he pointed a long finger in Emma's face. "Stay away—"
"Put your hand down or I'll break it," Don said, moving toward Tahir as he spoke.
"No, Dad!" Emma cried.

"Please," Sufyan said softly to his uncle.

Tahir lowered his hand, but not his voice or eyes. "You stay away from him. You are not his kind. You are not our kind."

Sufyan stared at his uncle. He looked scared.

"I love him, and he loves me," Emma said, taking Sufyan's hand. "So good luck with that attitude."

Lana, for the first time, was happy to see her daughter's defiance. Tahir had not only insulted her, he'd come close to slandering Emma.

"Keep her away from him," Tahir growled at Lana. "This is dangerous."

Don seized Tahir's arm as the man started for the door. "Don't you ever come in here again and start threatening anyone."

Tahir looked down at Don's grip, then gazed at both of Emma's parents. "You really don't know, do you?" He ripped his arm free and pulled out his phone.

"Know what?" Lana demanded, no longer so even-keeled herself.

Tahir raised his phone, showing them the Steel Fist website. At the top of the screen clenched fingers gripped a brutal-looking band of chrome knuckles. Right below it was a photo of Emma and Sufyan. Scrolling down, he revealed an angry command: "Ammo Up!"

"Now they want to kill you, too," he said to Lana. "But you are grown up. He is not. His life is ahead of him. I saved that boy when he was nine. I took him away from soldiers who were killing everyone in our village. His father was already dead. I brought him and his mother to America. I am not going to have him die for the love of *her*." He stared at Emma, then pointed to the screen. "See, they show how they go to school. To *school*."

His voice shook, no longer with anger but agonized fear, and in that moment Lana understood how much he loved his nephew.

"You, too," he said to her, regaining his composure. "They show how you get to work and come home." But he wasn't through with Emma. "Wrong skin," he said to her. "Wrong religion. *Wrong*."

He threw open the door. A single glance at Sufyan drove the young man out the door.

"What was that picture?" Emma asked as soon as her dad locked up, pulling out her own phone. "Why was he showing you that? And what's Steel Fist? You're going to stop them, right?"

"Yes, we'll stop them," Lana said, putting her arm around Emma. "Come on, let's get some sleep."

Her daughter pulled away. "I'm not going to stop seeing him. No way."

"Can we talk about all of this in the morning?"

"No," Emma said, bolting toward the stairs. "Not if any part of the discussion involves my not seeing him." She pounded up the stairs and disappeared behind her door, no doubt to grab her phone and find out about those photos.

Lana turned to Don. "From now on, we need to start double-checking all the locks and the alarm system. I'll talk to Holmes about getting you licensed to carry. Meantime, we'll keep the 12 gauge on your side of the bed. I'll hold onto my Sig Sauer."

Lana had taken firearms training at the FBI Academy at Marine Corps Base Quantico in Virginia. Don's martial tactics had been honed less formally among dope dealers and armed guerillas in the jungles of South America. Over the summer, they'd upgraded their home security with steel doors and polymer-coated windows to stop bullets. Don had yet another idea to up their defenses:

"We need a protection dog. It's too easy to short-circuit alarms."

"I'm all for it," she said. "Can you look into it?"

"I'm on it," he replied. "Who's Steel Fist?"

"The worst," Lana replied, pulling out her laptop. "The worst."

CHAPTER 4

I'M THE GUARDIAN ANGEL.

It's such a Christian idea—and so at odds with my own beliefs—that I take particular delight in using it. But it's true: I've been looking over Steel Fist's shoulder for almost four years. Actually, let's use his real name—Vinko Horvat—and dispense with the juvenile theatrics of his macho *nom de guerre*. I have one, too: Golden Voice. But it's a tool to me, nothing more, whereas Vinko takes his pseudonym seriously. He believes he's penetrated CyberFortress and the NSA, and he did, but only after I left him a trail of cyber breadcrumbs. Without me, Vinko would be nothing but another American demagogue shouting into the vast echo chamber of the Internet.

Instead, he's championed by millions because he—*I*—give them what they want most in a time of devastation and deprivation: an eager outlet for their grievances against their government. And let us not overlook the importance that naturally underlies their most vociferous complaint—the legitimate fear that the U.S. military can't protect them from the forces now killing citizens with abandon.

To put it yet another way, the people Vinko reaches and enrages really do have reason to hate their leaders, and he plays off their anger with the mordant skill of a born Machiavellian.

Their loathing grows daily, and hatred is a great galvanizing force. It not only brings angry, frustrated people together, it sticks to everyone it touches—just like the blood it spills, which is as red as the fires I stoke every night.

I built this home on a mountain ridge in central Washington state nine years ago, carefully crafting wood forms for the fireplace and chimney. Hard work was better than grabbing an automatic rifle and finding a bell tower, though that impulse—born of good reason—haunted me long enough to buy the weapon and search out possible locations.

But I stuck to homebuilding, at least for awhile, pouring a ton and a half of cement to make that chimney rise up. The wood grain is visible on the concrete that faces me now. I never covered it with tiles or metal cladding. I like the bald utilitarian appearance. It's at one with the Douglas-fir logs I used for the home itself, eight hundred square feet. But don't go confusing me with the Unabomber because this is no shack, and I cared nothing for his anarchism. By comparison to his hovel, my home is like living in a finely constructed armoire with cedar walls, fir floors, cherry wood cabinets, and a three-hundred-foot sleeping loft.

The chimney draws smoke smoothly. Nevertheless, I prod the logs every now and then with a wrought-iron poker just to see sparks fly. They might have inspired me because it didn't take me long after settling in here to realize that I could also prod Americans every day by stoking their fears, and that my best weapon wouldn't be an Army-issue automatic rifle but an even deadlier weapon: the computer. And I'd been well-trained to use it.

So every day I stoke the panic of Americans. But they're not fools. Fools fear ghosts in the attic and voodoo at their back door. Americans face real terror. And Vinko? He's the accelerant I throw onto their fire.

I've done a lot to make his threats blaze even brighter. You must have figured out by now, for instance, that the government did not inadvertently release those thousand pages detailing the weak links in America's most vital infrastructure, along with fanciful methods for how they could be hacked. You don't really believe that pap, do you?

I hacked those files and released them on the Homeland Security website. But the Department of Defense could hardly stand before the

American people and say, "We gave away the keys to the kingdom." Of course not. They fell on the sword of "inadvertence," preferring to look vaguely incompetent than definably weak, failing to realize that in cyberwar those two words are synonymous. That was why they offered such a dense technical explanation when they announced the "penetration." (Well, they had been royally fucked, now hadn't they?) Their exegesis was so bewildering that it made no sense, especially to me. But I was hardly going to point out that the emperor had no clothes. Besides, Vinko did exactly what I expected of him. He pounced on the government's purported failure like a cougar on a hare.

I play the long game. I always have. Vinko believes he does, too, because he's been hacking government sites for six years without getting caught. But the long game is the length of your life *and* what you pass on to those who will carry your flame.

I've come to know Vinko better than he knows himself. I've sensed the excitement in his fingertips when he's gained access to Defense Department secrets. And when he released those NSA files last night I remembered how he used to smile with every success. But that was years ago, before he discovered that someone had turned on his computer camera. He immediately ended my surveillance by sealing the lens and has remained far too stealthy for that kind of exposure now.

And his shrewdness came through, once again, when he dispatched those photos of Lana Elkins, her daughter, and the girl's black Muslim beau. Red meat for that crowd. And the maps of their daily commute? Vinko's very own cyber crumbs.

He knows how to pander to his subscribers. That's where *he* excels. My effectiveness with him lies in giving him the truth. It's taken a long time but I sense that he's beginning to trust me. I noticed that he blamed his takedown on Lana Elkins *before* he made any attempt to confirm what I'd told him. The confirmation will come easily enough—I've made sure of that—but taking my word for what happened to him was a critical step.

When he does his own digging, he'll also find that while the attack originated at CyberFortress, it was not from Lana Elkins exactly. It hailed from Jeff Jensen. When he discovers that, it will make him feel smarter than his anonymous helper. I want him to feel smarter than me.

Eventually, I'll even let him find that Elkins has a weakness for gambling. I know she won a hand of *Texas Hold 'em* online yesterday by drawing a second jack. After compromising that gambling site and installing a back door, I'd waited months for the alert that Elkins had returned to it. And it was I who made sure she got her second jack. I'd have happily dealt her a third, if she'd needed it.

I'm luring her in much the same way I lured Vinko, by playing to what might prove her greatest weakness. Her $137 win will twitch in the back of her mind. That's the seductive nature of addiction. The desire burns softly, invisibly, until it bursts into flame with the sudden onslaught of irrepressible need. Elkins and those like her can turn the flame back down, but the memory of pleasure doesn't die quickly; its dissolution is slow and inversely related to the speed of a quickening pulse.

So the heat lingers for the Lanas of the world, wrapping them in temptation until they succumb, blinding themselves to everything but pure want. Until that delicious tipping point comes, Lana will tell herself that she can beat her addiction, but I will do my best not to let that happen. I'll replace the ads on her phone with ever more enticing ones. Cards will appear on her screen with jingle-jangle casino sounds, and when she sees them landing on green felt they'll whisper of the silent thrills she's known so many times before.

She'll submit.

But . . . if she manages somehow not to compromise herself with gaming, then in all likelihood she'll be at those Gamblers Anonymous meetings to rendezvous with others who share her weakness, a move that will expose her mercilessly.

Fascinating, the way the holders of the nation's secrets unburden themselves to complete strangers in a church or civic meeting hall. Not everyone who attends those sessions is of good will. That was how I observed Lana firsthand. Once I even sat next to her. We exchanged knowing, empathic nods when a man spoke of emptying his family's nest egg to bet on the "ponies," as he referred to them affectionately. When he finished, Elkins rose to admit that she had also squandered unconscionable sums. I nodded at her again, lying once more. Gaming does not appeal to me in the least, not when I double down on my life every day. But my hatred of Lana Elkins is so strong I could kill her.

But I might not have to. Vinko has made it demonstrably clear that he wants her dead, too, now that I've linked Elkins to the hacking of his site.

He and I share so much more than our dislike of that woman. We both despise moderate Muslims. Vinko's absolutely correct when he says they are really wolves in sheep's clothing. He must be greatly encouraged right now because federal authorities blamed his previous provocations for vicious attacks on Muslims in St. Paul, Dearborn, Oakland, Omaha, even in the liberal bastion of Cambridge, Massachusetts. The FBI is asking anyone who might know his real identity to step forward. Fat chance. Vinko's secrets are safe with me. A few dead here, a few maimed there... the list of attacks will only grow longer and more welcome.

And I will make sure Vinko's fire burns brighter.

CHAPTER 5

LANA DIDN'T SLEEP WELL. Too much unfinished business loomed in the darkness. Emma had stormed upstairs last night, more upset over Tahir's threat to her relationship with Sufyan than a neo-Nazi's online threat to her life. *Steel Fist isn't real to her, but her boyfriend's uncle is*, Lana thought, swinging her feet out from under the covers and easing on her slippers.

Don lay on his back, still sleeping, arms flung wide. She let him grab a few extra winks and headed downstairs, knowing she'd have to drive home the gravity of Steel Fist's words to Emma before she went to school. Lana wished she could just lock the girl up for the duration. *Of what?* Lana asked herself immediately. *Because this is our life now.*

She pushed a button on the automatic espresso machine and heard the grinder go to work. Sitting on a stool, she glanced at a wall clock: 6:36 a.m.

The steam hissed and the beans gave off their enticing aroma. The last drips dimpled the dark surface.

Lana cradled the cup, blowing softly over the steamy brew. She remembered the windswept waters of the Black Sea and Don sailing her to a perilous rendezvous with Galina Bortnik. Lana and Don had been forced to work together after having had no contact for most of Emma's life. And to think they'd not only survived that mission but been reunited. A potent brew of danger, physical chemistry, and rekindled love had brought them back together. Lana still couldn't parse the appeal. She just knew it was as real as the rings they'd slipped back onto their fingers. They'd already talked about making it formal—again.

"'Morning, Mom."

Emma glided past, putting the espresso machine back into service. "How'd you sleep?"

"So-so."

"Same here. We need to talk."

"I'm pretty sure I made my position clear last night."

"This is not about saying you can't see Sufyan. I wouldn't do that, Em. That's not on my agenda."

"It's sure on Dad's," Emma shot back.

"Your father's been worried about the whole religious thing with Sufyan's family, and after last night I think we both have to admit there were grounds for that."

"He's never liked Sufyan."

"I honestly don't think that's true, Em. They've talked plenty about basketball and—"

"They've talked plenty about everything but Islam. He won't say a word about that to him."

"He's not comfortable with it. Give your father—"

"Neither are you. Admit it."

Emma's arms and legs were crossed, her coffee mug pressed against her shoulders hard enough to whiten her fingers. *Closed up like a bank vault.*

"I'm a skeptic about all religions. That's no bulletin. But I've never tried to sway your beliefs. Who drove you to church for choir practice and Sunday services? And if you become a Muslim, I'll be driving you to a mosque."

"I can drive myself now."

"Point taken."

"Yours, too."

"Look, *your* happiness is most important to me, not whether you believe what I believe. I could be wrong about all that stuff. Maybe St. Pete's going to meet me at the Pearly Gates and give me the old heave-ho." Which eked a smile out of Emma.

"Do you really mean you'd accept it if I became a Muslim?"

"Absolutely. I just want you to know that your choice is yours alone, and not confused with feelings for someone else."

"I don't think that's what's happening here, Mom, although I do love him."

"So what are you going to do about his uncle?"

"This is America, not the Sudan. Tahir's going to have to deal with our feelings."

"Did Sufyan text you after they left?"

Emma nodded. "I'm picking him up for school just like always. He says his uncle can't stop him from seeing me."

"You can't blame Tahir for being worried, not after what that family's been through. And you can't go the same way to school anymore." Lana pulled out her phone: "Here's the route that creep put up on the Web about you two."

Emma studied the screen. "What the hell! That's *exactly* how I go. How did he even know that?"

"That's the shortest distance between those two points," Lana said, hoping that Steel Fist had simply been guessing; the thought of neo-Nazis already tracking her daughter's movements was too horrifying to consider. "But you've got to start changing how you go every day. It's not hard to do. Look at this."

She slid a map in front of Emma. Before going to bed, Lana had highlighted half a dozen different routes her daughter could take to and from school, which included stops for Sufyan; a small red dot designated his home. She'd also colluded with Don on another security measure.

Emma ran her finger along the yellow lines, shifting the map to read the street names.

"I figured you'd be doing the driving," Lana said. Sufyan didn't have a car.

Emma looked up. "Do you think those threats are going to become news?"

"I hope not, but the *Post* probably has someone monitoring the Steel Fist website. They did a piece about it a few weeks ago when he registered his ten millionth follower. Whether the paper will spread the word about you two, I can't say. Let's hope not."

"Can't you stop them?" Emma asked.

"No, I can't. But I'll talk to Deputy Director Holmes and see what can be done a little higher up the food chain, maybe get someone to nudge the publisher. We could make the argument that neither of you is even a legal adult yet."

A point that usually made Emma bridle. Not today.

Don straggled into the kitchen, hair bunched to one side. His robe hung open, exposing his prison stripe pajamas. Emma had given them to him for Christmas as a gag gift, which Lana hadn't known about until he opened his present. She'd held her breath when he took out the top, replete with a prison number—his birth date. But he was smiling and wore them most nights, joking that after years in prison they made him feel right at home.

He was the last of the clan to activate the espresso machine. "Everybody sleep okay?"

"No," Emma and Lana answered at the same time.

"Me, either. I don't think I really fell off till about four. You tell her about the dog?" he asked Lana.

"What dog?" Emma lowered her mug.

"We're looking at getting a Malinois," Lana said.

"I've never heard of them."

"Remember the story about the Belgian military dog that was on the Osama bin Laden raid?" Don asked.

"Uh, no?"

"That was a Malinois. They're like German shepherds but they have shorter hair." Don pushed his own out of his face and grabbed his java. "They make excellent guard dogs."

"Who's going to train it?" Emma asked, clearly at odds with any thought of doing it herself.

"None of us. No time for that," Don replied. "We're going to have to buy one all ready for duty."

"Is he going to be okay with me?"

"Of course, but the three of us are going to have to be trained to work with him."

"You're kidding," Emma laughed. "*We* have to be trained for *him*? That's classic."

• • •

Emma opened the garage door and looked over her shoulder. Her Ford Fusion was two years old, white, and spotless. Her parents had insisted on a safe car. She'd wanted a sports car, an argument had ensued, and they'd won. But Emma liked the Ford, and it made her feel like an adult to drive to school and park it in the lot.

She backed out, looking for bad guys. That was how she thought of them, but she had a hard time figuring what they'd look like. *Skinheads?* She knew cool punk skinheads. And she doubted anyone trying to kill her would be that obvious.

What she didn't see as she pulled away was her father, shotgun by his side, waiting down the street to follow her in his old Chevy pickup. By taking the pump action, Don was risking a fast return to prison for violating his parole guidelines. It had been fine for him to be armed on the high seas, but bad news for him to try that in Bethesda.

Emma turned into one of the town's few modest neighborhoods and parked in front of Sufyan's house, a small clapboard two-story, freshly painted by his uncle in a cheerful yellow hue with refrigerator-white trim. A red door provided a flash of bright color when Sufyan hurried out with his knapsack. His uncle stood in the doorway staring at the departing young man. He never lifted his eyes to include Emma. If he had, she would have waved. She wanted Tahir to warm up to her, but it felt like trying to melt a block of ice in a blizzard.

Sufyan slipped his solid frame into the front seat and dropped his pack to the floor. He smiled, but didn't kiss her. He avoided that with Tahir always watching them until the car was no longer in sight. The man had piercing eyes, like he could see right through you.

So her first kiss of the day never came until they braked at a stop sign at the end of the street. But this morning Emma pulled a U-turn and headed back the way she'd come.

"Hey, where are you going?" Sufyan asked. "We're going to be late."

"We've got to change the way we come and go to school. Didn't your uncle show that website to you?"

"No, but he tried to take me to school today."

"And you told him no?"

"My mother told him to let me go with you, and then he pounded the table and walked away."

Emma gave him the URL and waited while he looked up the Steel Fist website on his phone.

"I have six ways to come and go from my house to yours and school," she told him. "My mom had that ready for us this morning."

"I like your mom. She's cool."

"And my dad?" Emma asked.

"He scares me. I don't think he really likes me seeing you."

"He's old school. Not about race," she hastened to add. "With the religious stuff. Both my parents just don't buy any of it."

"I don't see how people can't believe in God," Sufyan said. "Look at all this." They were passing a city park near Bethesda-Chevy Chase High School. Flowers everywhere. "It's so beautiful."

Emma nodded. "Talk to him about it sometime. See what he says."

"Did you say your evening prayers?" he asked.

She shook her head, unwilling to lie.

"Morning?"

"No, but I had a latté." A non sequitur she hoped would make him laugh.

Sufyan suffered a smile. "Me, too." He said nothing of his prayers, which he never missed. They were as important to him as breathing.

They finally came to a stoplight and kissed. Emma had put on lipstick before driving to his house especially for this moment. She loved his lips, his looks, everything about him. When he took to the court as a point guard, she always thought of Wesley Snipes in *White Men Can't Jump*, an old movie her father had insisted she see when she showed the slightest interest in basketball. One look at Snipes had her thinking *OMG, I want a guy just like him.* She'd hardly noticed Woody Harrelson. Then she'd seen Sufyan playing summer ball at an outdoor court and felt a shortness of breath. Not long after she'd brought him round to meet her parents.

Sufyan had enrolled a few weeks before, having just moved to the district in June. He could shoot, drive to the hoop, spin in the air and pass behind his back. And he was deadly with three-pointers from any spot along the perimeter. The school was expected to move from also-rans to contenders this year. She was proud to hold his hand as they strolled onto campus.

He was also the most sensitive guy she'd ever met. Sufyan was the first man she'd ever made love to. "Same here," he'd revealed as they cuddled on her bed afterward. He believed their lovemaking had formed a sacred bond between them. That a guy could even talk in such terms proved no small part of Emma's sudden interest in Islam. There was nothing remotely "hook-up" about him.

Sufyan wrapped his arm around her back to escort Emma to her first class, AP World History. That was where her friend, Mindy Wellstrom, stood waiting.

"Did you see this?" she asked Emma as the bell sounded. She was holding up her phone, hand visibly shaking.

Sufyan took hold of the young woman's wrist so they could see the screen.

"Shit!" Emma said to Sufyan's immediate consternation. She was staring at a *Washington Post* headline: "Suburban Teens Targeted for Terror."

• • •

Lana laid her Sig Sauer 9 millimeter semi-automatic under a nubby summer-weight sweater that she'd draped casually across the passenger seat of her Prius. Looking around, she backed out of the garage. It was about fifteen minutes after Em had left with Don on her heels. He'd already texted to say the young couple arrived safely at school.

As Lana drew within feet of the tree-shaded street, Em also texted: "See WA Post."

Lana braked, groaning at the headline and photo. She scanned the story and texted Emma to avoid reporters.

Lana took side streets through Bethesda, eyeing the rear-view mirror as much as the lovely gardens in their fading summer glory.

She made decent time to Fort Meade, passing through security at the gate. The Marine guard knew she was licensed to carry her gun.

"Keeping that close to you today?" he asked her.

She nodded.

"We all are," he replied, perhaps to reassure her. He failed, but she doubted any comfort would come until Steel Fist was identified and arrested.

Or killed.

Lana hurried straight up to Holmes's office. His longtime executive assistant Donna Warnes waved her in to see their boss.

He looked up, every one of his seventy-eight years imprinted in the lines on his forehead, cheeks, and chin. The bags under his eyes looked packed, the orbs themselves weary as a winter sky.

She noticed his electric razor sitting on his desk and guessed he'd slept on the base. It was an option for all of them whenever circumstances grew especially tense. Bob, as she called him when they were alone, might not have moved farther from his duties than the long leather couch nestled against a wall.

"You're getting protection," he told her without preamble. "So's Emma and Don when you're all together. It'll be 24/7 for the foreseeable future."

"You saw the *Post*?"

"We've already contacted the publisher. Showing those kids like that, a pair of seventeen-year-olds?" He shook his head. "How's Emma doing?"

"Emma's in love, so that's all she's really thinking about."

"He seems like a nice young man," Holmes said, as if by rote, though Lana figured he'd probably had Sufyan thoroughly vetted.

"He is. His uncle's a handful." Which Lana guessed would come as no surprise to Bob, either. She filled him in on last night's confrontation.

The deputy director leaned back. "He could be more than just a handful. The CIA thinks he was Al Qaeda in Sudan. He was on their radar long before his nephew took up with Emma. Now that there's a link directly to you, the FBI is keeping a very close eye on him."

"Seriously? Al Qaeda?"

"The uncle and the boy's dead father."

"What about his mother?"

"Nothing, but if it's true she must have known. The agency's still digging."

"And Sufyan?"

"Nothing on him yet, but they could be using him."

"To get to me?"

Bob nodded.

"I don't think so. The uncle was really agitated last night. Either that or it was an Oscar-winning performance. He forbade Sufyan to see Emma again."

"How did she react?"

"She shrugged that off and picked him up for school today as always."

"So the boy was allowed to go with her after his uncle's big display in your living room?"

"They're seventeen, Bob. I don't know how it was when you were raising yours, but there's no forbidding a romance at that age now unless you're part of some fundamentalist religious community."

"Which they are. They're Sunnis."

Neither spoke for long seconds. It was hard for Lana to imagine the young man as a zealot when he'd been up in Emma's bedroom breaking all his faith's rules about premarital sex.

"I'm not saying the boy knows," Bob went on. "He probably doesn't. I'm not even saying Tahir is Al Qaeda now, much less when he was back in Sudan. I'm just saying Sufyan and his uncle and mother are being watched. And now I'm hearing Tahir's been in your home."

Lana's turn to nod—uneasily. *Al Qaeda in my house?* A chilling thought. "Don should be licensed to carry."

"I'll make sure we talk to the Bureau of Prisons. It's definitely subject to parole conditions."

"He was armed on the Black Sea." Don had been doing a six-year federal sentence when his drug contacts in Colombia had made him valuable to the DEA. Then his high seas sailing skills made him even more useful to the Defense Department.

"That was then and this is now," Bob replied.

"They make exceptions," she said.

"And he'd be a good candidate for that. We'll do what we can."

In Lana's experience, that meant Don would be locked and loaded by nightfall.

"Tell me about the security detail you're arranging for us."

"Three rotating one-man shifts per day."

"A little on the thin side with Emma, Don, and me coming and going," Lana said.

"I agree, but getting any coverage is really tough with our domestic challenges. The threats to just about everyone on Capitol Hill are increasing almost every day. And the White House?" He waved his hand as if there were no telling the level of hatred directed toward the incumbent.

"Don's thinking we should get a Malinois."

"I can help you with that." Holmes was smiling for the first time in days. He suddenly looked years younger. "I had one myself for eleven years. His name was Bingo, like the old song. My son raises them up near Hagerstown. Superb dogs."

"We're going to need an adult for guard duty."

"He trains them for that if they don't go to the military. Or for special security details if clients have unusual requirements. He may have one suitable for family work. I'll check."

"So what did you want see me about?" Lana asked.

"Steel Fist."

"Of course..."

"I don't know about you, but I'm not buying that any one person is capable of what he's done. The release of all those files on citizens was not supposed to be possible. You told me so yourself."

At Bob's request, Jeff Jensen had tried to hack NSA's domestic surveillance files last month, though neither Lana nor Jeff had any idea of the extreme nature of their contents. He'd failed to make a dent in the agency's deeply layered encryptions. It irked her to no end that another hacker had succeeded.

"So all that private data was real?" Lana said. "Not some stab at propaganda?"

"They were old. They were supposed to have been destroyed. Now members in both houses are demanding to know why we ignored the post-Snowden reforms."

"That's not all they're demanding." She showed him the subpoena from the Senate Select Committee on Intelligence.

"I see we're scheduled for the same day. I wish I could say I'm surprised, but I warned you. We're going to want you to push back hard with testimony about the need for even stronger national anti-terrorism standards. The agency's legal counsel will prep you. Oysterton's a prime example of that, but we're going to have to fight this battle with facts, not anecdotes, which is what they're doing with stories about good old boys holding down the fort. That's what they're going to hit you with. Me, too. We'll coordinate our testimony." He handed her back the subpoena. "I want you to try to attack our files again. Use that Bortnik woman instead of Jensen this time."

"Really?"

"A fresh perspective. Just try it. Indulge me. See where Bortnik's forensics take you."

She realized he wanted Galina to search for the footprints of the hacker who'd succeeded where Jeff had failed. If Galina could find the hacker's trail, it might reveal the weaknesses in the NSA's network that had led to the release of those embarrassing documents—and ultimately lead to the identity of the cyber culprit.

Bob lowered his voice. "I suspect we've got a mole in this operation." He looked out his window at the wide expanse of NSA facilities. "There are thousands of possibilities here. A mole's the only way we could have been penetrated."

"A Snowden?"

"No, someone who's probably still working on the inside, passing it along to an openly declared enemy."

"Well, Galina's very good. She's excellent, in fact, at detecting patterns in metadata."

"Meantime, be very careful out there, Lana." Bob had returned his gaze to the window. "You're an open target now."

"When do I meet the security detail?"

"Anything else you want to talk about first?"

"No."

"Then the answer is now." Bob picked up his phone. "Donna, send in Robin Maray."

The deputy director hung up. "He's one of the three agents who'll cover you every day."

Holmes rose as a tall, broad-shouldered man walked in. "Robin, meet Lana Elkins."

She turned, working hard not to show her shock. Lana knew the agent, though they'd never exchanged more than first names.

And hers had not been Lana.

CHAPTER 6

VINKO'S MOST INSPIRED THINKING came when he first awakened. Lying under the sheet, eyes still closed, he'd revisit whatever had been nagging him before going to bed. He'd grown to depend on the answers provided by the unconscious mind. But this morning brought only more questions about his mysterious guardian angel, the most grating of which was whether the creature who'd put him back online was the same person who'd taken him down.

He needed to suss that out quickly and make absolutely sure Lana Elkins was responsible. Not because he had any qualms about calling for her death, along with the murder of her daughter and her black Muslim boyfriend. Hardly. Vinko couldn't have cared less if a prominent member of the cybersecurity state, much less her spawn, were gunned down, run over, or had their damn throats slit with a gutting knife. The sooner the better, in fact. What he cared about was whether he'd become an ox with a cyber ring in his nose to be led here, there, and everywhere at the whim of another hacker. One rule of cyberspace was you never surrender control because you never know whom you're surrendering it to.

It had even crossed his mind that the guardian angel might have forged his path to those NSA files, acting as the cyber equivalent of a machete-wielding jungle guide. But why would anyone want to bolster his standing? If they supported his beliefs, why not come on board directly? More questions without answers.

As he opened his eyes to the daylight, all he knew was that the guardian angel had an agenda. Everybody did. And it was rarely so selfless as the heavenly name might suggest.

Vinko eyed his digital alarm clock: 10:35 a.m. He avoided using the alarm, spurning ranchers' hours. He liked to work late and sleep in. The goats adjusted to his schedule. They weren't like cows. At all.

Biko understood. He already had his eyes on his master, ready to obey the orders of the day. The border collie was a smart workaholic.

"Isn't that right, Biko?"

The dog stood as soon as he heard his name and stared intently at him. Biko had a vocabulary of about four hundred words. More than a lot of humans in Vinko's experience.

He rubbed Biko's scruff, rose, and threw on a pair of Levi's before letting his dog out. He watched him bolt to the barn, sniffing the door. Then Biko backed up a few steps and barked. The goats bleated. Biko began to circle the barn, checking for trouble. An uncanny animal.

Vinko headed into the bathroom for his morning ablutions before carefully combing his boot-black hair straight back.

He was back in his bedroom reaching for a shirt when Biko started barking. Vinko heard a car pulling around toward the barn.

He slipped his short-barreled .357 Ruger revolver into the back of his jeans and threw on his shirt, then headed to the back door. He couldn't believe it: a black man and white woman in a Porsche 911 Carrera. His first impulse was to reach for his weapon so he could shoot out the raked-back windshield and the pair perched behind it. They had to be tourists. Nobody local would have dared intrude. But they weren't tourists. He saw that with his next breath.

Is he out of his mind?

With his gun still hidden, Vinko pushed open the screen door and whistled Biko to his side.

Bones Jackson uncurled himself from the Carrera's driver's seat. "If it ain't the white man's white man. How you doin', Stinko?"

Bones actually waved at him, as if they were old friends. Then he had the temerity to close the Porsche's door, as though he planned to stay longer than the few seconds it would take Vinko to jam his gun into Bones's black face and send him packing.

The white woman climbed out the other side in a skirt shorter than an old man's memory and tighter than a drug dealer's fist. She looked like a supermodel, with blond hair smartly cut to an inch above her distinct collarbones. Her face had a vaguely Asian cast. No, Russian, he realized a moment later.

So Bones had landed himself a beauty. Vinko figured that was one of the perks that came when you'd started for more than a decade for the San Diego Chargers and made the NFL Pro Bowl seven of those years. His career having ended four seasons ago, Bones was a shoo-in for the Hall of Fame.

"What do you want?" Vinko moved with deliberate speed toward his former tight end. Bones had lost some weight, some muscle. Vinko smiled at the man's reduced stature. Maybe he wouldn't shoot him. Maybe he'd just beat the shit out of him.

"I wanted to see what the white man's white man was up to. Ludmila and I were in Coeur d'Alene, and I remembered my old QB lived within striking distance on his family's land or compound or whatever it is. Jesus, you got more warning signs out there than a nuclear plant."

"Which you ignored."

"I figured you'd be glad to see me."

Bones wasn't serious, Vinko could tell, but that made him feel toyed with, teased in front of Bones's girlfriend or wife, whore or hooker. Bones had teased him plenty back at Boise State, nicknaming him Stinko as soon as he'd found out the quarterback was chilly toward any shade of skin darker than a tan line. Pretty soon, the whole school had picked up on it, the moniker following him right through graduation.

"You figured wrong. Get back in your car and get the hell out of here. And take Lugnut with you."

"I wasn't planning on leaving her. Though she was a bit curious. You played ball with *who*?"

"I could ask the same about her being with *you*. You're nothing to me," Vinko said. "She's even less for being with you."

Ludmila was standing by the front of the car. "You are fucking idiot," she said in an unmistakable Russian accent. Vinko had been right about that much.

Vinko felt the Ruger pressing against the small of his back, luring him with its swift promise. He didn't resist. He drew and pointed it right at Bones.

"You're trespassing. I shoot people for less. You drove right past those signs. That's a dangerous thing to do." He stepped closer to Bones, only an inch or two shorter than himself. The ex-tight end had played at a rock-solid 220 pounds, but he looked forty shy of that now. Shirt hanging off him like a tent.

Cocaine. Of course. Vinko would have bet the ranch on it. The guy had always partied hard. So now he'd gone to drugs. Bones sure wasn't smiling anymore. All his cockiness had vanished. Ruger magic.

Biko started sniffing Bones's pants leg. Vinko wished he'd taught his dog to pee on command. He gave him one he did know: "Biko, heel."

"Biko? Did you really name him after Stephen Biko?" The black South African anti-apartheid activist had become famous after being killed in police custody. He'd also been known for coining the slogan "Black is beautiful."

"Yeah, and I got a big fat barn cat called MLK. So what of it?" Vinko was enjoying himself immensely now. He'd resented every pass he'd ever thrown Bones, and he'd fired off hundreds in the two years they'd played together. Now he stood as close to him as he once had in the team huddle. Never next to him, though. Bad enough he had to touch the same ball.

"Fair is fair," Bones said. "I got a hamster named Stinko. Fact is I got a whole string of them because I feed them to my boa. I always say, 'Here comes Stinko,' and that boa, he comes *alive*."

"You don't look so good, Bones. Been sucking on a crack pipe with your bros and hoes?"

"You are one sorry son-of-a-bitch," Bones replied.

"So I guess the answer is yes. Guess what else? You're about to be one dead n—"

Vinko froze at the sound of a semi-automatic racked inches from his head. Ludmila had the muzzle pointed right at his temple.

"Put it down," she said.

Vinko realized he'd made a huge mistake by taking her for granted.

"See, she actually loves me, Stinko," Bones said. "She'll blow your fucking head off if you so much as blink, so why don't you do like she says before your dog has to find a new home to go with his new name?"

Vinko glanced at her without moving his head or gun, hoping to see something that would give him the upper hand. But she'd gotten the drop on him and held a Browning with practiced ease, nice and steady. That was when he realized they would both be witnesses to his killing, should that come to pass. He also knew police would probably believe they'd shot in self-defense because Vinko had threatened Bones before millions of viewers after a bowl victory their senior year. When a post-game interview ended, a pack of photographers had wanted the quarterback and his receiver who'd caught the game-winning pass to hoist the big trophy over their heads. Not what Vinko had wanted, and as soon as the media mob had moved on, he'd turned to Bones and said quietly, "You ever touch anything I'm holding again, I'll kill you, nigger."

But his microphone had still been on, and his use of the n-word reached the ears of millions. It turned his name to mud. Not one team in the NFL dared to draft him. It made the gun trained on his head right now seem as predictable as death itself.

"I never forget," Bones said, "and I'm guessing right about now you're remembering the last time we were together, too."

"I might as well shoot you," Vinko replied. "I'm a dead man anyway. Isn't that what you're saying?"

"Nope, not what I'm saying. You're the one who threatened to kill me. Ludmila just wanted me to have some closure with the worst man I've ever known. She thought it would be good to give you another chance. 'People change,' she said. And the truth is she couldn't believe anybody could be as foul as you. So I said, 'Sweetheart, you want to meet Stinko, you better bring your gun.' Aren't you glad, hon?"

She nodded. "Not waiting one second more," she said evenly. "Put it down or I put bullet in your stupid brain."

Vinko lowered his pistol.

"Better put that on the ground and step away," Bones said.

Vinko complied. The late morning sun glinted off the stainless steel chamber.

Biko growled at Bones.

"Keep him by your side or get ready to bury him."

"Quiet," Vinko said. The dog stopped growling.

"Why do you hate me?" said Bones. "I just have to ask." He'd picked up the Ruger and held it by his side. Ludmila, however, maintained her easy aim at Vinko's head. "I never really got that. All I ever did was make you look good."

"I never needed you for that."

"Yeah, you did. You needed someone to catch the crap you threw, Stinko."

"There were plenty of white guys who could've done that."

"Not on that team, there wasn't."

"The team still would've been better without you."

"And seventeen other blacks? Are you delusional?"

Bones stared at him. He looked like he was earnestly trying to figure Vinko out. He also looked exhausted, as if no amount of effort could ever make sense of Vinko's hate. Or maybe Bones had just driven too far for too little.

"Come on, let's go," he said to Ludmila. Then he turned his attention back to Vinko. "I'd hoped you changed. I really did. We did a lot together. You were a loose end in my life. I thought maybe I could tie it up. It wasn't really her. She didn't care if she met you. She thought I was crazy to even come."

That was when Vinko knew the real reason Bones had driven hours to see him: Bones must be dying. It's what a man does when the end is near—if he's weak and sentimental.

"What is it?" he asked his old teammate. "Cancer? What kind you got?" Vinko was smiling now. "How much time you got left? I'll bet not much."

Ludmila pressed the barrel against his face.

"Don't," Bones said to her. He locked eyes with Vinko. "I got time. I just don't have any more for you. No regrets."

He got back behind the wheel, but Ludmila didn't move. Vinko wondered whether she'd actually shoot him. Two witnesses and a history of white pride that would be used against him. But the worst part would be dying at the hands of a race traitor.

"He's a good man," she said in his ear. "He just wanted to make peace with the one asshole in his life. You are scum."

"And you sleep with filth," Vinko dared. He shook his head in genuine disgust, pressing hard against the muzzle. Yes, daring her to shoot him, because now he knew she wouldn't. She loved Bones too much to fuck up their last weeks or months together.

She backed away, relaxing her aim.

"Come back when he finally dries up and dies. I'll show you some real fun."

Ludmila fired right above his head. Vinko never flinched and, to his credit, neither did Biko, though the dog's haunches began to shake.

Bones yelled for Ludmila to get in the car, and Vinko watched them drive away with his Ruger, kicking up dust that hung in the air like a bad odor.

He let out the goats and put Biko back to work. Then he walked back inside, trying to put aside the unpleasant encounter.

This was the greatest reward in life, he told himself: outliving the ones you loathed. Some died all on their own. Others had to be taken down.

He headed straight to his office with Lana Elkins foremost in mind.

CHAPTER 7

FBI AGENT ROBIN MARAY trailed Lana silently into the office she used at NSA headquarters. He settled across the room from her, checked his phone, and studiously avoided all eye contact. It was as if they had no past. But they'd packed plenty of history into a lone night two years ago, potent enough that Lana now struggled to focus on her work. She had to. The security of the nation might be at stake, though fortunately there had been no bombs or other terrorist activity in the past twenty-four hours. Noting an absence of gruesome violence for a single sweep of the clock actually said reams about the otherwise miserable status of the country.

Well, there was one bomb, she thought, casting a quick glance at Robin, whom she'd met in a trendy Georgetown bar, just days before the grid went down and launched the cyberwar era in earnest.

Since Don had left Emma and her to smuggle boatloads of pot from South America up through the Caribbean, she'd directed almost all her free time to her growing daughter. But Emma had had a trusted babysitter so Lana could maintain a social life, mostly meeting work friends for drinks and dancing about once a month. And she'd met only a handful of men in Don's fourteen-year absence, twice in bars, once after a colleague had stood her up. Less *Looking for Mr. Goodbar* than a slightly sybaritic Jane Goodall on holiday from the chimps.

To the point: nothing scandalous, which was precisely why she'd spurned online dating. She knew as well as anyone in the world how little she could depend on real privacy with the porous security of most of those websites. Rather than slipshod encryptions, she had trusted her gut, though the whole of her had been attracted to Robin in the time it took to make eye contact. Basically, a blink.

Of course he'd drawn her attention in that crowded bar. *Look at him*! she thought now, glancing away from her monitor. Curly blond hair, closely cropped; blue eyes, very bright; and a strong jaw and body. You could tell a lot with a glance, especially when your eyes were wide open, which Lana's had been on that evening.

He'd bought her a drink, Glenfiddich straight up, intelligence he must have garnered from the barkeep, then moseyed his way through the Saturday-night thicket to greet her in person.

"I can't believe you're here all alone," were his first words, not that an avalanche of them would follow. But he'd said enough that she'd liked his baritone.

"My husband's out of town." Which was true—for a number of years at that point. It was also her response on the rare occasions she was interested. It said: *I'm married*. It said: *Whatever this is, it's unlikely to happen again*. It said: *But I might want you within those strictly prescribed limits*.

He'd used his real first name. Lana had not. She couldn't recall the name she'd assumed.

After the requisite chitchat, they'd ended up at the Four Seasons in Washington.

He'd never told her what he did for a living. When she'd asked, he replied, "Nothing important." Which immediately signaled quite the opposite.

When he'd asked the same of her, she'd given him the exact same response, the unwritten code of those who worked in the most sensitive arenas of government.

She'd even kept her purse and ID with her when she'd used the en-suite bathroom, recognizing that while she would trust him with her body, she would not trust him with her career. And she'd been well rewarded, for the sex had been explosive, as if he hadn't been with anyone for months, either, though she never believed that. More to the point, he'd been the best choice she'd ever made on those rare forays, so good she'd almost reconsidered the anonymity she'd established for herself so carefully.

That said, she'd been eager to destroy his: when he used the bathroom after their first round of lovemaking, she'd rifled his wallet and found his FBI identification. He'd screwed up, and that meant he could screw up in other ways. Desire was pitted against discretion, and the latter won out, but only after Lana made love to him for the last time at five in the morning. Then she'd left, fully satisfied, yet shadowed by the paradox that always prevailed in the face of great physical pleasure: sated, she'd wanted only more.

Can't have it, she'd told herself driving home at daybreak. She'd never looked back—till now.

"I've got to get back to my office in Bethesda," she said to Robin without glancing up. "Have some things I need to discuss with my associates."

"I'll follow. I've got a Charger, but you won't lose me this time."

What's he saying?

As they stepped outside NSA headquarters, he spoke up more directly. The timing was not coincidence: he was sparing them both surveillance within the building.

"You didn't even use your real first name," he said quietly.

"I know."

"Do you remember what you did use?"

"No, I don't."

"Lucinda. Don't you remember my saying that I loved Lucinda Williams and had been listening to *Car Wheels on a Gravel Road*?"

"Nope." But Lana was lying because the conversation they'd had was coming back to her. So were other memories, like cinders in a burn pile of forgotten feelings. She didn't need any sparks right now. She and Don had talked of remarrying. Which prompted a question from her that could keep things simple: "Are you married?"

"No," Robin said. "I've been waiting for the right one. Actually, I thought I'd met her in a bar in Georgetown."

Don received a call from Donna Warnes, who identified herself as Deputy Director Holmes's executive assistant.

"He asked me to tell you about his son, a Malinois breeder and trainer up near Hagerstown. He said the dogs come from a strong bloodline and there are three good possibilities for family security work."

Don thanked her and went online, pleased the younger Holmes had video of the three dogs in question, but only them. He figured the ones headed for secret government work were not made public, a thought that sent him on a diverting Google search, which revealed that the dog on the bin Laden raid had been a Malinois named Cairo. It boggled Don's mind to think the government hadn't kept that secret. None of the SEALs' names had been made public, not by the feds, anyway. Don could only imagine what jihadists would do to Cairo if they ever had the chance.

He returned to the breeder's site, deciding he liked the look of Jojo, the biggest dog. Also his name: two syllables with two hard vowels. Easy for a dog to hear, and Jojo was an unusual enough sound to stand out when a command had to be heard.

The dog also had an intensely alert look. He'd peered into the camera lens as if he were trying to solve the mystery of sight itself.

Don called and made an appointment to meet the dogs tomorrow afternoon, no sooner hanging up than his phone rang. Warnes again: "The deputy director just asked me to tell you that you're approved to carry. I'm sending a courier to your home with the necessary materials."

"When?"

"He should arrive in about forty-five minutes."

"Could he meet me at the corner of Waverly and the East-West Highway instead?"

"In forty-five minutes?"

"Yes."

Twenty minutes later Don slipped the loaded shotgun into the cab of the pickup and backed out of the three-bay garage. A beautiful late-summer day, balmy as he headed to the high school. He planned to trail

Emma as she drove to Anacostia for choir practice. *Bizarre*, he realized, to think she'd be attending Quran study in two days.

He arrived at the school about ten minutes early to make sure he snagged a place across the street from the parking lot. He was sure a vehicle with a shotgun was verboten on campus.

It's not legal out here, either, he reminded himself. *Till you see that courier.*

He discreetly pulled out his compact binoculars and scanned the lot for Emma's white car. He found one in the third row from the street. Don couldn't see the plate so he glassed the rest of the lot to make sure there weren't two white ones.

He expected her to be moving along quickly because of choir, especially with Sufyan not around to lure her attention. She'd told her parents that he and the rest of the team were scheduled for pre-season physicals today. Don remembered them from his own playing days, squirming when he recalled the command "Cough, son."

There she is. Emma was rushing toward her car. Then she turned; Don thought another student must have called to her. But it was Sufyan's uncle Tahir, hurrying up to her. Grabbing her arm.

Don swore and threw open the old Chevy's door. He locked it and sprinted across the street in seconds, dodging kids driving away from school as fast as they could.

"Let me go!" were the first words he heard as he moved within earshot.

Tahir looked up and saw Don running toward them. He let go of Emma's arm. She backed away, rubbing a red mark above her wrist.

"What did I say about threatening my family?" Don stepped just within striking distance of Tahir, who was a couple of inches shorter than him and lighter. He told Emma to get in the car. "And lock up."

Emma jumped behind the wheel.

"She didn't listen when I told her to stay away from my nephew," Tahir said. "She picked him up this morning."

"I'm proud of her for that," Don said, glancing quickly around them. "She's not going to let you intimidate her." Nobody was paying attention to the two adults. Satisfied, Don delivered a sharp blow to Tahir's midsection, expecting to fold him over, the best position, he'd learned, for talking sense into bullies. But to his astonishment, his fist felt as if it had struck a knight's breastplate. Tahir didn't even flinch.

"Don't do that again," the Sudanese said evenly.

Don had fought FARC guerillas and unscrupulous drug dealers in Colombia—the kind who'd tried to rip off honest pot pirates, as he'd viewed himself back then—but he'd never punched anyone that hard to no avail. "Next time I'll take you down for good," he said with measured calm. "I know what you survived. But you don't know what *I've* done. She doesn't even know." Don nodded toward the car; Emma had started the engine. "If you think I'm going to let you hurt my kid, you're dangerously mistaken."

Tahir walked away unbowed. Don knew that as surely as he'd read the murderous anger on the man's face. Don turned back to the car. Emma was gripping the wheel. She looked terrified. He realized that she and her boyfriend were caught between two veterans of violence.

As long as they're not caught in the crossfire.

He slid into the Fusion's passenger seat.

"You punched him." Emma looked as if she'd been struck.

Don nodded. "He threatened you. I threatened him. We speak the same language."

"What are you doing here?"

"Making sure you're safe."

She dropped her forehead to the steering wheel and started crying.

"Em, I'm sorry, but that guy—"

"He said he was going to kill me if I didn't leave Sufyan alone. I'm not stalking him! He loves me."

"I know. Tahir's got to know that, too. But it's not just him I'm worried about. We've got those neo-Nazis, too."

"I know." She sat back and wiped her eyes. "I feel like I've got a big bull's-eye on my butt." A smile creased her lips.

Don was glad to see the levity. It showed that his daughter hadn't lost her grit.

"You might as well go with me in this car to choir," Emma said, "since you really are a stalker."

Don's turn to smile. "Do you want me to drive? I have two quick stops."

"No, I can drive. Where? They've really got to be quick."

The first was at his truck; he couldn't leave his weapon in the cab in front of a high school, of all places. He rested it between the two front seats.

"So you're actually riding shotgun?" Emma said, resting her hand on the barrel.

"Looks like it."

The second stop came at Waverly Street and the highway, where the courier was waiting. He handed Don a padded envelope. Don signed for it, knowing from the weight that more than a gun license was sealed inside.

He climbed back into the car and pulled out a Glock G30S semi-automatic. He checked the magazine: packed with .45s ready to pop. A spare had also been included in the envelope. Lana really did have clout with a capital C these days.

"Jesus, Dad. Things have sure changed since you got back." She didn't sound so approving now. Sometimes reality set in slowly.

"I didn't bring any trouble with me, Em. I'm just here to make sure none of it sticks to us."

"Can you really do that?"

He nodded. So did she. She believed him. Trust was a good place to start. It meant she'd probably listen to him if things got bad.

Emma merged back into traffic, heading toward the city.

"We'll get an injunction against Tahir," Don said.

"An injunction? Are you kidding?"

Emma was right: a court order would never stop him.

"We'll have him arrested."

"Don't!" She turned to him. "Then he'll be deported."

"Watch the road."

"He told me he'd take Sufyan back to Khartoum if I kept seeing him. It's like Mom says—caught between a rock and a hard place."

"We'll figure something out."

Don glanced down at the Glock, wondering if the best solution lay on his lap.

Son-of-a-bitch might have a hard body but he's not made of Kevlar.

• • •

Lana pulled up to CyberFortress with Robin right behind her in his broad-bodied Charger. He hurried ahead to get the door, which she didn't mind because she had both her shoulder and laptop bags in tow.

His eyes roved over everything in sight but her, and she realized that getting the door gave him an opportunity to scan behind them without drawing attention to what he was doing. An important skill when a man with ten million hateful subscribers was calling for her death and the murder of her daughter and Sufyan.

She brushed past the FBI agent wondering *Why Robin? Of all the possible agents? What were the odds?* Worse than craps. But she'd have to grant Robin this much: he'd taken her mind off gambling with cards or dice, perhaps because her strongest impulse right now was to gamble with her heart.

Lana had never told a soul about him. At times she'd wished she had a close friend to confide in, but she didn't. And her work had trained her long ago not to talk, not to give away much of anything to the everyday world of her fellow citizens. Maybe that was why she'd given everything *but* her heart during those steamy hours with Robin.

She waved Jeff Jensen and Galina Bortnik out of the war room to introduce them to Robin. Galina gave him a big smile, which Robin didn't appear to notice.

"I need to talk to them privately," she said to him.

"I'll park myself outside," he replied equably.

Once settled with Jeff and Galina in her office, Lana asked for an update on the ISIS men in Louisiana. "The last I heard, they were being transported to Camp Blanding by an army detachment."

"That's right, a big military escort," Jeff agreed, "plus the sheriff, who insisted on going with them. Turned out he even had his picture taken with some of his prisoners."

"Are you—"

"Nope, not kidding."

"Otherwise, everything went okay?" Lana asked.

"One of the prisoners was sick by the time they got to Blanding. He's on lockdown in sick bay. They're going to hold them all there for questioning, then they'll be taken to the supermax in Florence."

She nodded. The supermaximum prison in Florence, Colorado, had become the detention facility of choice for terrorists awaiting trial or serving time.

"What's the prisoner in sick bay for?" Lana asked.

"A bad sunburn," Jeff said. "A few of them did. It sounds like he had heatstroke, too. I guess they didn't have much cover on their boat."

"Do they know where they sailed from?" she asked.

"They're still working on that. Nobody's talking."

"What about your work?' she asked Galina, whom she'd tasked with trying to run down Steel Fist.

"He's not working alone."

"What makes you say that?"

"He's secretive, right? Never gives away a location. Could be in St. Petersburg for all we know. He has all this data uploading, but he's the destination of streaming data, too."

"From NSA?"

"I don't know yet," Galina replied. "Could be from other places but it's hard to tell. So many people support him and they fill the Web with chatter. Ten million subscribers, and they are active. It's like a big cyber smokescreen. Hard to run trace routes against the various streams."

"Or he could be scattering it himself," Jeff said. "Throwing up his own camouflage."

"Yes, could be," Galina agreed. "He is slippery. He is good."

"Jeff, we've got a change in plans. Holmes wants Galina to try to crack NSA security, specifically anything related to files on domestic intelligence gathering."

"I already tried, remember?"

"I do, and Holmes does, too. But he wants a fresh approach. She's had no experience with NSA."

As soon as she spoke, it occurred to Lana that she was making an assumption about Galina that might not be true. Galina could have gone after the agency when she was hacking in Russia. "Have you ever hacked NSA?" she asked her directly.

"No, only the professor," she answered. A Harvard computer engineering genius, whose murder had been ordered by the man employing Galina.

"A lack of experience is supposed to be an advantage?" Jeff asked. He didn't sound affronted, only surprised.

"He thinks it might be. Galina, I'll take over your work on Steel Fist. You get on those NSA files. You're free to use any attack vector you want. I'll give you the rundown when we get back to the war room."

As they started there, Don texted her about Tahir.

Goddamn him.

She was grateful Don had been with Em, replying to him accordingly.

When she caught up with her colleagues at the war room, Galina was talking to Robin, asking about his job, making sure her hair was in place, and smiling as she had earlier.

Flirting. Unabashedly.

Lana filled with a most unfamiliar feeling: jealousy.

What am I turning into? What is this place turning into?

"Galina, we need to get moving here."

The young woman appeared to snap out of a trance, wheeling around and heading toward her workstation. Lana couldn't read Robin's reaction, and tried to tell herself that she didn't care, but the jealousy wouldn't let her.

She did explain to him that he wouldn't be permitted in the war room, either. He caught her eye as she talked. She tried to look away but was drawn right back.

No, she told herself sternly. *A thousand times no.*

But her arm brushed against the sleeve of his navy blazer as she walked past him. Wholly unintentional *and* wholly unnerving.

Lana worked hard in the next few minutes to put aside these fleeting excitements. She contacted her liaison at the CIA to see if they'd learned anything more about Tahir's history in Sudan.

"The jury's still out," the voice on the other end of the line replied.

Like Holmes said.

Lana hung up, shaking her head. The CIA strongly suspected Tahir had been Al Qaeda in Sudan. And he was behaving like a jihadist toward her daughter. *And the jury's still out?*

Wouldn't the agency want to know everything possible about a man with that background now living so close to the nation's capital?

Time to do her own digging. Time to go as deep as she could. As deep as she needed to. Her daughter's life might be on the line. She doubted anybody in the CIA possessed her fear-fueled motivation.

Despite the liaison's words, Lana strongly suspected the "jury" at the highly driven agency had heard all the staggering evidence against Tahir *and* rendered its verdict.

If so, the only question remaining was the nature of the sentence—and who would bear the full brunt of its potentially lethal burden.

CHAPTER 8

THE SUN'S LOW IN the sky. I can see it shining directly into the windows of my log home in the distance. It's been hot up here on the ridge. Summers are getting longer and the heat lingers late into the day. Right now it's in the mid-nineties and it's almost six o'clock. That surprised me when I first moved to the Pacific Northwest. I expected the worst heat at midday, but it'll last into the early evening. The climate is deceptive that way.

I can appreciate that approach. I come at people slowly, too, building up the pressure as I move in on them. Hiking clears my mind when I need to think about my latest targets. The truth is, there's not much to distract me. The beauty of April, May, and June has paled. That's wildflower season when the Indian paintbrush, balsamroot, lupine, and a promiscuous variety of lilies drape the hillsides with reds, yellows, purples, and blues. When a thousand feet below me the apple, pear, and cherry trees bloom. Now they're growing heavy with fruit.

It's even warmer to the east because the ridge forms the border between the lush western part of the state and the drier expanses to the east, where ranching and wheat farming prevail. Within a mile or two I can move from one climate to another, though the differences at this time of year are minimal. The danger from wildfires is severe everywhere.

It's been that way since mid-July. By then it gets so dry that I have to have everything cut down to the nubs—natural grasses, wilting wildflowers, bushes—in a three-hundred-foot swath around my house. It's my first line of defense against fire. If I had Vinko's goats I wouldn't need to hire a guy to do it for me, but I can't bear those creatures, their sour odors and noisy rutting. And I can't abide goat milk.

I prefer to simply relish the solitude and slow flow of seasons up here. I'm completely off the grid. I have solar panels on my roof and a Powerwall from Tesla to store all that precious electricity. A well supplies my water, hikes give me a great deal of time to think.

I am an island.

And I'm concerned about Lana Elkins. She hasn't placed a single bet since her $137 win. She's installed an ad blocker to stop the targeted casino ads I'd been sending her. I looked for any indication that she's been going to Gamblers Anonymous to avoid inflaming her relapse, but she appears to be doing nothing but working and sleeping, though clearly she could be slipping away to meetings. Maybe *she's* focused on that ISIS brigade now held at Camp Blanding.

I'm sure the intelligence services are putting enormous resources into trying to figure out just what was going on down Louisiana way. Let them try-try-try. I've researched those men completely. Other than ISIS's Fahad Kassab, they are a blank slate, the *tabula rasa* of terrorism. But Tahir Hijazi is not. Even if I knew nothing of him, his nephew's and Emma Elkins's many texts would tell me much about his role in their Romeo and Juliet playlet. The pair are fast and loose with their communications, as you'd expect from a couple of teens. That gives me ample insight not only into their movements and plans but also, by extension, into those of their caregivers, including Tahir. It's another dimension of a most curious man.

Interesting, isn't it, that he landed in Bethesda, Maryland? Doesn't anybody wonder why an immigrant of severely modest means from a war-torn nation eventually ends up in a pricy suburb that's home to so many spies and other government officials, including Lana Elkins? *And that his nephew then starts seeing her daughter?* Apparently not. He's certainly active online, though even by my strict standards he has sophisticated encryption.

If I were Lana, I'd be wary of what he could put under my car, like a bomb or electronic locator. But I'm not her. I'm better at this game. And I've been playing it as long as she has. We have what you might call common roots. Which is to say that if I were her, I'd suspect there's more at play here than Tahir's objections to Sufyan's love interest. In fact, wouldn't the smart money—and Lana would certainly know about that—say the conflict over the teens could be nothing but a means for Tahir to draw attention from his real goals? Not that Tahir, a bona fide Muslim fundamentalist, doesn't truly loathe the young white woman. But hate is rarely exclusive, and I rather like my confluences of interest with him. He certainly has some with Vinko in their genuine distaste, to put it mildly, for Lana Elkins.

My stomach tightens as I now walk up to my second defense against wildfires. It's an emergency water tank sunk into the earth—eight feet across, fifteen feet deep, and lined with heavy black plastic. The nearest fire district ends twelve miles from here, so I'm glad I have the means of holding a lot of water, along with an engine to pump it through a hundred feet of thick fire hose.

Lately, the tank has also been holding a lot of dead rats. And . . . it's no different today as I lift the heavy wooden cover.

The odor is abominable. The heat must be drying up every source of water for miles. My tank has become the Golden Gate Bridge for rats because once they take the plunge, they're dead.

I've taken to keeping a long-handled fishing net nearby to pull out their rotting bodies. I count as I net them and throw them far from the tank. There, the seventeenth and last one—for today.

My task complete, I lower the cover and walk around it. I still can't see how the rats can get inside this thing.

Too bad Vinko's subscribers don't avail themselves of drowning. It would be good to see his mindless millions similarly bloated. They've been chatting up a storm about his call-to-arms, along with vows to murder Lana Elkins, her daughter, and Tahir's nephew. In yet another intriguing twist, I found Tahir himself mouthing off in chat rooms devoted to Steel

Fist, doing a credible job of impersonating a white racist. He was actively joining the calls for violence against Lana and Emma, though even in his guise he said nothing of Sufyan. He certainly had the vernacular down, saying it was time to "take names and kick ass." Does that sound like a Sudanese immigrant to you?

Tahir *is* intriguing. Not so much to me, but I would think Elkins would be playing catch-up as fast as she can. That he appears to be operating without any concentrated attention by Vinko or her speaks of blinkered obsession as much as anything else. But when a project consumes you, it's easy to get blindsided. Both Lana and Vinko, from what I can see, are preoccupied with terrorists slipping across the country's borders.

I have my own interests to consider. Some, as I said, could be served by Tahir, some only by Vinko. I find myself moving back and forth between those two political climates, much as I move between two real climates when I hike the acreage I call my own. On the western flank, fir trees common to coastal forests grow, while Ponderosa pines flourish in the warmer drier reaches to the east. But both political climates are moist with hate, arid of feeling.

Just the way I like them.

CHAPTER 9

LANA STARED AT "THE Today Show" in the corner of the kitchen. "Do you believe this?" she asked Don and Emma, who were eating the blueberry waffles she'd cooked from scratch.

A shaggy-headed young guy in a Hawaiian shirt, khaki chinos, and flip-flops was walking onto the set.

"Gimme a hug," he said in a southern drawl as he hauled Matt Lauer out of his seat.

"Well, you know who this is, don't you?" Lauer said to the camera, breaking the clinch with an awkward smile. "Jimmy McMasters, the brave young man who fought ISIS, and our show's new terrorism expert."

"Reality is getting so bizarre that I don't see how satire can survive anymore," Lana said, shaking her head.

"How can they say he's a terrorism expert?" Emma asked, wolfing the last of her waffle. "He looks total surf punk to me."

"Maybe that's what we need nowadays, if we're going to get serious about terrorism," Don said.

Lana threw him a startled look but Don was already giving in to laughter.

She'd fixed breakfast with him especially in mind, solicitous of Don since FBI Agent Robin Maray had rekindled old emotions yesterday. Penance for the guilt she was feeling.

"He reminds me of someone," Don said, studying McMasters.

The TV *tête-à-tête* was well underway: "So what do you make of those bad sunburns the terrorists got?" asked Lauer. "You'd think they would have been prepared for that. One of them's in the infirmary at Camp Blanding with what's being reported as sunstroke."

"That's some bad stuff," said McMasters. "I guess the sun's our first line of defense down on the bayou. And out on the Gulf, man, it's brutal."

"From what you saw, did those terrorists have any shade?"

"Nope, not much. Their boat was super crowded."

Don's right, Lana thought. McMasters reminded her of some fifteen-minutes-of-fame guy. *Who?* It was starting to drive her crazy. The tip-of-the-tongue that won't let go. Then it did:

"Kato Kaelin," she blurted. "He's the Kato Kaelin of this case."

"Exactly," Don said.

"Who's Kato whatever?" Emma asked.

"You don't want to know," Don answered.

"A footnote to a nightmare," Lana added. "So you're going to head out with Dad?"

She and Don had urged her to go with him to look over the dogs they were considering, though Emma appeared to have voted for school with her attire: short skirt, sleeveless summery top, heels.

"I can't," Em said, rinsing her plate and sticking it in the dishwasher. "I've got three AP classes." Advanced Placement. College credit, if she did well. "The only reason you're pushing me to go is Dad can't stalk me today so you want me with him."

"First, you're right, we want you covered," Don replied. "Second, you're a smart kid. You can miss a day. And third, I really would like your company."

"If you're not stalking me on the way to school, who's going to protect Sufyan?"

"His uncle. Trust me, he's got Sufyan's back," Don said. "Don't you think?"

Emma had to agree. "Okay, but I better go change."

Lana grinned at their back-and-forth, relieved they got on so well. Don was lucky to have reentered his daughter's life when he did. Another year or two and he might have missed the boat entirely.

Missed the boat? She wondered whether he did miss his forty-four-foot sloop on which he'd plied the Caribbean. She was deeply grateful to have him back—and felt just the opposite about the undeniably disturbing presence of Robin Maray.

She didn't even think about the agent again until she backed her Prius out of the garage and saw him parked in front of a neighbor's house in the Charger.

With a quick wave she acknowledged him as she drove down the sunlight-dappled street, making an effort to put aside any intrusive memories. She had far too much on her mind with the workday looming ahead.

Lana pulled into her spot in CyberFortress's underground parking garage and hurried to the elevator. An armed security guard stepped in behind her and pushed the button for the lobby.

"Good morning," Robin said, slipping in as the doors began to close.

Lana replied in kind with an effortless smile, then remembered her guilt. *For what?* she challenged herself. *It's not going to happen again.*

But the fling two years ago felt as near as yesterday when Robin had walked into Holmes's office.

Robin let her exit the elevator first. She felt peered at from behind and acutely aware of her body. She'd dressed modestly, as she always did for work, but after brushing out her shiny black hair she'd dabbed on Byredo's *Seven Veils*, a scent she adored. She hadn't even thought much about it till now. She'd just done it. *Like a few other things that you're now regretting.*

"Ask Maureen Henley to come to my office," Lana said to Ester Hall, her new executive assistant, an amateur tennis champion at fifty who smiled when Robin came into view.

Lana closed her door to him. He understood that he would not have access to her office or the war room, while young Maureen Henley was escorted in moments later by Ester.

"Have a seat," Lana told the MIT grad whose senior thesis on the economics of scale in the development of macro cybersurveillance systems had landed her a prestigious position at CyberFortress.

Maureen settled and shifted her silky red hair off her long graceful neck.

"This is a first," Maureen said.

"A first what?" Lana replied with her eyes on her inbox.

"The first time I've been in your office for a one-on-one since you interviewed me for the job."

"I think I'm about to disappoint you. What I need will call less on your cyberskills than your analytical ones. I want you to systematically review the posts of Steel Fist's followers. Hack where you need to, but you should start with the public sites because they'll be the most heavily trafficked. I'm guessing they'll also be on private sites, on social media, in chat rooms, all that stuff. I'm not interested in the threats against my family and me or Sufyan Hijazi, unless they depart from the usual fare. I want to know what's the story here, and, more importantly, I want to know when the story *changes*."

Maureen read at more than one thousand words a minute, even faster than Lana who clocked in at about eight hundred. So while the assignment was daunting, given Steel Fist's ten million subscribers, Maureen could race through the cyberclutter faster than anyone else in the war room.

"The first idea that strikes me," Maureen said, "is to construct a filter to screen out the typical neo-Nazi stuff. The n-word, Jews, kill, murder, gas, that kind of stuff."

"That might work. I'm not going to micromanage you. I just know we can't overlook the most easily accessed info."

"I'm on it."

Before Lana turned to Steel Fist's website, she knew she had to look as closely as possible at Tahir. She was back to triaging terror again.

And hack where you need to, she thought, echoing the advice she'd just given Maureen.

• • •

Don and Emma headed north in the old pickup. She busied herself texting Sufyan until school started, then bemoaned her boyfriend's unwillingness to stay in touch during class time. "He's so serious!" she complained, putting aside her phone.

"You are, too, taking all those AP classes. Does he take any?"

"All of them, including AP physics."

"No kidding."

"He's really smart, Dad."

"I guess. That's all college-level stuff, right?"

She nodded. "And I'm guessing you weren't like Mom in school."

"If you mean 4.0 and all that, you're right." He shook his head. "I'm a terrible role model."

"Not so bad now."

"Thanks, Em. That's generous. My biggest regret was missing so much of you growing up."

"Better late than never."

She put her earbuds in and propped herself against the passenger door.

Don looked over to make sure it was locked, then glanced at the road ahead before checking the side- and rear-view mirrors. He'd been keeping a discreet eye on them while he and Emma talked, though he expected no problems today; by heading north to meet the dogs they were breaking all the driving patterns Steel Fist had put up on his website. And Don's pickup hadn't gained any notice yet. Nevertheless, he had the compact Glock in the door pocket next to him. It was far less cumbersome for travel than the shotgun.

Once they escaped the grip of morning traffic, the trip took less than two hours. The kennel was about seven miles southeast of Hagerstown, Maryland, not far from the Pennsylvania border, marked only by three numbers on an eight-foot steel gate. It closed off a formidable stone wall that might have hailed from colonial times.

Don had to call the kennel to announce their arrival. Then Emma and he waited a few more minutes before a dusty SUV pulled up and the gate opened.

A portly middle-aged man in a Baltimore Orioles cap checked Don's driver's license.

"I was kind of surprised there were no guard dogs to greet us," Don said.

"They're too valuable. I had one killed in a drive-by shooting about five years ago, and that was the end of that." The man stuck out his hand. "Ed Holmes."

Don introduced himself and Emma.

"You can follow me in," Ed said.

The kennel grounds spread out over more than a hundred acres. As Don drove they heard gunshots. Emma tensed.

"They're training dogs, Em. Dogs for the military and police work are exposed to gunshot sounds from a pretty young age. You don't want them freaking out over live ammo."

"How do you know that?" she asked.

"Google."

Ed led them to an open, large white barn with cyclone fence kennels along both sides. Don could see that each kennel extended indoors via a dog door.

The breeder and trainer walked up to the pickup as Don and Emma climbed out. "How much experience do you have with dogs? You grow up with them?"

"I did," Don said. He glanced at Em, who shook her head.

"Security dogs?" Ed asked.

"No. Just an old mutt," Don replied.

"Time for a primer then. Our home security dogs are very different from the ones we train for the military or police. They've been socialized a lot. My wife has personally taken Jojo into Hagerstown from the time he was six weeks old. We wanted to make sure he was comfortable around people, unusual sounds, alarms, all that city stuff. So he's good that way. But he's still very much a guard dog and we're going to show you just what that means."

"I thought you had three dogs for us to check out today, including Jojo," Don said.

"Not after my dad briefed me about who you are and what's going on with you folks. I was sorry to hear all that, but I knew Jojo was the right one for you. He's the brightest, the biggest, and, I gotta say, the *baddest*."

Ed smiled. Emma laughed.

As the trainer led them along the kennels on the right side of the barn, a Malinois with white whiskers and graying facial fur joined them. The close resemblance to a German shepherd was clear at a glance.

"Who's he?" Emma asked. "He looks old."

"Oh, he's old," Ed said. "He's got the run of the place. He's retired now."

"From what?" Em asked.

Ed paused and looked at her. "The navy."

"They have them on boats?"

Ed shook his head. "No, not boats. This guy was really famous once, but not too many people know his name."

"That sounds like a riddle," Emma said. "How could he be famous if not many people knew his name?"

"You could be known to most folks as 'the dog' on a secret mission that became international news."

"Was he Cairo, the Malinois that went on the bin Laden raid?" Don asked.

"I could never say that," Ed replied.

"Could never or would never?" Don asked.

"Could never," Ed said. "But a right-thinking man or young woman might be okay coming to that conclusion."

"Really?" Emma said. "My father was telling me about that dog just last night." She looked closely at the old hound, sounding awed when she spoke again: "So he's that hero dog?"

"He's the real deal. I would not mislead you."

"Is he safe here?" Emma asked.

"You bet. Nobody knows where he's living out his life in peace. And look at him. He's not the spry young guy he once was. But you guys don't strike me as suicide bombers or paparazzi. And your mom knows how to keep secrets," he said to Emma. "So I'm guessing you can, too. Promise?"

"Yes. Can I shake his hand?"

"Sure. The President did. So did the First Lady."

Emma reached out, but the old dog lifted his paw and pushed it toward her for a high-five.

"He prefers that," Ed said.

Emma high-fived him.

A beautiful young black and tan Malinois stood just inside the gate peering at Ed with a look of eager anticipation.

His master opened the gate and ordered Jojo to heel. He minded immediately, coming to Ed's left side, keeping his eyes on him. The older dog wandered off.

Without looking down, Ed said, "Jojo, sit"

He turned to Don and Emma. "Let's walk away."

Jojo stared intently at the departing trio.

Ed stopped after they'd moved about twenty feet. "You notice I didn't say 'stay.' Just 'sit.' This is as basic as it gets, but that's where we have to start. If you command him to sit, he'll sit. Don't confuse that with the stay command. If you order him to lie down, he'll lie down. The same goes for all basic obedience commands. Forget 'stay.' That's always his default mode."

"Can I pet him too?" Emma asked. "Or is that off limits?"

"Absolutely you can pet him. Say, 'Jojo, come.'"

Emma complied. The dog raced up and sat right in front of her.

"Go ahead and pet him," Ed said.

Emma surprised Don by stroking Jojo's head confidently, then using both hands to rub his scruff.

Ed ran Jojo, Emma, and Don through the rest of the dog's basic obedience, which included the command "quiet."

"What you need to know about the Malinois," he added, "or a breed like the German shepherd and Doberman pinscher, is that most will naturally protect their families. What we do with our dogs destined for that kind of duty is evaluate them in this regard."

"How do you do that?" Don asked.

"Oh, you'll find out soon enough."

That must have been the cue, because a large man in a protection suit stormed around the barn and ran toward them. Jojo raced toward him and bit a camouflaged protection sleeve—and hung on. The man stopped resisting.

"Stand down," Ed commanded.

Jojo released his bite and stared at the man.

Ed put Jojo in the heel and went on. "We evaluated him for the first time when he was about nine months old. That was precisely how he reacted when one of my trainers launched himself at me. So we knew he had plenty of natural drive for protection. That's when we started working on the stand-down command."

Without warning the man in the protection suit ran toward them again. Jojo raced toward him. Ed shouted "Down." Jojo dropped to all fours.

"That's critical, too," Ed explained. "You've got to be able to stop his attack."

"He'd protect me like that?" Emma said.

"He'd give his life for you," Ed replied. "Usually we want to work with you for at least two long sessions before turning over a family security dog. We don't have that luxury with you. You need help as in yesterday, as I understand it from my father. That's one of the reasons you're getting Jojo. He's got a great temperament. We've tested him at each stage of his training. You'll also get a manual that you're going to have to study. Your mom, too," he said to Emma. "This is serious business. By the way," he added to Emma, "he likes you."

"I'll bet he likes all the girls," Em replied.

"Only the one's he's going to be protecting."

"What about my friends, if we're horsing around and I shout or something?"

"That's an excellent question. He'll be good with them. They can pet him, but you'll notice he's standoffish around them."

In the next two hours, Ed ran them through all the advanced obedience, which included hand signals for each command. Then he put Jojo through his security-dog paces, including preventing a suspect from moving by barking aggressively at him from about three inches away, backing a suspect up, and chasing one down.

By mid-afternoon Don and Emma had worked with Jojo for several hours and fed him for the first time.

"You two and your wife will be the only ones he'll take food from. We always worry about poisoning. He's poison-proof. But you guys can't let anyone else feed him. If someone tries to give him a treat, it won't be an issue because he won't take it. But to keep him poison-proof, you guys have to be the ones to feed him. If you have to leave him for a vacation or for any other reason, you leave him with us."

"I'm guessing you have a lot of demand for dogs like him these days," Don said.

"A lot of demand is right, but we've always sold every dog we've bred and trained, unless they were unfit for service. And we're still very careful about who gets them."

Don leaned over to pet Jojo. He could've sworn the dog was looking right through him. When he straightened Don saw the old dog wandering back up, as if to say good-bye.

"How old is he?" Don asked.

"Old as the hills. He's got some health issues. He's not going to be around much longer, I'm afraid."

"That's so sad," Emma said. "Can I give him a hug?"

"Nope. Sorry," Ed replied. "Good you asked, though. That old salt was trained for much harder stuff than hugging, so we don't push our faces into theirs. Family security dogs are different. You can hug Jojo. But this old guy?" Ed shook his head. "He's just not the cuddly type. You can high-five him good-bye."

Emma and Don both did. Then she asked for a picture of her with the dogs. Ed nodded his approval and Don took it with his daughter's phone. Ed snapped one of father, daughter, and Jojo.

It was now Don's turn to take the lead, this time to Bethesda. Jojo shared the pickup cab with his new owners.

Don wasn't the only one watching their backs now.

• • •

Lana settled into researching Tahir. She had Maureen combing through the posts of Steel Fist's fans, Galina trying to penetrate the NSA's military-grade encryption, and Jeff Jensen back to his primary role of insuring CF's own cyberdefense, a constant struggle.

Lana found it easy enough to check on Tahir's record in the U.S. It was in all the papers he'd submitted for political asylum, along with his background in Sudan. He'd run an import/export business there, as he had since coming to the States. He'd done well enough by Sudanese standards to have been considered a successful entrepreneur in sub-Saharan Africa. He now had a small shop in a mini-mall on the outskirts of Bethesda, where he sold African artifacts, carpets, and hand-carved furniture. Not bad for a man whose home country's chief exports were little more than peanuts and impoverished people.

He was Nubian from Khartoum in the north, Sudan proper, as opposed to South Sudan, which had been established after two civil wars had torn the country apart. Khartoum was the city to which Tahir had threatened to return with Sufyan. Lana didn't believe he'd actually do that. He was clearly devoted to the boy's future, and Sudan was plagued by the same problems afflicting much of the sub-Sahara: poverty, drought, hunger, war, inadequate medical care. Misery appeared to penetrate every realm of Sudanese life.

As she looked at Tahir's history, she was reminded immediately that Osama bin Laden and the core of Al Qaeda's leadership had headquartered in Sudan from 1991 to 1996. Bin Laden himself had been instrumental in seeing to the construction of two hundred miles of highway in the largely roadless land.

But what really grabbed Lana's interest was when she read that in addition to a construction company and massive farms, Al Qaeda had helped support itself by setting up an import/export business. How many people in Sudan could have been involved in that line of work back then? There were also news reports that in the pre-9/11 era, Al Qaeda had used the cover of legitimate businesses to smuggle weapons. She would have been surprised if they hadn't. But had Tahir been involved with that? An even more critical question concerned Tahir's import/export business now. Carpets, cabinets, and chests could be used to move bomb-making materials, including weapons of mass destruction.

But surely the CIA and FBI had vetted him for any kind of nefarious activity. Which had Lana asking herself whether she really wanted to reinvent that particular wheel by doing research that likely had been done by others. If the NSA knew about any of that, she should have been informed of it. She also knew that if she penetrated the NSA defenses right now, she would have some cover: Holmes himself wanted to see how porous the agency's cyber perimeter had become.

But that was for domestic surveillance files.

Correct, but she knew that a lot about Tahir could fit under that rubric.

She chose to share none of this with Galina, undertaking her own efforts in her quiet cubicle just feet from the industrious Russian émigrée.

Using codes she had been privy to in the past, Lana accessed the NSA system with ease. This was no violation of the spirit or letter of the law. As a prime contractor she was well within her purview. What she found in the next hour was ample official attention on Tahir, which came as no surprise. What she couldn't grasp was why—if he warranted so much focus—he'd even been permitted into the U.S. But as Lana worked, each step along the cyber highway became slower and more difficult to take. She did manage to unveil pertinent data repositories, which led her to a surprising keyhole. She hesitated only briefly before entering it.

More like a black hole. For Lana was swept in a nanosecond into the CIA network. But there she faced dense encryption.

"Aha," she said to herself softly when she realized the formidable security was a variation of code she'd written under contract for the NSA. A smile widened her face.

Adjusting quickly, she navigated for another twenty minutes before unearthing Tahir's CIA files. The revelations proved stunning.

In situ agents and their intrepid informants had linked Tahir to Al Qaeda in Khartoum in the two years preceding bin Laden's arrival. Tahir, in fact, appeared instrumental in setting up the terrorist group's import/export business, exactly as she'd suspected at first glance. He'd even rolled his own firm into what became Al Qaeda's.

But what chilled Lana to her fingertips and left her staring dumbfounded at her screen was learning that in 1996, when bin Laden and his two hundred closest supporters fled Sudan for Jalalabad, Afghanistan, Tahir and his brother went with them—*and stayed with Al Qaeda as the group established itself as the guests of the Taliban.*

It was from that base of operations that Al Qaeda had launched its September 11 attacks five years later. Both Tahir and Sufyan's father were full-fledged members of America's sworn enemies. American bombs then killed the brother when the U.S. struck back at the Afghan militants who'd provided safe haven to those who had organized, trained, and dispatched the box-cutter brigade. So, in fact, his brother hadn't been killed in their home village but by U.S. warplanes. Ample cause for anger.

But the rabbit hole Lana had plunged into then took an even more unexpected twist. In the month after his brother perished at American hands, Tahir became a CIA asset, providing information to an agent whose name was not revealed in the file.

Tahir had switched sides.

Or had he? People who changed their loyalties worried Lana. How pliable were their beliefs? Most jihadists who'd lost loved ones became more determined than ever to defeat their *kuffar* enemies. But according to these documents, Tahir had embraced the U.S. Did he do it because he felt deep responsibility for his brother's son and wife, which was certainly part of his Muslim and Nubian traditions? Or was Tahir playing a longer game?

Whatever the reason, the U.S. had soon paid a huge price to protect him, Lana learned when she began to read a file earmarked "Top Secret." It reported that Tahir had been among the Al Qaeda members, led by bin Laden, that had been run to ground by U.S. military forces at Tora Bora near the northwestern Pakistan border. The failure to deploy an adequate force of U.S. troops to tear the raggedy remains of the terrorist group from those mountain caves had long been the subject of great criticism and speculation. While two hundred jihadis were listed as killed, bin Laden and his key lieutenants, including Tahir, had escaped into Pakistan's Federally Administered Tribal Areas.

Scores of commentators in the U.S. and abroad had wondered openly why the U.S. could possibly have let the reviled terrorists slip away. Lana now stared at the answer: to protect Tahir Hijazi, a spy for the U.S. in the fight against radical Islamic terrorism.

According to the top-secret report, Tahir had been prominent among bin Laden's advisors in urging the retreat to Tora Bora and, therefore, had come under deadly suspicion by his fellow jihadis when their forces were attacked at the infamous cave complex. Tahir saved his own life, and the lives of his nephew and sister-in-law, by contacting an agency operative and hammering out a deal—quickly approved by the highest U.S. military command—to let the shredded Al Qaeda leadership escape to Pakistan. That deal protected not only Sufyan and the boy's mother, but preserved Tahir's invaluable role.

In exchange, though, he also had to agree to the devilishly tricky role of becoming a lifelong double agent under deep cover, a commitment to the agency that had saved the three of them. In the years that followed, Tahir's loyalty turned him into the most important spy in the U.S. War on Terror. It also placed Tahir firmly in CIA hands. He could never waver from his assignment without risking the lives of those he loved most.

But he's reneging on that now, Lana thought. *He's backing away from whatever he once agreed to.* No CIA asset threatens the life of a young woman who's the daughter of a major player in the country's intelligence community, not if he's trying to become a good citizen of his newly adopted land.

Maybe there were other motivations for Tahir's desire to return to the Sudan. And maybe because of her personal link to him, she'd glimpsed a whole lot more of what he was really up to than the CIA operatives who were running him now.

Lana wondered if Bob Holmes knew. If he did and had hidden it from her, it would only reinforce the veracity of what she just read because it would strongly indicate that Tahir was known only to the highest echelon of the intelligence community.

And if that's the case, he's not going to confirm anything.

But Lana had known Bob for more than two decades. She might be able to read the old spymaster's reaction.

Donna Warnes put her right through to her boss. Bob sounded as tired as he'd appeared when she'd seen him yesterday.

"You okay?" she asked.

"Fine, fine," he replied quickly, always dismissing any interest in his health. "Do you have Galina trying to hack into this place?"

"I do."

"Good. Don just picked up my son's best family-security dog. I told Ed to send the bill to us."

"I appreciate that." A fully trained adult Malinois could easily cost more than $25,000.

"They're on the way home now, in case you're wondering. Ed sent me a photo of Emma with her new dog. She looks really happy. What's up on your end?"

"It's Tahir Hijazi. Do you know anything about him being a CIA asset?"
"Only that it sounds possible. Why do you ask?"
"Because given where he's from, and where he's ended up, it makes sense that he could have been, or still is, on the payroll."
"I could look into it."
"Would you? I'd also like to know if it was ever confirmed that he was Al Qaeda."
"I'll see what I can find out."

She wondered if Bob were phrasing his answers carefully, or just as casually curious as he sounded. "It's important," she went on, "because he threatened to kill Emma yesterday afternoon if she keeps seeing his nephew."

Bob groaned. To Lana he sounded like a man who'd just learned that someone he'd had on a short leash had just bolted away. But she couldn't challenge him further without heightening the risk that he would figure out what she'd found. Besides, if the deputy director were dancing around his replies, pressing him harder would achieve nothing. So she tried to sound concerned, but companionable:

"I know. It scares me, too."
"Don't let Emma out of your sight."
"That's hardly practical, Bob. But we're doing all we can to try to keep her safe. Don's on the job. Thanks for rushing through his license."

Lana ended the call and sat back, wondering . . .

But not for long: Maureen, though only across the room at her workstation, sent her a screen shot from Steel Fist's website. A photo had been posted showing Em with the dogs in front of a barn. Don's pickup and an SUV were parked in the background.

The message below the photo read:

"Lana Elkins's daughter, Emma, just got a guard dog from a CIA-connected breeder and trainer in northern Maryland. Look at the plates on the pickup and SUV. The pickup is registered to the girl's father, Don Fedder, a convicted drug dealer who just got out of federal prison. He's back living with the kid and his ex-wife, Lana Elkins. The SUV belongs to Ed Holmes, the breeder working for a government that can't keep you safe, but is doling out thousands of dollars for a damn dog to protect the daughter of a drug pusher and her black Muslim boyfriend. Holmes is the son of Robert Holmes, a deputy director of the NSA. These people are all in bed together in every possible way.

"So the Elkinses now have a dog at your expense. Look at that kid. Don't you want to just wipe that smile right off that rich bitch's face? You can because we don't need a dog that can bite. We've got bullets!

"Ammo up!"

CHAPTER 10

VINKO STOOD UP FROM his computer and stretched. It was true: a chain was only as strong as its weakest link. And right now Lana Elkins's weakest link was her kid.

Emma Elkins represented everything he'd always *hated* about a certain sort of girl. Brought up rich, or nearly so, and goddamn beautiful—if he were feeling generous, which he was not—she'd already chosen at age seventeen to live in the world of mongrels.

How pathetic is that?

And from what Vinko had gleaned from intercepting her texts, she was smart, too, but not in the most important ways when you lived—and *died*—based on your online privacy. Emma was too lazy to even bother using her tight-ass OpSec—operational security—most of the time. He guessed her mother had put it on her phone because it sure wasn't standard-issue. But guess what, Emma? It's just like a condom: you don't use them, you don't have *any* protection. And that means you get seriously fucked. He figured she was realizing that right about now.

Vinko had intercepted the photo of her with their new dog as soon as she'd sent it to her boyfriend.

A photo's low-hanging fruit in the cyber orchard, especially the way you sent it.

Just like her texts, which he'd been hacking for weeks. The two of them were definitely sexually active—something that nauseated him every time he imagined the white girl slapping skin with the dark one. Recently he'd read an elliptical text from the boy apologizing, once more, for the "mishap" when they'd been "doing it."

Mishap?

Not when push came to shove with a Muslim man. *Just try getting an abortion, Emma, if you're pregnant.* Vinko couldn't wait to intercept those messages, if she lived long enough to send them.

The very thought of her trying to explain to a Muslim why she had to terminate a pregnancy had Vinko shaking his head as he stepped outside. He shaded his eyes with his hand and spotted the goats in the shadow of a giant beech tree.

Time to milk them, but he relished another moment imagining Emma Elkins pregnant—and the messages he could send out with that news. The responses would be volcanic, and that was important because he wanted to move his followers to take real action, not simply brag and snort in chat rooms about their guns and who should be killed. They needed a breakthrough moment to understand their power. The assassination of the Elkins family would do it. Even murdering only Emma could accomplish that much. Nothing destroyed a family faster than the death of a child.

So he luxuriated in thinking about the aftermath, the militant mobilization that would follow, including the exterminations necessary for the building of a self-sufficient nation. He'd already seen to his own needs. Others should, too. Vinko had solar panels on his roofs, and a well drawing the purest water from a depth of four hundred feet.

He also raised his own food—chickens, turkeys, fruits, and vegetables—on three carefully tended acres. You didn't need a thousand acres, or even a hundred. Three acres could raise it all. Add a deer or elk or bear to the larder and you were set.

"Herd 'em inside," he commanded Biko, who'd risen from all fours as soon as he'd seen his master. Now the border collie nipped at the goats, driving them toward the barn.

Biko moved back and forth, methodically funneling them toward the open doors. The Gallas hated Biko—until they needed his protection. Then they'd do whatever the dog wanted. The perfect relationship between the herd and the one that kept them safe.

Vinko felt the same about his followers. Nitwits, by and large. But they needed milking too, for their anger and firepower. And they definitely needed direction.

Biko was still nipping the legs of the last of the nannies. They brayed in protest but ran into the barn, straight for the milking pen, leaving their kids behind. People idealized animals, Disneyfied them, believing the mothers would never abandon their young. Horseshit. Even bear sows were known to leave their cubs for lunchmeat when their own lives were threatened. And as a kid he'd personally witnessed a guinea pig mom gobble up her pink offspring as soon as they were born. Nature, red in tooth and claw.

Get used to it, America.

Biko turned his attention back to Vinko. It made his master recall the first time he'd seen a border collie work. Wasn't in Idaho, but down in Baja, Mexico, during spring break in college. Some of the white guys from the offensive unit had caravanned down to spend a couple of weeks fishing, kayaking, and mountain biking.

On an early morning solo ride Vinko had come barreling over a rise and almost plunged straight down into a large herd of sheep. He'd locked his disc brakes and skidded wildly to a stop.

The sheep scattered like snowflakes in a storm, white fleece swirling left, right, and center, revealing a border collie at the very heart of the chaos. The dog had been a portrait of calm, staring Vinko right in the eye. The QB had taken a good guess at what the canine was thinking: *I got this, asshole.*

And then the dog went straight to work on those crazed sheep.

Vinko, off his bike, had figured he could sneak by while the herd dog spent the next hour or so chasing down the flock.

Wrong as wrong could be. Vinko had made it only about halfway past where the herd had been congregating before that dog had rounded up every last sheep, and there were at least two hundred of them. Astonishing to watch. It couldn't have taken the hound more than two minutes.

Then the border collie started back for him. He hadn't run toward Vinko. He'd trod like a stalker, deliberate, eyes blazing. No more than forty pounds of animal but he'd looked loaded for bear—or Vinko.

Vinko had placed his mango-colored full-suspension bike between the dog and him—and kept moving along. But every step he took was matched in the next instant by the border collie.

Curiously, the animal never drew within six feet of him. When he'd stumbled over a small boulder, the herder had barked, as much as saying, "No excuses. Move!"

Vinko had recovered his balance and hurried away faster, wishing like hell he'd had a can of pepper spray. Just in case.

But "just in case" never happened. After ten minutes of their step-by-step, the dog stopped and watched him leave.

Vinko knew he'd always remember that border collie. He'd *respected* that canine. The animal had exercised his proper authority and power with great care, doing no damage to Vinko but sending him on his way. That was all Vinko wanted to do to the mongrels in his nation. He wasn't out for blood, not at all, though he recognized, as any reasonable white man would, that spilling a lot of it was probably inevitable because mongrels were by nature stupid and understood only the power of pain. There was nothing to be done about their limited aptitude but nip at their heels—*hard*. After all, even goats and sheep had to feel the bite if they refused their masters' wishes.

Look at them. The nannies were compliant, yielding to his ministrations with the milking machine, though it challenged Vinko at a time like this to be patient with the demands of husbandry when, more than anything, he wanted to get back on his computer and rally his followers.

But Vinko also needed to visit the gun shop in town. That bastard Bones had taken a very valuable Ruger from him. If Vinko had had any faith in the sheriff, he would have reported the theft at gunpoint. But the sheriff hated Vinko and the dozens of other white supremacists still hanging around Hayden Lake. The lawman made no secret of his disgust for their beliefs. But there were ways other than running to the sheriff to deal with Bones. And, regardless, he needed to replace the .357 because he wanted to have a killer weapon on hand at all times.

Right now he carried his dead father's Pony .380. But he just didn't trust the Pony's action as much as the Ruger magic he loved so much.

He'd get his gun back, and it wouldn't be hard. Bones had glioblastoma, GBM, the most devastating form of brain tumor. He was on a downward path with no way back. And when Vinko once more had his Ruger in hand, he might even do Bones a favor. Or maybe he'd just let him waste away to nothing.

The *Idaho Statesman* in Boise had published a story about Bones just a week before he'd rolled up in his Porsche. Vinko had missed the tearjerker when it was published because he hated American newspapers. They all obeyed *sharia* self-censorship when they should be telling the real story of the country's undermining from within.

But he'd endured a few minutes with the *Statesman* report, which of course included an obligatory resurrection of the ESPN interview with Bones and Vinko, and a line that had made the former QB curdle with anger: "While Bones Jackson went on to the NFL Hall of Fame, and has raised millions for charities ranging from childhood nutrition to Alzheimer's research, his former quarterback, Vinko Horvat, is now an all-but-forgotten goat farmer in Hayden Lake."

All-but-forgotten.

No question that the line stung. But being considered all-but-forgotten was good. It was better to have people think he had settled wholly into the hick life. That wouldn't add up to a man who was also a computer mastermind with ten million followers. They'd find out the truth soon enough. He'd emerge more triumphant than he'd ever been on the gridiron.

Vinko gathered up the milk canisters and poured them into a vat for pasteurization. Then he released the nannies. The kids ran up, sure to be disappointed by the empty teats.

He saw to the cleaning of the milking machine, turned on the drip irrigation for a half-acre of greens and a row of rhubarb, then hurried inside to settle in his office. The shades were drawn. They always were. Nobody would ever get a glimpse in there.

Now it was time to up the ante:

"You saw my words last night. You saw Emma Elkins's photo earlier today. You saw her guard dog. And I know you've seen the photo of her black Muslim boyfriend. You've seen Emma's father, too. And you know who her mother is and where they all live. Even the routes they take to school and work. What are you waiting for?

"You've told *me* time and again that you're organized into cells. You've told me you're armed. You've told me you're all ammoed up, too.

"Now *show* the world what you can do to a rich bitch and her guard dog. Take down the father and mother if you can, but KILL THE GIRL. Slaughter her and you'll destroy her mother. Destroy her mother and you'll puncture the armor of the police state we still call America.

"Talk is cheap.

"Blood is priceless."

CHAPTER 11

LANA'S PHONE RANG AS she sped down the Beltway. She'd just finished an early morning prep session with Deputy Director Bob Holmes for their testimony tomorrow before the Senate Select Committee on Intelligence and was headed to her office in Bethesda. With cars and trucks ripping past the Prius at 85 to 90 mph, she pulled onto the shoulder to take the call, trailed by Agent Robin Maray in the Charger. The nation might be enduring gas and diesel shortages but drivers weren't slowing down. Full-bore ahead, wherever that might lead them, as if what really fueled them was a general, underlying panic. There were ample reasons for it.

The flooding of coastlines continued unabated, with hundreds of thousands of refugees from shoreline communities pressing inward. The number of displaced Americans had yet to be calculated with precision but the estimates now ranged upwards of three million—on the East Coast alone. Southern California was seeing similar numbers. Communities on both coasts stood abandoned, roofs now low-lying islands in the rising seas. Long Island, with the geometry of a table top, had shrunk by twenty percent.

The news on Lana's phone was no less disturbing. The fashionable young sandy-haired lawyer who'd briefed her and Holmes had just sent Lana what could be a preview of tomorrow's hearing, video of a corpulent member of the Select Committee on Intelligence denouncing CyberFortress: "They're getting massive, million-dollar contracts, letting

Lana Elkins fatten on the fear that grips our great land. That money should be going straight to the fine law enforcement officers who now form the front line of our mighty nation's defense." Then the senior senator from Louisiana castigated Lana further for "stealing" Galina Bortnik: "Elkins not only drains our treasury, she drains our brain power, too, spending taxpayer money to hire a brilliant young Russian computer hacker who's only here because brave members of our military saved her from the treacherous claws of Russian thugs."

Lana winced at the memory of the SEALs who'd died on that mission, but the senator wasn't playing fair: she and Don came close to dying as well, and both had received secret commendations from the President for their heroism. Not the first time in Lana's case.

Will this crap never end? The political wars.

Lana had so much going on right now her head felt as if it would explode. The single most harrowing message on her phone today had come from Jeff Jensen when she'd been on her way out to Fort Meade: a Steel Fist diatribe against her daughter that included a command to his followers to kill Emma—and ended with the words "Blood is priceless" that had almost sickened Lana.

First, Tahir had threatened her daughter's life, and now the other end of the political spectrum, Steel Fist, had openly called for his followers to "slaughter" Emma to "destroy her mother."

Those goddamn animals.

The latest threats from Steel Fist came in the midst of a short breather from terrorism. More than seventy-two hours had passed without an attack or bombing. Commentators were claiming the relative calm reflected the "stiffening backbone of the country in a time of crisis." Other partisans were heralding a new age in national defense as "local law enforcement steps up to the plate."

Their chorus of clichés was joined by senators and members of Congress offering paeans to the locals while also urging the appropriation of billions of dollars for the nation's biggest defense contractors for more fighter jets, aircraft carriers, and pricey missile defense systems that would do next to nothing to fight the asymmetric war in which America was now engaged. Fighter jets to try to stop small bands of terrorists determined to slip past the country's flooded borders so they could create large-scale mayhem in crowded cities and rural outposts? Whoever had said you couldn't possibly burn the candle of national defense at both ends clearly hadn't anticipated politics and budgeting in an era of invasion. With her entire country under attack, Lana felt strongly that centralized command was the *sine qua non* of an effective *national* defense.

As for cybersecurity, amazingly enough, it had gone begging once again. Voters saw kinetic war because it showed on their video screens—bombs, blood, and broken bodies—so they supported steps to stop it. Understandable. Steps needed to be taken. Clearly. But what too many influential voices on the Hill and in the media failed to recognize was the "invisible invasion" of the country's infrastructure that was taking place every second of every day by cybersaboteurs.

Those attacks came from carefully deployed electrons. Try selling that to a science-starved electorate. Not as sexy as a new class of fighter jets, nor as immediately powerful as next-generation smart bombs with their own visuals, but terrorists had formed a fifth column from afar by infiltrating millions of private and government devices to create botnets that hijacked the country's own vast resources into an attack against their very hosts: jiu jitsu in the cyber age.

Lana took a breath and checked her rear-view, where Robin sat in the Charger with his aviator sunglasses fixed on her. She put the Prius in drive just as her phone went off again. She was tempted to take off, but couldn't: a glance at a text showed tension on the home front now. Emma wanted Sufyan to come over. She couldn't go to school. The principal had said the district didn't have the resources to ensure the safety of its students with Emma in their midst.

At least she's asking permission. And using her encryption. Finally. Maybe she'd even remembered to keep her Mace around, though Lana had her doubts; every time she'd checked, Em had come up empty-handed.

"U can c him @ home," Lana texted back.

Tap-tap-tap.

Robin was at her window. "Everything okay?"

"Everything's fine." Lana glanced up. Couldn't see his eyes behind those shades. *Just as well.* "I'm going to get moving here."

But everything wasn't fine. Her personal life was flooded, too—with confusion. Which might have explained her sudden itch to gamble, so palpable it felt like psoriasis of the psyche.

She grabbed her second phone. Her fingers stabbed the dial pad. Not for texasholdem.com: a Gamblers Anonymous meeting. Tonight at seven o'clock at the Hope Center in Bethesda.

You're going, no matter what.

She got back on the road, pulling into CF's underground garage fifteen minutes later.

Robin remained in her wake to the elevator where they stood silently as the security guard brought them up to her company's reception area.

She noticed that Robin received "Good mornings" and smiles at every turn, already a fixture. Even the men, Jeff Jensen included, appeared impressed by him.

Maureen gave him a big smile *and* a wave. Lana could scarcely believe her youngest employee, at twenty-three, could be interested in a man about twice her age.

But fit, Lana thought.

Don't remind me.

Maureen tugged Lana aside. "May we talk privately?"

"Sure."

Lana led the young woman into her office, where Maureen spoke up quickly: "I found something incongruous in the most popular Steel Fist chat room."

"Shoot." Lana arranged herself at her desk and started up her desktop computer.

"Almost all those guys rail against you, Emma, and Sufyan. Some are now raging about your dog and Don, but you and Emma and her boyfriend are the chief recipients of their animus."

Lana nodded, pleased by Maureen's use of language at a time when so many others were dumbing down their speech.

"But there's one self-proclaimed white supremacist who conspicuously, at least to my way of thinking, omits any reference to Sufyan."

"That is odd. Does he talk about any people of color?"

"Plenty. He's got nothing good to say about Senator Booker or a certain President, and he hates—he puts that word in caps—the Reverends Al Sharpton and Jesse Jackson and their friends on the left, like Cornel West and Amy Goodman. He's quite vociferous, too. I've compiled three pages of those comments."

"So where do you think we should go from here?" Lana knew the route she wanted Maureen to take, but waited to see if the cyber swallows would actually land in Capistrano for the MIT grad.

"You should give me the go-ahead to hack Tahir Hijazi."

Conspicuous, indeed, thought Lana, who quickly gave her permission.

Lana's own effort ranged far from both Steel Fist's chat rooms and Tahir's efforts to stir up hatred against her family. Assuming it was Tahir, which felt like an eminently reasonable supposition.

She was far too busy digging into deeper vaults where Tahir's quietest secrets apparently hid. And if her work and Maureen's converged, it would give Lana a chance to observe the young woman's skills firsthand.

Lana settled at her workstation to return to her probe of Tahir's background, which had confirmed his strong associations with Al Qaeda and the CIA and—by extension—the NSA.

Now let's see just how many hands that Sudanese ex-pat is playing.

She paused over her use of gambling lingo, which sometimes could infect every other thought—a sure sign of the tumult she felt. Another appeared in the next instant when she checked her watch for the third time since talking to Maureen and saw that she had seven hours and forty-three minutes until the Gamblers Anonymous meeting.

Then four hours and thirty-seven minutes.

An hour and twelve minutes.

After her least productive day in memory, it was finally time to leave. Which meant that Tim Angier, the FBI's second-shift agent after Robin, would learn that one of the nation's top cyberwarriors was an addict.

Lana shrugged off the concern. With five million Americans enrolled in one twelve-step program or another, high-ranking members of the intelligence community were likely represented in significant numbers.

Still, the thought of the meeting made her nervous. The anonymity she sought was also the anonymity she feared.

Emma glared so fiercely at Don he felt as if she'd reduce him to ash if she could. He'd just told Em he didn't want Sufyan and her going to the mall. The young man was standing by her side.

"It's less than a mile away. I'm sick of being stuck in this house all day long. It's like a prison."

She sounded screechy, every word a drill bit to Don's brain. Even Jojo's upright ears were rotating like satellite dishes. So was his head as he followed the argument, as if he understood the words.

Don tried to keep his response soft. "Em," he pleaded, "you saw the message from that madman. You know he's got ten million racist followers. I'm not Superman—"

"That's for sure," she cut him off to say.

Breathe. "Which means I can't protect you everywhere."

"We don't need you to. I've got this." She pulled a blond wig out of her shoulder bag. "Nobody's going to recognize me if you're not ten feet behind me all the time. I'll be fine."

He sighed. "You really think that's going to throw them off your scent?"

Long straight hair parted in the middle, it looked like it had been modeled on Gwen Stefani.

Or Stefani's just been scalped, which Don felt would be more in the spirit of the times.

"And I'll wear some shitty-looking shorts, totally out of style so nobody will recognize me."

"And what's Sufyan going to wear?" he asked patiently, wishing he hadn't when Emma nudged her boyfriend and the young man whipped out an afro wig that he'd been holding behind his back. It looked like it had been lifted off the head of boxing promoter Don King.

Don couldn't stifle a laugh. *Bad* move. Emma now glared so hard her eyes were slits.

"Look, you two won't be going to a Halloween party for a few weeks. And in those get-ups you're not going to fool anyone."

"With sunglasses," Emma protested, "I think we will."

Interestingly enough, Sufyan hadn't said a word. Don figured Tahir's nephew wasn't nearly so practiced at defiance.

"No, sorry." Don shook his head.

"Let's go," Emma said to Sufyan, throwing her wig on hastily. The middle part ran at a diagonal across her own hair, which hung down and looked so bizarre it would have drawn more attention to her than the wig itself. "Put it on," Em said to Sufyan.

The young man demurred, but scooted out the door to the garage right behind Emma.

Jojo looked back and forth, as though unsure of what to do. "Don't look at me," Don said to him. "I don't know, either. But duty calls. Come."

Don and the dog trailed the pair into the garage. The electronic door was rising. Emma fired up the Fusion. Sufyan was closing the passenger door. Em started backing up.

"Sit," Don commanded Jojo.

He ran inside and grabbed the Glock from the top shelf of a kitchen cabinet, then bolted back into the garage, determined to try to keep them safe.

Em had closed the door.

He swore, raced to the panel and pressed the button to open it. Lana had ordered him a remote from the security company but it hadn't arrived yet. Then he opened the door to his pickup, signaled Jojo into the cab, and backed out as daylight appeared behind him.

Emma was long gone.

Don backed onto the street fast, thankful that at least he knew their plans, unless . . . she wanted to dodge him completely at this point.

Swearing profusely, he gunned the old truck, which had more ponies under the hood than a lot of newer cars.

He tore through the neighborhood, watching crosswalks and corners for children, then turned onto a main boulevard to the mall, which soon loomed before him, a colossus of consumerism.

God knows what entrance they might have used.

Don turned into the first one, making a sweep of a parking area the size of FedEx Field. Lots of Fusions, but none was Emma's. No cockamamie blond wigs or Don King lookalikes, either.

He circumnavigated the mall, which took almost forty minutes, acutely aware that his was a cursory search at best.

Don felt panic creeping up his spine. He trolled all the surrounding neighborhoods and mini-malls, even making a pass by Sufyan's house. Nothing, nothing, nothing. Jojo sat beside him, looking back and forth from Don to the parking lot. Ninety minutes more passed by the time Don was done. Still no sign of them. He was frantic.

And then he heard the sirens.

• • •

Second-shift FBI agent Tim Angier hung back as Lana walked into a meeting room of the Hope Center in Bethesda, which hosted a number of twelve-step recovery fellowships. She'd briefed him in her office, pointing out that it was a closed meeting. "Addicts only. There won't be any family or friends. And just so you know, nobody here knows about my addiction."

"I understand," he'd replied. "Am I going to have to say anything? Fake it?"

"Not at all. Some people don't talk at all for their first few meetings. There's no pressure to do that."

About twenty gamblers were seated when she arrived. Only a handful were women. The meeting was to begin in three minutes. Lana helped herself to a cup of coffee, spurning the cookies.

Tim walked in a minute later, sitting at about two o'clock from her. Three other African Americans were also at the meeting. Asian Americans and Caucasians, including Latinos, formed the rest of the multicultural group.

Lana recognized seven regulars. One was the woman she'd sat next to at the last meeting. She avoided Lana's eyes. Lana didn't feel much like socializing, either; she wanted to get this monkey off her back. And if she couldn't pry the tenacious beast loose, she wanted to sedate it somehow.

A man with short, oily curls sitting to her right did nod at her. In a leather vest, he was the only one who looked like he could have come from central casting.

The troubled-looking woman was the first to speak, revealing that she'd taken her maximum out of her ATM. "Then I went straight to the MGM Casino." A new one that had opened near DC. "I promised to limit myself." Lana had sung that tune too many times herself. "I sure didn't *plan* on going back to the ATM every day last week. By the time I was done, I'd lost all the money I'd saved to fly out and visit my mom in San Leandro. She's dying. That was going to be my last visit." The woman began to cry. "I can't take this anymore."

No one said a word. They watched to see if the woman wanted to go on. A moment later she did: "I felt sick every second and I just kept doing it."

"We've all got the sickness," Oily Curls said. "I hear you."

The woman nodded. She was finished. Her sponsor reiterated her support for her.

Lana talked about her own disturbed state over the past several days, telling them how she'd rushed into a stall in a restroom, pulled out her phone, brought up texasholdem.com, and placed a bet before she'd even let herself think about what she was doing. "But I stopped after playing one hand and winning $137. Only the desire hasn't stopped. It's like it's feeding on that win every minute. I'm having a hard time getting it out of my head. It's as real as this room. I just want it to go away."

"It will," said a distinguished-looking man Lana happened to know worked at the Federal Trade Commission. His white beard looked bleached against his dark skin. "First step is the one you took. You put the phone away. You walked out of that bathroom. You walked the walk."

"Amen," said Oily Curls.

When Oily Curls said that, Lana looked at him and felt the gambling sickness slip away. But what replaced it wasn't calm. Nothing so soothing. What replaced it was fear. Her sixth sense was screaming, *Who is he?*

• • •

Emma and Sufyan had decided not to go to the mall because she was sure her father would have found them and made a huge mortifying scene, so they snuck into a dimly lit video arcade nearby that Sufyan favored.

Emma had more than a video game in mind.

Snuggling together, she felt confident they'd drawn no attention. Both had made sure their wigs fit properly. Emma liked her look so much she had her compact mirror out and was flirting with the idea of dyeing her hair.

"Come on," Sufyan said. "Put that away and let's play."

He brought up a *Jurassic World* game on a large screen a few feet away, then clobbered her in short order. A second time as well. Emma wasn't really into gaming, mostly indulging him. But she enjoyed taking a break to make out, vigorously enough that Sufyan's hairpiece came off as three guys barged in to see if the station was available. One of them did a double take and looked away so fast that Emma knew they'd just been made.

"We've got to get out of here," she whispered to Sufyan, spying the guy who'd eyed them; he'd stepped away and was on his phone. Coincidence? Possibly—everybody Emma knew was on their phones most of the time—but she couldn't take any chances.

As casually as they could they headed toward the entrance, the sounds of games—guns, explosions, and angry commandos—dogging their every step. Even so, the guy on the phone shouted above the din and clicked his fingers like a waiter calling for a bus boy. His two friends rushed up. The larger one stepped in front of Em and Sufyan. "Where you guys think you're going? Stick around."

When he grabbed Emma's arm and yanked off her wig, Sufyan clocked him and kicked the legs out from under his buddy, then took Emma's hand and raced toward the rear exit.

Bursting from the shadowy arcade, they were almost blinded by the light of late afternoon.

Running hard, they jumped into her car. Out of breath, Emma drove away, making it to a four-way intersection where a windowless van screeched to a stop, blocking them.

The van doors flew open. Four guys spilled out, including the one at the arcade who'd been on his phone as soon as he'd spotted Emma and Sufyan.

The Sudanese started to open his door and was halfway out when Emma screamed "No," grabbed his belt, and jerked him back onto the passenger seat. She floored the Fusion in reverse. The guys chased her for a few feet before sprinting back to their vehicle. As the van started to turn toward them, an old white Corolla plowed into the front bumper.

"Stop!" Sufyan yelled at Emma as his uncle climbed out of the subcompact.

Sufyan was opening his door again. Em still had the car careening in reverse. She braked, fearing he would hurl himself out while they were still speeding.

He sprinted to the intersection as Tahir ducked a bat swung by the driver. The much younger man was twice as wide as Tahir, but his attack proved half as fast: Tahir landed blows to the man's throat and crotch, leaving him gasping and doubled over. His aluminum bat clanged on the asphalt.

But two other lunks piled on the bone-stitched older man from behind and started dragging him to the open side of the van, as though to abduct him.

Sufyan launched himself into the fray, freeing one of his uncle's arms.

Emma raced up. The guy who'd been on the phone came around the rear of the Corolla, charging her. She backed up, then Maced him at the last second. He reeled away, blinded.

She looked over as Tahir pummeled the man still clinging stubbornly to his arm. Then the assailant let go and tried to throw *himself* into the van.

Tahir grabbed his foot and dragged him halfway out before stomping his knee so hard Emma heard bones crack and the man scream. It took less than three seconds, the leg now bent as nature had never intended.

Sufyan's arm was bleeding. The guy he'd been fighting had used a knife on him and was charging Sufyan again, as though to finish him off. Emma shouted. As soon as the man looked over, she Maced him too.

Tahir grabbed Sufyan's arm, looked at the stab wound, and said, "Hospital." He pointed to Emma, his expression furious. "Take him. Get out of here."

Neighbors were staring out their windows. More than looking; in several cases they were shooting video with their phones.

Emma and Sufyan rushed to her car. Her legs felt rubbery. They hadn't till now. The fight had happened so quickly.

Shaking, she piled herself behind the wheel and headed to Suburban Hospital with Sufyan.

"Did he cut an artery?" she asked, near tears.

"No, but he stuck it deep. It hurts. Thanks. You were great."

Only then did Emma realize she still gripped the Mace in her hand. Only then did she hear the sirens in the distance.

• • •

By the time Don found his way to the four-way, police, ambulances, and a growing crowd had converged on the intersection. There was ample chatter about two white cars that had fled the scene.

"A skinny old black guy put the crazy on them," an impressed young man said.

A detective immediately took him aside. Don tried to listen in and was told to back away.

With Jojo in the heel, he walked over to a fellow using his phone camera to shoot two white guys on stretchers getting loaded into an ambulance.

"You see much?" he asked him.

"I saw it all," the guy said.

"I heard there were two white cars."

"Yeah, an old Corolla and a Fusion. Everybody was fighting, man. A chick with pepper spray took two of 'em out. One of them had a damn knife he used on a young black dude. But it was the old guy who waled on those honkies. No offense," he added as if he'd just registered Don's race.

"None taken. Where'd they go, the ones in the white cars?"

"Different places. I think the old guy told the white chick to take the brother to a hospital, then he was out of there, too, in the opposite direction. No plates on his car. He knew his business."

• • •

Don left Jojo in the pickup and rushed into the emergency room at Suburban, finding Emma in the waiting area.

"I'm so sorry, Dad."

"Put it aside, Em." He figured natural consequences spoke far more loudly than he ever could. "Are you okay?"

"I'm fine."

"How about Sufyan?"

"Fifteen stitches. He wouldn't let them use an anesthetic. I thought I was going to throw up. He's finishing up in there. But Tahir's out for blood."

"From what I heard, he already got some. And so did you."

"I mean Tahir's freaking angry, Dad. I could see it in his eyes. At *me*."

"Can you blame him?"

"No." Em shook her head.

Sufyan walked out, gauze wrapped around his right arm from his elbow to his wrist. He had a pill bottle in his uninjured hand.

"Did you call home?" Don asked as he pulled out his own phone.

"I left a message," Sufyan said. "I hope he's okay."

"Your mom didn't answer."

"His mom never does," Em said in a way that suggested that Don should leave that subject alone.

"I expect the police will be here any time," Don said, calling Lana.

"A detective already came and went," Emma said. "He took statements from us and gave us his card." She handed it to Don. "Those guys attacked us and then they tried to blame us. But the detective said five people got video of it, all from different angles. Can you believe that?"

Easily, Don thought as he heard his phone ringing Lana's. "So you guys are in the clear?"

They both nodded. "The cop made sure we were all right, and he said he'd be back in touch. We're probably going to have to testify and stuff."

Don nodded, knowing that as much as the video might have exonerated his daughter and Sufyan, it would also make them absolutely notorious to those who would drag them from cars and beat them to death.

Lana answered on the fifth ring: "Don, where are you?"

"I'm with them. Emma's fine. Sufyan's fine. They're safe. I can tell you what happened when we get—"

"Hold on," Lana said quickly. "Tahir's pulling up in front of our place. And—"

"I think he's going to be pissed."

"He's definitely pissed. He just slammed his car door. I saw him on the news. Now he's running up here. Where's Jojo?"

"Sorry. I've got him, too."

"Got to go. He's here."

In the background, Don heard thunderous pounding.

Lana hung up.

CHAPTER 12

LANA RUSHED THROUGH THE living room to her home office and grabbed her Sig Sauer 9 millimeter, racking the slide and jamming the barrel into the back of her pants. She draped the tail of her shirt over it as Tahir pounded on her door again.

She approached it without a word. He might not have heard her anyway; the door weighed almost fifteen hundred pounds and was made of reinforced steel, the kind used most often for panic rooms in homes. She figured her whole house qualified for panic status with all the security upgrades. She'd had them added when the seas rose and domestic "disturbances" escalated.

Lana looked at the screen of her digital door peephole. Tahir's angry face loomed close; in the background she saw that the small blue car he'd driven was not the smashed-up Corolla he'd used to save Emma and Sufyan. She also noticed that he hadn't drawn a weapon, though on the video she'd watched minutes ago online he'd acquitted himself handsomely with nothing more than his fists and feet.

She unlocked the door, and stepped back quickly, keeping her distance from Tahir. He moved past her without saying a word in greeting. He smelled of sun and sweat.

"Where are they?" he demanded in a hoarse voice.

"They're coming. Don's with them." She mentioned him, lest Tahir assume he'd be facing only the teens and her.

Tahir didn't respond. He looked around as if he still might find Sufyan lurking in the living room.

"Can I get you something to drink?"

"Water."

He sounded dry. But at least he'd answered her.

When she turned her back on him to go to the kitchen, she listened for his footfalls. If he'd taken one step to follow her she would have wheeled around with her weapon. But he remained by a bay window and stared at the street.

Lana filled a plastic cup with water, unwilling to give the apparently unarmed man a weapon of any kind; she knew the damage you could do to someone's face with a simple glass because she'd been trained to do it. She suspected the maiming and blinding potential of a glass wouldn't have been lost on a fighter like Tahir, either.

So be it. She offered it to him with her left hand to keep the right free for drawing her gun.

For a man who'd sounded parched, he sipped slowly. Maybe if you were born and bred in a desert, you always savored every drop.

"Do you want to sit?"

He turned his wide unblinking gaze on her, the whites as unblemished as any she'd ever seen. That was all the answer he gave her.

She perched eight feet away on the armrest of a chair, keeping her body free of cushions or anything else that could impede her reach.

"Thank you for what you did earlier." She couldn't leave that unsaid, even with malevolency alive in every moment since he'd stepped inside.

He shook his head, as if she'd just piled annoyance onto his fury. But after several seconds passed, he said, "Your daughter is not the problem."

"I know that, but you're the one who threatened her life right in this living room."

"I hoped that would stop them."

"Stop them?"

"Stop the two of them with all this"—he threw his hands outward—"this love." Spoken like an epithet.

"You've also been trying to incite people to attack her, me, Don, our dog." He stared at her. Didn't disagree. "That's right," Lana went on. "I know it's you. You're in those chat rooms trying to whip those fools into a froth."

"That will stop. My threats were part of my cover..."

My cover?

He surprised Lana by revealing that he was anything more than an immigrant, although he might have suspected his appearance on the video would soon have reporters digging into his background.

Or he's found my cybertrail and knows I'm already looking into him.

"I'm watched, too, not just by you. We're all watched, even when they say we're not. Eyes are everywhere."

His gaze roamed the room, as though for cameras that weren't there.

"You almost got them killed."

"You think I do not know that. But I saved them," he pointed to his chest. "If I wanted you or your daughter dead, or Don, you would not be sitting there."

They both turned as Emma pulled into the driveway with Sufyan. "And she would *not* be with my nephew."

Don drove in behind them in his pickup.

Neither Lana nor Tahir spoke. It seemed an hour had passed before the door from the garage opened. Don led Emma and Sufyan into the house. Jojo came up and sniffed Tahir, who ignored the Malinois.

"Hello, Tahir," Don said.

The Sudanese didn't respond. He stared at Sufyan, who quickly bowed his head.

That can't be good, thought Lana. *Not if he's that cowed already. He knows his uncle a lot better than we do.*

"Sit down," Tahir said to him. "You, too." He pointed to Emma.

Lana saw Don bristle and eyed him to be silent.

Tahir took a deep breath. "Do you love my nephew?" he asked Emma. "I mean really love him. No games now."

"Yes, I do."

"Sufyan, do you love Emma?" The first time he'd ever used her name.

"I do, Uncle."

"Enough to die for her?"

"Yes." Sufyan answered without pause.

"And you," he turned back to Em. "Would you die for my nephew?"

"I would," Emma said, eyes pooling.

Tahir looked at the ceiling. Perhaps he was seeing more than the smooth white surface. Perhaps he had his eyes on whatever he viewed as Paradise. The very possibility had Lana reaching back and placing her hand on her gun.

He shook his head at her, as if he knew what she'd just done, then sat across from the young couple. "I ask you these questions because today you almost died. I know killers. I know your mother and father have killed for their country, Emma. They have not told me that, but I *know*." His fist thumped his chest to punctuate the last word. "And I know those men in the van were killers. But I will tell you both something: neither of you is a killer yet. You were both fine fighters out there, but I do not want Sufyan to have to kill. That is not why I came to America. And your parents do not want you to have to kill," he told Emma.

He looked at Lana and Don. "Do you?"

"No, we don't," Lana said. Don shook his head.

"Each generation wants peace for its children," Tahir said to Emma and Sufyan. "But you two have chosen love in a country that is having difficult times and won't let you know peace with your kind of love. That is why I ask if you are ready to die, because if you are ready to die for love, then you must be ready to kill for it, or you will surely perish. Can you *do* that?"

Sufyan said yes immediately. Emma paused. Tears ran down her face. "I don't want to have to kill."

Lana wondered if her daughter was remembering the bloodshed on a bus about a year and a half ago, when Emma had tried to murder a madman, and the nightmares she had suffered in the aftermath of that sickening violence. Emma had been so young to learn—with such vicious visceral force—that sometimes you had to try to kill someone or be killed. Em had failed to slay that jihadist, but she'd injured him and saved countless lives with her courage. Now she was learning another side of that macabre equation: sometimes you have to kill for love.

"If you stay with Sufyan," Tahir went on, "the decision to kill might be made for you. It is better to make that decision now. Your father and I are running around trying to keep you two safe. I am watching you while I am watching him, and he is probably watching me while he is watching you. It is likely that you will get yourselves killed doing this, and you might get us killed, too.

"We cannot keep doing this. You cannot be children running around like this is a game. If you choose love, you *must* grow up now. If you are willing to die for love, you *must* be willing to kill for it. That was how it was in Sudan, and that is how it is in America now. Do not try to fool yourselves. Do not play childish games. Or you will die and so will the people you love most." Tahir settled his eyes on Emma. "You are welcome in my home. My nephew loves you and I will protect you with my life as I would protect him."

Lana swallowed hard at his apparent sincerity.

He turned to Lana and Don. "We are in this together. I did not want this," he looked at the young couple, "for their sakes. And I know you did not. But it is life." He stepped over to Lana. "Now we must survive. All of us. Together."

She couldn't have said it better or more honestly.

Tahir took her hand in both of his and bowed his head. He repeated the gestures with Don.

"We three are strong," he said, "because of those two." He looked at Emma and Sufyan. "We have such powerful reasons."

Forty minutes later, they sat at the dining room table and ate their first meal together.

CHAPTER 13

IT'S GOING TO BE incredibly tight making the Gamblers Anonymous meeting in Bethesda. I've got to catch a flight leaving Seattle-Tacoma International in an hour and fifty-five minutes—and I don't even know for certain that Elkins will be attending. But she did search for a time and place, then texted her family that she'd be home late. All from a phone that is not the one she uses for work. At least the defense establishment better hope she doesn't because I've had no trouble hacking and tracking it. She's installed an ad blocker to stop my flow of casino ads, but I changed the content and had them come from a new server. Lana's clever. She switched to a new virtual private network. It didn't stop me, though. I sniffed out messages to Emma coming from a new IP address and located Lana's "gambling phone." I've yet to hack into her work phone, however.

SeaTac is more than an hour away. It's not a given I'll make the flight, so as soon as I jump into my SUV I open Waze. It looks like clear sailing, and there don't appear to be any police lurking in the firs to nail speeders, though I'm not too concerned about them. State patrol officers have been pressed to take on so many additional duties that America's interstates feel more like autobahns.

People hurry from place to place as though they know how exposed they are to harm when they're out and about. Major league baseball teams have been playing to empty stadiums for the past few weeks as media-savvy

UNHOLY CODE

ISIS propagandists threaten "convocations of death," spectacles only nihilists could enjoy. I am not a nihilist. My agenda is so much richer, if equally crimson. And I know how exposed Americans are, even at home. I know because I make a point of visiting them at random.

I'll often split my screens into quadrants and turn on computer cameras just to see what strangers are doing as they watch *their* screens. Mostly, not much. They sit and stare, eyes like glazed donuts, and just as empty in the middle. What's repugnant, frankly, are the extreme numbers pleasuring themselves. I take no pleasure whatsoever to see boys and girls—or men and women, for that matter—in various states of undress. I have no interest in voyeurism, but I do find cultural anthropology in the age of terror fascinating. Here's the most curious thing I've noticed: Since the nuclear attack, *nothing* has changed in the privacy of people's homes. If anything, more of them than ever are sitting in front of their computers touching themselves or Skyping with friends or dawdling over cat videos.

I think one big reason they are at their computers so much now is that unlike the physical world, which no longer proves comforting with fixed shorelines and geological features, the virtual world remains a steady, stable, predictable presence . . . if eminently penetrable.

My Mercedes averages ninety-seven miles an hour and I make it to the airport in only fifty-eight minutes. With only my computer case and shoulder bag, I'm seated in first class with four minutes to spare. I used to loathe flying when I was consigned to steerage at government expense. But now I deny myself nothing of wealth's prerogatives. I skim from accounts in the States and abroad. Dollars, euros, Swiss francs, they're all the same to me. Sometimes I pay the banks back by stymying the efforts of others queued behind me who also want to sack the virtual vaults. But I'll admit it's in my interest to keep the banks' losses to a minimum so that my own efforts can continue as unimpeded as possible. I'm not greedy. I take only what I need to be comfortable. I couldn't care less if Bank of America, Deutsche Bank, Credit Suisse, or Banco Santander, to note only four institutions that have endowed me of late, lose a few hundred thousand here or there. It all goes to a good cause, which at the moment is flying me comfortably to Reagan International so I can arrive at the Hope Center in Bethesda, Maryland, in time for Lana's Gamblers Anonymous meeting.

We have one stop in Denver. I've always enjoyed flying over the Rockies in daylight, but it's downright disconcerting to see the near absence of snow. While it's never flush in the fall, there have always been peaks that remain covered year round. Now they are few and far between and Denver, like most western cities, suffers from drought.

We land in the Mile High City exactly on time. There's no deplaning for those of us flying all the way to DC. The new passengers board hastily. A size fourteen sits next to me on the aisle. She has the most comely face I've seen in ages, attractive in the ripest way possible. Large women don't get a fair shake. She smiles at me in that certain way that sails across the seat divide as easily as it can reach across a room, but I know nothing will come of it. I have no real interest in her.

The pilot warns that we'll be facing turbulence as we pass over the Midwest. It turns out to be an understatement. The wind shear shakes the plane like it's a maraca, and we passengers rattle in our seats like dried beans. I can see the woman beside me white-knuckle the armrest.

"We'll be okay," I tell her. "This is nothing."

What do I really know about such things? Not much, but I simply can't believe the plane is going to get ripped apart, not with my life's work so clearly before me.

We stop shaking well before we begin descending. Even so, I've never been so glad to get off a plane. I request a driver from Uber, canceling twice before a woman with a Honda Accord responds.

She pulls promptly up to Arrivals. Her name is Sam—red-haired, round-faced, and as freckled as Little Orphan Annie. She's friendly, effusive, and I'm reminded of why I'll never again stand in an endless cab line waiting for some sleepy-eyed taxi driver to roll up and stare insolently at me as I shoehorn my body and bags into a filthy back seat.

Sam ferries me to the Hope Center in the downtown area. There's angle parking in front set off by a black, slatted fence. Lots of empty spaces. Sam slides right into one and I pay her, bidding her adieu.

I watch her drive away, pleased that she's gone, unlike a taxi driver, who might have wanted to pick me up in an hour—for an added fee, of course—so that he could take a dinner break at my expense. With the sky darkening, I notice that it's that time of day.

I don't want anyone looking out for me. I have plans. Left to their own devices, our leaders from the President on down would have us all spying on friends, neighbors, and strangers. How despicable is that? Like the reprehensible Operation TIPS program after 9/11, which would have given the U.S. more citizens spying on one another than the Stasi had in the former East Germany. Popular opinion drove the proposed TIPS operation into the ground, but the weight of public opinion these days is driven more by paranoia than it was even back then.

I enter the facility, which looks less like a healing center than an office building for boiler-room brokers. So much for the architecture of awe in the design of a sanctuary.

Carrying my briefcase, which hides the main reason I've made this trip—it surely wasn't just to observe Lana grovel with guilt over gambling—I walk up to the meeting room on the second floor and see that she's not there. I look at my watch. There's still time. *Come on, Lana.*

With only five minutes to go, my impatience makes me squirm in my seat. And then she walks in.

I observe her only at an angle. While this will be the third meeting we've shared, we've hardly talked at all, although a few words did pass between us at the coffeemaker a month ago. That encounter definitely gave me a thrill, making me wonder when we'd meet for the last time. Now I know the answer: never. This will be it, if I'm successful with the device I'm carrying. I had wondered how surprised she'd be if there had been a revealing, climactic moment, an unveiling of me, if you will. I think she would have been shocked to find out who I am. But maybe I'm giving myself too much credit. She might have her suspicions already, for all I know, but there have never been fewer than fifteen of us at the meetings. Tonight it's especially busy with Lana the twenty-first person to show up. I wonder if she's counting, too. And if she'll find that propitious, a winning hand at a game I know she plays. I suspect she's savvy enough to be a card counter.

And here comes number twenty-two. He slips past the door less than ninety seconds after his charge. I'd give odds—and it's fun to put it that way in a room full of repentant gamblers—that the African-American man is her FBI-issued security. He might as well be wearing a blue jacket with the Bureau's acronym blazing across his back in iridescent letters. He has chiseled features and looks alert and intelligent. Too much so for the circumstances. Most of these people look beaten down by debt, doubt, and their affliction. He looks like a winner all around, a warrior. No, I'm not buying him for a man with a gambling problem. I'm buying him as a man with a security problem: Lana Elkins.

It'll be interesting to see if he tries to join in at some point.

He never does. There's not a lot of talk during the meeting; it seems to reflect the lack of interaction beforehand. A dourness pervades the room, as if something has sucked out all of the oxygen. I finally nod in what I think is an encouraging manner when an older man with a bright white beard speaks up in support of Lana. Yes, she was strong. Yes, she blocked my efforts to flood her phone with casino ads . . . for awhile. But my goal wasn't simply to have her gamble. My goal has always been to keep her distracted so Steel Fist can kill her, or have her killed, which would only encourage his subscribers to commit more mayhem. And gambling is sidetracking her. She just said, "I can't get it out of my head." That's the idea, Lana. I want you thinking about gambling when you could be thinking about your survival.

After the meeting ends, she hangs around long enough not to attract attention for leaving in a rush. Predictably, the man I picked out as her FBI agent follows suit.

Between him, Lana, and me, there are two gamblers. No one's behind me, but that's just luck. If someone appears, I'll have to find a reason to delay, a sudden return to the center as though I've forgotten something. Thankfully, I don't need to. What is even better is I immediately see that Lana has angle-parked her Prius by the dark, slatted fence. I dressed in black slacks and a dark top, knowing what I planned to do. I'd imagined executing my next maneuver by stepping away from the meeting for a bathroom break. But as soon as I saw the likely agent, I knew he might decide to follow me if I left that room, and I could ill afford to have been caught sneaking around Lana's car then. *Or now.*

What I plan should take less than ten seconds, but if I'm caught it'll get ugly fast. I *can't* be caught.

I'm planning to drop low behind the fence when she climbs into her vehicle. Then I'll reach through the slats and try to carry out my plan. And that might still work, but right now she's stopping again to talk to the handsome guy who's been trailing her all evening. To anybody else it might look natural enough: an attractive woman with a striking man chatting after a meeting they've both attended. But Lana's not flirting, not with her arms folded tightly across her chest. I sense tension, possibly for reasons all my own.

But now it's getting interesting. As they start to wander toward her car once more, they turn away from me. I'm no longer in their peripheral vision, if they ever noticed me at all. Recognizing this, I slip behind the slatted fence and move through the darkness along it toward her Prius. They're still turned away. I can almost hear them, which means they can almost hear me.

With a breath I drop down to my knees, dig into my briefcase and pull out an electronic tracking device. They're standing by the rear hatch of her car. I swear silently when they shift positions again. I worry this *pas de deux* is planned, that they've spotted me somehow and are coordinating their coverage. In fact, his gaze drifts over to the fence. I flatten myself on the sidewalk and listen for long seconds.

Just do it, I tell myself. It worked for Nike.

I reach through the slats and under the car. I have to stretch so hard the side of a board digs into my armpit. It hurts like hell but the magnet on the locator is not finding metal. There's so much plastic crap on cars now. I stretch so hard I'm cutting off blood to my arm. This is taking a lot more than ten seconds. My fingertips tingle and start to go numb. The device finally clicks when it clamps to the chassis. A soft sound that to me is deafening.

I freeze, not even breathing. I withdraw my arm carefully, feel the blood starting to pound through my veins. I try not to make the slightest noise. I listen intently to see if they're talking—or walking toward me.

They're saying good-bye. The normalcy of the moment is undisturbed. The *click* didn't register . . . apparently. But I take nothing for granted.

I have to get away before she gets in her car and puts on her lights and backs away. The slats won't hide me.

I hear her take a few steps. She opens the car door, then closes it. But the Prius doesn't move, and Lana's friend or FBI agent or whatever he is stands off to the side, as if to watch her back up. I fear making any sounds.

As soon she starts her engine, I look behind me and, staying low, I scramble backward, commando style, disappearing just as Lana backs up and her headlights throw shadows from the slats I'd been hiding behind seconds ago.

She drives off, followed by the man in a Dodge Charger. It looks government issue.

I spring to my feet and look around. I see no one. In the next instant I'm brushing myself off and requesting another car from Uber. I walk down to the corner and a new female driver greets me. I ask her to take me to the Watergate Hotel.

The device on Lana's car is not super-sophisticated. The first time she goes through security at Fort Meade they'll discover it. Which is fine; she'll know people are getting dangerously close to her. But I don't think she's going to make it to Meade.

In the morning, she'll be going to the Senate to testify before the Select Committee on Intelligence. That's on the public record. I presume the senators are planning on a circus, which is no more prophetic than suggesting that a monkey will scratch its scrotum in the course of a day. The deputy director of the NSA will be there to testify as well.

So there's time to put everything and everyone into play.

I'm smiling when the driver pulls up to the broad curved exterior of the Watergate. If it was good enough for Nixon's cronies to break into, it's good enough for me to launch my far more elaborate crimes from above its opulent, chandeliered lobby.

I order room service. The kitchen offers an excellent hamburger, which might sound downmarket for the Watergate but it really is superb, and I'm an unabashed carnivore. I remind the staff to send up the freshest possible fries.

After I eat I go immediately to work online. First, I must send a message to Steel Fist. It's short: the code he needs to track the electronic beacon.

I'll leave it to him to decide how to disseminate it. It's not as though he can put it out to ten million subscribers without it getting back to Lana in seconds. But he must have some killers he trusts. We all do, even if it's only ourselves.

I certainly feel murderous sending him my anonymous message. I wouldn't give Lana Elkins twenty-four hours after this, if Vinko Horvat truly knows his business. And his business lately has been whipping up his troops to kill Lana and her family.

"Have at it," I say to myself as I issue another *click*, dispatching the code to his Idaho stronghold.

But I'm not through with Vinko just yet. I decide it's time to give him another tip, almost as juicy. I'm tired of waiting for him to figure it out on his own: in the background of the photo of Emma, her dad, and their new guard dog was an old Malinois with a gray muzzle. That was Cairo, the hound that went after bin Laden.

If Steel Fist is really serious about showing how poor the country's defenses are—and how necessary he is to the nation's resurgence—he'll have that dog killed. And he'll do it in the most public way possible. Americans have learned to stomach a great many indignities in the past two years, but a "revenge" murder of Cairo would be the *coup d'état*.

Leaving nothing to chance, I also give him the address of the kennel near Hagerstown, Maryland. I even write a headline for Steel Fist so he can immediately grasp the powerful nature of the potential propaganda: "Islamic Terrorists Kill Hero SEAL Dog. 'Skinned Alive.'"

Just do it.

CHAPTER 14

DEPUTY DIRECTOR BOB HOLMES looked as gray as his suit when Lana spotted him starting up the stairs of the Russell Senate Office Building, a Beaux Arts beauty of marble, granite, and limestone on the north side of the Capitol.

Historic events had taken place inside those walls, but Lana had no illusions that today's circus would produce the drama or statesmanship that had emerged so memorably in the past.

She reached Holmes as he neared the double-door entrance, trying to hide her dismay at his peaked appearance. He'd sounded tired when they'd spoken on the phone yesterday, and now she had to remind herself that he was seventy-eight. On this morning he looked his age.

"How's that dog working out for you?" he asked by way of greeting her, jovial despite his washed-out look of weariness.

"Great. He's moved right into our daily routine like he's always been part of the clan."

"Well, that was the plan," Holmes rhymed with a smile. "You ready for these fools?" he asked as Agent Robin Maray held a door for them.

"Ready as I'll ever be."

"Don't let them get your goat." He leaned closer to her as they strolled into the rotunda with its stately columns and coffered dome, adding,

"They're assholes, the ones gunning for you. Long as you stay cool, you'll look great compared to their bombast."

Lana and Holmes, with Agent Maray now a few steps behind them, entered the Dirksen hearing room, a generously wood-paneled expanse with green marble accents. It smelled of old leather and coffee, and made her think of men and their politics, though two women did hold seats on the Select Committee on Intelligence. This would be Lana's first testimony before the committee.

Another woman was settling in at the witness table, Madeline Emberling, the sandy-haired lawyer who'd spent hours prepping them. After greeting them, Madeline settled back behind a table loaded with her impressive collection of briefing materials. She had two co-counsels assisting her. They perched on the edge of chairs behind her, as though ready to spring into action. Holmes sat to Madeline's right, Lana to her left.

More than two dozen senators assembled before them. The corpulent Senator Bob Ray Willens of Louisiana nodded at Holmes, but offered Lana only an amused expression, as he might a sausage roasting on a grill at a Fourth of July weenie roast.

Spare me, she thought, breaking eye contact quickly. His rapt attention felt unbecoming.

The chair of the committee was the senior senator from New York, known for his curt manner, cutting remarks, and remarkable intelligence. He banged the gavel and the assembled fell silent at once. Lana glanced around. Standing room only, which told her the media and Capitol Hill cognoscenti expected the circus Holmes had predicted.

Three rings, no doubt.

What none had expected—what shocked and horrified everyone— was the ringing explosion of a bomb so nearby that the walls and floor shuddered.

As long-dormant dust loosed from the ceiling, every head turned toward the rear. Senator Willens was no longer looking so entertained by Lana's presence; his startled eyes peered right past her.

Capital Police officers burst through the doors. One of them announced an emergency evacuation of the hearing room. As swiftly as he spoke, the men and women with him fanned out and directed those attending the hearing to the exits already filled with the receding backs of the senators.

Agent Robin Maray appeared suddenly at Lana's side, telling her to follow him. "You too, Deputy Director Holmes."

But Lana's old friend was gripping his chest. Without warning, he pitched forward heavily, head and upper body coming to rest on a three-ring binder.

Agent Maray was already on the radio transmitter tucked under his suit jacket lapel, calling for emergency medical personnel.

Lana checked Holmes's neck for a pulse, finding it thready and slow. He did not react to her touch.

"We've got to get *you* out of here." Robin signaled one of the security guards, who arrived as two paramedics raced into Dirksen. He took Lana's arm. "We don't know what's coming next," he said into her ear.

Loathe to leave Holmes, Lana asked, "Is he going to be all right?"

She immediately recognized the juvenile futility of her question, with the paramedics only beginning to attend to the deputy director. But Robin was already rushing her toward the door through which the senators had exited moments ago. From ahead, gunfire erupted abruptly. Outside the walls of the Senate building, she hoped. A second bomb, farther away, exploded as they passed quickly through a smaller room, rattling windows they were sprinting past.

"Stay low," Robin ordered as they burst into a light-filled hallway.

"Where are we going?" she asked as they scrambled down the broad corridor.

"A secure room," he replied.

Senate staffers were stuffing themselves into an elevator.

Turning to Lana, he pointed to two Capitol Police officers rushing down a flight of stairs about thirty feet away. "Follow them."

She nodded and fled.

He bolted to the elevators, ordering the mostly younger men and women out of the packed space, grabbing a callow-looking man frantically working his phone, oblivious to Robin's commands.

"All of you, use the stairs!" he shouted.

That was the last Lana heard of Robin as she headed down them herself. Even in the rush she noticed people on their phones, swearing in exasperation. Then she overheard a man say he couldn't get online.

Here? Lana wondered if the attack included the Senate's ISP. She'd have to check.

In seconds she was sequestered in a crowded basement corridor, awaiting entry into what appeared to be the Russell's very own panic room. She tried to use her phone. No service for her, either.

She looked up as the door to the panic room was locked, leaving her and about forty others in the hallway.

"The rest of you must stay down here for the time being," a blue-suited woman announced with great authority. "We're here to protect you."

Officers in full SWAT regalia flanked the crowd. The men and women were armed with automatic rifles, helmets, grenade launchers, and belts heavy with weapons and gear less readily identifiable to Lana.

She could not let herself believe ISIS or any other terrorists had actually laid siege to the nation's capital. This wasn't Ramadi. This wasn't even San Bernardino. This was Washington DC. But neither would she have believed that Liberty Square could ever have been the scene of a massacre of innocents.

She heard children crying and wondered how they'd ended up down there. She also remembered an alarming episode of *Homeland* from years ago, in which Washington's elite were jammed into a supposed secure room—with a suicide bomber in their midst. What had unnerved her then was what frightened her now: the very real possibility that a mass killer already stood among them.

With no Internet access, Lana could do nothing but think and worry. She found hope in every minute that passed without an explosion in the corridor or terrorists trying to shoot their way through the Russell.

A tall man wearing lanyards and laminates walked through the crowd, eyeing everyone carefully. She figured he was searching for a suicide bomber. *But what do you look for?* The would-be bomber on *Homeland* had been among the least likely suspects.

Turned out the man with the laminates was looking for her.

"Ms. Elkins, come with me."

"Why? Who are you?"

"Detective Adams, Capitol Police. You were scheduled to testify, weren't you?"

"That's correct."

"So you were in the hearing room when the bomb went off?"

"Yes."

He was already guiding her up stairs near the rear of the building. "I'm going to put you in the hands of the Secret Service. They want to talk to you."

A special agent of the Secret Service intercepted them on the staircase. The woman wasted no time getting to what appeared to be her most critical question: "Did anybody in Dirksen react strangely, in your opinion?"

"No, but all I noticed was dust falling down from the ceiling before Deputy Director Holmes collapsed onto the table. Do you know how he's—?"

"So no one ran off right away? Nobody was praising God or Allah or anything obvious like that?"

"No, nothing. People just looked shocked. I don't even remember anyone asking what it was. It was like everyone knew."

"We want you out of the Capitol zone as soon as possible. You might well have been a target. Did you drive?"

"Yes."

"FBI Agent Stan Pence will get you to your car and accompany you home. He'll be here shortly. Do not go to Fort Meade. The marine detachment there is fully activated. We want you to go home. As we understand it, your residence has bulletproof windows, a guard dog, and that you've been trained with firearms."

"That's correct," Lana replied.

"Ms. Elkins, we also need to tell you that there was a bombing just outside CyberFortress, almost to the second with the one that went off outside Dirksen. We don't believe that's a coincidence."

"Oh, my God." Nightmare images appeared, unbidden, in her mind's eye. "Was anyone injured? Or killed?"

"No injuries, no deaths, except for the suicide bomber."

"We have blast-resistant exterior walls over there, too."

Lana tried to text Emma immediately. Failed. She tried calling. Failed. And still no Internet.

The special agent went on: "The bomber was a woman. She made an attempt to enter your firm but was repulsed by security personnel."

"I should be with them."

"No, you should not. Except for security personnel, they've been evacuated until we can secure the surrounding blocks."

"How is Holmes?" Lana asked again.

The woman rested her hand on Lana's shoulder. "Headed for the ICU at the VA Medical Center."

"But he's alive?"

"Yes, he is."

"May I go *there*?"

"Honestly, we don't want you doing that. There have been numerous casualties. We're trying to get everyone away from the District so we can lock it down and help those in need. Are you armed?"

"I have a Sig in my car."

"Excellent."

A blue-suited man ran up, early thirties, glasses, perspiring, as though he'd been in motion since the attacks began.

"This is Agent Stan Pence. Agent Pence, Ms. Lana Elkins," the Secret Service woman said, then started walking away.

"Wait," Lana called to her. "What about Agent Maray? He's part of a security unit assigned to me full—"

"Not now. We can't spare him. Agent Pence will accompany you home. Once you're safely locked in your house, he'll return to duty here. Thank you for your cooperation."

Pence was on his radio when she looked back to him, signing off quickly.

"How many casualties?" she asked right away.

"I'm not permitted to disclose that information, Ms. Elkins. Where are you parked?"

She told him, talking as they moved out of the Russell Senate Building and down its stone steps. "Look, I'm not trying to pull rank on you, but my security clearance is probably higher than yours, Agent Pence. You can tell me, for God's sake. Do I look like a terrorist? I was here to testify before the Select Committee on Intelligence."

"Take it up with my commanding officer. Let's keep moving."

He gripped her arm and led her toward the parking structure on Massachusetts Avenue. Sirens screamed. The roads were chockablock with cars. To avoid the gridlock, ambulances and other emergency vehicles were rolling down sidewalks and across the Capitol's wide expanses of neatly manicured grass. The cacophony was ear-splitting. The whole time Agent Pence kept them walking at a furious pace.

She wondered how the bomb- and rifle-toting terrorists had forged their way so close to the nation's seat of power. Then again, several years earlier an unauthorized man had made it into the living quarters of the White House, and another guy landed a gyrocopter on the West Lawn of the Capitol.

"Can you tell me about the gunfire?"

The way Pence was looking around, with his handgun by his side, he appeared to be ready for more of it. "No, there's an embargo on all info."

"Can you tell me where?"

He shook his head. "Here we go."

The garage was half a block away. Amid all the turmoil, Lana hadn't noticed their progress.

Still holding her arm, Pence led her into the parking structure. "Now you take the lead," he said.

He still held his semi-automatic close to his hip.

Lana pointed their way to her Prius. Pence took the passenger seat, his handgun in plain sight now.

She reached past him and grabbed her Sig Sauer from the glove box. The agent nodded in approval, but cautioned her to follow his commands on any action. "Don't start shooting until I do."

Presuming you're still alive, she thought reflexively.

She tried to text Emma from her car.

"Service is spotty," Penn said, shaking his head.

The agent gave her step-by-step directions, and in minutes they were speeding down the Washington Mall.

They passed hundreds of people. Most looked scared. Many were running. She hadn't seen this much panic since the grid went down. Not even the nuclear bombing of Antarctica had produced so much transparent fear. But that explosion had taken place at a great distance, and the seas had risen over weeks. They were still rising, but even flooding of coastal communities lacked the immediate drama of suicide bombers and armed skirmishes in the District of Columbia.

They made it to Bethesda in good time, given the challenges. Lana had taken mental notes of the byways she hadn't been aware of in the past. Don's truck was gone.

Jojo greeted her at the door. He looked right past her to Agent Pence. "He's okay," she said to Jojo.

The Malinois might not have agreed: he followed Pence into every room on the ground floor and then up the stairs to the second level.

"Your dog never let me out of his sight, but kept his distance," Pence reported when he came back down to the living room, where Lana had just checked her phone and seen there was still no service. "He's a good dog."

She nodded. "I think so, too. I really like him."

"Nobody's gotten into your home. I've contacted Bethesda PD. They're dispatching an officer in a marked car to sit in your driveway. Meantime, keep your weapon on hand at all times. I wish we could spare you one of our agents but we're in crisis mode at the Capitol."

Lana nodded.

"Are you okay?" Pence asked with finality.

"I'm fine. Thank you. How are you getting back?"

He pointed outside, where a full-size gray sedan waited on the street. Right then the Bethesda cruiser pulled up.

Before Pence was out the door, Lana checked her phone again. Nothing.

Minutes later, though, her phone beeped. She had service. "R u ok?" she texted Emma at once.

"Yes @ Suf. U?"

"Fine @ home"

"Thank Allah"

That gave Lana pause. "Do u want 2 stay with him?"

"Yes"

As if I had to ask. "ok"

She called Jeff Jensen, who answered on the first ring.

"Where are you?" she asked.

"Here at CF."

"I thought everyone was ordered out."

"I pulled rank. I don't have to tell you that we've got intelligence stored here that no FBI agents are cleared to see."

"Are they there?"

"Yeah, they've secured the perimeter."

"I'll be right down."

"I think that's smart."

Lana stopped to draw a glass of tap water, downing it in gulps. Then she texted Don, unsurprised that he was parked near Sufyan's house. She knew the jury was still out for him regarding Tahir. Lana told Don she was heading to CyberFortress, and that Em had just said she'd be staying put.

When Lana headed for the garage, she was shocked to see it wasn't even noon yet. So much had happened.

Jojo tailed her. She looked at him. "Ready to work? Let's go."

She led him to her car. The Malinois jumped onto the passenger seat, looking exceptionally alert.

Lana was backing out of her driveway thirty seconds later. She told the officer in the cruiser she was leaving. When he objected, she flashed her federal government ID and said she wouldn't return for at least an hour. She expected the drive to CyberFortress to take no more than fifteen minutes, even in the worst of traffic.

But more than cars and trucks were on the road.

CHAPTER 15

STEEL FIST EXPECTED COLONEL Williams and his cadre of killers to go after Lana Elkins with "extreme prejudice," but he'd never anticipated *this*: live video of their murderous operation that Vinko could stream on his website for the voyeuristic pleasure of his most volatile subscribers.

He'd met the colonel in person more than a year ago when Vinko had attended a large gathering of neo-Nazis and right-wing militia members down in Boise. He'd never let on that he was Steel Fist, enjoying the fly-on-the-wall experience of hearing people speak glowingly about the mystery man behind his website. The only comment he'd made about his alter ego was to speculate aloud about whether Steel Fist was in attendance.

He'd been inspired enough by Colonel Williams's call-to-arms, issued behind the conference's closed doors, that he'd made a point of shaking his hand and finding ways to praise the ex-Army officer on the Steel Fist website without implicating the man in committing or abetting any crimes.

So when Vinko received the electronic code for the locator on Lana Elkins's Prius from the same anonymous "guardian angel" who'd proved so helpful in the recent past, he sent it along to Colonel Williams, warning that the window of opportunity would be brief. He'd closed with "Good luck!"

"Don't need luck," Williams fired back at once. "Just tell me it's good intel."

"Good intel," Vinko confirmed, hoping like hell that was true, because you didn't get a second chance with men like the colonel.

All the telling clues that could identify Williams's men on-camera were hidden. The three beefy bruisers wore urban camouflage clothes—dark green, gray, and dark blue. Their full face masks bore the same dull colors. Even Vinko, a fan of the conventions of terror, thought the colonel's heavily armed crew looked daunting.

He watched them inspect their weapons, hearing the encouraging slide of steel on the semi-automatic pistols getting readied for business, and the *shush-shush* of camo pants legs brushing against each other. When Vinko still hadn't spotted the tall, lean colonel he realized the officer must have been the one with the camera mounted on his head.

The men's diligence reminded Vinko of how impending violence can bring out a studied sullenness in men. Yet the four also moved with such purpose that he would have known they were ex-military even if the colonel hadn't assured him that his crew had seen plenty of combat.

Years ago, the colonel had been cashiered out of the 75th Ranger Regiment after a night raid in Ramadi, Iraq. Not dishonorably. Quietly. When the Army has a colonel who leaves behind seven dead noncombatants, and a severely wounded four-month-old baby girl whose leg had been severed by bullets fired by the officer's own M17—her hearing lost to a percussion grenade—you don't advertise your failures by making any of that public. For the colonel, speaking behind closed doors in Boise about what had happened on that night raid was a point of honor. Unfortunately for him, though, the entire incident had been captured by the unit's cameraman and made available to his superiors, who did not agree with his self-serving assessment. But Vinko admired the colonel's steadfast refusal to apologize. "They were there. They were in the way. They made the mistake. Not me or my men."

The one-legged baby without eardrums was now a deaf seven-year-old who shared a bed with three other girls in a Baghdad orphanage. Something the official newspaper of *sharia* law—*The New York Times*—would not let its liberal readers forget. More aid and comfort for the enemy. One of these days they were *all* going to learn their lesson.

Vinko was content to watch the men moving about on screen. He didn't plan to go live online until the last possible moment. The colonel had noted unnecessarily that the propaganda value of the video would fail dismally if he and his cadre were caught, so there would be no signposts viewed along the way, no advance notice of the target, and no identifiable locations until they closed in for the killing of Lana Elkins and whoever else might be in her car. Vinko hoped Emma, most of all, would be in that Prius.

Already the colonel's camera was focused tightly on the blinking light of the locator on a tablet screen. His voice was electronically disguised, making him sound echoey, froggy, and plenty scary.

"The target is in motion. Operation Intercept American Evil is underway."

The ambient sounds of footfalls accompanied them to an enclosed parking area with whitewashed walls. Could have been anywhere. Could have been the moon. The killing crew approached a pair of dual sport motorcycles and a gray Hummer H3 parked in the lot. As soon as two of the men gunned the motorcycle engines, Vinko felt his pulse quicken. He double-checked his website, making sure it was ready to receive the video. He'd been sending out a cryptic message all morning to his subscribers: "Countdown to Killing." That was all. Not who, where, or when. His subscribers didn't need to know. They trusted him. Just like the colonel. They knew Steel Fist didn't bluff.

The colonel and his men were only minutes away from the blinking locator. They'd had all night to move into position, since Vinko had passed along the guardian angel's electronic code for the device. Whoever the guardian angel was, he'd proved himself a useful son-of-a-bitch. Clever, too, even if he'd outsourced the placement of the locator on Elkins's tin-can car, which was Vinko's suspicion.

If he regretted anything about the need to move on Lana so quickly, it was that she'd never get to hear those two words from Emma: "I'm pregnant." Vinko couldn't remember ever wanting anyone pregnant as much as he wanted that seventeen-year-old bitch to be knocked up by that Muslim.

Vinko caught a quick reflection of the colonel's mask-covered face on the passenger-door window. Yep, there was the camera, strapped to the top of his head.

Otherwise, Williams kept the lens focused on the locator. But Vinko figured they were getting very close, confirmed within moments when the colonel pointed his eyes—and that lens—at the Prius driving down a tree-lined suburban street.

Where's her protection? Vinko wondered. The guardian angel had warned him that Elkins would probably have an FBI escort, which Vinko had told Williams.

Vinko smiled. *This is going to be a turkey shoot.*

"Go!" the colonel commanded over a radio in his froggy voice.

Vinko sat forward, feeding the video for the first time onto his website.

The bikers were getting down to business, racing past the Hummer. They came up alongside Elkins's car, shooting out her front tires. But they didn't shoot her.

Intriguing. The colonel must have a flair for drama.

Vinko wondered what he had in mind.

But his cadre would have to move very fast now. Anyone familiar with these streets could be watching, and in a town that was home to many government employees, including intelligence and military officers, there might be a few who would be on their computers and outraged by this attack.

Gunshots flared on screen.

Elkins had just fired a shot out her driver's-door window, hitting the biker on her left, who was spilling off his dual sport on the fly. But she was slowing down, running on her front rims.

She angled sharply right and shot at the biker on her passenger side. She missed him with car and bullets as he veered off, speeding up over the curb. He chewed half a donut into the lush front lawn before braking, no longer an easy target.

Vinko smiled. Elkins didn't appear to know the real threat was racing up behind her.

• • •

Lana had fired four times, leaving six rounds in the magazine. She had another one loaded and waiting in the glove box.

Silencing Jojo with a command, she then yelled "Down." The Malinois dropped to the floor in front of the passenger seat as his master pulled behind a Chevy van and in front of a large Buick, grabbing the scant protection available to her crippled car. A large chestnut tree towered over the spot she'd claimed, trunk thick as a whisky barrel.

Lana opened the electronic locks and looked left before moving to exit right. She glimpsed the biker she'd shot, bleeding from his neck on the street. His arm rose feebly, drawing her attention to a large SUV turning to a stop about fifty feet away, effectively blocking the street on that end.

The biker on the lawn shot out her rear window. She pushed past Jojo, then opened the door, determined to grab the protection of the tree. The Prius now felt like a goldfish bowl. She doubted it could stop a .22. She'd bought it before chaos had come to America. Time to trade it in for a vehicle more up to the grim challenges gripping the country.

She signaled Jojo to heel as she scrambled behind the tree, wishing like hell her one-time lover, Agent Maray, hadn't been shanghaied by the crisis at the Capitol.

Two men were throwing open the front doors of the Hummer. She couldn't tell if there were more in the back, certain only that at least three were still alive.

The biker on the lawn fired two more times at her, having claimed cover behind a Toyota RAV4. His second shot shaved bark off the chestnut tree inches from her head.

In the corner of her eye she saw someone snatch a toddler from the wide front window of the house fronting the shoot-out. A drape fell back, closing off any view of the interior.

Through the RAV4's side windows, she saw the biker's shoulders move, guessing he was reloading. She made a split-second decision: "Jojo, attack!"

The exceedingly fleet Malinois, moving at twice the speed of the fastest human, cleared forty feet of lawn, wheeled around the RAV4, and launched sixty pounds of rippling muscle at the masked man as he raised his weapon.

The shooter was too slow.

Thank God.

Jojo's powerful jaws locked onto the man's gun hand, driving him backward into a garage door. Lana could see them clearly now. It looked like the tenacious warrior was crushing bone *and* metal and would never let go.

The biker beat Jojo's head with his fist—to no avail.

Rip him to pieces, Lana thought.

But she couldn't help Jojo; she would risk shooting him by mistake at this distance, and the men from the Hummer had taken cover behind the Buick less than thirty feet away.

• • •

Vinko was so excited. *I did this.* He felt like a commanding officer who'd deployed his men on a vital mission. And millions would see this video. He imagined thousands already messaging friends and alerting online groups, even as he stared lovingly at his screen. But he'd also make sure no interested party would ever miss seeing the action by streaming the video over and over for years. A battle to remember, with the colonel and his closest cohorts in a position now to terminate Elkins.

What did Vinko care about the biker who was shot in the neck and now bleeding to death on the street? It was good bang-bang, as the news crews always called the battles in a war zone. And make no mistake about it, Bethesda was now a war zone. He was just as glad to see the dog hanging off the other biker's arm because the man still had his wits about him and was unsheathing a knife.

Yes, stab the beast.

The biker was—over and over.

But not for long. The big dog fell away and the man bolted right back to the protection of the RAV4 in the driveway, switching his gun to his left hand. The right didn't look so good anymore.

The dog—*what a pathetic animal*—tried to crawl after him, leaving a blood smear a foot wide behind. Vinko saw the dog's shoulder bone glinting in the sunlight. He reached down and patted Biko. "Don't you worry. I would never let that happen to you."

But Biko's eyes opened wide a beat later when the Malinois howled in pain.

• • •

Lana's first impulse was to retreat. *Where?* Then she saw one of the men from the Hummer lob an object toward her.

She had time only to swear at the grenade and tuck herself tightly behind the tree before the explosive ripped apart the Prius. The blast sent plastic and metal fragments into the tree trunk with such force that the stately old chestnut shuddered and the big window where the toddler had stood shattered. Tiny bits of flaming Prius also tore into Lana's calf. The pain was searing.

She heard footfalls and spotted one of the men from the Hummer ducking and running around the far side of the Buick. She aimed low, guessing he was in body armor, reasoning that if he'd come bearing grenades, he'd be equipped in every possible manner. As soon as he moved out from behind the roof, she fired three times, nailing both of his upper legs. The bullets sprawled him onto the pavement.

That son-of-a-bitch. The man was wearing a head-mounted camera. She aimed to kill but heard two men advancing on the lawn side of the tree.

One was the driver of the Hummer. He darted behind another chestnut about twenty feet away, making him no longer a viable target.

Elkins didn't see the biker with the chewed-up hand. He was targeting her from the behind a big lilac bush.

• • •

"Look out!" Vinko yelled at his screen. Not out of any concern for Elkins.

A man from the house, whose big front window had been blown out by the grenade, was aiming a hunting rifle out the opening at the biker who'd just taken cover behind a lush lilac. Hard to see clearly, though: the picture was turned on its side because that was the position of the wounded colonel lying on the street not far from the man Elkins had shot in the first seconds of the attack.

Vinko twisted his screen to straighten the view just as the rifleman fired at the surviving biker. No armor was likely to stop a high-caliber bullet designed to take down a buck from five hundred yards. Vinko sat stunned as blood burst from the exit wound in the biker's chest.

The colonel's camera switched perspective again, jittery, bouncing, apparently moving backward. Vinko could only conclude that the driver of the Hummer was retreating, dragging the colonel with him back to the vehicle. Close shooting continued; the man laying down covering fire at Elkins or the homeowner who'd just killed his cohort.

The camera juddered again, the colonel now clearly half-sitting half-lying in the Hummer's spacious back seat. The stout driver piled into the vehicle behind the wheel.

The windshield shattered, chunks raining into the front seat area. The colonel's camera caught his own arm and hand as he pointed out something to the ducking driver. Vinko couldn't make out what either of them shouted over the din of the continuing gunfire.

Now the Hummer was backing up fast, the sound of gunshots fading; but the plinking of lead into steel remained audible as the colonel and his man continued their furious retreat.

Vinko collapsed back in his chair, swiping Biko aside with his boot. He had been sure the video would show the slaughter of Lana Elkins, but the planned *coup de grace* had turned into a *coup de disgrace*. Soon to be replayed hundreds of millions of times on the small screen—but not by *his* followers.

• • •

The pain in Lana's leg was excruciating. She forced herself to focus first on the Hummer to make sure it wasn't getting ready for a drive-by. The driver was backing wildly onto a lawn five houses away, then peeling out in the opposite direction.

Now she started toward Jojo. So was the man who'd fired his rifle from inside the house. If she'd counted correctly, she had one bullet left in the gun to put the dog out of his misery. She felt responsible for his injuries, and they were horrible: the dog's fur was soaked with blood in four places on his back and shoulder. He looked like he might have been stabbed in the spine.

Jojo was panting, tongue hanging out, flews slick with foam. His eyes were open wide, wild.

"I don't have a vet," Lana said to the man who might well have saved her life. "I just got him."

"I do," he said. "I'm on the line to her right now." He turned from Lana. "This is Harry Riggs. I'm bringing in a Malinois guard dog that's been knifed by a madman. This is trauma work."

"You'll get my dog to a vet?" Lana said after Harry hung up and called 911 for the two men sprawled on the ground.

"Of course I will. And I know who you are. It's an honor to meet you." Then he noticed Lana's bloody leg and immediately dialed back 911. "We have an injured woman." He stated the address again. "Lower leg wound. Do you hear me? A casualty who needs treatment ASAP."

Lana felt tears running down her face. Not from the pain, but for Jojo. And for the man who'd stepped forward to help her when she'd needed it most. The country was riven, to be sure, but there were plenty of brave people out there who'd had all they could take of crazies of any stripe.

"Who are you, Harry?"

He told her.

Bethesda, it turned out, home to spooks and spies and retired military, also had one hell of a retired park ranger.

"Who are they?" Harry asked.

"I'm not sure," Lana said.

"But you have your suspicions and would rather not say?"

Lana nodded, then looked him in the eye. "Thank you."

"No problem."

The first ambulance raced up as she and Harry were loading Jojo onto a dark plastic tarp. As gently as they could, they lifted the dog into the back of Harry's small SUV.

"I'm going to grab my granddaughter from her crib, and then I'll get Jojo here to my vet. Here's my card. You call me when you can."

"Do whatever you can to save him," Lana said. "I don't care what it costs."

"No worries about that. I've spent my whole life saving animals whenever I could. He's going to the best vet in the region."

For the first time in hours, Lana's thoughts returned to another of the day's casualties: Bob Holmes. She took one last look at Jojo, who was staring at her. Then she glanced at her watch. Barely two o'clock.

Lana pulled out her phone, staggered, and felt herself blacking out. Waves of pain were overwhelming her. Two paramedics caught her before she fell.

CHAPTER 16

VINKO STARED AT HIS screen, stunned by the setback. All he could see was the view from the camera strapped to the head of the colonel, who remained still slumped in the back seat. The driver was racing away from the debacle toward an intersection, leaning forward and peering through a bullet-shattered windshield. Vinko could just make out a black man on the far side of the intersection leveling a handgun at the Hummer.

Vinko had another urge to shout a warning but no one would hear him, so he remained silent as bullets ripped into the hulking vehicle. The fourth one took off half the driver's face, leaving him screaming and slumping against the door, hands no longer gripping the wheel but what had to be a gruesome wound.

All of it caught by the colonel's head-mounted camera, as the SUV barreled past the shooter.

Not for long.

The Hummer smashed into three parked cars before rolling up over a curb and crashing into a tree.

The colonel lurched forward, then fell back. The camera reflected those wild movements, then settled on the driver as his hands fell away from his bloody face and his head lolled left, smacking the driver's-side window. A moment later he spilled forward, chest, shoulders, and head collapsing against the steering wheel.

Vinko heard groaning, realizing it hailed from the colonel when he saw the man's head-mounted camera pointing toward a semi-automatic pistol on the floor. As the colonel grabbed it, a man with an unusual accent yelled, "Put it down!"

"You are so dead," Vinko growled, furious with the colonel for the mess he'd made of what should have been a simple assassination. Those motorcyclists should have shot Elkins 1-2-3, not the fucking tires in some Hollywood attempt to take her alive.

But Vinko knew he had to take some of the blame for that lame maneuver. He'd posted at various times that POWs in the war on American traitors should be subject to online trials. "Show trials," Vinko had called them, "and then we'll execute the people who betray their race." Of course they'd want to seize Lana. Seize her and try her on video.

So the colonel had swung for the fences and failed.

And now he's about to die.

Or was he? The colonel was scrambling gamely despite his leg wounds to grab the 9 millimeter.

"Good. Yes!" Vinko whispered to the screen, as though he were in the Hummer's back seat beside the wounded man.

The colonel had the gun in hand, but as he pulled himself upright the weapon was blasted out of his grip, bloodying and mangling his fingers. Someone wanted *him* alive.

But the identity of that person remained a mystery because a black hand ripped the camera off the colonel's head. After a quick repositioning, the device must have been strapped to the African American's brow, for it now revealed a horrified expression on the colonel's face.

"No," the colonel begged. "Not that."

Not what?

The answer came quickly: Vinko watched a serrated blade plunged into the colonel's throat. With the man still very much alive—with his eyes bulging in horror—the sawing of his neck began.

A black hand grabbed the colonel's head and yanked it backward for the final deep cuts.

With the colonel's eyes still open—the head was placed upright on the console between the two front seats.

The camera was in motion again, this time returning to the colonel's head where the lens peered up at the decapitated, blood-drenched torso.

Vinko heard footfalls recede, but not quickly. He detected no sense of panic. The killer who'd beheaded the colonel might have been cruising stalls at a Saturday market. *He's killed like this before. He'll do it again.* Which scared Vinko most of all.

He stared at the colonel's blood-soaked shirt and, for the first time, had no doubt: *This was ISIS. They're really here.*

• • •

Lana woke in the ambulance, finding herself strapped to a gurney with her wounded calf packed in gauze.

"How are you feeling?" asked a female paramedic sitting by her side.

"Better," Lana lied. She felt on the verge of delirium but wanted straight communication with the people around her. The shrapnel in her calf burned like a torch.

"Police and federal agents want to talk to you when we get to emergency. Do you think you can handle that? You don't have to. We'll be arriving in a few minutes."

"Yes. What happened to me?"

"You passed out," the woman replied. "It looks like you caught some fragments from an explosion and they severed an artery down there." She nodded at Lana's lower right leg. "Not a major one," she added quickly. "We've got you hooked up." Lana saw what appeared to be a plasma line feeding into her arm.

The ambulance braked, turned, and slowed even more. Next, the rear doors flew open and she was wheeled into the emergency entrance.

A woman in a Bethesda Police Department uniform rushed up, trailed by Agent Robin Maray in jacket and tie. Lana managed a smile. The two law enforcement officers hurried alongside the gurney as the paramedics wheeled her into the hospital. Lana noticed that Agent Maray was looking her over carefully, then caught her eye and nodded, she assumed in reassurance.

The gurney came to a stop in an area that was quickly curtained off. A doctor entered as Maray leaned over Lana, she assumed to ask him questions. But the doctor waved him away. "Not now. Step aside."

A nurse hooked her up to a blood pressure cuff and heart rate monitor, then started cutting off Lana's pants leg.

"You'll have to leave," the doctor said to Agent Maray and the officer. "I need to examine her in privacy."

Robin nodded and followed the officer through a gap in the floor-length curtains.

"I'm Dr. Rivera," he said, filling a syringe. "I'm going to give you something for the pain, then I'll be examining for shrapnel wounds. You caught some in your calf so you might have caught others."

He injected the painkiller while the nurse methodically removed or cut off the rest of Lana's clothes. Just as systematically, Rivera examined every inch of her, turning Lana over to complete the task.

"Just your leg," he pronounced minutes later.

The nursed draped Lana with a sheet. "Do you want the FBI and Bethesda Police back in here? Can you handle that?"

"That's fine," Lana replied.

Robin swept to her side first, asking if she'd seen an African American male anywhere near the attack.

She shook her head. "Why?"

Dr. Rivera turned back to them. "I wouldn't go into that now."

"I can handle it," Lana snapped. "Why?" she asked Robin again.

"There was a beheading down the block from the scene. A black male cut off the head of the man who appeared to have been in charge of the assassination attempt on you."

"I don't think it was an assassination attempt," Lana said. "They could have killed me right at the start, if that's what they wanted. I think they wanted to take me alive."

"How many did you see?"

"Four men. Never their faces. But I saw their hands. They were white. A beheading? Really?"

Robin nodded. Dr. Rivera tugged on the agent's jacket sleeve. "Do you have enough for now?"

"How long will she be under?" Robin replied.

"I don't think we'll put her under. I'll use a local anesthetic. But I want her focused on the procedure. If she feels any serious discomfort, I'll need to know right away."

Robin backed out of the curtained cubicle for a second time, already on his phone. The Bethesda police officer followed him.

Dr. Rivera might have wanted Lana thinking about the procedure but all she could do was wonder why Tahir—she figured that was a solid guess—had cut off the man's head. Did he want to leave the impression that ISIS had advanced into the District's toniest suburbs? Wasn't he worried he'd show up on video? Or did his convoluted relationship with U.S. intelligence agencies grant him a special form of immunity? But even if that were the case, why would he want to generate the widespread fear that a beheading would bring?

Or maybe he wants to fight fire with fire?

"Ouch," Lana squealed as Dr. Rivera probed her wound.

"Sorry," he muttered. "I'm putting you under," he said a moment later, nodding at an anesthesiologist. "I've got to go deeper than I expected," he said, turning back to Lana. "Just so you know, you'll have some scarring down here."

Lana smiled. That was the least of her . . .

She hadn't finished the thought before the drugs took over.

• • •

Vinko brought up YouTube, hoping against hope that the failed abduction had not been posted.

1,257,546 views in the first hour and a half.

He groaned.

"Cyber Spy and Park Ranger Heroes" was the website's headline. All four of the dead attackers were on vivid display. But they didn't show the colonel's severed head, though Vinko had no doubt that that grisly sight would show up somewhere, probably sooner rather than later.

He didn't know how he'd get to Lana Elkins now. And then he told himself to return to basics.

Get her kid. That's what you were thinking before the colonel fucked things up. Emma's the bait.

He murmured her name to himself, as if invoking those two smooth syllables would grant him mantra-like powers. Then he got to the point: "I'm coming to get you, Emma. And then I'm taking down your mom."

It was personal for Vinko now. He'd make sure it would be no different for Lana Elkins.

CHAPTER 17

LANA SAT WITH HER injured leg propped on a hassock in the living room. She had two wounds from the fragments that had ripped into her calf, which were now closed with twelve stitches. The surgeon said the cuts were deep, down to the bone in one case, and insisted that she keep her leg elevated for four days.

She worked effectively enough from the couch, where she glanced up periodically to see if the breeder and dog trainer, Ed Holmes, had arrived yet.

Bob Holmes's son had been aghast to learn about Jojo, but relieved that the young Malinois would survive, the latest report from the veterinarian's office. Ed Holmes had phoned Lana last night to say he'd be bringing her a replacement.

"Which one?" Emma had asked when Lana got off the phone.

"I don't know. Does it matter?"

"He had two other younger dogs, I'm pretty sure."

There was Ed now. Lana saw Robin greeting him in the driveway, where the FBI agent had just completed another circuit around the house. The dog by Ed's side looked heftier than Jojo. Actually, he looked ... older.

Robin escorted Ed and the hound into the living room.

Better than a butler, Lana thought of Robin, smiling to herself.

Ed introduced himself as Don walked in from the kitchen. He'd been anxious, too, about Jojo's successor.

"You're kidding," Don said, staring at the hound. "That old guy?"

Lana thought Don sounded insulting, but before she could come up with some meliorating words for Ed, Don turned to her and said, "Do you know who this is?" He gestured at the dog.

"No."

"This is Cairo, the dog that helped take down bin Laden."

"Seriously?" Lana was now staring at Cairo, too.

"He's the best I've got right now," Ed jumped in. "The demand is very high. The navy took my two younger ones," he added with a knowing nod to Don. "Cairo's not as fast as he once was, but he's smart, experienced, and has a better sense of people than any creature, including humans, that I've ever met. Thing is, he's not a family dog. He's all business. Think of him as a battle-hardened grandfather who can't suffer fools, and you'll pretty much know what Cairo's all about. And *nobody* cuddles up with Cairo. Just feed him, air him, and he'll secure the premises."

"So we have a celebrity guard dog?" Lana said.

"Lower case c," Ed replied. "Don't go dining out on stories about him, though. There's a price on his head, and I understand there's a pretty hefty one on yours, too, so you don't want some enterprising jihadist aiming for a twofer with both of you in this place."

Ed did introduce Cairo to her. Lana petted him. He appeared to tolerate her touch, but that was about it. And he barely glanced at Lana, eyes on his new digs. Emma got a reintroduction, and asked if Cairo still high-fived.

"Sure," Ed replied.

She and Cairo slapped palm and pad.

While Don, Emma, and Ed gave Cairo the tour of the house and grounds, Robin remained in the living room long enough to ask Lana how she was doing.

"Fine. Do you need anything?"

"No, nothing. I'll leave."

She didn't mean to be curt, but realized that must have been how she'd sounded. As he exited the front door, Ed, Emma, Don, and Cairo returned through the kitchen.

"I brought along special senior dog food for him," the breeder said. "You can pick it up at Whole Pet Central in Rockville when you run out. Or from us if you happen to be up in our neck of the woods. Thing is, don't ever let anyone else try to feed him but you two and Emma." He went on to brief her about the importance of Cairo's rigid feeding regimen. "Now, if you're going on vacation—"

"We won't be taking any vacations for the foreseeable future," Lana interrupted.

"I hear you," Ed said. "Nobody is. Not even the President's taking any time at Camp David. I'll go get that dog food from my truck. Just remember, Cairo does not cuddle."

Lana didn't need a reminder. Cairo looked all business to her, like most of the SEALs whom she'd gone into battle with.

• • •

Lana's leg wounds paled in comparison to the shocking medical nightmare unfolding down south. The ISIS fighters who'd surrendered so readily in Oysterton, Louisiana, at the End of Summer Jamboree had apparently infected themselves with smallpox well ahead of the attack. So they had, in fact, carried ashore suicide bombs—their own bodies—and spread the deadly contagion to more than a hundred of the men, women, and children who'd crowded around them during the perp walk to take photos, including tons of selfies and videos. Also infected the same day were the news crews, reporters, and sheriff's deputies who'd proudly paraded their prisoners past all the lookie-loos.

The sheriff himself was stricken with the disfiguring disease; his exposure came after he'd insisted on taking selfies with the handcuffed and ankle-chained men en route to Camp Blanding in central Florida. Now the terrorists he'd treated like trophies he'd bagged on a big-game-hunting expedition were on the verge of killing *him*. In turn, the sheriff had infected countless others by glad-handing constituents in his boisterous bid for November reelection. The polls were unlikely ever to open for the incumbent sheriff: His voter-ready smile on the campaign trail had been replaced by deeply scarred features on what now appeared to be his deathbed.

All the stricken were housed in isolation units in poorly equipped and vastly overwhelmed rural hospitals in Louisiana, Florida, Mississippi, and Alabama. Parts of east Texas had also drawn close scrutiny from the Centers for Disease Control in Atlanta.

The sheriff was in the same hospital as Jimmy McMasters and the pert piccolo player rescued by the boat racer in the early moments of the beachside invasion. The eighteen-year-old band member had spent many hours smacking skin with Jimmy and exchanging vital bodily fluids, ensuring her own infection and that of five family members, including two older brothers who now promised to tear Jimmy "limb from limb for violating our sister."

In the past twenty-four hours, she had broken out with the mouth sores that presaged the full onslaught of the disease. She was also running a 104-degree fever.

Jimmy was doing better—so far. His doctors described him as having the constitution of a rhino. Considering what the girl's brothers wanted to do to him, he wished he had the hide of that creature as well, though it might not be needed: The furious pair now appeared unlikely to last long enough to fulfill their heartfelt vow. But Jimmy wasn't past the disease's danger zone yet, and his Kato Kaelin physical charms were succumbing to more pustules with each passing day.

Jimmy sat up in bed and watched a cute nurse exit the room now occupied only by him; a young man had died at sunrise, only an hour ago.

Jimmy could hardly believe how fast his downfall had come. Not only the smallpox and death threats from piccolo's thuggy brothers, but also his descent from national hero to national goat in a matter of days. Masochistic though it always proved to be, he tuned into the *Today Show*, where much of the viewing audience was now fixed on Matt Lauer's battle against smallpox, for which millions blamed Jimmy. NBC's executives stoked the audience's anger by replaying, at least once a show, the moment when Lauer had introduced Jimmy, only to have the sturdy good ol' boy pull the sharply dressed host to his feet for a Louisiana-style bear hug.

Why'd I do that? Jimmy shook his head in regret. He really liked Matt the man. And then he'd gone and fucked him over but good.

The video came right up, as if on cue.

Sheeeee-it.

"Right there," Lauer's excited female co-host gushed. "That was when poor Matt got infected, according to his doctors. Right when that boat guy grabbed him."

Boat guy? I don't even have a name anymore?

"Doctors say that was point of contact," the co-host added, shaking her head as she looked directly into the camera.

The beautiful woman could not have sounded more disgusted if she'd been describing the vivisection of a pregnant pig.

The entire news division of the Peacock Network—from multi-million-dollar anchor monsters to the lowliest interns—was now isolated on three floors of 30 Rockefeller Plaza, scrutinized daily by roving teams of medical professionals looking for any signs of sickness—just like the audiences for the NBC's news shows.

Jimmy glared at the screen. Hugging Matt had been such a great moment for him. How was he to know he'd been contagious?

He'd sent an email apology to Lauer. Jimmy hadn't heard back. Didn't expect to. Lauer was said to be running a high fever with pustules weeping pus all over his body. Jimmy figured a simple "I'm sorry" wasn't going to cut it with Lauer. He wondered if he should go to Lauer's funeral . . . if it came to that. Maybe even speak as a great admirer and newfound friend.

He wished he could do something to make amends, anything that would make people stop comparing him to Typhoid Mary. One guy on TV even called him "Smallpox McMasters." Jimmy swore he'd go to the caliphate himself and spit in the furry faces of ISIS leaders if he had half a chance. But he was unlikely to slip past the end of the corridor, where armed guards kept patients in and visitors out.

You're not going anywhere. You're sick, dude.

As if to confirm his status, he walked into the bathroom to check himself in the mirror. *Yup, still got it.* Not too bad . . . considering. Like a bad case of acne. His fever this morning had even dropped to ninety-nine, which by smallpox standards was nothing. Staring at his reflection, he knew that getting laid night after night by hero groupies had ended. He was contemplating that dark, lonely future when he heard a *Today Show* report that fifteen ISIS fighters were battling right at that moment to take control of a poorly defended BP oil rig platform a couple hundred miles off the Mississippi coast.

Jimmy stumbled back to his bed to see helicopter footage of the heavily armed fighters seizing weapons from BP's defeated security force. Out came the big knives.

Oh, Christ.

No, the network would never show . . . But they did, and then another head rolled. Those ISIS monsters were tossing them into the Gulf like coconuts. Bodies, too. *What the fuck!*

And they were hoisting their big black flag with the white circle and weird writing.

Three men on the BP crew had been spared. The reporter in the helicopter said the man in the middle—bald, portly, and wearing nothing but his undershorts—was the platform's chief engineer. The other two were oil workers. A statement from the attackers, just received in news centers around the world, said the terrorists intended to blow up the well. "We will make the five million gallons from BP Horizon look like a puddle. We will sabotage every emergency device that could cap the well. The Gulf will be poisoned forever."

To underscore their point, a crew of ISIS suicide bombers had taken the chief engineer's family captive and threatened to cut off the heads of his three children if he didn't comply with their wishes in the next seventy-two hours.

"Jesus H. Christ," Jimmy said to the TV. "Everything's going from bad to worse."

He stared at BP's three men standing under the Gulf's brutal sun. They looked shiny from sweat. He knew how hot it got out there. He'd even worked on a BP offshore oil rig for three weeks before he'd been fired for partying in the rec room with a pair of exotic dancers he'd smuggled aboard. BP's execs were *very* touchy about regulations after the Horizon fiasco. So Jimmy did know something about their operations. *Probably just enough to be dangerous*, he thought.

But then Jimmy realized that knowing just enough to be dangerous might be just enough, indeed.

• • •

Lana checked on Holmes's condition almost hourly. The deputy director was still in the ICU, still not permitted visitors. His longtime executive assistant Donna Warnes said his condition was grave. She'd sounded weepy when Lana had spoken to her by phone. That Donna was upset worried Lana, and not just for deep personal reasons. The interim deputy director sitting in for Holmes, Marigold Winters, was clearly vying to remain his replacement *and* had already made strong efforts to coerce Galina to leave CyberFortress and come to work for the NSA.

Winters, dubbed "Flowers" by her many male friends at the agency, hadn't even had the decency to consult with Lana before telling Galina that Louisiana Senator Bob Ray Willens was prepared to introduce a bill that would force Galina to work for the NSA for seven years from the time she was granted political asylum by the U.S. The legislation already had twenty-five co-sponsors in the Senate, 151 in the House.

Flowers's move didn't shock Lana. The pair had started at NSA the same year, but while Lana's cyberskills had moved her up the agency command quickly, her envious antagonist had refined a different set of talents: she'd become a consummate in-house backstabber and power grabber, and a demagogue of the first order, casting aspersions on some of the most talented Arabic-speaking experts in the intelligence community. She'd drummed up enough suspicion on the "questionables"—her term—to drive them out of government work.

The woman wasn't without smarts, of course, or extraordinary physical appeal—and she'd deployed both successfully enough to have been named Holmes's interim replacement.

Galina had rebuffed Flowers's recruitment efforts, but that bill was set to be introduced in Bob's absence, and the President had said he would sign the Bortnik Aid and Comfort Act, BACA.

As in "Back atcha," Lana thought, sensing the real target of Flowers's insidious machinations.

In the White House Daily Briefing, the President's press secretary had quoted him as saying, "We must all pay our dues if we want to enjoy the great benefits of living in our proud country."

The President could have added that the country was also profoundly broken, but Lana knew that would have been asking too much of an incumbent hungering for reelection.

After texting Galina to continue to do Bob's bidding by trying to penetrate the NSA's defenses, Lana turned her attention to Tahir, whom she was all but certain had decapitated the man in charge of trying to abduct her. But no video of the person performing the gruesome act had appeared anywhere. How was that even possible? Every catastrophe or public act of violence was recorded these days. Why would this be any different?

The only video that had surfaced so far was the close-up taken by the man who'd put the camera on his own head before cutting off the target's.

It made Lana wonder if Tahir was so connected to the intelligence services that video of him committing the crime had been surreptitiously vacuumed up by his superiors, which was entirely plausible. Meantime, the beheaded man had been identified as an ex-Army colonel and white supremacist. Video of his macabre death had been viewed by tens of millions of viewers.

Lana was tempted to apply her skills to finding a definitive answer about Tahir's role in the ending of her abduction attempt, but with Bob Holmes in the ICU, she not only lacked her longtime ally at the agency, she also faced her longtime nemesis occupying his seat and likely looking for any excuse to terminate CyberFortress's contracts. So Lana could wonder about Tahir, but she dared not wander across any inter-agency boundaries. At least for now.

Lana's previous forays, revealing Tahir's past in Sudan, Afghanistan, and Pakistan—and his critical association with both Al Qaeda of the Arabian Peninsula and the CIA of Langley, Virginia—had been stymied by her wounding: When she retraced her steps from her perch on the couch, Lana found that her previous penetrations had been patched up.

With no easy access to the cyber routes she'd trodden, Lana had to forego any further incursions, for they, too, might be used by Flowers to terminate CyberFortress. Only Galina, ironically enough, had the right to search the NSA for vulnerabilities. And only, Lana believed, because Flowers didn't know that Holmes had given the Russian émigrée her secret assignment.

Lana turned her attention to the smallpox outbreak—the CDC, she'd noticed, had been careful not to call it an epidemic—in the South and New York City, where 30 Rockefeller Plaza had become ground zero for the highly contagious disease in the Big Apple.

Right from the start, Lana had been suspicious of the easy surrender of the ISIS fighters. But even she had never conceived that the terrorists had turned themselves into biological bombs.

The CDC had started issuing hourly updates on the spreading smallpox, still carefully avoiding the "e" word. But the agency's graphics showed ample red tendrils, which represented newly identified cases, reaching out of the South and New York. The exposed now included residents of cities and suburbs in more than half the states. Only older Americans, inoculated before vaccinations against smallpox ended in 1972, had immunity. Fortunately, after 9/11, American fears of biological warfare had prompted the resurrection of smallpox vaccine production, so there were doses sufficient to inoculate every American. But the challenge of actually getting the vaccine to each of them was formidable. The CDC was rapidly deploying teams to every corner of the country to coordinate those efforts, but these tremendously difficult attempts were coming when much of the country's coastal infrastructure was severely compromised, which had already impacted the movement of basics, such as food and fuel, throughout the nation.

Now, as Lana checked the latest news on her screen, she saw the American flag lowered on a BP oil platform in the Gulf and learned about the latest atrocities committed against her fellow citizens. In seconds, the ISIS flag was raised. A wild-eyed man with a distinctive Maine accent was pointing to a camera and shouting, "We will turn your waters black as your infidel souls."

Sleeper cell, she thought right away.

A thousand miles away, Jimmy McMasters watched the same angry announcement, then saw the ISIS spokesman, who looked so American he could have been brought up in a logging town, throw gas on Old Glory and light it up.

He held it over the platform railing and then dropped it. The flight of the burning flag was brief, but it was still nothing but char when it hit the water.

"Like you, America," the man shouted. "Burning to death in your own filth."

Not if I can help it, Jimmy thought. *You worthless sons-of-bitches.*

He was already slipping off his hospital gown.

CHAPTER 18

STEEL FIST IS HOPELESS and, quite frankly, as good as dead. That's my decision as I sit here at my computer, watching the debacle that's getting huge play online and in broadcast news for all the wrong reasons. The man he enlisted to kill Lana Elkins made a grisly mess of the whole operation. And now they're making a hero out of Elkins and a game warden.

I gave Vinko Horvat a veritable paint-by-numbers approach to throttling that woman *after* taking considerable personal risks to put an electronic locator on her car to make the assassination—*not* abduction—possible. Then I barely got back to the mountains of Washington before coverage exploded with Vinko's dismal failure. Turning Lana Elkins into a larger-than-life heroine was not on my agenda.

And it's Vinko's fault, plain and simple, although I'm kicking myself for not having connected his public enthusiasm for show trials with the possibility that he might prove just thick enough to try that with such a high-risk prospect as Elkins. I'll admit, a show trial would have been a coup, but all the "would have beens" that have failed in the past five years alone could provide data enough to shut down the Pentagon with a distributed denial-of-service attack.

But instead, the world salutes a woman who survived a *grenade* and four killers. Granted, her victory came with the help of a game warden with a hunting rifle and a black man whose identity now intrigues millions, but who kept the camera off his own face.

Now Elkins looms larger than ever in the eyes of the public. Which does make taking her daughter a bigger prize. Steel Fist could redeem himself—if I were fool enough to give him a second chance.

That is *not* going to happen. Here's what I mean:

Emma Elkins must be abducted to Hayden Lake, where cyber clues will lure her mother to the lair I have in mind. There are few people whom I'll trust with that task, mostly myself. When her mother comes calling for her—and I know precisely how to manipulate her hunt so she doesn't arrive in the company of the SEALs who have saved her in the past—I'll dispose of mother and daughter, along with Vinko. Nobody will be the wiser about my role. Few even know I exist, and Vinko's a complete loner. I've checked his communications. Never a word of a personal nature. He lives in isolation up there. But he doesn't deserve to live any longer. I'll remind him of that as I start to lop off his head. Just before I finish, I'll offer him another old line: "Live by the sword, die by the sword." Let Vinko hear that as the blade severs the last few inches of his neck.

Besides, I'm better suited to snatching Emma. I have a quality Vinko lacks. Actually, as I've seen of late, I have a number of them that he could use, so I'm confident Emma will find me eminently approachable, were she to need some emergency assistance. And she will. She drives a Fusion, after all. I know the exact nature of the malfunction she'll soon experience. So does J.D. Powers and Associates.

But I do have one final task for Steel Fist, for which he's shown supreme ability. Disgusted as I am by him, even I have to admit the man knows how to drum up hatred against Muslims. And now he's got plenty of ammo, thanks to those ISIS fighters who have spread smallpox throughout the Southeast, though an honorable mention must go to the boat racer named Jimmy McMasters for transporting the deadly virus to New York City.

Could we have asked for a more beloved victim than Matt Lauer? Probably. But he'll certainly do. He looks like he's going to die. Even if he doesn't, he's probably going to be scarred from head to toe, and all because boat racer boy gave Lauer a nice big hug that went, well, *viral* in the original sense of the word.

As for the government's response, the CDC is doing a splendid job of keeping the public up to date and scared to death. The venerable *New York Times* reports on its website, right at this very moment, that the CDC has identified outbreaks of smallpox spreading from tightly knit Muslim communities in Dearborn, Michigan; Patterson, New Jersey; Los Angeles; and, of course, New York City, particularly Bay Ridge in Brooklyn. In fact, the CDC has finally called the spread of the disease an epidemic, and it's pointing its finger right at Muslims, blaming sleeper cells of infected believers for mixing with large crowds wherever they can find them.

"It's no coincidence," a CDC official is quoted in the *Times* as saying, "that this is taking place as ISIS claims responsibility for the epidemic in North America. ISIS is everywhere."

And the *Times* reports that local officials from coast to coast are cooperating with the panic by calling for the quarantining of all Muslim neighborhoods. Delightful: a whole series of our own Warsaw ghettos.

And those are the mild reactions. Others, including the men and women who cluster in Vinko's chat rooms, are calling for the "culling of all Muslims" from their cities and suburbs. The *Times* is giving that quote and the rest of the chat room chorus lots of coverage, too.

While a handful of officials refuse to sanction such efforts, there are reports of organized groups of "red-blooded Americans," as the *Times* puts it, attacking Muslim "cells" in five cities. Apparently, police in those communities have refused to intervene to stop the vicious assaults and murders. The tacit approval of vigilante violence has set off similar beatings and killings elsewhere. So it's not just smallpox that's spreading.

"There are no moderate Muslims," the mayor of Birmingham, Alabama, said flatly after the city's Islamic center was reduced to ash, along with fourteen of its members.

None of the coverage is true, but people who want to believe what I wrote on the *Times* website, after hacking it, are having no trouble accepting the "news." And by flipping their online edition's servers to read-only I've made sure there have been no corrections or updating on the part of the paper's editors. Fox News is reporting the lies as if they come from its own "reliable" sources.

This is my fourth hacking of the *Times*; my earlier efforts were all alpha runs. I've also hacked the *Wall Street Journal* twice, which has marginally better cyberdefenses.

When the *Times* finally regains control of its website, which I expect is still several hours away, even more violence will be underway against Muslim communities throughout the country. And when the paper's brass tries to make its predictable claim that they were hacked, they'll be widely accused of conspiring with, and kowtowing to, government efforts to support Muslims "in their time of need." In the malleable minds of millions, it'll stand as another example of the *Times*' self-imposed *sharia* law.

So . . . Elkins, her daughter, Vinko, and the American public. Check, check, and check. Simple as cyber—to me. What I can't put my finger on so easily is how that African American beheaded the colonel and vanished so completely. Whose side is he on? He's got me wondering.

Let's look at what he's done. By chopping off the colonel's noggin, he's created yet another incitement against mainstream Muslims, or, to put it in patently American terms, the Uncle Toms of their religion who so proudly hail their moderation and patriotism. We'll see how steadfast they remain in both regards when their fellow citizens continue to burn down their homes and slaughter them in the streets. That will certainly drive many survivors into the arms of ISIS.

So separating the colonel from his head could be part of a neat divide-and-conquer strategy—if you're a radical Muslim. I understand and appreciate that. It will spread the violence against moderates as fast as the fear of smallpox is moving through the country at large.

But it could also serve as an incitement to Muslims to behead their neighbors in retaliation for violence visited upon them. So it could cut—please excuse the pun—both ways.

Still, I wish I could be sure of the man's game.

I'm dipping deeper into the nether regions of the Net to try to find out. I haven't found anything yet that would link me to him; nothing, in short, in the realm of arms dealers, terrorists, or bomb makers, all of whom have left many a head behind. And the obvious video of *him* committing the beheading is missing. How does that happen in a wealthy community like Bethesda? Even in the poorest, blackest ghettos of America a cop can't sneeze without it showing up on someone's smart phone. But, then again, those purveyors of instant history are primed to react, while the more affluent among us presume degrees of safety and justice not so readily accessed by those further down the food chain.

Okay, here's the beheading proper. It's emerging everywhere. There he is, casually sawing away, totally unhurried. Like "another day, another head."

And there's the colonel's head on the move again, from his body to the front seat console, the camera focused once more on the colonel, *sans* skull. I've had enough. I don't need to see any more blood spurting from his open neck. What I want to see is the guy doing the sawing, and he's not giving us a glimpse of that.

But this . . . this is interesting. I'm back where I was earlier today, when I discovered Al Qaeda in the Arabian Peninsula, AQAP, trying to hack the Pentagon, NBC News, a navy shipyard, and one of the giant sump pumps trying to drain the last floodwaters from the Washington Mall. AQAP hasn't made much headway in its intrusion attempts. I could give them a helpful nudge in the right direction—it's obvious to me and I've done it before—but I won't, not yet anyway.

I have more critical nudges in mind, so I look once more at ISIS's social media campaign. ISIS does know how to inspire Muslim youth, and they're at it 24/7, displaying photos and videos of testosterone-driven young warriors waving AK-47s and their black flags from the barricades and backs of trucks racing to battle. "Hear the commands of Mohammed in your heart and join us" scrolls across the screen in one language after another.

Farther down, I find them urging those "blessed with courage" to become lone wolves. "Our enemies are your enemies, and they are all around you."

There are so many lone wolves out there they could form packs at this point, at least in cyberspace.

Maybe not only there, though.

I've made numerous forays into both AQAP and ISIS online. They have their individual strengths. What they've always needed to do was come together to form one big pack. But to accomplish that they needed a persuasive voice that could coordinate their actions to advance their effectiveness.

They're both Sunnis, after all. They both hate Shias. And they both belong to the branch of Islam that claims eighty-five percent of all believers. They have so much in common. It was only a matter of time before ISIS and AQAP recognized that they had more to gain by cooperation than competition. And wouldn't a reconciliation that began right here, in the heart of America, prove most fruitful?

That time is now.

I certainly can claim my role. Chainsawing Lana Elkins and her daughter to death will be a tangible demonstration of what can be accomplished when ISIS and AQAP join forces. The *khilafa*, caliphate, will grow exponentially, for if AQAP and ISIS can cooperate here in the harsh land of unbelievers, they can kill at will anywhere at all.

CHAPTER 19

JIMMY MCMASTERS CRACKED OPEN the door of his hospital room. Guards armed with automatic rifles stood at each end of the long corridor, eyes on anyone seeking access to the patients. They were there to keep the quarantined inside, but looked ready to repel an invasion.

He swore softly to himself. He was dressed and ready to roll, and they were still there. *Don't they ever take a damn break?* The hospital was in lockdown, a prison term that sounded painfully appropriate to Jimmy. If he could just get out, he could start rehabilitating his name, if not his health. But he wasn't feeling too bad. No worse than some epic hangovers he'd known, and he'd managed to race *Sexy Streak* almost two hundred miles per hour during one of them.

As he eased the door shut and backed away, he glanced again at the mirror in the small bathroom. Not as bad as most of the cases he'd seen on TV, or on his now-dead roommate. But Jimmy had been a good-looking piece of work; he wasn't so sure of himself now. Dozens of women—he was pretty certain he'd passed the half-century mark—had thought enough of him to show their appreciation. Piccolo—the one who really knew how to play a flute—had said he'd "rocked her world." Now she'd probably like to stone him to death.

He wanted to feel like a hero again, and he had a plan, a *risky* one, admittedly, but he'd go for it—if he could just get the hell out of there.

Jimmy was on the third floor. The old bedsheets ploy wouldn't work. By the time he tied them to a radiator—the hospital had been built in the 1930s—and ran them across the room to the window, he'd be lucky to make it to the top of the second floor. Jumping twenty feet in his condition was not a cool idea.

He thought about tackling a nurse and stealing her baggy blue clothes, but the one who breezed in and out of his room every hour outweighed him by a good eighty pounds and looked pretty frickin' angry about having to come anywhere near him. She called him "Matt killer," even though Lauer wasn't dead yet, a point that Jimmy had made to her more than once.

"But he's dyin' and you're lookin' like you got nothin' but a couple of zits," she'd said on her last visit, shaking her head as she left. It was as if she'd just discovered there really wasn't any justice in the world if Matt Lauer might die and Jimmy McMasters actually got to live.

He peeked out the window. Starting to get dark, for all the help that might bring him. At least he spied no guards on the hospital grounds.

Christ!

He heard the XXL nurse in the hallway just as he caught sight of a possible way down.

Jimmy rushed to his bed and in seconds had his eyes closed, gown over his pants and shirt, and the sheet over everything but his face.

A moment later she barreled in. "You dead yet?" she asked, sounding far too hopeful for Jimmy's comfort.

He cracked an eyelid. *Yeah, XXL all right.* "No, but I feel like I'm dying."

She promptly stuck a thermometer in his mouth. Pulled it out seconds later. One of those fast-acting ones.

"Don't be such a wimp. Ninety-nine degrees. You're no worse for wear. Not like my boy, Matt," she humphed. "Not that you care."

"Hey, I liked him, too."

"Yeah? With friends like you, Matt sure don't need no enemies. And don't be talkin' like he's already dead. That's disrespectin' him even more. Makes me wonder if you've been workin' with those terrorists the whole time."

"If I was working with them, I wouldn't have let myself get sick."

She humphed again. "They got sick and now they're dyin', so it seems if you was workin' with them, you'd be sick, too. And there you are, a waste of space and fresh as some damn peaches and cream . . . for a supposedly *sick* man. Tell you what, though, we're bringin' in someone in a few minutes who's sweatin' blood he's so gone. See how you're doin' with him around."

"That sucks."

She looked at her watch. "Ten minutes. Sendin' up the orderlies. Be seein' you soon." She smiled at him for the first time, then slammed the door.

Jimmy swore to himself again, burst from the bed, and raced back to the window. What he'd spotted before XXL showed up was a drainage pipe about five feet from the edge of a six-inch-deep windowsill.

He cranked the handle for the window and watched it open sideways. Might give him just enough room to squeeze by.

Nope.

His pecs wouldn't compress enough. All those incline presses and drop-sets had left him a little too pumped, even after days of sickness.

He scraped himself, seeing if he could fit through the window, but no one saw him. Tore open a pustule right through his favorite Lynyrd Skynyrd T-shirt, the Greenville show, Ronnie Van Zant's last before the band's fatal crash on the way to Baton Rouge. The tee was a collector's item—and Jimmy only had five more of them. That was when he remembered the salve XXL had applied to his worst sores. She'd grimaced applying it.

He found the tube in the bathroom and smothered his bare chest with the greasy ointment. Hated to leave the tee behind, but he had no choice. He was giving someone a real fine gift, even if it did have some of the ooze that came out of those sticky sores.

Now he squeezed right through the open window and found himself thirty seconds later perched near the edge of the sill, a good leap from the drainage pipe.

One more step, dude, and you're free!

But when he pressed his foot down to get ready to launch himself from the last brick, a chunk of the outer sill broke and the brain buster flew loose. Almost took Jimmy with it, landing and bouncing on brown grass that looked hard as concrete.

He steadied his nerves, tested his footing one more time, and reassured himself all he needed was one good jump and he could slide away to freedom, just as he'd done as a kid after climbing light poles.

But you never were Spider-Man, a meek voice inside him said.

He nodded in agreement and studied the pipe, shadowy now under the ever-darkening sky. *Oh, no.* He'd spotted rust on the length of it. Hadn't been painted in forever and a day.

His palms felt sweaty as he shifted his weight back to help propel himself over the gap. Not just sweaty, he realized when he rubbed them against the gown: greasy. Really greasy.

"Shit."

He did his best to wipe off the salve but the reason it proved so soothing was the ointment had been designed to penetrate the deepest layers of skin.

Voices arose in the hallway outside his room. He wasn't sure if it was XXL, the orderlies, soldiers, or someone else.

Just go!

He hurled himself at the drainage pipe, regret throbbing through him the moment he felt himself falling short.

But no. With a desperate reach he grabbed it and jammed his fingers between the rusty metal and the brick wall, skinning his knuckles. Then he started slipping. *Good God!* And the rusty metal strips holding the pipe to the brick wall began to break loose.

The whole apparatus fell backward. The only blessing—if you could call it that—was Jimmy could now wrap his arms and legs around the pipe and hold on, no longer hampered by greasy hands.

Down he went, faster and faster in gravity's sure grip, a nail stuck to the mighty head of a magnetized hammer.

• • •

Emma was pregnant. No doubt about it. She'd used up five test sticks. Every one came up pink. She had no idea what she was going to do.

Here she was waltzing down the stairs with Sufyan to have dinner with her folks *and* Tahir—this was happening way too often—and she hadn't even told her boyfriend the nightmare news. Even so, for all her casual airs, she feared he sensed her doom already. He'd sure been asking her a lot of questions: "What's the matter?" "You feel all right?" "You sure?" No surprise why: she'd vomited in his presence four times. Morning sickness. Except not always in the morning; the fourth time had come five minutes ago.

"Stomach flu," she'd lied.

"You have got to tell your mom. You should see a doctor."

"No!" she'd snapped. "She's got too much to worry about. Don't say anything. Promise?"

Sufyan might not have figured it out but she knew her mom would put two and two together.

He wasn't promising. He'd stopped on the stairs and was staring at Em as her dad called them down to dinner again.

Em knew Sufyan was going to have to own up because it was the condom that broke, not that that excuse would wash with her mother who'd been telling her the same message since she'd first shown interest in boys: "The pill is to stop pregnancy, and the condom's not a bad backup but it's also good to stop STDs." Always reminding her that even a condom could fail to protect her from herpes.

Em had got something a whole lot worse than an STD: she'd gotten pregnant.

"The last of the halibut," her dad announced as they walked into the dining room. "Cooked it in a creamy dill sauce. Your favorite," he said to Em, who felt like hurling all over again. It really was her favorite fish dish, so why did it smell worse than a septic tank?

"Great. Thanks." He was always trying to fix foods she liked, but she'd been eating less and less because of morning sickness. Maybe he'd noticed; her portion tonight was smaller.

Thank God.

Em urged herself to eat. She felt a hint of her gag reflex when she flaked off a forkful of the white fish, but managed to swallow it.

Tahir's eyes were on her. He rarely said much but his gaze felt penetrating. She and Sufyan had talked about that. Her boyfriend said there had been times when he would have sworn his uncle could read his mind.

What else could he read? Em wondered. *My body?*

"So what have you been up to?" Don asked Tahir.

"Not too much," Tahir replied, his manner of speaking as stiff as ever.

"You work on your computer all the time," Sufyan said, a prod that didn't appear appreciated by Tahir, who replied crisply:

"Like you on your phone."

"Do you work on it a lot?" Lana asked Tahir.

You're real subtle, Emma thought.

"It is the only way I can stay in touch with our friends and family in Sudan." Tahir smiled at Lana, which is to say his lips parted just enough to flash his perfect teeth.

"I thought you didn't have any surviving relatives there," Lana replied.

"Cousins. Our clan." That smile again, sneaky as a snake bite.

Em watched her mother eye him the way she always stared at her when Lana expected Emma to say more. The silence trap. That was what Em called it. She'd learned to avoid it—after years of fumbling verbally and trying to fill it, often with self-incriminating information. She saw immediately that Tahir was a much faster study: he simply went back to eating.

• • •

"Awkward. *Awkward*," Em said to Sufyan when they walked outside to wait for his uncle, who'd stopped to thank her parents for dinner, as formal in parting as he'd been at the table.

The FBI agent, Robin Maray, smiled at Emma and Sufyan. *Good-looking, for sure*, Em thought, smiling back. Too old for her, though. Old as her mom and dad. And she loved Sufyan.

"We've got to slip away from your uncle and my dad soon," she told him.

"Why?"

"I'll tell you but you have to promise to keep it secret."

"Of course."

"No, I mean it. Say—"

"I promise I'll keep it secret."

"I'm pregnant. I need to get away from those two and get to Planned Parenthood as soon as possible."

"Why?" Sufyan exclaimed. "This is glorious news."

Glorious?

"No, it's not gl—"

Tahir was walking toward them. She doubted he could read her mind—or his nephew's—but she had no doubt that he'd at least heard her last few words. Among them might have been "I'm pregnant."

"Text me." Sufyan said, as if they'd been discussing his latest basketball drills. He bounced a ball up and down the court every day.

She nodded and said good night. She still didn't dare kiss him, even on his cheek, not in the presence of his uncle. And here she was, carrying his child.

He'd be bouncing a baby on his knee if they didn't do something fast.

• • •

After the rusty brackets holding the pipe to the wall broke loose—and feeling himself falling backward at an ever-increasing rate—Jimmy heard a sound even more ominous: the pipe itself snapping apart where it was coupled to the bottom length that ran about fifteen feet to the ground.

Which was a "break" for him because the pipe's ancient steel peeled apart slowly at the seam, with the gentleness of a new mom laying her baby in a bassinet.

Jimmy even had a chance to lower his feet to the ground and step out of the way. The words "in the flow" came to him, one of Janey the piccolo player's favorite expressions when they were humping and bumping.

In the deepening shadows of night, Jimmy pressed his back against the building and took a breath, wondering if Janey hated him as much as her brothers did. One brother now: XXL had told him the younger bro died last night, shaking her head like Jimmy was to blame, once again. And there she was, big head sticking out the window. He pressed himself flat against the brick. There would be no missing the pipe, though.

"Where are you, McMasters?"

He heard her tell someone "Pipe's all bent. That walking sack of smallpox must have fallen with it. Can't get far."

Yes I can, Jimmy thought, racing along the hospital wall to the employee parking lot.

He had to check seven cars before he found an unlocked door. He couldn't believe how untrusting people were these days. But the owner of the old Toyota 4x4 had been kind enough to stash the keys on top of the sun visor.

Jimmy never looked back, driving to a warehouse district not far from the boat garage for *Sexy Streak*. He hoped like hell BP hadn't changed the push-button combination for the gate to the compound.

Jimmy punched in the five digits. The lock didn't open. Tried it again. Still didn't work. He looked up, wondering if the old coot security guard was still around. Didn't see him. Then Jimmy looked back at the buttons and made himself take a breath, realizing he might have been off on the last number. True enough.

Third time's the charm.

BP's warehouse—one of many, but the only one he'd been in when he worked for the company—rose before him. A city block wide, two stories high, and filled with the tools of the oil trade, including explosives. He needed just enough dynamite to blow the pipe that ran from the seabed to the platform to set off the blowout preventers, BOPs. If the ISIS assholes caught him, they might even think he was doing their work for him. That's what he planned to tell them, anyway.

When? Right before they chop off your head?

Then he spotted the old security guard shuffling along. He looked harmless. He wasn't. He carried a pistol and stun gun, using the latter mostly to fry stray cats.

Wilbur. His name made him sound sweet as a teddy bear. Fact is, he smelled sour as an old sock and cussed faster than a Lotto loser. And he loved his nightstick, tapping everything as he walked along. Right now he was cracking it against the concrete walls of the warehouse every few seconds, warming up, no doubt, for surfaces less resilient.

Jimmy huddled by the steps to a loading dock, shoehorning his body into the slim shadows thrown by the security lights.

Knock-knock. Pause. *Knock-knock.*

Getting closer.

Wilbur, called "Burr" by his friends, all two of them, walked right above Jimmy without looking down. Burr must have patrolled this stretch ten thousand times without ever seeing a soul.

Jimmy stuck to the shadows till the *knock-knock* softened, then he peered over the edge of the loading dock and watched Burr amble around a corner.

Jimmy hurried across the well-lit concrete to an unlocked door in the center of the building. The interior had night lights outlining the tall shelves and, as Jimmy knew from his brief and spectacularly unsuccessful stint at BP, the outlines of anyone entering the facility after hours.

But if the oil giant was as cheap with security in the warehouse as it had been with the men hired to protect the offshore oil platform now under ISIS control, then there would be no one monitoring those cameras. But Jimmy couldn't count on that so he crawled in the shadows till he was down the third aisle to his right, hoping the dynamite hadn't been moved. Not exactly. It was still there, but the sticks were now locked in a steel case as large as an upright freezer.

Getting awful formal around here. Not like the good old days when he had helped himself to a stick or two for some fast nighttime fishing. *Let her rip and catch some fish.*

Knock-knock. Burr was entering the warehouse. *Knock-knock.*

Jimmy swore, worrying the guard had spotted him with the security cam. He might be watching a video feed on his phone.

Knock-knock. Getting louder.

But Burr didn't sound like he was rushing to get to him. Just tapping his nightstick as he'd always done.

Jimmy wedged himself between the steel case and the crisscrossing brackets that supported the shelving rising high above him. He felt no more effective than a kid playing hide-and-go-seek.

The nightstick struck the locked case, then cracked against Jimmy's knee.

Burr paused with his searchlight pointing down at Jimmy, pulling his Taser out so fast that Jimmy knew the security guard must have practiced on plenty of kitties.

"It's me, Burr."

"Who's 'me'?" Burr demanded, peering through his thick glasses. "I don't know no 'me,' shithead. All I know is you're crouching like some goddamn cat next to the 'plosives. 'Course, I *love* finding cats."

Jimmy put his hands up. "I'm coming out. I'm coming out."

"What? You must think this is the Queer Pride Parade. 'I'm coming out,'" Burr mocked. "Get the fuck out of there 'fore I fry your testicles."

Jimmy cupped himself instinctively. "I'm Jimmy McMasters." Hoping his name still meant something to the cussed old creep.

The light flashed right into Jimmy's eyes.

"Hell if you ain't," he said, taking a step backward. "What the fuck are you doing here? Last time I saw you was on the outtakes from the surveillance cam they showed at the Christmas party. You was rootin' and tootin' with those high-tailed strippers. Man, they were treating you like the prize calf in a ropin' contest."

"You like that, huh?"

"'Least you went out in style, not like these other half-dead fuckers. But let's get to the issue at hand, Tit Fucker. What the—"

"'Tit Fucker?' I was doing other stuff, too," Jimmy protested.

"Yeah, but that shit was funny. And Jimmy, you should be proud of yourself. Those pictures got themselves a rerun on the Fourth of July picnic up on a big white sheet."

"Thank you." What else could he say?

"But what the fuck are you doing here?"

"You see me coming up on that beach with those ISIS terrorists?"

"Yeah, I saw that on the TV. Then I heard you stuck it to that *Today Show* guy, laid him up faster than a run-down dog." Which probably explained Burr's immediate retreat when he recognized Jimmy.

"I didn't mean to, Burr. I was just feeling so great I thought I'd—"

"Fuck him. I hate his smiley ass anyway. So what do you need the dynamite for? Goin' fishin'?"

Jimmy told him.

Burr smiled. "Glad to oblige. How much you need? And don't go gettin' greedy."

"Six would be perfect."

Burr opened the steel case, grabbed the red sticks, and handed them over to Jimmy. "You ever let on I did this, I really will fry your testicles. My brother's the sheriff. He survives, he'll help me."

"I won't say a word, but since you're helping me this much, you got a gun you could spare?"

"Now that could be traced to me—"

"I'll throw it in the Gulf when I'm done. I swear."

"—if I hadn't already filed off the numbers."

Burr reached down and pulled a .38 Saturday night special from an ankle holster. "I always keep a drop gun on me, case I need to shoot some loser and say he drew on me."

"You are a first-rate thinker, Burr."

"Don't bullshit me, Jimmy. Take the sticks and blow them shitheads to bits."

"You got it, man." Jimmy tried to shake Burr's hand, but the old guy backed up farther.

"Do I look like Matt fucking Lauer? Get outta here."

Jimmy didn't breathe till he was beyond the reach of that stun gun. Then he rushed across the loading dock and jumped down to the pavement.

Seconds later he was back behind the wheel of the 4x4 and heading to the home of *Sexy Streak*, asking himself if he really wanted to do this. That platform was more than 140 miles out in the Gulf. He wasn't sure he could even carry enough fuel to get out there and back. Be right on the margins of the boat's range.

It's a goddamn suicide mission, he thought, swampy Gulf air thickening as he drove up to the boat garage.

But facing down that boatload of terrorists could have got him killed, too.

And you did that. You got the hero in you, Jimmy.

Janey had told him that over and over, panting those very words into his ear.

She could be right. And "hero" would sure sound better than being remembered as "Tit Fucker."

He unlocked the garage and opened the big wide door. *Sexy Streak* still had bullet holes high on her starboard hull. Otherwise, she looked sweet as ever. Hell, Jimmy had a few holes in his own face now. Pull off this caper, though, and they'd look different. Heroes had scars, sometimes lots of them.

If they survive.

He started the engines, their rumble music to his ears as he slipped into the Gulf and left Oysterton behind, maybe for the last time.

CHAPTER 20

A THOUSAND MILES NORTH of Jimmy's bold incursion into the Gulf, Lana sat on the couch with her laptop as the blackest hours of morning arrived. Typically, she would have succumbed to weariness long before two a.m., but pain had subverted the best intentions of sleep. That was the price of refusing the powerful palliatives prescribed for her leg wound. She needed mental clarity, and the drugs had made her not only drowsy but, in a word, stupid. She could not afford stupid. Neither could her family nor the country. So her leg throbbed. How could a goddamn piece of Prius plastic hurt so much?

"It cut through a nerve," Dr. Rivera had told her. "I did microsurgery, and it should heal nicely, but nerves are, shall we say, touchy? You're going to be uncomfortable. Take your meds. Don't be a hero."

Hero? She'd never cast herself as one. But Lana did see a confluence of her own interests with those of her family and nation, so she was doing everything she could to keep her mental resources as sharp as the fury she felt toward the forces intent on destroying her country.

The mystery of Tahir Hijazi commanded all of her attention as she stared at a freeze frame of his chiseled face on her screen. She was certain he'd beheaded the colonel, though she'd shared that conclusion with no one. First, she wanted to know what he was really doing in the U.S., besides watching over his nephew and—if his words the other night were true—her daughter.

The revelations she'd unearthed so far about his role with Al Qaeda and his emergence as a double agent on behalf of the U.S. had been startling. But had he added "triple agent" to his portfolio by working with ISIS as well? Moreover, the very thought that Em's welfare might at times be in the hands of a man who'd decapitated Lana's own would-be assassin proved an unnerving prospect, no matter how much she had welcomed Tahir's timely intervention. She would have brainstormed with Deputy Director Holmes about the Sudanese, but her boss was still in the ICU.

Maybe it was time to open an early morning line of communication with another colleague.

Using a data tunneling protocol Lana felt confident was secure, she texted Galina Bortnik on the off chance that her employee was working. Galina had reported keeping odd hours to care for her daughter Alexandra, who was ending chemo for her leukemia. The cyberspy had also been using her late nights and early mornings to shoehorn in efforts to breach NSA security, per Holmes's assignment to her. His replacement, Marigold Winters, whom Lana found so repugnant—and a control freak of the first order—was apparently unaware of Galina's mission. If Flowers had any knowledge of it, Lana felt her old nemesis would have stopped Galina immediately, fearful of revelations about security lapses on her newly established watch.

In these dark hours, Lana wasn't even comfortable with the notion that she herself would be around long enough to see the results of Galina's investigation. Just after midnight, Lana had been shot through with adrenaline when she'd found her own face plastered on a poster on an ISIS website. Modeled after the iconic ones of the American West, it read "Wanted Dead or Alive, Lana Elkins. $100 million reward."

A hundred million? Lana couldn't help but feel flattered—in the worst possible way. Surely the FBI would counter by providing protection by more than one agent per shift.

Surely? The bureau was stretched to the breaking point by domestic challenges that ranged over the rest of the country.

The ISIS site then noted what Lana had registered instantly: the reward was the biggest ever offered, more than three times the bounty paid for Uday and Qusay Hussein, Saddam's brutal sons, who had made their infamous father seem puppyish by comparison; and quadruple the bucks posted for bin Laden.

ISIS was also calling for all true warriors of Islam in the States to hunt down and kill Cairo, though their financial commitment to those who achieved this goal was considerably less: $100,000.

Lana looked up, checking on the old Malinois as he rose a few feet away to begin one of his periodic patrols of the house. Then she knocked off a text to Galina: "Have you come across anything involving Tahir?"

The irony remained that Galina, whose employment at CyberFortress was tenuous—thanks to senatorial efforts to try to force the recent Russian émigrée to work for the NSA—had more power to investigate that agency than anyone else in the nation.

Within seconds of sending off the message, Lana's private phone rang, the one she'd used for gambling. She answered it warily.

"It is me, Galina," the younger woman said in her distinctive accent.

"I'm not sure this is a safe phone," Lana found herself whispering.

"It is safe for me and you right now, but you should know that it took me only forty-five minutes to break the secure connection to your phone."

Had Galina done more than figure out Lana's encrypted connection? *The gambling*? That was the real worry, but Lana couldn't ask. She could only trust that Galina hadn't come across her visits to texasholdem.com. Failing that, might she trust that Galina, hailing from the free-for-all corruption of post-Soviet Russia, would think little of her vice? At least Lana had forsworn any gambling of late.

But it still left her acutely uneasy about talking on the phone—and highly dependent on Galina's assessment of her security. *Which she just broke*. Lana's sense of vulnerability was only heightened by recognizing that untold hordes would want to claim the $100 million price tag recently placed on her head, including many Americans of a distinctly non-Islamic, but highly greedy, persuasion.

"Tahir says his nephew, Sufyan, is in 'difficulties.' That was how he put it. He has been communicating with people in Sudan. I think he wants to get the boy out of the U.S."

"Does he say that specifically?"

"No. I am saying what you call the 'tone' of his words."

Galina was being modest. Her English was excellent, other than her reluctance to use contractions, which was not unusual for those for whom English was a second or third language. Better than Lana's Russian, which she considered fair at best.

"I followed Tahir to ISIS and AQAP sites," Galina went on. "Access logs. I have not cracked their actual messages yet. But there are so many of them to ISIS and another one from him to AQAP. A lot of men go between those two, like they are trying to decide which one to join, but Tahir's back-and-forth is much more sophisticated. I do not know if he is communicating with them or trying to hack them. He might be working with both of them."

Lana agreed, having done that kind of double duty herself on numerous occasions.

"But he seems to know his way around the websites. He does not hesitate. He enters them easily. Then he disappears into them in ways I have not been able to follow. Like he finds black holes in their security, or already knows their keys. I am working on it."

"Are you finding any evidence of him compromising NSA's perimeter?"

"Yes, but I am not sure he got very far."

Doesn't matter. That was great news, as far as Lana was concerned. It would give Galina ample justification, beyond Holmes's order, for targeting Tahir, a legal resident, should a Senate committee ever threaten to crucify her for investigating him. Lana wouldn't put it past those senators to use any tool in their box to try to pressure Galina into working for the NSA.

"I wonder if he detected me watching him," Galina said. "He is very good, so he could have given me a trail to follow to the NSA. It was like he wanted me to see what he was up to—or anyone else doing online surveillance of him. Sending a signal even. But I do not know why he would want to do that."

To alert us? Lana wondered. *To key us in?* Was he another spectral presence leaving cyber breadcrumbs behind? *In case something happened to him?*

"You said he didn't get very far?"

"That was strange. He hacked five upper-level operatives with the highest security clearances. But once in their domains, he vanished."

"Meaning you lost him?"

"No, he left the agency."

"That is strange."

"Show and tell, maybe." Galina appeared to like her newfound Americanisms. "He might be as good as Oleg."

Oleg Dernov, for whom Galina had been hacking at the time she and Lana first encountered each other last year. Dernov was as vicious—and talented—a cyberterrorist as Lana had ever met.

Until Tahir? Possibly. Lana still couldn't figure out the Sudanese's game. "So his nephew is supposed to be having 'difficulties,'" she said. "Did he give any indication of what they might be?"

"No, that was the only reference."

"Did he mention my daughter, Emma?"

"No."

"How's Alexandra?" Galina's seven-year-old.

"Maybe good. We have to wait to see if the cancer stays gone. She is starting to sleep better. I am not. The doctor says she has a good chance."

"I'm so glad to hear that."

"I pray it is good enough."

"I hope so," Lana replied.

"She must see the doctor in a month."

Cairo lumbered back into the living room, completing another of his nightly patrols. She called him over and rubbed his head. She had the urge to pull him close, but remembered Ed Holmes's warning: "Cairo doesn't cuddle."

"I should tell you about something I found about Alexandra in the NSA files," Galina said, as if she'd been mulling it over.

"Really?" *What the devil?* "Whose?"

"Marigold Winters."

"Did Tahir break into hers? Did you follow him there?"

"No. I went there because she replaced the deputy director. I thought I should check her security. I found emails from Flowers to Senator Bob Ray Willens of Louisiana telling him to threaten me with the loss of Alexandra's medical care if I did not go to work for the NSA." Through Lana's efforts, Alexandra had been receiving cancer treatments at Children's Hospital of Philadelphia, one of the highest ranking pediatric facilities in the U.S. "Can they take that away?"

"No." Lana felt her blood pressure shoot so high so quickly the roots of her hair burned. It was as if someone—Flowers, perhaps—had grabbed a fistful of it. "Are you thinking of going to the NSA?" She had to ask. If anything could compel a parent to surrender to threats, it would be one to their child's health.

No, not health. Her life.

"No. This Flowers woman must be a bully. I know you can take care of her, right?"

"I will. Absolutely."

But how to fight back flummoxed Lana, although she had a chit or two she could cash in at the White House that might get her a few minutes with the President. Whether she could work her way past the palace guard to actually make her way into the Oval Office was another matter entirely. But Flowers was engaging in a grotesque abuse of power. She needed to be reined in—or exposed. Threatening a child's health care might even be sufficient to send her packing for good.

"I'll need a copy of what you found," she told Galina.

"It could be traced to me."

"Not after I launder it."

Lana signed off, sitting back with the phone by her side. The one she'd always used for gambling. The one Galina had found all on her own. The Russian was an amazing digital analyst.

And then it hit her again: the itch to gamble. Lana found herself imagining face cards, then a pair of aces, on her phone, with "YOU WIN! YOU WIN!" flashing in red. She noticed the time, almost three-thirty.

You can't.

For so many reasons. Without question, someone else would now know. And that someone had a cancer-stricken child who needed Lana's support and strength, not her weakness.

Buck up.

Cairo rose quickly from his resting place. He must have heard something. He might be older and slower, but his ears were as alert as radar dishes.

Lana had her Sig Sauer under a cushion by her right hand, racked and ready, though she couldn't fathom anyone slipping past her door without the security system signaling her.

What she hadn't planned on was a person close to her slipping out a door with her own deep secrets.

・・・

Jimmy ran *Sexy Streak* without lights till he was far from Oysterton. Then he set the GPS for the oil platform on the electronic navigation charts and watched a white dot blink alive on the blue screen. It looked so harmless it was hard to imagine the horror of the beheadings that had taken place 140 miles ahead of him.

They're crazy, he thought.

"Maybe as crazy as you are for going after them," he said aloud.

He turned on a bow light, keeping the beam on low for another mile, then switched on the big headlights and pushed the chrome throttle forward.

The race boat responded with a bolt, racing up to 80 mph in seconds. It felt like the Lamborghini one of his rich clients had loaned him for a weekend.

The onrush of speed thrilled Jimmy, as it always had, but it also brought alive a deep fear of the industrial refuse floating in the Gulf. Hard enough to avoid at times in daylight. In darkness it could prove deadly.

Without looking away from the water, Jimmy put in ear buds and switched to CNN on the boat's communications console. The network was reporting that widespread inoculations of Americans with smallpox vaccine had been scuttled after a suicide bomber blew himself up in a line in Rockville Center, New York. ISIS then pumped up the terror exponentially by announcing that infected Muslims were in lines across the U.S. "They will infect everyone who tries to defy Allah's will."

That announcement, according to the news network, was leading to widespread panic and fighting, with attacks on anyone perceived as Middle Eastern or Muslim. The CDC had advised health authorities in all fifty states to suspend the vaccination program, "pending the full restoration of civil order."

"Good luck with that," Jimmy said to himself.

He feared he'd done nothing but help those ISIS terrorists from the time he'd forced them ashore from these very waters.

All you can do now is what you're doing.

Jimmy felt like he was in the middle of a war movie in which a soldier goes off on a solo mission to save the day. But he heard no stirring music in the background, only the powerful rumble of those twin outboards pushing him ever closer to the oil platform.

To destiny, he thought.

Or to die.

Or to save someone worth saving. Maybe a whole lot of someones called Americans.

...

Lana finally dozed on the couch, waking ninety minutes later to Cairo's nails clicking on the hardwood floor. His dark eyes stared at her from above his white muzzle, as if to say, "You okay?"

She nodded at him, just to see his reaction. He turned away and continued his umpteenth tour of her house. She realized she admired his ingrained sense of purpose—protection—and shared it fully.

Aware once more of her throbbing leg wound, she went back online, shocked to find video of an attack on Long Island that had targeted people who'd been waiting half the night to get their families vaccinated. She saw shredded children's clothing and shoes and copious quantities of blood.

That grim account was followed by a report of an assault on Ed Holmes's kennel near Hagerstown by two self-styled, homegrown ISIS terrorists, one of whom had posted on Facebook a minute before the attack took place that they were going to kill the dog that had gone after bin Laden.

And claim the reward, she thought.

When they didn't find Cairo—saved by the call of duty down in Bethesda—they killed a ten-week-old Malinois puppy. Two retired Army

Rottweilers ambushed the pair, killing the one who'd left the Facebook message.

Reuters reported paramedics on the scene had balked at treating the Islamist radical who'd survived. Despite severe wounds, the man was vociferously taking credit for the attack on the puppy.

Police officers forced the EMTs to offer him emergency medical measures and take him to a nearby hospital.

Lana heard Cairo heading up the stairs slowly.

It's come to that? Killing a puppy?

She checked on Deputy Director Bob Holmes, who was still in the ICU and still seeing only family, which in his case included Donna Warnes.

Lana then received an email from park ranger Harry Riggs, who said Jojo remained immobilized. The dog's spine had been almost severed during the knife attack. No word on whether he'd ever walk again. Riggs said Jojo would be kept sedated until he'd healed enough to safely assess his mobility.

Lana thanked Harry and checked the time, 4:42 p.m., before turning her thoughts to what she'd say to the President, if she ever got the chance for an Oval Office meeting.

• • •

Jimmy drew within ten miles of the rig. He spied the sky turning from starlit black to the darkest shade of gray. He had to risk racing closer without lights. He needed to reach that platform before they could see him. Otherwise, his mission would fail.

And they'll have a boatload of fun killing you.

He gunned *Sexy Streak* up to 140 mph, racing blind until he shut down the engines one mile out. He let momentum and current take over from there. Normal security would have alerted those on the platform to an incoming vessel, but he hoped ISIS would be ill equipped to take over the more technical aspects of perimeter security, after killing almost everyone up there. Even more likely was that a specialist had activated a self-destruct program before ISIS could take full control of the facility.

Jimmy thought the odds *might* favor him so far.

A little more than a half-mile from the installation. *Sexy Streak* slowed almost to a stop. He stripped to his briefs, tied a line around his waist and the end to the bow, and slipped into the water.

The Gulf felt cold, which he attributed to his low-grade fever more than the water, which had been warmed by unseasonable highs all summer.

With the current still running with him, he started swimming and towing the boat toward the pontoons that supported the BP operation looming before him. If all went well, he'd have *Sexy Streak* tied up under them before dawn made visibility his greatest enemy.

And if things go to shit, Jimmy boy?

Then nothing's gonna matter, he answered himself. *Least of all you.*

CHAPTER 21

JIMMY WAS SHIVERING BY the time he towed *Sexy Streak* under the Blue Ring oil platform and hauled himself up onto a floating dock, tie line hanging from his hips.

Happy Daze, the forty-two-foot cabin cruiser that ISIS had hijacked to launch its assault on the rig, rested in a slip some twenty feet away. Jimmy had no intentions of leaving it afloat so ISIS could escape. That boat was getting a stick of dynamite on his way out.

If you get that far.

The oil rig was similar to BP's ill-fated Horizon, which blew, burned, and killed eleven oil workers in 2010 before spilling five million barrels of crude into the Gulf. But Blue Ring's potential for catastrophe was even greater—all ISIS had to do was sabotage the rig's automatic shut-off valves, called BOPs, or "blowout preventers," before destroying the oil pipe proper and subsea wellhead.

Jimmy figured if he knew that much from working just three weeks on a rig, then ISIS would likely know even more because the execution of the group's plans—and most of the rig's employees—had so far been both grisly and flawless. And the terrorists had made clear their desire to turn the Gulf into petroleum goo. But if Jimmy could blow the oil pipe running up to the platform before ISIS disabled the BOPs, the sudden change in pipe pressure should trigger the fail-safe mechanisms, if the oil companies had actually upgraded them after Horizon.

A big "if," he thought. But another "if" came to mind: *If* there had ever been a time to bank on hope, it had arrived this morning in all its shaky glory.

To get started, he tied up *Sexy Streak* and threw on his clothes, grateful for the warmth. Then he headed toward the nearest door, stilled by the sound of someone trying to key the lock.

Jimmy dug into his pocket and pulled out the Saturday night special the cantankerous Burr had loaned him, trusting the cheap .38 wouldn't jam or backfire and blow off his face. No choice about using it, though: Anyone stepping through that door would see the race boat at a glance.

But they don't need to see you.

He dashed to the side of the door that would open in front of him and give Jimmy cover for precious seconds. The person on the other side seemed to be trying a second key.

Must be ISIS. A Blue Ring employee wouldn't have been fiddling around.

Now a third key. Jimmy was sweating now instead of shivering.

The lock opened and the steel door swung toward him. He caught a glimpse of a lone man with black hair and beard stepping out to the boarding area holding a Kalashnikov by his side. As the door slowly closed behind the fighter, Jimmy watched him turn toward *Sexy Streak*.

"Don't move," Jimmy said.

The man froze. The door swung back slowly. *Too* slowly. Jimmy wanted it closed to block the sound of gunfire.

"Drop the gun and turn toward me."

The Kalashnikov clattered on the deck.

Jimmy aimed right between the man's eyes, but another pair greeted his gaze: The fighter had a head hanging by his side, middle and ring fingers plunged into each socket and his thumb hooked into the mouth. Could have been a bowling ball.

A beat later the door did click shut.

Jimmy fired exactly where he'd aimed, and one of ISIS's finest crumpled to the deck. The head he'd been holding started rolling toward the water.

Jimmy swore and lunged for it. The last thing he wanted was to fish it out. Right before it would have fallen off, he grabbed a shock of hair and rested the head upright on the deck so it wouldn't take off on him again, though it now gave the distinct appearance of bearing witness to the macabre goings-on in the immediate vicinity. Only then did Jimmy recognize the victim from television as one of the two oil workers who'd been taken prisoner with the rig's chief engineer.

Jimmy commandeered the Kalashnikov and a beauty of a Browning 9 mm semi-automatic pistol, then tore open the dead killer's shirt hoping to find body armor. None. But he spotted a long knife sheathed in black leather and pulled the blade out, wondering how many heads it had severed. The knife was clean. He slipped it back in the sheath and hung it from his belt.

With a wary eye on the door, he climbed back on *Sexy Streak*, put in one ear bud, and scanned news channels to try to find out the extent of the violence up above. Had all three been killed?

An AP report on a New Orleans radio station said an oil worker had been beheaded because the chief engineer had claimed he couldn't shut down the BOPs.

Just as Jimmy wondered why they hadn't dropped the head into the Gulf, as they had the others, the reporter quoted from a terrorist communiqué: "We will use the heads of the last three men on this rig as soccer balls on the White House lawn as soon as we take Washington."

"You're not getting anywhere near the White House, you sons-of-bitches," Jimmy said to the dead man. "And neither are you," he added in more soothing tones to the roughneck's head a few feet away.

He checked out the Kalashnikov. He'd never handled one but knew their reputation for reliability, as well as a lack of accuracy.

Are you really going to use that?

Jimmy had no choice, not in any world in which he wanted to live. They'd started killing the innocent again. He couldn't in good conscience merely blow the oil pipe and leave. He'd have to go up to that platform and do whatever he could to save the last two men and the Gulf of Mexico, which he loved as much as the Louisiana land on which he'd been born.

He grabbed the keys from the dead man and headed back toward the door.

• • •

Emma had stuffed the essentials into her book backpack: change of clothes, phone, makeup, toiletries, and an extra pair of shoes. After silencing the security alarm to give her thirty seconds to slip out of the house, she'd eased out the back door, held her breath, and stood in the darkness, hoping her mother and father were still asleep.

Cairo, thankfully, hadn't barked as she left. He simply watched her. That was when she realized he'd been making sure she was okay. She wished she could have taken him with her. She felt safer with him around, and she needed to get to Planned Parenthood in Baltimore. Em figured if she tried any of the agency's clinics in DC, Sufyan would find her and try to stop her from ending the pregnancy. He'd been adamant that she should have the baby.

"I'm seventeen," she'd pleaded. "I have my whole life ahead of me. I can't have a baby."

He'd glowered at her for the first time. "Our baby has her whole life ahead of her, too."

Why'd he think it was a girl? It was a collection of cells. Still, aborting was a horribly hard decision, but also heartrending because she loved Sufyan and wanted to have a family with him someday. Not now, though, not in high school.

That's crazy.

"I'm so sorry," she whispered to the night as she headed down the street to where she'd left the car. Her mother's mobility was limited, and Emma had correctly foreseen that Lana wouldn't drag herself to the garage to check on the Fusion. Or her father, for that matter. They trusted her, which made her feel even guiltier.

Earlier, Emma had parked two blocks away, then came in through the garage, as she did every time she came home. She'd known better than to think she could raise the garage door in the middle of the night without setting off alarms and Cairo.

The engine started smoothly. She drove away with her pack beside her, tears blurring her vision. She wiped them away, not so much scared as sad. She didn't know Baltimore well, and now that she was on the interstate, every minute was taking her a mile closer. In an hour she'd be there. The sky was graying. She'd have to hide out till the clinic opened.

And then what?

Would she have to wait a day or two? She didn't want to make her parents insane with worry. Maybe she'd just call them from a pay phone, if she could find one, and leave a message that she was all right and would be home soon. She didn't want them coming after her, either. She'd already shut off her "find my phone" app.

When it was all over, and her mom recovered fully from the grenade attack, she'd tell her about the pregnancy. But right now Em needed to be alone.

And she thought she was.

CHAPTER 22

I'M GLAD EMMA ELKINS switched off that app. Of course shutting it down didn't stop me at all. What Emma couldn't know (without a great level of cybertise) was that I could just as easily track her movements by hacking her car's computer system. I've found the Ford Fusion easy to access remotely and was delighted when I realized her mother had bought it for her. Now, of course, the sleek-looking coupe was about to become the Achilles' heel of the whole family. Lana Elkins was renowned for providing superb cybersecurity on an international scale—and she had avoided the Jeep Cherokee, which had made headlines for getting hacked at speed—but when it came to the Fusion? Not nearly so wary. And why would she have been? The Fusion had escaped notice until recently. Not by me, though.

What young Emma did achieve in shutting off her "find my phone" app was to foil less sophisticated users, like her boyfriend. After reading their emails, I knew precisely why she needed to get away from him: to quiet her conscience.

It was easy for Emma to put Sufyan off her trail. What she doesn't know is that with a little help from me, Vinko Horvat is no longer able to hack her.

He'd been showing far too much interest in her, even after screwing up an assassination attempt on Emma's mother. Maybe he was looking to redeem himself. Too bad. Pay for therapy on your own time, Stinko. Not mine. It took me three arduous hours to sever his links to Emma's phone and computer, which entailed cutting off all the young woman's service for forty-three minutes, an eternity for a chronic phone user like her. But with all the ISP disruptions these days, she gave no indication of being alarmed, nor did she take any action to try to root out the source of the problem by going to her mother. Not that Emma was likely to, given her new need for secrecy.

I'm certain Vinko is much more frustrated at this point than his young target because my perusal of his emails showed that he knows about her pregnancy. That must have whetted his appetite: white girl coupling with a black guy; the worst kind of beast with two backs to the likes of him. For those who loathe interbreeding and embrace Islamophobia, Emma and her beau would be a sweet target.

But Vinko isn't going to find her unless *I* want him to. I would say the same for Lana. The manipulation of those two must be coordinated, and I'm in the position to do that, with Vinko now relegated to watching from the sidelines. I'll cue him when I'm good and ready, *if* I need to.

Originally, I'd thought of corralling Sufyan as well. I even feel some gratitude toward him. His rift with Emma has driven her away from those who could protect her, making his girlfriend little more than chum in the turbulent currents she's trying to swim.

As for Vinko, he's already switching his attention to the death of Bones Jackson. The famous receiver had took up residence recently in Oregon, presumably to imbibe the deadly, legal dose of secobarbital that killed him. I don't blame him. A gentle death versus the ravages of brain cancer? Not a difficult choice.

For all Vinko's professed hatred of his former teammate, I found it amusing to see that he'd viewed online video of Jackson's memorial service six times. But what really surprised me was an email Vinko drafted to Bones's widow Ludmila. I thought Vinko might have expressed a scintilla of regret over his teammate's passing, but no. He called Ludmila a "slut" for having sex with a "black monkey." His parting words to the bereaved widow: "You are a degenerate."

Seriously, Vinko? You wrote that to her right after the service?

At least he didn't send it. I see that it's still in his "draft" folder. I'm tempted to delete it. Wait a sec. Vinko's opening it. I can almost see him subvocalizing as he rereads it.

No, don't, Vinko. Even for you, that's going too far.

But he just hit "send," and there it goes.

Why?

Well, why not? I realize. That's who Vinko Horvat really is: a racist. And that's what racists do.

I wonder if he realizes Ludmila is Russian. Does he know the well-deserved reputation of Russian women?

I feel like I'm taking a bath when I leave his site. It's a pleasure to return to Emma's Fusion. She's driven sixty-three miles, so she should be inside Baltimore proper now.

Yes, the GPS agrees.

The sun must be coming up. Her mother must be waking, too. In the next few minutes both she and her husband will start to panic. They'll wonder if their daughter has been abducted. But how? They'll check their tight security and find it intact. Then they'll review the electronic history of the system and learn that it was opened from inside the house by someone who knew the code. They'll check Emma's room and discover no signs of struggle. And they'll see that her phone is missing, along with key personal belongings, if my guess is good about the latter.

Most painfully, they'll realize their only child is no longer protected by the extensive measures they've taken to insure their family's well-being. And if they're particularly insightful parents, they'll also understand that they could protect their daughter from so much, but not from herself.

A seventeen-year-old is impulsive.

A seventeen-year-old feels immortal.

A seventeen-year-old doesn't understand that death can come in a whisper.

Emma. I imagine my hot breath on her ear. *I can help you.*

So her parents will be right to shudder at the fact that Em is now vulnerable to the scores of terrorists stalking American cities and hinterlands, hunting for ever more horrors to visit upon the nation.

But don't worry about all that.

Those are the exact words I would tell them if I could. They need only worry about me. And it's too late for that. Their only child is trying to free herself of too much too soon, and all she's really done is seal her fate.

The one I've planned for her.

And you shall share it, Lana.

The chainsaws are oiled and calling. Can you hear them? Here, I'll start one.

How about that? Can you hear it now? The blade sounds angry, doesn't it? Like it could cut through skin and bone and the last scraps of hope in a dying girl's heart.

I won't let you die without seeing that, Lana. I promise.

That's how a mother gets to die twice.

CHAPTER 23

JIMMY PUSHED THROUGH THE door that had delivered the ISIS fighter to his death, entering a short, wide hallway. He immediately scanned the ceiling and corners for surveillance cameras. Didn't see any but that didn't mean there weren't fiber optics embedded in openings no larger than the head of a finishing nail.

Better move faster, then.

He headed to the only interior door, finding a digital pad for the lock. Jimmy tried the handle—a non-starter, as expected—but didn't dare touch the pad. A false code could alert the security system.

He retreated back to the deck, resigning himself to climbing the rig. His best bet appeared to be a massive chain near the end of the dock, one of four that anchored the facility to the seabed. They ran all the way to each corner of the upper platform, where he'd seen the chief engineer and the roughnecks displayed like human trophies.

Each steel link was half his height and thick as his thighs. But the openings were ample enough for solid footholds. Keeping his pistol in hand, knife belted, and the Kalashnikov strapped across his back, he started up slowly. Nothing like those Greenpeace maniacs who'd climbed a Shell rig like they were spiders. Then again, they hadn't just survived a boat crash and a nasty case of smallpox. Nor had they been facing armed ISIS terrorists on the platform above them.

Jimmy climbed up the anchor chain methodically, but the steel was slippery from an early morning mist that shrouded him. Good cover, bad for climbing. He paused with every advance, hearing nothing till he'd moved thirty feet above the water—Arab gibberish drifting down through the thin fog, which would burn off soon enough. It already appeared to be vanishing to a frightening degree.

Speak English. He shook his head, but otherwise remained as still as the steel that held him—except for his stomach, which felt queasy. He tried to clear his belly with a big breath, and it might have worked. Feeling better, he looked upward, listening intently for a chopper. There had been a number of them keeping watch on the platform, including some news crews that could give him away in the time it took to hit a camera switch.

Would they do that? he wondered.

Hell, yeah, they would, he answered himself a beat later. It'd be a scoop: Smallpox McMasters climbing the towers geared up like a Gameboy commando? *Are you kidding? 'Course they would.*

Move.

He had to get up there before the mist disappeared completely and someone spotted him. He had no allies in the sky, and the only ones on the platform probably had knives at their necks.

He moved up several more links, passing girders and metal handrails and mesh walkways beside him. Corrosion everywhere he looked. The salt air was an omnivore, eating everything it touched.

An agonizing groan froze Jimmy. It arose about ten feet above him. Then more gibberish violated his ears. Definitely not from the groaning guy.

Jimmy hated the sound of Arabic. He didn't feel that way about Spanish or French, the two languages other than English that were spoken in the Gulf. But Arabic made his ears curl. Yeah, he knew there were millions of right-thinking Arabs who were great people, and had met a few who spoke English, but unfortunately he wasn't dealing with the great mass of nice ones. He figured he'd be coming face to face with the most bloodthirsty killers he'd ever heard of, and the sound of their voices made him want to start shooting.

The groaner grew silent. Jimmy had little doubt about the language that man had been speaking: agony.

What the hell are they doing to him?

Jimmy looked up to see if he could get any kind of visual. Nothing. He took little solace in having his gun ready; firing it would be an act of desperation, for it would alert everyone. It wasn't like that Saturday night special, which had sounded like a cap gun, and he was drawing ever closer to the ISIS brigade that could hear it.

He did spy overhanging walkways and ledges that would make murdering him a challenge. *Unless they also come at you from below.*

But he moved as quietly as he could on his bare feet—heavily callused from beach life—and hoisted himself up onto the next link. It was right below a recessed area that was painted red, which he realized must be where the groaner was feeling so much pain. He had no idea what purpose that area usually served. A lookout, maybe?

Should have paid a little more attention. And partied a whole lot less on his three-week stint.

A damn seagull landed on the link above him and squawked. Christ, they were loud. He saw others gliding around the rig, guessing the roughnecks fed them when they got bored.

The gull squawked again. The Arabic speaker shouted at it and lunged toward its perch right above Jimmy. He caught a glimpse of another bearded man long enough to know the guy hadn't looked down, which saved Jimmy's life—for the time being.

The gull flew off, leaving a fresh deposit that dripped down the link. Jimmy moved up, careful where he held on, stopping when he was just below the overhanging ledge; the chain continued straight up to the left of it.

He peered over the four-foot section of red-painted steel. A hulking man was facing the lone surviving oil worker, other than the chief engineer, whom Jimmy could only hope remained alive. The roughneck had a grease stain on his face, and was gagged so hard his cheeks had whitened from loss of blood. His eyes betrayed his pain and terror. So did the muffled groans still rising from him. Then Jimmy saw why: ISIS's finest was cutting off a six-inch strip of skin from the man's knee. It looked like he was peeling him alive: The roughneck's entire calf and shin had been stripped and glowed bright red with fresh blood.

Jimmy wanted to shoot the torturer, but couldn't. Not if he wanted to live long enough to actually get off the platform.

Instead, Jimmy slipped the gun into his belt and drew the long knife. He'd have to rise up slowly, scurry across the four feet of steel ledge, and drive the blade into the bastard's back. First, he looked at the pale sun to make sure it wouldn't throw telltale shadows from him.

Not a problem, thanks to the dim light.

Then Jimmy checked his footing, glad that he did: His left foot was half an inch from the gull's greasy waste, which could have given him a noisy slip.

He drew a long steady breath, which was interrupted by the *whup-whup-whup* of a helicopter.

Using the noise for cover, he lifted himself up as the knife-wielding man gazed at the sky. Jimmy hurled himself across the ledge as the man glanced back and spotted him. But Jimmy drove the blade into his back, shocked at the sudden resistance to such a sharp steel point. *A bone.* He twisted the blade in the next instant, plunging it past whatever hard matter had brought it to a halt—maybe spine—leaving the knife buried to the haft.

Not a scream or moan of protest from the bearded man, who pitched forward onto his victim. The roughneck's eyes looked right at Jimmy.

"Shush," Jimmy whispered, though the gagged man could scarcely speak.

Jimmy dragged the dying man off the oil worker and grabbed the knife that had been used to peel the roughneck's skin. Then he cut off the prisoner's gag and sliced through plastic cuffs binding his ankles and wrists.

"Man, you saved my life," the roughneck said softly. "He was skinning me alive. Who are you?"

Jimmy was about to say "A boat racer," when the man recognized him.

"I saw you on TV, and in a *great* video. I can't believe it. Tit Fucker just saved me. That's so cool. But, hey, don't get too close, okay?"

• • •

The heat woke Emma up, sun streaming through the windows of her Fusion. Last night she'd locked the doors and reclined the front seat after parking near the Planned Parenthood clinic. She'd recognized it from news reports about the protests at the facility.

She sat up as a woman unlocked the clinic's front door. Adjusting the rear-view mirror, Em put on lipstick and brushed out her hair. Still unhappy with her rumpled appearance, she surrendered to urgency and climbed out of the car, knowing she looked half-baked, like some of her stoner friends at school.

Emma hurried across the street, glad nobody was outside the clinic wielding those graphic posters.

A nurse greeted her from behind a counter. Emma told her why she was there. The woman handed her a clipboard with a two-page form. "You understand that we'll need to confirm the pregnancy first, but for now it would be good to answer those questions."

After complying, Em looked up, realizing she was still the only person in the reception area.

The nurse returned, took the paperwork, and led her to a room with a small table and four chairs. Not an examining room, as Em had expected. Neither had she been asked to provide a urine sample. The nurse looked up from the form.

"I see that you're seventeen. Is that correct?"

Emma nodded, taking a seat. The nurse stood in the doorway.

"In Maryland, we like to have at least one parent who's aware of a minor's decision before we perform the procedure. They don't have to approve, but we like to know that one of them knows what you're doing."

"You said Maryland likes that. You didn't say it was required."

The nurse nodded. "That's correct. There are exceptions. If the physician believes that you're mature enough you may have the procedure without parental notification."

"I'm really mature," Emma said. "I don't want to bother my mother with this. She's recovering from a wound from a hand grenade last week."

The nurse's eyes widened with recognition. "Was that *your* mom who almost got killed in Bethesda?"

"Yes," Emma replied, eyes flooding at once. She tried to stem her tears—not very mature to start bawling—but couldn't stop. "She doesn't need to be dealing with this right now. She's in a lot of pain." Which was true, damn it.

"What about the person who got you pregnant? Does he know?"

"Yes, but he's Mus . . ." Emma checked herself. The nurse smiled. "He doesn't want me to end the pregnancy. Look, I'm not going to have a baby. I'm still in high school."

"What about your father? Does he live with you?"

"He does," Em allowed, wiping away her tears, "but that's kind of recent. My mom basically brought me up alone till he came back."

"Are you saying he'd have objections to your terminating your pregnancy?"

"No, I don't think so. I mean, it may sound weird to say this, him being gone most of my life, but he's a pretty good dad."

"I'm glad to hear that. Emma, please call him. Let him know what you intend to do. Then we can confirm that you have a parent onboard, okay?"

"I really don't want them to know."

The nurse eyed her closely. "I'll have the doctor talk to you. But at least think about your father. It's just a call. We have a simple approach to this. He sounds like a decent guy."

He is. But Em had never felt a greater need for personal privacy.

The woman started to leave, then turned back to her. "The doctor will listen to whatever you have to say. Just tell the truth. It goes a long way around here."

"Thank you."

"Here." She handed Emma a pamphlet. "That has answers to a lot of the questions that patients have."

"What's the doctor's name?"

"Dr. Mohammed Abbas."

Mohammed? Abbas?

Emma watched the nurse walk away—and felt an instant urge to rush out of the clinic.

• • •

The roughneck's name was Cal. Strips of his skin had been laid aside carefully by the ISIS fighter. Jimmy stared at them, one at least ten inches long.

What a son-of-a-bitch. Jimmy had never killed anyone. Seeing the peeled skin left him with no regrets.

"He was working his way up my body," Cal said. "The only reason he left my foot alone was when he was all done he wanted to march me around up there for the news choppers. This hurts so fuckin' bad."

"We should wrap it up," Jimmy said, stripping off his T-shirt. "You don't want to be bleeding all over the chain. You'll slip and fall and we've got work to do."

"Don't put that shirt near me. Man, you got smallpox, right?"

"Sorry, sorry. I wasn't thinking," Jimmy said. "Come on, let's just head up."

"Head up? We gotta get the hell out of here."

Jimmy shook his head. "The chief engineer's still alive, right?"

"Maybe. They've got him trying to disarm the blowout preventers."

"Is he doing that?"

"He's trying. They're threatening him with all kinds of shit. They want to turn this place into a tar pit."

"I heard that. Look, they're going to kill him no matter what he does," Jimmy said. "We've got to save him."

"Listen to me. No way we're gonna do that. They got him on the computers in the operations center, and it's surrounded by these murdering assholes. Be easier to break into Fort Knox."

"Why are you down here?"

"Because that dead shithead won me for cutting off the most heads the fastest when they took over this thing. I shit you not. It was a contest and I was the prize."

"There's really no way to save him up there?"

Cal shook his head. "I ain't lying. You want to commit suicide, you go right ahead."

Jimmy looked up at the platform. Saving the chief engineer did sound impossible. "Do you think you can climb down this chain?" Blood now covered Cal's foot.

"To get off this hellhole I'd climb down razor wire."

"I'll lead the way, but we got one thing to do before we take off down there."

"Yeah, what's that?"

"We're blowing the oil pipe so the BOPs kick in before they get disabled."

"That's going to really piss 'em off. We better be ready to tear ass out of here."

"Pissing them off is the plan, and tearing ass out of here is a big part of it."

Jimmy helped Cal to his feet.

When they looked up, a pair of eyes were staring down.

CHAPTER 24

LANA WAS UP AND performing her morning rituals by five-thirty, though greatly hampered by her crutches, cumbersome fixtures since the surgery on her calf. She had a six-thirty video teleconference scheduled with the President's Chief of Staff William Evanson. She presumed the marginal, break-of-day appointment time reflected Evanson's lack of priority on their meeting. But Lana found awakening so early a welcome change, even after her middle-of-the-night phone call with Galina. She liked the peace and quiet and trusted it would continue for at least a couple of hours.

With Don and Emma safely tucked away—and no hint of the mayhem at large in the world—Bethesda could seem like an oasis; one purchased, she understood, at the cost of bulletproof glass and steel doors. Recognizing this tempted Lana to check on Emma upstairs; but her daughter, once the proverbial log in bed, had become such a light sleeper that she didn't want to disturb her. Em was, after all, fighting a stomach bug. And Lana didn't relish navigating the stairs on one good foot and two clumsy crutches.

After arranging her hair carefully and applying lipstick and a bit of blush, she donned a blue blouse that she kept fully buttoned. For a videoconference, she only needed to look professional from the middle up—"table date acceptable," as she and her friends had once joked about pear-shaped men. So her shorts would do fine and spare her the ordeal of putting slacks on over her wound.

Lana made short shrift of her first espresso before hobbling into her home office. She was adjusting the lighting for the computer camera to avoid freak-show shadows when she heard the front door burst open. She assumed it was Agent Robin Maray, but switched on the screen that showed her home's entry points. Robin, indeed, was slamming the door behind him and yelling "Go to the safe room, I've got it opening right now."

The panic room?

"What about Emma and Don?" Lana yelled, jamming her Sig Sauer into her shorts, grabbing her crutches, and starting down the hallway.

"I'll get them. You get in there *now*."

The steel cubicle had been placed off the living room behind a bookcase that swung open at the touch of a switch, a location central to the home's traffic patterns.

"Emma," Lana yelled as she limped along. "Emma!"

When Em didn't reply, Lana launched herself toward the stairs. As quickly, Robin swept her up into his arms and carried her toward the door to the secure room.

"Sorry," he said as he deposited her into the steel-reinforced confines, "but I said I'd get them, and I've got my orders."

"What's going on?" she asked, but Robin was already closing the panic room door.

Lana flipped on the room's monitor and switched to her home's exterior cameras as two men in black ski masks set off a charge by the big front window. She felt the violent vibration in the one foot she had on the floor and sheer panic at the sight of the pair piling into the house.

Switching quickly to a living room cam, she saw swirls of dust and Robin staggering across the floor toward the safe room with a long shard of glass sunk in his shoulder, blood already soaking his white shirt and darkening his suit jacket. She called 911 as he tripped on a length of mangled window frame and spilled to the debris-ridden floor, not far from where Cairo lay unmoving on more rubble. Wincing in pain, Robin tried to lift himself up and draw his gun. Too wounded and too late: before he could even raise it, the men ripped the gun from Robin's hand and dragged him toward the safe room, visible through the broken remains of the bookcase. Volumes lay strewn on the floor. The men kicked them out of their way and stuck their guns to Robin's head right in front of the cam that framed all three of them.

"We will kill him, if you don't open up right now," said a man who sounded like he was trying to affect a Middle Eastern accent—and failing miserably.

He pounded the door with the butt of his gun. Lana saw this on the screen, but barely heard the impact through the thick steel. She studied the features beneath the ski masks, searching for any evidence of beards. No billowing at all.

"Don't open it," Robin said in a barely audible voice.

Lana wouldn't have, regardless. You never negotiated someone else's release by offering yourself, but she didn't recall from security briefings that a terrorist or money-grubbing criminal would—without further warning—shoot an FBI agent in the foot to demonstrate his viciousness.

Excruciating pain twisted Robin's face. Lana saw him grinding his teeth but he didn't make a sound. The gunman who'd shot him in the foot now offered a warning: "His knee is next. Then his balls."

In his excitement, he'd abandoned any attempt at an accent. Which made her sick with worry about Emma.

Where is she? They'd do the same to her daughter if they got their hands on her. *And where's Don?*

She hoped Emma was climbing out a window, running away as fast as she could. Lana could do nothing to protect her, not from in here, although she knew without question—or hesitation—that she'd give herself up for her daughter, no matter how fruitless the move might be.

But there was absolutely nothing she could do for Robin. Open the door and the gunmen would sell her to ISIS as fast as possible, and then those killers would do whatever they found necessary to drain every last secret of U.S. intelligence to which she'd ever been privy—along with her last pint of blood.

Good to his word, the eager gunman blew Robin's knee apart on screen. Robin now howled and writhed in agony, still held tightly by the men.

The high-caliber bullet left a gaping wound in the agent's leg.

And the gunman now pressed his weapon to Robin's crotch.

With $100 million on the line, Lana couldn't believe they'd shoot off his scrotum. Blood loss would likely kill him in minutes—and their chance at a monstrous payday. But the intruders were agitated, screaming for her to open the door: "We know you're in there, bitch!"

She stared at the screen. The gunman had his eyes on his pistol, jamming it harder into Robin's crotch. Then Lana glimpsed Don's shadow fall on the rubble in the living room. His arms rose into view, a two-handed stance with the semi-automatic that Deputy Director Holmes had finessed for him. Don fired two fast head shots, spilling both gunmen to the floor, their last dying move.

Robin fell against the door to the safe room, barely holding himself up. Lana pulled out her phone again and called back 911: "FBI agent's down. Shot in the foot and knee. Major blood loss."

Don helped Robin from the door. Lana threw it open as a Bethesda police officer ran into the living room.

"Put down your gun!" he yelled at Don.

"He just saved an FBI agent's life," Lana shouted, pointing to Don, who dropped his weapon anyway.

Without lowering his own gun, the officer called for help.

Robin flashed his FBI badge at the cop. "He's a good guy." Then he looked at Lana. "You did right." The agent's pain was so grievous that he spoke through a locked jaw.

She thanked him for saving her. "I'm so sorry I couldn't do anything for you."

"He did fine," Robin managed, glancing at Don who was reaching with his free hand to clear debris that had been blown onto the couch. He eased the agent down onto a dusty cushion as Lana shuffled away, shouting for Emma, grateful she hadn't tried to engage in any heroics like Don.

But after searching every corner of the house, she limped back into the bombed-out living room, accepting that Emma was gone, probably long before the shootings. The final clue was the absence of her phone.

She tried calling her. Got her voicemail.

Then she saw Cairo, draped in dust, but trying to stand. She rushed to help him; but when he growled, she kept her distance.

The old dog rose on his own and shook off the dust, as he might water from a splash in a lake. He took hesitant steps, as if taking inventory of his injuries, the way she would if she'd just regained consciousness. And then Cairo regained his stride and started sniffing, back on the job. Lana guessed it wasn't the first time he'd found himself in the midst of an explosion. No more rattled by the experience than you'd expect from a grizzled old war vet.

Lana returned to her study and turned on her computer. The power had gone out briefly before the back-up batteries kicked in. It took her only a few minutes to discover that Emma had deactivated her "find my phone" app. Lana had installed the secure connection on her phone, so she needed only a couple minutes more to reconfigure it and switch the locator on.

With EMTs and a trauma doctor crowding the living room, Lana found Emma's phone in downtown Baltimore. She used Google Earth to comb the area, searching for what might have attracted her daughter. The answer came in seconds: Planned Parenthood. There it stood, bold as brick.

Not sick, Lana thought as her own belly roiled in recognition of Emma's plight: *Pregnant.*

Lana tried calling her again. Still no answer.

What about Sufyan?

She started to work on his phone, finding immediately that it had security protections, probably installed by Tahir.

She called Galina, rousting the Russian from bed, and put her on the task. Galina had already followed Tahir's breach of the NSA so she was aware of the Sudanese's techniques. Then Lana looked at her watch and saw that she had all of a minute before her videoconference with William Evanson.

She linked quickly to a secure server for the White House, to the extent that any lines of communication were actually safe anymore.

The chief of staff was not yet present. "He's with the President," Evanson's personal assistant informed her. Like his boss, the young man had worked on the President's campaign staff.

Lana started to tell him about the attack on her home, but was interrupted by Evanson's appearance.

"We heard," the chief of staff said, settling in. "You're okay, and your husband is the man of the hour."

"Yes," Lana replied, realizing that Don had saved the life of the only man she'd cared about romantically in his absence.

"So what's so critical that you requested the President's time?"

Lana took a deep breath, knowing every word counted because anyone seeking the chief of staff's time got about twenty seconds to make her case: "I wanted him to know that interim Deputy Director Marigold Winters is back-channeling a request to Senator Bob Ray Willens. He's threatening to cancel medical care for Galina Bortnik's cancer-stricken daughter, if her mother doesn't go to work for the NSA."

"And how do you know this?"

"I have her email."

"Don't make me ask the obvious," Evanson said.

"You know perfectly well that's privileged information."

"You're talking to *me*, Ms. Elkins."

What an imperious ass. "I am because I know that you know what an egregious abuse of power this is *and* how poorly it could reflect on this administration, were it to be revealed."

"Are you threatening us with its disclosure?"

"Of course not. But if I got my hands on it—and I did not hack either party—then others might get it as well."

The most obvious suspect, Galina, was hiding in plain sight, but it was highly unlikely that Evanson would know of her secret assignment from Deputy Director Bob Holmes.

"I could have you polygraphed over this."

"But I won't be," she shot back. Her boldness spoke of an underlying threat that all superb hackers could deliver—the unearthing of a powerful man or woman's own secrets.

"Who else knows?"

"You and me and whoever did the hack."

"A friend?"

"Are we playing twenty questions now?" she replied. "It might be safe to conclude that a friend gave it to me. It would not make it true. Look, Winters needs to be reined in."

"Did it ever occur to you, Ms. Elkins, that you might be fighting above your weight?"

Lana smiled. "No." She paused before going on: "But what has occurred to me is that this could look far worse for you and the President. And I know that you know that."

"I'll look into it. This will not involve the President. Is that clear?"

"Absolutely."

Mission accomplished.

Senator Willens was up for reelection. If he wanted a wartime President throwing his considerable popularity behind him, he'd ignore Winters's request—unless she had something on him.

Lana watched the chief of staff disappear from her screen, realizing with a glance at her watch that their conversation, barbed as it was, had taken less than ten minutes.

Back on her crutches, she emerged from her office to see Robin wheeled out on a gurney, lines running into his arms. That chunk of glass was still embedded in his shoulder.

She waved, surprised when he managed a thumbs-up.

Lana navigated around the rubble in her living room to the kitchen. Plopping onto a stool, she noticed how silent her home had become, as quiet as it had been at daybreak. The FBI's Evidence Response Team hadn't arrived yet. She expected them at any moment and knew they'd be working there the rest of the day.

She spotted Don outside talking to an FBI agent. The bureau would be reconstructing every step of this attack and studying it eventually at Quantico.

Lana's phone buzzed. She turned from watching Don and checked the screen.

Galina.

Lana took the call.

"I got into Sufyan's phone. Do you know Tahir hacked Emma's last night?"

"He got into hers?" Now *that* alarmed Lana: Tahir knowing his son had impregnated her daughter.

"Yes, he got in."

"Then he knows."

"Yes, he knows," Galina confirmed.

You must think we're quite the American family. Galina had already alerted Lana that she'd hacked into her private phone—and no doubt learned that her boss had certain gambling issues. Now Galina had found out Emma was pregnant. Lana couldn't help feeling that she'd failed as a person and, more important, as a parent.

"Has there been any communication from Sufyan to her? Or from Tahir to her, for that matter?" *Is the boy's uncle threatening Em?*

"Only from Sufyan. He wants to talk to her. He keeps texting. She has not responded."

"Any other content from him?"

"He has told her four times that everything is going to be okay."

"Please keep monitoring him and Tahir. I need to know if either leaves Bethesda."

Or both, Lana thought after hanging up.

• • •

I've monitored Emma since about four this morning. I'm still doing it as I drive once more to SeaTac, this time for a flight to Baltimore. But all I'm seeing are Sufyan Hijazi's texts. He's so lost, all but pleading for Emma to tell him what she's doing. He wants to know why she won't respond to his earnest entreaties. And there she is, trying to end her pregnancy in Mobtown. A dying city. A dying baby. He must suspect that, too.

But annihilating the innocent takes time. A day or two at least. The murderers at Planned Parenthood will insist that one of Emma's parents at least acknowledge the dirty business their daughter is up to. And if I read Emma Elkins correctly, she's going to resist those efforts. She'll try to convince the staff that she's very mature, perfectly capable of making a decision to kill her child. Why else would she have left Bethesda in the middle of the night all by her lonesome? That's dangerous. Anything could happen to her. Terrible things.

I must beat Sufyan to her. I've known many Muslim men. They can take it very personally when a woman refuses his family seed.

What worries me even more, though, are Vinko's efforts to hack into Emma's phone. Minutes ago that was done by someone but it wasn't him. I've set up alerts for any more exploits Vinko attempts to make on that device. He could use a back door into Emma's world by hacking the hacker of her phone, or by accessing Sufyan's. End runs abound in the cybersphere.

Unfortunately, there's a limit to how much I can do while driving to an airport. This is high-end security work, but it's not as important as the relatively simple task of finally putting my hands on Emma Elkins. The weakness in her security has been apparent to me for some time. Talk about a vulnerability. She's been keeping it close, depending on it daily.

Get Emma and I'll get Lana. Get them both and I'll have all I need for a tremendous coup.

I will simply trust that Emma will proceed toward the murder of her child. I will simply trust that she'll need more than a day to make that happen. And I will simply trust that by day's end, she'll be in my hands at last.

With those comforts now so close, I pull into the airport parking lot with ample time to board my plane. In fact, I can take my leisure in the airline's private club, reserved for valued flyers like me.

But as I enter I receive another alert on my phone. With a single glance I look up at the big screens on the wall. Each is split between video of Lana Elkins's home in Bethesda, which looks like its face has been ripped off, and aerial shots of that offshore platform that ISIS took over. Jimmy McMasters and one of the oil workers are trying to shoot their way down the side of that rig. I can hear the gunfire.

He's such a nutbar, I can't look away.

CNN goes full screen for the bang-bang. It's live, happening right now. And what a show it is.

CHAPTER 25

JIMMY HAD NEVER DRAWN a gun from his belt so fast. He didn't now, either. That was all Cal's doing. When the ISIS fighter looked down from the ledge, the oil worker Jimmy had just saved shot the bearded jihadist right between the eyes.

"Nice aim," Jimmy had said in open astonishment.

"Top of my class, Southeast Shooting Regionals, High School Division."

Now they were descending the platform's anchor chains. Cal was right below him.

"They actually have that in schools here?" Jimmy asked.

"Don't know about *here*, but in my part of 'Bama they sure as hell do."

"We gotta move a little faster," Jimmy told him.

Trouble was, Cal's skinless calf, which looked like one of those healthy chicken thighs Jimmy never much cared for, was dripping blood on the links below, making them slippery as seagull spatter.

Jimmy tried to avoid both the human and avian splotches while keeping his AK-47 raised up so he could spray any gunmen appearing above them.

Oh, shit. Here they come.

He heard their footfalls on the metal catwalk up there. Could have done without seeing their bearded faces or weapons—but both appeared a second later. M-16s, if Jimmy glimpsed that right.

Wasting no time, he sprayed the whole area, hoping the bullets wouldn't catch him on the rebound. He got lucky, as you could with a barrage, splitting open the face of a man who peered over the catwalk's rail.

The rest nosed their barrels down at them, popping off single rounds, frugal with their firepower. Parceling out your ammo might be smart, Jimmy realized, because he had no idea how many rounds were left in the Kalashnikov's magazine. And those *pop-pop-pops* were keeping him and Cal clinging to the links for cover, which made for a hellishly slow descent.

"Keep moving," Jimmy urged, unleashing another round while the *whup-whup-whups* formed a bizarre contrapuntal response to the *pop-pop-pops*.

From the catwalk, one of the gunmen nailed Cal with a round that tore into his left triceps, leaving inches of flesh to dangle grotesquely. Looked like bait in the hands of a dolphin trainer.

Now the young marksman, grimacing even more, was forced to wrap his arm around each link as if he held them in a series of headlocks. In that awkward manner, he kept sliding down to the loading area, which seemed a lot safer than remaining open targets on the chain, though there was no telling when someone might come out that door to the deck.

Guess we'll find out, thought Jimmy, as Cal's feet touched down.

He spilled aside to make room for the boat racer, who jumped from six feet up, landing as the door swung open with a blaze of bullets. The fusillade would have sliced both Cal and him in half if they hadn't found themselves in the corner of the loading area, far to the left of the closest shooter, who couldn't see them.

Behind their precautionary fire, the two terrorists emerged from the doorway looking satisfied by what they'd found. Jimmy felt pretty good himself, spraying back in the next instant, catching the nearest one in the chest. He fell away nicely, clearing a path to the other's back, which Jimmy quickly targeted.

"Which boat is yours?' Cal asked, pointing to the cabin cruiser and *Sexy Streak*.

"The fast one," Jimmy said. "But we're blowing that oil line first."

"Yeah? Well, you can blow me," Cal responded. "I'm getting the fuck out of here."

"No you're not," Jimmy said, running over to *Sexy Streak* for the bag of explosives and three bungee cords. "You strap them on that oil line and I'll shoot the shit out of anyone trying to stop us."

Cal pointed Jimmy's own pistol at him. "We're leaving *now*!"

Jimmy rued not taking back his gun. "You got the keys to the boat? I don't think so. And neither do I. I stashed them, and I'm not saying where till you get the fuck in the water and do the deed."

Cal fired. Not at Jimmy but over the boat racer's shoulder, taking out the deck's three security cameras in three shots.

"Good man," Jimmy said.

"Fuck off."

Jimmy tossed Cal a life preserver and pulled a beer cooler from the boat. His lucky one; he hoped filling it with dynamite wouldn't mess with the mojo. Then he told Jimmy to hand over the pistol. "You're going to want me to cover you."

Cal swore again, but handed it over. Then he threw on the PFD and dropped into the water.

"Goddamn that hurts," he said as salt water soaked into the raw wounds on his leg and arm.

Jimmy handed him the lucky beer cooler, top snug as a manhole cover. "The lighter's in there, too. Fuse will give us five minutes, max. Keep that shit dry. Go!"

Cal swore again and pushed off, trailing blood from his arm and leg, but keeping the cooler high and dry. He made fast time to the pipe that rose from the water between the giant pontoons that kept the rig afloat.

A minute later he was stringing one of the bungee cords around the oil line. That was when Jimmy spotted a dorsal fin surfacing about ten feet behind Cal. Didn't look like Flipper, either. Tail reached almost to the deck below Jimmy. A real moral dilemma for him: Should he tell Cal now or wait until he had that fuse burning? The greater good of the Gulf was at stake. Killing those ISIS madmen, too.

Jimmy had no choice but to take the high moral ground: silence. But he did suggest to Cal that he hurry up.

"I'm not exactly taking comp time out here," Cal fired back.

Damn dorsal was moving forward. Cal might see it.

Oh, no. Swishing its tail back and forth, making Jimmy think about the way he'd rev *Sexy Streak*'s engines before shooting across the starting line of a race.

Cal cinched the second cord.

"I wouldn't bother with the last one," called Jimmy, trying to keep his voice even, which was a challenge because dorsal fin number two had just shown up. Another tail swisher, no less, but only about half the size.

"I'd already planned to forget about that," Cal snarled without looking back. Good. He might have seen something upsetting.

But what the hell are you gonna do? Jimmy asked himself. He couldn't just let Cal get munched up like a big ol' chew toy.

He came up with a plan. It was a little better than *Let them eat him.* But not by much.

Cal slid the last of the dynamite under the bungees and reached for the lighter. Which necessitated looking at the cooler. The frightening fins lurked feet way.

"You son-of-a-bitch. You never said shit about—"

"I got your back." *Liar, liar.* "Light that sucker."

Cal lit the fuse and started swimming toward the deck on the other side. The first shark, the monster, perhaps seeing lunch slipping away, started after him. A second later he bumped Cal from behind; a shark's way, Jimmy figured, of testing the tenderness of his meal.

Jimmy fired into its back and head, then the smaller shark's tail. And just that fast he'd emptied the AK's magazine. Four piddly rounds, no more effective than jabbing pushpins into elephants.

Jimmy pulled out his pistol as he raced around the deck to where Cal was heading, wishing like hell he had the Southeast Regional shooting champ's eye. But he didn't need Cal's expertise to pump three quick shots into junior's back, which finally drew some serious blood as it surged up alongside Jaws. The big beast responded by taking a savage bite out of his smaller brethren, setting up a titanic thrashing as Cal virtually catapulted himself out of the water.

"I want to kill you, Jimmy."

"Get in line, but you're gonna have to be patient 'cause it's a long one." *Beginning with Piccolo.*

Both guys raced to the boats amid the furious splashing from the sharks' thrashing tails and heaving bodies. But the fuse was still sparking like the Fourth as it neared the dynamite.

Jimmy started the engines. Then he swore aloud. He'd forgotten to save a stick of destruction for the boat ISIS had hijacked.

He gave the pistol to Cal, yelling, "Shoot up the dashboard on that thing." Pointing to the larger boat.

And that might have worked but the door to the deck swung open again, sending Cal to *Sexy Streak*'s deck and Jimmy to the throttle.

Cal rose to his knees and picked off one of the bearded men bursting onto the loading area, and a second who'd spotted the fiery fuse and started running in its direction. But killing those two used up the last of his bullets, leaving three other men free to sprint to the cabin cruiser. An instant later the big boat's engine roared to life.

Jimmy forced the throttle forward and raced out into the Gulf, adding up the ISIS body count. At least seven: six by gunshot, plus the skinner Jimmy had knifed in the back.

Sexy Streak was up to 70 mph in a handful of pounding heartbeats. Five choppers now circled above them. The only thing blazing up there were camera lenses reflecting the sun.

Didn't matter. The salt spray had never felt finer to Jimmy. They were flying over the swells. He looked back and raised his fist in victory. That oil line would blow any moment, and they were well out of range.

Putt-putt-putt.

And out of gas.

CHAPTER 26

LANA NEEDED TO GET to Baltimore as soon as possible. She threw a change of clothes and her toiletries into an overnight bag and called downstairs for Don. "I need some help up here."

Damn crutches.

She'd be driving north in her new Dodge Charger. Quite a change from her blown-up Prius—and a reflection of how sharply the world had changed since she'd walked into a Toyota showroom four years ago to buy a gentle, environmentally responsible vehicle. She needed speed and power, so she'd bought the Charger, the four-wheeled beast federal agents preferred.

"Don, I've got to get moving."

He was getting questioned by the FBI about his killing of the two men who'd bombed their house and tried to kidnap her. He was cooperating, of course, taking them through the entire shooting step by step, but the agents had made it clear he wasn't going to scurry off to Baltimore anytime soon. Lana thought it might be better to leave him on the home front, anyway, in case Emma returned; they didn't want her coming back to an empty house, especially in its current condition.

What am I forgetting? Lana wondered. It was always something. Then she spotted her hairbrush. Two swipes at her shiny black locks and it was in the bag, too. She zipped up the overnight as Don came through the bedroom door.

"Can you grab that?" Lana asked.

"Sure. Is she still at Planned Parenthood?"

"It looks like it."

"Have you texted her?"

"Too risky, Don. If she thinks we're monitoring her, and really wants to avoid us, she could toss the phone. I want to know exactly where she is till I'm by her side. And I want to get there as soon as I can. She's got no protection. There'd be a huge prize in taking her."

"Yeah, *you*. I wish to hell I could go. This business of going back over the shooting is taking forever."

"It always does. They're dotting the i's and crossing the t's. They have to."

Don looked over at Cairo standing in the doorway, staring at them. "Take him."

"I don't think I need—"

"No, definitely take him. His primary job is to protect you. He can't do that from here."

"Okay, Cairo, you're coming."

The dog brightened at the sound of her voice. Maybe he knew from long experience it was the call of duty.

Don grabbed Lana's bag. She packed one more item—her Sig Sauer in the belt of her pants.

• • •

You're so good about being in touch, Emma. I could almost take it as an invitation to join your little escapade. Of course I will. I might be thirty thousand feet in the air but I could be right on the ground beside you for all you'd know. I'll bet anything—no, I'll bet *everything*—that very soon I'll walk right up to you without your paying me any mind. Not that I needed your phone to track your larger movements, but it's good to know how close up and personal I can be, hiding in your pocket. That's where I imagine your phone is, in a nice warm place. A place so redolent of . . .

Emma. I notice that you've turned off your sound. I'm so tempted to send you a message just to make you vibrate.

Now look at that. Your locator is back on. Do I have you to thank for that, Em, or is your mother somewhere in cyberspace spying on you? How dare she encroach on my terrain? But whoever it is has my deepest gratitude.

Oops, your locator has gone dark again. I'm guessing Mommy's doing that, trying to protect you from the likes of me. I'll bet you're not even aware of her fiddling yet. You're probably distracted by the care and treatment you've been getting at the hands of those abortionists. Interesting, isn't it, that by making you wait for your "procedure," they're making it possible for me to kill you *and* your baby?

I'll keep an eye on your half of the screen, but for now I'm going to attend to the other half, where Jimmy McMasters can't seem to stay out of the public eye. He's been speeding away from the oil rig with one of the hostages, but he's slowing down. That's weird.

Oh, my God.

The oil line just blew up. But the flames are already dying. And I don't see oil pumping into the Gulf. This is not BP's Horizon, which I guess was the point. And Jimmy's pumping his fist in the air, so he must have done it.

Jimmy is the Energizer Bunny. Make that "was" because now his boat's dead in the water. And he's got a boat full of bearded men with big guns descending upon them.

• • •

Jimmy and Cal's victory over ISIS lasted about as long as a sneeze. Yes, the blowout preventers worked, choking off the oil flow, but what they needed most right now, ironically enough, was a little fuel for the boat. They had no bullets, no dynamite, nothing but the most abject fear to keep them company as a full complement of heavily armed ISIS fighters raced toward them in the cabin cruiser.

Where's all my good karma?

"We are so fucked," Cal said. "I hope they didn't notice who shot most of their buddies." He raised up a lethal-looking gaff. "I swear I'll slit my fucking wrists with this before I let them get their claws on me."

Jimmy understood the impulse, but grabbed the gaff just in case Cal was serious. A tug of war ensued.

The choppers were still hovering above them, feasting the way sharks might soon on their dismembered bodies down below.

"Wait, what's that?" Jimmy said, pointing to a U.S. Navy Cyclone-class patrol boat streaking toward them.

They both dropped the gaff, which barely missed Jimmy's big toe.

The patrol boat was a long ways off but it sure gave the bearded killers pause. *Happy Daze* had slowed way down, though the 150 yards still separating it from *Sexy Streak* left Jimmy and Cal well within rifle range.

A chopper pilot, maybe sensing some serious bang-bang potential below, brought his camera crew closer—and promptly drew fire from the ISIS warriors.

Then the real guns started to roar. The navy opened up with a Bushmaster, sending a screaming trail of 25 mm shells that tore across the water and into the large white cruiser. Jimmy heard the boat's fiberglass hull ripping open. It sounded like bubble pack getting stomped by a dozen fat bikers. It sounded *good*.

But *Happy Daze* was still afloat, and ISIS was still fighting back. A furry-headed guy with a shoulder-mounted rocket launcher fired his mini-missile right at the navy boat. Not a heat-seeker, though, judging by the way the American captain veered out of the way.

But a sophisticated missile did make an appearance moments later. In a wild flurry of return fire, sailors sent a laser-guided Griffin racing directly toward the cabin cruiser. The newly anointed captain of *Happy Daze* was the only member of his crew with reflexes fast enough to dive into the water.

"Down," cried Jimmy.

BOOM.

A heated shockwave flew over *Sexy Streak*'s gunwales, rocking Cal and Jimmy sharply.

Jimmy raised his head and searched the sea for where *Happy Daze* had been.

The navy had thrown a strike.

And you're out.

Jimmy was cheering. The cruiser had been blasted to melted bits, a furious geyser of flame rising from its ruins, fiberglass and flying limbs falling into the sea around it.

"I'm never complaining about my tax dollars again," Cal said. "That was so fucking great."

Jimmy and Cal watched the patrol boat motor within a couple hundred feet of the destruction. Men with automatic rifles stared down their scopes, searching openly for survivors. Jimmy couldn't fathom anyone living through that onslaught.

But somebody had.

The captain who'd dived from the cruiser was hauling himself over *Sexy Streak*'s outboard motors, wielding a blade as long as a ruler. Cal, closest to the stern, backed up in shock. A sailor shot and missed the intruder, who ducked and lunged forward.

"You stupid Americans," he screamed in a distinctly Boston accent. Christ, he sounded like JFK.

Then he lunged toward Cal, growling, "I'm taking you with me."

Jimmy swung the gaff as hard as the Louisville Sluggers he'd used to smash home runs in American Legion baseball, sinking the steel hook into the side of the bastard's head. The dude fell to the deck, flopping like a big game fish.

Cal smashed the anchor down on the man's bloody skull.

No more flopping.

Cal raised up the weight to finish him off.

"No," Jimmy yelled. "He's still breathing. He can tell us stuff."

Jimmy heard the helicopters right above them. He was so sick of the *whup-whup-whups* that he raised his middle finger and waved it freely at them, less forgiving of the media in that moment than of the madman bleeding at his feet.

Then he turned to the sailors, gave them a thumbs-up, and shouted, "We got us a live one."

Don marveled at McMasters. So did the FBI agents who'd stopped their interview with him to watch the action on Don's kitchen TV. He'd seen wild times himself in the smuggling trade, but nothing to rival the near capture of two brave young Americans by terrorists, the wholesale destruction of an oil line to save the Gulf of Mexico from a much bigger disaster, and the launching of a laser-guided missile to obliterate a boat full of bad actors.

And then hand-to-hand combat, featuring McMasters and a man with a blade big enough to skin a lion. After watching all that Don felt guilty for ever agreeing with Lana that McMasters was the Kato Kaelin of the Gulf Coast. Hell, Jimmy McMasters felt like someone whose company Don would enjoy. That young man was, in a word, incredible. *You go, boy. You go,* Don thought as another agent yelled that he had a visitor.

"You mind?" Don asked the pair who'd been reconstructing the shooting with him.

"Go for it," said the senior agent. Both appeared more engaged at the moment by the action on screen.

As he eased himself off a stool, the last Don saw of McMasters was the boat racer flipping off the TV crews that had probably just immortalized him. Don was certain that billions of views would agree: The country needed its heroes, even the most unlikely ones.

He headed out to the rubble that had once been their living room, spotting Sufyan Hijazi standing in the street outside the taped-off evidence area. The young man looked worried.

"Is she okay?" he asked as Don made his way over.

"She wasn't here," he replied. "Have you heard anything from her?"

Sufyan shook his head. "How about Mrs. Elkins?"

"She's fine. But an FBI agent was badly wounded. Some fools blew up the house trying to get to Emma's mom. It got ugly."

"What do you mean?"

"I had to shoot them."

"Did you kill them?"

Don nodded. "I'm getting questioned about that now. It should be over pretty quick, and then I was going to check on the agent. You want to come with me?" He thought it would be good to get Sufyan away from the scene of the bombing; the young man looked disturbed by what he was seeing. But Don also wanted pick Sufyan's brain about Tahir, if he could do it subtly enough.

Turned out, subtlety wasn't necessary.

"My uncle's gone," the boy blurted. "Sometime during the night, I think. He just disappeared."

"Did he leave a note? Anything?"

"No. Maybe one of his old enemies grabbed him."

"I doubt that. Your uncle's one tough son-of-a . . . gun. How's your mom?"

"She's worried, too."

"I'm guessing your uncle has good reasons for whatever he's doing."

Nothing but empty words, and Don knew it. Tahir could be plotting the final death throes of the entire country. "Let me finish up inside and we'll take my truck."

But first he texted Lana the news about Tahir.

• • •

Lana and Cairo were racing toward Baltimore when she received Don's message. Instinctively, she checked her rear-view, half expecting to see Tahir on her tail. Which made no logical sense—he could have left for Baltimore hours ago, if that was where he'd even headed. But she had reason to suspect that he might be pursuing Emma because he'd been trying to hack into her phone, according to Galina.

The Russian had texted her twenty minutes ago with good news: Senator Willens had canceled his demand that she appear before his committee.

"Like a miracle," Galina had added.

She and Lana both knew better, though. Galina was wisely avoiding any allusions to efforts her boss might have undertaken on her behalf. The real miracle workers were the doctors and nurses trying to save the life of seven-year-old Alexandra. Now they wouldn't be obstructed by Marigold Winters's petty power grab.

Lana looked over at Cairo. The Malinois held his gaze firmly on the road ahead. Her own eyes returned to the phone as they sped toward Baltimore. She spotted Em's GPS signal in front of a building. Em was likely entering Planned Parenthood.

"Stay there, kiddo," Lana murmured. "And don't do anything rash. I'm coming."

• • •

Emma waited in an examining room for Dr. Mohammed Abbas. She didn't feel good about a Middle Eastern obstetrician. Probably a Muslim. *With my luck.* Which hadn't been the greatest lately.

Dr. Abbas walked in moments later. He wore black-rimmed glasses and sported a neatly trimmed beard. He put out his hand in greeting. Em took it. "Let's check your blood pressure," he said next.

And her pulse, as it turned out. A nurse had done both less than ten minutes ago, which Emma mentioned to him.

"But I bet you're a little more anxious now because you're meeting a doctor named Mohammed, and I'll bet you're thinking, 'What's he doing working here?'"

"No, not really," Emma lied.

He smiled, pausing to look at her numbers. "Anyway, your blood pressure's up a little, but nothing to worry about." He sat in a chair across from Em, who was perched on the end of the examining table. "Are you anxious?"

"A little, maybe."

"Most women are when they find out they're pregnant, especially for the first time. You've shown good sense coming in. Do you have any concerns about your pregnancy?"

"Are you kidding? I don't want to be pregnant. I've made that pretty clear to everyone. I'm in high school. I'm going to college. It's the last thing I want."

"So please tell me what you want."

"I want to terminate."

"It says here," Dr. Abbas looked down at his tablet, "that you don't want your parents to know. Why is that?"

Emma told him about her mother's wounded leg. "And she's got a very important job in Washington. She has no time for this."

"I know who your mother is. I know she's very important, but I'm sure she has time for you. At moments like this a girl needs her mother, and I think your mother would want to be with you, unless there's something about her that makes you think otherwise."

"It's not about her. It's about me. This is *so* private."

"Did you leave a note at least, to let them know you're okay?"

"No, and I realized last night that I should have. I'm sorry."

"Don't be sorry about that." He pulled out his phone. "Call them. At least tell them you're okay."

"I can't. She'll know where I am. I've been so caught up with getting away I never thought to—"

"Emma, find a way to let them know you're okay. I have a fifteen-year-old daughter. I would be petrified if she did this to me. We love our children more than anything in the world."

Emma believed him and had to force down tears.

"So you don't know what's happened, do you?" he asked.

"What are you talking about?"

"I know you've been caught up with other things, but I have to tell you something."

"Is my mom okay?" she asked quickly, suddenly terrified.

"Yes, your mother is fine, but your house was attacked this morning and part of it was blown up. Your mother and father and dog are all fine, and—"

"Wait a second! My house was *bombed*? Are you kidding?"

"No, I'm not kidding. Two men blew up the front of the house but everyone is okay. The two men were shot and killed, and only one person inside was injured. That was an FBI agent who was wounded. But he's doing well. Look, I'm not sure you should be making this decision on your own when so much is going on in your life."

"It's really *private*. Can't you understand that? And I'm seventeen. I'll be eighteen soon."

Don't get all worked up, Emma warned herself. *Be mature.*

"What about your boyfriend?"

"He knows I'm pregnant.

"What does he want? Do you know?"

"Yes, he's"—she paused, and in hesitating felt as though she had said the word that now had to follow—"Muslim."

He nodded. "So am I."

I knew it. Here it comes.

"But that doesn't mean I can't understand *and* respect your feelings. That's what's most important here. I'm not making any judgments about you, and it would be good for both of us if you didn't make any about me. Maybe your boyfriend isn't, either."

"No, he definitely wants the baby."

They talked for another ten minutes. Dr. Abbas appeared to listen carefully as Emma did her best to sound level-headed. Inwardly, she experienced a growing sense of panic that despite his reasonable demeanor, Dr. Abbas would insist on bringing her parents and Sufyan into the discussion.

He took off his glasses and cleaned them with a tissue. "Where are you staying while you're here? Where did you sleep last night?"

"In my car."

"That's not safe, Emma. The receptionist has the address of a residence we refer women to. It's safe and comfortable, and it's nearby. If you need money, we can arrange your stay for you. I want you to think about your decision for twenty-four hours."

"Is that so *you* can think about it?" She was so tired of waiting.

"No. If tomorrow you want to terminate, I will have you scheduled. You have my word."

Your word? She didn't want his word. She wanted to be on his schedule for the abortion as soon as possible.

At the front desk, Emma got directions to the home where other clients had stayed, and then headed out to her car. The location was about two miles away.

They would be the longest two miles of Emma's life.

CHAPTER 27

EMMA FELT OUT OF her element in the heart of Baltimore. She wished she could hurl herself forty-eight hours into the future when she'd have all this behind her: pregnancy, abortion, the city itself.

But maybe it won't ever be. She'd read about women who'd regretted ending their pregnancies, but also others who'd been doubly glad they'd had them. Almost all agreed, though, that it was complicated and made *you* more complicated. Your body, your mind, your soul. Changed you in so many ways. After everything Emma had endured in the past two years—almost getting blown up by a backpack nuclear bomb; kidnapped by a Washington DC drug lord, who turned out to be an old business associate of her father's—she didn't know how much more complicated her life could get. But she supposed the women who'd been writing about abortion on the Web—pro and con—knew a lot more about the subject than she did.

She swore when she saw a parking ticket on her windshield. *The whole country's falling apart and they're still giving these things out?* She wanted to tear it up, but didn't dare.

Instead, she pulled it out from under the wipers and threw it on the passenger seat. Then she looked around and put the address into her phone. Right away her phone told her to drive north, adding, "Turn right on West Mulberry Street."

"Okay, okay," Emma replied to her phone. "Just give me a chance to get this thing started."

She fired up the Fusion and drove dutifully north.

More directions followed, taking Emma past men with grocery carts, sleeping bags, filthy blankets, and plastic bags filled with empty cans and bottles. One stumbled to the driver's-side window, his vacant eyes staring at her.

"Get me out of here," Emma whispered, as if the voice on her phone might respond to a desperate request.

Instead, it told her to turn left in one block.

Emma did.

"Oh, crap."

From the homeless to the nearly so: dilapidated housing with broken porch railings and rotting stoops loomed before her, along with the people sitting on them.

Watching me, she realized.

A second later, the vehicle stopped running. Died right in the middle of the street. Cars parked on both sides, leaving her to block the right lane.

Emma tried the starter repeatedly. Not a spark. *Dead-dead-dead.* She pounded the steering wheel. A car eased around her. Then it was gone. She was alone.

No you're not.

Two guys were walking up. Gold chains around their necks, jeans around the bottoms of their butts, undershorts showing. Ball caps askew— Orioles and Wizards.

"Hey, girl. Need some help?" asked the bigger, bulkier one. His short bony friend looked on, smiling.

The smaller one promptly started talking a line, too. "Sure she does. Come on, sweet sister, pop the hood on your Fu-sion." Making a dance out of those two syllables.

"I'm going to call Triple A," she said through the closed window.

"Sure, you do that," the big guy said. "You must think you're in Bethesda and they'll come running." He was laughing now, looking at her high school parking permit in the corner of the front window. "Good luck with that shit. Last time I called, I waited days."

The shorter one laughed, too, and slapped palms with his buddy. "Triple A. Yeah, you'll be waiting. Least you got some company. Pop the hood. I work on cars. I might be able to help you."

Did she dare? Did she dare not?

She released the hood. It rose before her. She couldn't see what the bony guy was doing. The bigger one tapped her window.

"What do you think we're gonna do? Eat you alive? You can come out."

Shit. She froze. She wished Sufyan were here. *Or his dad.* That would show she wasn't prejudiced. But maybe she was to react like this. Or was it just showing good sense? She didn't know, wondering if some bigot banging around her brain really was making this seem so much worse.

There were now five guys crowding around. No women.

Emma called Triple A, giving the dispatcher the cross streets. "How long?" she asked.

"I'm guessing they'll be there pretty quick. Half hour at the most."

"A half hour?" Emma knew she sounded panicky.

"That's right," the dispatcher said. "Hang tight."

"Turn it over," the big guy outside her window said.

Emma looked at him, unsure what he meant.

"The car key, or the button. Whatever you got in there to make it go."

Emma pushed the ignition switch. Dead.

"Let me try it," the guy said. "Open the door."

Push was coming to shove. *Sometimes you just have to put your faith in people.* Which felt like the thinnest of reeds. She unlocked the door.

"Now get your skinny ass out of there and let me check it out."

My butt or the car?

The car, apparently. He exchanged positions with Emma with nary a glance.

"The key?" he asked.

"They're in my bag." Which was on the passenger seat next to him, home to her wallet, credit cards, ID, *money*. "It'll start with it over there." She didn't want him to touch her bag.

He grabbed it anyway and put it on his lap, trying the ignition button again. Still nothing.

"You seeing anything up there?" he asked his friend, who was still under the hood.

"Nothing. Everything looks cool."

"I'm seeing something," one of the hangers-on said. He had his eyes all over Emma. "You wanna party with us? Come on." He grabbed her arm.

"Hey, Beast, leave her be," the guy in the car said.

"Why? You think you got reservations? You don't have shit, man." His grip tightened on Emma.

"I'd suggest you let her go right now."

A woman had walked up behind them. Tall as Em's mom.

"Go fuck yourself, bitch. You don't come into *my* hood and tell me shit."

The woman nodded. Maybe agreeably. Emma hoped not. She wanted this guy to let her go. His fingers felt like steel cables.

"Fuck it, you're coming, too," the guy holding Emma said to the woman. "We'll make it a big fucking party."

"Beast, cut that shit out." The big guy climbed out of the car.

"Stay right where you are," the woman said. She had straight dark hair and blue eyes like Emma's. Wearing jeans, sweater, heavy boots.

Combat boots. Em's mom had a pair. Dust colored. Didn't fit the woman's outfit at all.

"Now that was your mistake," the big guy said. "'Cause I'm on her side, but you're pissing me off."

He stepped toward her. The woman drew a semi-automatic from the back of her jeans, racking and raising it in a blink. Aimed it at his face.

"Freeze. And you," she eyed the guy holding Emma, "let her go or I *will* blow your balls off."

The shorter guy slammed the hood down. "You people are shit. I was trying to help her."

"He," the woman nodded at Beast, "put his hands on her. Game over."

"Beast, you're a motherfucker," said the big guy. "Let her go."

Emma stepped away, rubbing her arm.

Then the big guy tossed Em her bag. "Don't be leaving that here."

"Lock it," the woman told Em, who complied without question, using the key fob. "Now we're leaving," she said to the seven men. "Nobody gets hurt if nobody moves."

The woman kept her gun on the young men as she and Emma retreated to a utility van about fifty feet away. The front passenger door was unlocked. Emma climbed in, finding an open laptop resting on a metal stand next to the driver's seat, like the ones she'd seen in some delivery trucks.

The woman backed up, executed a crisp three-point turn, then sped off within seconds.

"Thank you so much," Emma said. "I didn't know what was going to happen."

"You're more than welcome."

"I'm Emma."

"Emma Elkins. I know who you are."

Emma figured she was one of her mother's friends in some super-secret intelligence service who'd been ordered to track her down. "Who are you?"

The woman smiled, then hit the childproof locks. She still hadn't put aside her gun. "I'm your guardian angel. But some people call me Golden Voice."

CHAPTER 28

LANA LEFT CAIRO IN the Charger and hobbled as fast as she could into Planned Parenthood, but her best efforts got her nowhere. The youthful receptionist wouldn't even acknowledge that Emma had been in the clinic.

"That is confidential information between a woman and her doctor. And we're closing for the day," she added crisply.

"Look, I don't have a problem with your confidentiality. I respect it. But my daughter called and told me she'd been here." Lana leaned forward. "Her life is in danger. My house was bombed this morning." She indicated the crutches supporting her. "It's been all over the news." Lana glanced over her shoulder where the waiting room television was tuned to CNN.

"You're—"

"That's right," Lana said.

"Let me check with someone," the receptionist said. But as she reached for the phone, a bearded man in a white coat walked toward them from the back of the clinic.

"Carly, let me talk to Ms. Elkins." He turned to Lana. "Come on back here," he said, holding open a gate for her. "I'm Dr. Abbas."

He led her to his office, Lana crutching noisily down the hall behind him.

"Have a seat," he said, although he remained standing, leaning against a cabinet with his clipboard held to his chest. "You say your daughter called you? Did I hear that correctly?"

"Yes, she did."

"What did she say?"

"That she wanted to see me," Lana lied. "She knows she can call me anytime, any place, for any reason, no questions asked and no recriminations."

"We ought to have that painted on the bedroom of every parent we deal with," he replied with a smile. "We helped her find a place to stay. Did she tell you about that?"

"No," Lana replied, glad that Emma had found a place for the night. "Can you tell me?"

"Why don't you call her?"

"To be honest, I've tried, but her phone must be out of service." Lana rued saying "to be honest." A bad habit; even when she wasn't lying it made her sound as though she were.

Dr. Abbas raised an eyebrow.

"There are service problems across the country," Lana insisted, trying to make her story plausible. Emma simply hadn't returned her calls or texts.

"I asked her to call you." The doctor looked straight into Lana's eyes, then put his clipboard down and wrote on a prescription pad. "I've never violated a woman's confidentiality, but I've also never faced these circumstances. I saw the video of your home. I also know who you are, and I can understand your concern for your daughter's safety." He handed her the paper. "Your daughter should be at this address. A friend of the clinic rents rooms or provides them for nothing, if someone doesn't have money. Her name's Anna Hendrix. She's a good person. She's handled all types of situations. Abusive boyfriends, batterers, that kind of thing. Emma will be safe there. Anna knows there could be trouble."

"Is Anna armed?"

Dr. Abbas paused. "She . . . ah . . . finds that advisable. I can't disagree. Our opponents can be brutal."

Lana thanked him and was out the door as fast as she could manage. She read the address into her phone and followed the directions. They led her to the Fusion, which was getting loaded onto a flatbed tow truck.

Lana climbed out of her car, bracing herself against the door of the Charger. "Do you know where the driver is?" she called to the tow-truck operator. "She's my daughter."

He got out of the cab and walked toward her. "Cops just told me to clear the street. That's all I know."

A tall, muscular man sporting chains and dropped jeans sauntered over. "Was that your kid?"

"Yeah, did you see her?"

The tow-truck operator stayed close, as though he expected trouble.

"Yeah, I saw her. Friend and I tried to help her. Car just stopped dead. Then some dude grabbed her arm and a chick comes out of nowhere. She looked kinda like you, and pulls out a big barrel like she means business, and your kid left with her."

"In a car?"

"Big white van. Chevy Express. Kind without windows. You're not hearing from your girl?"

Lana eyed him carefully. "No, and there's a lot of money in finding her."

"Shit, I'm not looking for your goddamn money. I'm telling you 'cause I got a kid about her age and none of this shit makes any sense. Her car just stops for no reason. My buddy's good, and he was under the hood and everything looked fine to him. Then some chick with a Glock comes up at just the right second, aims it right in my face. So I hope you find your kid, and fuck over that bitch. She would've killed me. I could see it in her eyes."

"Thanks. I appreciate your help."

Lana was slipping back into the Charger, the tow-truck driver his cab. She called Baltimore police and reported her missing daughter and the description of the van. Ditto after dialing the FBI. Then she glanced at the car as she started backing up, thinking about what the big man had just told her: *Stopped for no reason.* Could have been a malfunction that wouldn't have been apparent to the naked eye, like a blocked fuel line. Or the vehicle's computer could have been hacked. She'd specifically avoided the Cherokee, which had become notorious for this vulnerability. Now she was doing an Internet search to see if the Fusion...

Oh shit.

Her stomach churned as she found the Ford among a recent list of cars that conceivably could be hacked.

Regardless of the cause—mechanical failure or computer hack—it all added up to the worst type of trouble: the kind that claims your daughter.

• • •

Emma shrieked. Some guy had just risen from behind her seat in the van and grabbed her. And he was dragging her into the dark cargo area.

"Don't fight me or I'll break you into pieces," he said.

The thought of fighting him hadn't even entered Emma's mind. The man was so strong and fast, he'd overwhelmed her.

"And don't move," he said in a softer voice, the city streets passing swiftly beneath them.

He threw a black curtain that closed off the cargo space from the cab, then switched on a light. He wore a Barack Obama mask.

"Put your hands out."

"What for?"

He grabbed them and jammed her wrists up behind her back, then cinched them tightly together with plastic cuffs.

"Lie down."

"Please stop. Please. Don't let him do this to me," she yelled to the female driver.

The armed woman didn't even acknowledge her.

"Next time I'll belt you in the face," the masked man said. "Get down."

She lay on her side. He cuffed her ankles together. Then he ran duct tape around her head, sealing her mouth and eyes. He left only her nose exposed.

Emma was so panicky she could hardly catch her breath. He leaned close. She smelled his mouthwash and felt the heat of his breath. "Calm the fuck down. Focus on breathing. The worst is over."

No, it wasn't. He rolled her onto thick plastic, then ran a zipper from her feet past the top of her head, sealing her in a body bag.

Lana followed her phone's directions to Anna Hendrix's house. She had little hope she'd find Emma there, but had to check.

Hendrix looked formidable at a glance. She stood at least a few inches taller than Lana, and though lean appeared strong as a braided whip.

The strength of experience were the words that came to mind as Lana took in the woman's curly hair, graying now in what appeared to be her forties, though she had the smooth skin of so many people of African descent.

"I'm so sorry," Anna Hendrix said, after establishing who had called at her door in the early evening.

"If my daughter shows up or you hear anything that could be helpful, here's my number."

Anna opened the door to take it but appeared no more hopeful than Lana felt.

"What are you going to do?" she asked Lana.

"I'm not sure."

Where do you go and what do you do when your daughter vanishes into the shadows of a big city? A detective had called Lana back saying they'd interview the witnesses, assuming they could actually round them up. Lana wasn't optimistic, knowing the BPD was looked upon with considerable cynicism in those precincts.

"How about if I take Emma's room, if that's okay with you?" Lana said.

"Of course, come in."

Lana set up her laptop on the bed in the spartan room. Knowing the abductor's van was a Chevy, she went to work on the Maryland motor vehicle database.

She'd hacked this sort of system before so it didn't take long to slip past its paltry security—she'd have given it a -1 on a scale of 10—and saw quickly that a lot of Chevy Expresses were owned by rental companies. It could take awhile to uncover recent activity, so she called the detective with this new info. But at heart Lana had little hope that whoever had grabbed Emma had been unprofessional enough to leave a trail with a rental company. And, no doubt, they wanted more than Em.

They want you, so let them come to you.

She was the perfect bait: wounded and just bloody enough to attract the biggest predators.

• • •

Emma felt cold sweat dripping off her. The kind that oozes from your pores when you're nauseated and scared so senseless you shiver with fear.

Her stomach roiled repeatedly, and she worried that with her mouth taped up she'd vomit and choke to death.

She could hear the murmur of conversation above the road noise. The two were up in the cab now. Only the murmur, though. No words that she could make out, other than the ones racing around her own head:

They came for you with a body bag. They're not fooling around.

• • •

I have her all zipped up back there, a body bag every bit as black as the sites Art's flown in and out of in the most remote regions of Central America and North Africa. We've worked together on and off for almost six years. He was cashiered by the CIA for making too much on the side. I know his history. He's a freelancer now. As soon as the agency gave him his walking papers, I got in touch. You see, I think greed keeps some men honest. It's clear what motivates them: money. And if that's all that moves them—if they're not hot for power or glory—then your contracts are direct and unencumbered. That's how it works with Art.

I'm fortunate to have his services, the loyalty he feels toward my money. The world changes all the time but the needs of people like me remain the same. Move the bodies. Use some as lures. Dump them when you're done.

As for Emma, she had no idea when I told her I was Golden Voice what that meant. Here I am, a figure of renown, known to many millions, and my prize catch is oblivious. My name will certainly ring bells for her mother, when the time comes for those revelations. And it is coming, Lana. It's coming very, very soon.

There's our airport. Crop dusters and small planes only, if all you do is look in the hangars. Only pilots might notice the runway is long enough to accommodate much more substantial craft. But nobody ever sees those planes and jets. They're in and out in the dark of night, loaded with all kinds of contraband, while the farmers and their families are fast asleep.

"No lights, not even on the runway," I tell Art.

"Don't need 'em."

While I know his history, he has only a skeletal outline of mine. But he does know who Emma is. He mentioned that as soon as he had her bagged. Now he's circling back to that subject as I expected he would. I'm guessing a warning is on the way. And, of course, I'm correct.

"You better know what you're doing. Her mother knows a ton of people."

A statement that doesn't bear comment, as far as I'm concerned. "Just get us on that plane and in the air."

"Turn at the fueling station. To the right."

As soon as I come around the pumps I see a twin-engine Beechcraft, white on top, butterscotch on the bottom.

"Was that the best you could get?"

"You wanted anonymity."

"It'll take all night. Are we going to need to refuel?"

"Once. Don't worry, this is the plane you want to be in these days. Jets and anything fancy get the wrong attention."

I know he's right but I still wish we had a Lear or Gulfstream.

. . .

Emma heard the van's cargo door open, then felt herself being dragged toward it. The two of them carried her. Not for long. Ten steps—she counted—before lifting her onto another hard surface.

She heard one of them climbing up next to her, guessing it was the masked guy. He dragged her a few feet farther.

The bag was unzipped. Up till then she'd managed to contain her claustrophobia. But now with the bag open—so close to being able to see again—she could hardly stand the tape across her eyes and mouth, or the cuffs—the unyielding sense of confinement.

Just take it off my eyes. Please.

She knew her urgency amounted to nothing more than groans.

Then Em felt someone close to her. Him, definitely him. But his breath had soured.

"Easy," he told her. "No need to panic."

A door closed. The floor shook. She heard propellers start up. They weren't taking off the tape or cuffs.

Oh, God. I can't stand it. I really can't.

Like a miracle, he was leaning over her again, slowly unpeeling the tape from her mouth.

Yes, thank you.

Now her eyes, but *so* slowly.

The plane was lifting off.

Mom's never going to find me.

Emma didn't realize she'd spoken till Golden Voice, tape balled up in her hand, held her gaze.

"She'll find you, Em. I promise."

Words that sounded like murder.

CHAPTER 29

CHIMES FROM LANA'S COMPUTER awakened her at three in the morning to a message from Steel Fist: "I have your daughter. We should talk."

She sprang out of the bed that should have been Emma's for the night. "Son-of-a-bitch!"

Lana had been so consumed with concerns about radical Islamists or bounty hunters that they'd nudged aside the threat from the neo-Nazi. *And what's this 'We should talk' crap? Like he was a businessman setting up a meeting with an investor. No, you should die.*

She tried contacting Emma again, to no avail. Her daughter's phone might as well have been on Pluto. Emma was gone, and Steel Fist had apparently used a woman to grab her.

But he wants more than Em. He wants you, too, she reminded herself. *So he's going to be in touch.*

She had to believe that. She couldn't accept that Emma would simply disappear. Steel Fist wanted propaganda. And now he had the means to leverage Emma's well-being to get Lana. And he would, because Lana was not going to back down. She'd find her daughter.

Whatever it takes.

She set up to work, once more, on the bed in Anna Hendrix's house, this time to try to find the trail that Horvat's message had taken through the cybersphere.

Without the slightest hesitation, given the hour, she first messaged Galina. Maybe she'd be up as she had been last night. Not this time. Sleeping, no doubt, as she should.

What about your sleep? Lana asked herself. An old line came to her—with fresh meaning: *I'll sleep when I'm dead.*

• • •

Emma awoke cold and short of breath. They must be flying awfully high. *Can't they do something about the cabin pressure in this thing?* But she had an even more pressing need to pee. She yelled out that she had to go.

"You're in that bag," the woman shouted back. "Just pee in that."

The body bag was zipped from her neck down. Emma didn't argue. Her biggest fear was they'd tape her eyes and mouth shut again and zip up the bag.

That's not your biggest fear. No, she was terrified that they'd kill her. She peed, unable to remember the last time she'd wet herself.

The back of the Beechcraft was black. No windows. The only light came from the instrument panel in front. Like the van. And to think Emma couldn't have been more grateful when her "rescuer" had whipped out that gun.

What a sick joke.

But now Emma was going to have to depend on another tall, dark-haired woman: her mom, who had to be the real target. *What good am I to them?* The answer hammered her immediately: *You're the bait.*

The realization was horrifying, as much for the slight comfort it provided—that they'd hold off killing her until they'd nabbed her mother—as the threat it represented to the one person who would do anything to save her.

• • •

Don checked on Sufyan, asleep in Emma's bed. *Not the first time,* her father thought. The boy's mother, Alimah, had a guest bedroom. He wished he could check on his daughter as easily, and that Lana hadn't been forced to take off on crutches to try to find and protect her.

The feds had moved fast to get a construction crew to the house to fortify it on a temporary basis. A Bethesda Police Department officer sat in a cruiser outside, while an FBI agent had taken up station in the backyard.

At least we take care of our own.

Springsteen's song came alive in Don's mind. This early in the morning, he knew he'd be hearing the Boss's catchy lyrics until he went back to bed to try to grab a few more winks, although that could be a challenge: those two law enforcement officers weren't sufficient to make him feel safe. Not after the day he'd had. Front of the house ripped off. Two men shooting up Agent Maray. And then his own killing of the pair.

That was a first for Don. He'd held a gun on men twice while smuggling tons of pot up from Latin America, but he'd never shot anyone until yesterday morning.

He was surprised and grateful over how little he felt. No guilt. No regrets. There might have been if there had been another option. But those two had shot Maray a couple of times and were threatening a gruesome wound that would have killed him. Don had lined up his shots just in time.

We take care of our own.

Right now, he wished more than anything that he could have been with Lana so he could help take care of their child. Staying behind, no matter how necessary, made him feel useless.

But he also felt something worse: the first pulse of panic.

• • •

The landing jolted Emma. If daylight had come, it probably would have awakened her fully; but through her barely sentient fog she heard the guy saying he was fueling up. Weariness claimed her quickly, but not for long: shortness of breath and her worsening cramps made for fitful sleep. Finally, the cramps doubled her over in the bag.

"Help me. I'm having—" She didn't want to say cramps and sound like some lame teenager. "I've got a really bad stomachache."

"You sound like you're having trouble breathing," the pilot said, as if she were a friend he was taking for a ride, not someone the pair had forced into a body bag, cuffed at the ankles and wrists.

From then on, Emma scarcely slept at all. What a time to be sick.

They finally descended enough that she could breathe without gulping air, landing minutes later.

She tried to brace herself for the taping of her mouth and eyes, and the sealing of the bag.

But once the plane stopped rolling, the guy who'd worn the Barack Obama mask didn't bother to put it on before he turned around to stare at her. That really scared Emma. When they showed their faces, didn't that mean they'd decided to kill you?

The two of them climbed back into the cabin. He opened the door.

"You're worried, aren't you, Em?" the woman asked.

A cruel question. But she sounded like she'd enjoyed asking it. Em couldn't help but nod.

"Well, now's the time to be very, very worried. So you have good instincts."

They hauled Emma from the plane. Not another person in sight, but in the distance she spotted snow-capped mountains whose peaks looked like the edge of a saw-tooth blade.

They carried her to the open trunk of a large car, laying her on the tarmac only long enough to tape up her mouth, take her photograph, and zip the bag.

Then they dumped her in the trunk.

• • •

I doubt she's going to die back there, but even if she suffocates on her own vomit from that bellyache, there's still plenty I can do with her body. That's what I needed and that's what I've got.

But before we move her any farther, I have to take care of a few items. It's easier to work on my computer at this elevation than on that plane bouncing around at ten thousand feet. That kid wasn't the only one having trouble breathing. Art said he had to fly at that altitude for "security reasons." I told him just now I needed privacy in here for "security reasons." I could tell he wasn't pleased but he's obedient and leaning against the trunk. Emma's kicking up a storm back there. I'm not quite sure what she thinks she's going to accomplish with that. She's such a moaner.

It doesn't take me long to get back into Vinko's website. He changes his password routinely, but the predictive algorithms I've devised come up with his new ones quickly. He's oddly unimaginative in that regard. Which I'm grateful for. He's also a convenient ruse to communicate with Emma's mother, though neither she nor Vinko knows they're being duped.

It's a pleasure to show off my skills, even if my audience consists mostly of me. Any hacker who denies the pure amusement that comes from deluding others is a liar. We all love it for that reason, among others, of course.

Vinko's been so vocal about his hatred for Lana and Emma—and his desire to see them truly hurt—that his old missives have done the cyber spadework for me. And his credibility with his followers is unquestioned—for now.

Let's see who's minding the Horvat store this morning . . .

What's that? Emma has stopped kicking. Settling down or suffocating? I'm in no rush to find out. At least she's in the body bag, if it's the latter. No muss. No fuss.

So it's the little Russian minx keeping her eye on Vinko, whom she knows as Steel Fist. He'd be so humbled if he knew how many of us are inside his system, which he believes so secure and sophisticated. NSA has some lines into it, too. I can see them, but they're not as nimble as I am. Not even close.

I'm just going to focus on Galina Bortnik for the moment and use the pathways she's forged. Minimize my presence. A few more clicks, a quick tour of some of Bortnik's data exfiltration, and that's all it takes. I'm back on your turf again, Vinko.

It's high time for you to get busy because, if all goes well—and it will—your hands will be full.

And then you'll be dead.

...

Galina was awake, alert, and active at her computer.

She'd only been slow in answering—busy, not asleep.

Now that's devotion, thought Lana.

In response to Lana's question, Galina messaged that Sufyan's uncle Tahir was booked on an early flight to Boise, Idaho. "First thing smokin'," was precisely how Galina put it, clearly sharpening her use of an American idiom.

"Boise? Are you sure?"

"Yes, and he has been hacking Steel Fist. So he might know something we do not. I used his entry point to get inside the Nazi's site."

"How long did it take you to do that?"

"Not long. It was fast today."

"What are you seeing right now?"

"A message board. It is active. Creeps are logging on. Posting. I see some photos of slaves in metal collars and chains. Steel Fist is responding."

"Anything of note?" Lana was surprised Steel Fist wasn't bragging about Emma. She wouldn't tell Galina about that, not at this point. It might affect her performance if it felt personal, and she was a mother, too. Lana needed pure, unemotional efforts from her.

"No, short messages. Same stupid Nazi stuff."

"What worries me is when Jensen got in and shut him down, Steel Fist was back online in a few minutes. He clearly had great cyber resiliency. But you got in easy and you're still in there."

"No problem. Very simple today. Probably for Tahir, too."

Maybe Galina's better than Jeff, Lana thought. After all, Deputy Director Holmes, still recovering in the cardiac unit, had asked for Galina to take over the testing of NSA's own cyberdefenses.

"Keep testing to see if you're being led around."

"Okay."

"But stay on as long as you can."

"Wait," Galina said. "Here is an alert from Steel Fist. That is what he is calling it. Big black letters. They fill the screen. It says 'THE PRIZE HAS ARRIVED.' The prize?"

A sinking feeling overcame Lana. "Let's see if he says anything—"

"He does." Galina interrupted. "I am so sorry, Lana. He says he has Emma."

"What does he say? Precisely?"

"This is bold too: 'I HAVE THE BITCH, EMMA ELKINS. YOU WILL GET TO SEE HER DIE SLOWLY. TELL ALL THE SOLDIERS OF THE NEW AMERICA THAT THE TIME HAS COME TO SLAUGHTER OUR ENEMIES.' There's a picture of her, Lana. I'm so sorry. She—"

"Tell me."

"Her mouth is taped. She is zipped up to her chin in a black bag of some kind."

A body bag.

In seconds, Lana linked to the Steel Fist website and saw Emma herself. But her daughter looked so different. It wasn't the duct tape wrapped around her head and mouth. It was the terror in Em's eyes. Deep as the oceans.

"The data flows," Lana said to Galina. "Can you access them?"

"Could be hard."

I doubt that, Lana thought. *He wants me to come, wherever they are.* "I'll hang on."

Lana shared Galina's screen but not her history of hacking this site. She had to sit back and wait, and she'd rarely considered patience a virtue.

"I am surprised. Here it is. See," Galina said, bringing up lines curving across the country, growing dense in the Pacific Northwest. "It looks like Boise."

He might as well have printed out an invitation.

"I've got to get moving. Let me know if anything else comes up."

"To Boise?" Galina asked.

"Affirmative," Lana replied, already sounding as though she were back in combat mode.

Chasing Tahir as well, it seemed. The Sudanese must have gleaned his own clues when he hacked the Steel Fist site, for he was already heading west.

Why? What game is he running? And who's he bringing?

She cut her computer connection to Galina and reached for her phone when a second direct message from Steel Fist arrived on her screen: "Bring no one."

Fat chance, you—

But Lana seized up over Steel Fist's next words: "I'll cut her open. I'll kill her slowly. I want you. You come, she lives. You bring anyone, I'll know and you'll watch her die slowly."

Lana's screen went blank. When she reached for her phone a second time, she did make a call, but not the one she'd planned. She rousted Jeff, the decorated navy vet, to call upon whatever chits he might have at the Department of Defense to get Lana and Cairo on a military flight to Boise as soon as possible.

She wouldn't bring anyone with her, but she would bring a dog.

• • •

Vinko was asleep while his alter ego online, Steel Fist, was busy conducting a forum for many of his followers. And before he awoke his system would lose every last trace of those exchanges. For Vinko, the activity might as well have been a dream that he'd never remember. After all, Golden Voice had organized all his replies from thousands of sessions, which left her fully equipped to field any query or expression of outrage with an appropriate response.

It had been an alpha test. And it worked splendidly.

• • •

Emma guessed the car was on the road for about twenty minutes, although it was hard for her to estimate with any confidence. Time felt borderless, so teeming with fear that she could have been suspended in a nightmare with no point of return.

Then they stopped and she expected to be pulled out of the trunk. Instead, the front passenger door, as much as she could tell, opened and closed, and the car sped up again.

So Art's gone. Nothing else made sense.

It felt black as a hearse in that trunk, even with her eyes untaped, as if it were, in fact, a coffin.

At least she could breathe, but her cramps were extreme. Yet her fear overrode even that pain. *I saw their faces.* She kept coming back to that. They thought they'd be done with her . . . soon.

The car started down what felt like a dirt road. The shocks were working overtime. Then the vehicle slowed almost to a stop before rolling onto a smooth surface for a second or two.

A garage?

All but confirmed when she heard the door closing.

Then the trunk lock was popped and the driver's-side door opened and closed.

The woman, who had yet to reveal her name, smiled at her as she lifted the trunk all the way up. It was the coldest smile Emma had ever seen.

She peeled the tape from Em's mouth. "How's your stomach?"

"Bad."

"I'm going to move you. You do what I say and I won't hurt you."

Now. You mean you won't hurt me right now. Just go ahead and tell me.

But Emma said none of that. Instead, she asked, "What's your name?" Desperate as it seemed, she was trying to make a connection to her captor. She'd heard her mom talk about how that had saved the lives of some victims.

"My name? Let's see. You can call me . . . Peggy."

Emma doubted that was her name, figuring the woman was gaming her. But she did what Peggy asked, rolling onto her side and pulling her legs to her chest, which actually relieved the cramping a tiny bit.

The woman grabbed the bottom of the bag, propping Emma's legs on the edge of the trunk, then reached in and grabbed the heavy black plastic by Emma's shoulders. She hauled her into a sitting position with little apparent strain.

"Now I'm going to get you on your feet. Have they gone to sleep?"

"No."

With her help, Emma stood, arms still cuffed behind her back. Peggy unzipped the bag all the way to the ground, then unfolded a pocketknife and sliced off the wet plastic cuffs on Emma's ankles.

Facing forward, Em heard her fold up the blade, then felt a gun barrel against her back.

"Walk through that door." It was straight ahead, already open.

In this manner Emma was directed down to a concrete basement with a drain in the middle of the floor, and an iron cage that looked like the one ISIS had used to burn to death an airman.

"Stop," the woman ordered as they neared the cage. "I'm going to undress you and hose you down."

"Can you take these off?" Emma asked, wiggling her hands behind her back.

"Once you're locked in there, I'll do that."

Again, she handled Emma carefully, slicing off her pants, shirt, and underpants before spraying her with a garden hose. The water was cold. Emma shivered, marching into the cage as soon as Peggy opened it. More than anything, she wanted to get away from her.

As soon as Peggy closed it, she slipped a thick padlock between matching rings and snapped it shut.

"Turn around." She reached in the cage and cut off the cuffs on Emma's wrists. "Now take off your bra."

"Please don't do this to me."

"*This* is nothing."

Emma reached back, undid the clip, and handed the bra over, noticing that the bars of the cage were heavily welded. No place to sit, no toilet, not even a bucket. And her cramps were getting brutal. She thought of curling up again, but the bottom of the cage was also crisscrossed with metal bars.

"Are you thirsty?"

"Yes, I'm really hungry, too." Even with the cramps. She hadn't eaten since yesterday.

The woman brought over the hose and let Emma drink her fill. She said nothing about food before walking up the stairs and closing the door.

But she did leave the light on. Emma was grateful until she looked up and saw why: a ceiling-mounted camera was pointed at her. When she moved, the camera moved.

She looked more closely at the ceiling and saw two more cameras trained on her.

What's she going to do to me?

That was when her eyes fell to the walls and floor. With the greatest apprehension she studied the room. And then she saw it. There could be no mistaking its purpose.

It was an instrument of unutterable pain.

CHAPTER 30

VINKO STARES AT HIS computer's blank screen. There's no electricity. That's clear, and the desktop doesn't have a battery capable of running much more than the device's internal clock. He jumps right onto his laptop, but those batteries aren't working. That makes no sense, unless he's been hacked and the batteries drained while he slept.

He's never bothered with a gas generator because his backup was always hydro from two streams that run across his acreage down to Hayden Lake. But the streams are nothing but a trickle, dried by an unusual yearlong drought.

Vinko points his binoculars up and down the lake, trying to spy lights or any other signs of power, but it's autumn, the slow season. There's nothing burning out there. Why would there be at this hour?

He grabs his phone. Why didn't he think of that first? But it's not working, either. Tiny pulses of panic thrum in the bottom of his gut.

The NSA. They know you're Steel Fist. They could be moving in on you right this second.

He feels marooned on an offline island. He has no idea of what's going on in the world—or even on his own damn website.

Biko stares at him from his spot on the floor in Vinko's office, the border collie the only consistent presence this morning. It's close to ten-thirty. They both hear the goats. The beasts need airing, food. Vinko swears and storms out of the house. He feels unhinged. The most critical time of his online life, and he's been shut off like a light switch.

He opens the barn. Goats spill out into the sunlight. Vinko eyes the lake. Same as it always was. The very normalcy is unnerving.

. . .

Golden Voice peers at Vinko through her high-powered telescope, taking great pleasure in his evident frustration. She couldn't very well let him go online this morning, now could she? Not after taking over his website and impersonating him with his subscribers. While he slept, she used her massive catalogue of his responses to their questions over the years to keep up appearances. He has no idea that Steel Fist has been hijacked. She'll be using his name for many years. But for the man who claimed it first, it's all over but the burial.

She must move quickly, though. Once he's done with his goats she can't give him any time to head into town to try to find out what's going on in Hayden Lake. Which is nothing, which would tell him far more than she wants him to know. She can't imagine that he doesn't have plans for his escape and his "bail-out bag"—phony passports, cash reserves, compact weapons, maybe even supplies for wilderness survival. She has all of that and more.

Golden Voice steps back from her telescope, smiling at the prospect of what she's about to do to him. Even more charming to her is what she'll do to his followers.

She walks down to the basement with a bowl of cold oatmeal for Emma Elkins. The girl squats in the corner of her cage, hunched over like a chimp. Golden Voice checked on her twice during the night. The girl didn't sleep well on those metal bars; she was tossing and turning every time her warder looked at the monitor.

She must be exhausted.

"Hungry, are we?"

Emma surprises Golden Voice by shaking her head.

"I'm bleeding," she says, "from down there."

"How's your bellyache?"

"It's more like cramps. But I don't think it's my period. It really hurts."

Golden Voice hears pleas for help underlining the young woman's voice. She sounds scared of her own body, when she should really be terrified of the one moving closer to her cage.

"You've probably miscarried. I thought that was happening when you started whining on the plane. I'm going to wash that mess down the drain." Golden Voice walks over to the hose. "You must be very happy. You got rid of your baby just like you planned."

"I'd decided to keep it."

"That's what you're telling yourself now."

"No, I did. I knew I'd get all the help I need because my mother is very—"

"Successful? Comfortable? She is. But not for long. She's on her way to *save* you. Isn't that sweet?" Golden Voice trills. "I'm sure you saw my chainsaw." She drops the hose and walks over to a hunter's orange Husqvarna case. It lies open, displaying a chainsaw long enough to cut through a thick tree. She jerks hard on the cord, bringing it to life.

"Better get up. Better get ready to *move*, Emma, because I can reach in with this. It'll give me a lot more to wash down the drain."

She lunges at Em, who throws herself from the corner of the cage, banging and scraping her elbows and knees on the iron bars. The blade comes within inches of taking off her foot.

"I'll get you when I really want to," Golden Voice shouts above the screaming saw. Exhaust pours from it, graying the air. "But I don't want to cut you too much before your mother joins you. You're such a performer, right? You love to sing, and every singer needs an audience. You'll have millions of people watching you, including your mom. You'll be naked and dead and I'll make sure to cut you right up the middle."

She shuts off the saw and pulls it out of the cage, then points it toward a ceiling camera. "I'll feed out to millions of viewers. They'll see every cut. They'll hear every scream. But they'll never know that I'll be overseeing your slaughter because I'll be wearing the mask. We'll have our own Halloween down here."

Golden Voice strolls to a cabinet and pulls out four iron stakes with steel cuffs attached to the ends. She carries them with no apparent effort to the center of the cellar. The drain sits a few feet away. She sinks each stake into an opening in the floor, locking them in place with a neat twist of the bar.

"Stand up," she tells Emma.

The young woman huddles as far from Golden Voice as possible. She shakes visibly. Golden Voice grabs the hose and hits her with a powerful stream, washing the blood from her legs. The water turns pink and foamy and floods across the floor, swirling down the drain.

. . .

Lana spots Fairchild Air Force Base in Spokane, Washington. From the air, the nearby city looks much like many of its mid-size western counterparts: a lone river amid ribbons of roads and highways that lace together urban areas, contiguous suburban towns, and exurban sprawl. All of it overseen by dusty mountains that look as dry as petrified rocks.

She reaches over and pats Cairo on the head. The hero of Abbottabad is strapped into a canine harness. She wonders how many missions he's been on and whether he'll survive this one.

Lana had caught up on news as she flew west, learning that the CDC had restarted smallpox vaccination programs in conjunction with the Army. Everyone seeking inoculation is now carefully searched by Army personnel or National Guard units. That precaution has led to massive lines but, so far, no more suicide bombings. The most recently declared quarantine areas are in the upper Midwest, eastern Mississippi, and, oddly enough, the U.S. Virgin Islands.

As they come in for a landing, Lana receives a short text message on her phone: "Directions on the ground will follow."

Cold comfort, those words—a recognition that someone thinks Lana will soon be on the trail of her own undoing.

By her best estimate, she's beating Tahir to Spokane by at least two hours. She wonders if he's flying in alone. Mostly, she wonders *why* he's flying in at all. Galina lost track of his device once he boarded a commercial flight out of Washington Dulles, which was par for the course.

But getting a seat on such short notice—given the crises and their consequences for civilian air travel—was remarkable. *Or was it?*

Lana told Jeff to alert the Department of Defense about her flight and Tahir's. They'll know they're both going to Spokane, but beyond that only question marks loom for her.

She has a locator on her phone, but can't imagine anyone sophisticated enough to hack the Fusion and grab Emma will overlook such an obvious means of having government officials track Lana.

True enough. Lana's first instruction upon landing is to drive a blue Ford Focus from the parking lot. Her second is to park at a convenience market three miles away. Her third has her take the keys from the ignition and walk over to an old Land Cruiser. The fourth instructs her to use a Toyota key on the ring to drive it to a nearby park. In effect, Lana whisks herself away from the air base and from surveillance cameras before changing cars.

Next, she's told to reach under the driver's seat of the Toyota 4x4 for a phone and throw her own device into a bear-proof garbage container.

Fresh instructions appear at once on the new phone, directing her to Interstate 90. "Turn left on the off ramp." She's heading east, racking her brain for the likeliest destinations. Coeur d'Alene?

Little more than a half hour later, the phone's familiar computer voice tells her to take exit 13 for North Fourth Street.

Hayden Lake? Naziville?

She feels as if a great hook has been buried in her belly and now she's getting reeled in.

Only twenty-four hours ago she was resolute about not trading herself for Robin Maray, even when he appeared on the verge of being murdered. *You never trade yourself for a hostage.* A cardinal rule of tradecraft.

But even then she knew that if Emma had been held at gunpoint, she would have opened the door to the panic room.

Now all of Idaho feels like it needs a panic room, and every mile north a step away from whatever safety Lana has ever known.

"Hayden Lake six miles."

As soon as she sees the sign, Lana thinks it's her destination. But when she tries to use the phone to signal Jeff or Galina, she finds it will perform only a single function: to lead her to the lair.

To the real horrors of the world.

• • •

I've seen Vinko in Hayden Lake a few times. It took some traveling but he's not that far from the ridge where I live on the cusp of Washington's Coastal Range. We're almost on the same degree of latitude. The trips took me past great wheat farms in the eastern part of the state. Where they rolled across gentle slopes they looked like Van Gogh's *Wheat Field and Crow* writ large. All that wheat could feed so many of the deserving. It will.

As my plans assumed shape, I bought a three-bedroom bungalow with a basement on seven acres near the lake, then made sure to run into him a half dozen times in the past year. Simple exchanges—nods, smiles, that sort of contact. Certainly nothing flirtatious, not until I forced myself to dress for the part this morning. Small town interactions, that was all, but enough to make sure he'd think of me as a local when the time came.

That time is now.

I'm driving another windowless van to his property. Not as new as the Chevy in Baltimore but that might stand out too much here. This is one of those four-wheel-drive vans Toyota made years ago. You still see them in mountain towns. I wanted a vehicle that would look normal, unprepossessing when I drove up. That's one of the great benefits of being an attractive woman. Men always underestimate you. Even online, if you make a particularly keen observation, the assumption usually is that you're a man, unless you state clearly that you aren't. That has, without exception, worked to my advantage. And when they do see you, they are biologically driven to think, if only for fleeting moments, that if all goes well they might just bed you. This is particularly true of better-looking guys, and Vinko, say what I will about him, is not bad looking.

I drive right up to his "NO Trespassing" sign at the gate and shoot off the lock. There's a proper technique for everything you do with a gun, and I long ago learned to do this without killing myself with a ricochet.

As for the report, this is rural America where gunshots are now as common as pine beetles.

Then I drive another half mile and swing around his house. And there he is with his border collie and those goats.

I wave. I can see he's not happy. I don't need much from him at the moment. I just need to keep him off guard long enough that he doesn't pull a gun on me before I pull one on him. But I will say, despite all my encounters with men in these situations, only one has actually done that to me. He's dead. And this morning I'm in a skirt that barely falls to midthigh. It's swishy, flirty. My legs are tan, my neckline low enough to hint at my modest cleavage.

"Hi," I say with neighborly enthusiasm. "I'm sorry to bother you but I live right over there," pointing across the lake—I could be pointing at the moon for all the specificity I offer—"and my power's out and so is my phone. I was wondering if I could use yours."

There. See. I've accomplished my first and most critical goal: establishing common ground with him by normalizing his power outage. His face relaxes. Even though my plight doesn't actually explain the loss of all his electronic devices, much less his batteries and whatever other reserves he might have, he has company for his misery. Attractive company. I sit on my heels to call his dog over. The border collie ignores me, but not his master, not with this much thigh on display. More as I stand. His eyes follow my every movement. *Voila!* His fears appear to have vanished, anaesthetized by the merest glimpse. But here lies the irony: We do have common ground. It's what lies between a target and the person aiming a lethal weapon at him.

That's precisely what I do the instant he wanders within ten feet. I level a small pistol at him. He knows he's in trouble now and he's probably beginning to suspect that it goes well beyond not having power.

"I can shoot out both your knees in the time it takes you to blink, so stop where you are."

I put out the flat of my free hand. He stares at it. Doesn't respond with words, but he's no longer moving. Victory number one. "Thank you, Steel Fist."

The name of his secret alter ego brings the first hint of open panic to his face. His lips part tensely, giving his countenance a square shape I hadn't noticed in our brief encounters. Whatever hope he had that this might be nothing but a simple robbery has given way to his worst nightmare—of being found out by someone who's subtly insinuated herself into his life. He probably thinks I'm some kind of crazy liberal out to even the score with a racist. He should be so lucky.

"I don't know what you're talking about."

He's got game, I'll give him that. But I tell him not to waste his breath. "I'm your guardian angel. Can't you tell?" I jab the gun at him. I'm smiling. He's not. His jaw is too busy dropping for that. That is not a figure of speech: his mouth falls open until I'm staring at his bottom row of molars.

I pull a plastic handcuff out of my skirt pocket. "I'm going to watch you cinch your ankles together. If you don't do a first-rate job, I will kill you right now, but I really don't want to do that. I actually have big plans for you."

I do, but he doesn't have to be alive for them to work. I spare him that detail. "Put them on tight."

His dog sniffs me, then never takes his eyes off me. "Tell him to go away."

He gives it a hand signal. It backs up. Clearly, the dog senses something wrong, but he's a herding dog. What's he going to do? Nip at my heels? Round me up?

Vinko finally takes off his boots and puts the cuffs on, cinching himself.

"Now put your hands behind your back."

He shakes his head. "I'm not doing—"

I shove the muzzle into the soft flesh under his chin. "I will shoot your face off and leave you sucking dust through your snot holes if you even try to say no one more time." Then I whisper, as though I'm sharing a secret: "I've done it before."

The great Steel Fist puts his hands behind his back.

I'm nimble enough to hold my gun against his spine and slip the male end of the cuff into the female. We women really can multi-task. I yank hard.

"Tell your dog to herd the goats into the barn."

"Biko, barn."

His voice remains impressively strong.

"Lie down."

He obeys.

I search him thoroughly. Nothing but a little pocketknife on his key fob, but used dexterously, he could have freed himself.

The dog, to my amazement, closes the barn door after herding the goats inside. "Tell him to stay over there. He's got creepy eyes."

Vinko orders his dog to sit.

"Get up, Stinko."

It's not easy with his ankles shackled, but he's an aging athlete and manages to bend and twist and stand without falling back down. Covered in dust, he looks like a cinnamon cruller.

"I'm going to pull the van up and you're going to crawl in through the side door."

But as soon as I start to drive toward him he tries to hop away. This is so ridiculous. I climb out, walk over, and grab him. "Who do you think you are? The Easter Bunny? *Get in the van.*"

He sits and rolls into the open back area. I climb in beside him and close the door. I wrap duct tape around his mouth, as I did to Emma. I leave his eyes alone, wanting him to see everything, though without windows that includes nothing of our route.

I drive back onto the road and on our way to my home pass an Audi R8 and a Porsche. Both have stunning women at the wheel. They sure love their German cars and trophy wives up here.

In less than five minutes I pull into my garage and close the door. He looks scared. I kneel beside him with his pocketknife open. The blade is little more than an inch long. "I have Emma Elkins down in my basement. She's in a cage. You're going to march down there and join her. If you so much as touch her," I unzip his pants and pull out his unimpressive penis, "I will cut this nubbin off and choke you with it."

I press the sharp little blade against the base of his manhood hard enough to leave an ample line of blood. The duct tape muffles his moan.

My threats and punishments will escalate, so I can't afford anything less than sincerity. I leave it hanging out of his pants. "Let's keep it handy."

After I open the side door, I swing his legs around and cut off the cuffs. "You're going through that door and down the stairs."

When we arrive, Emma tries to cover up with her hands.

"He's a rapist, Emma." The reason I made her take off her clothes is now clear to her: she's recoiling at my news. "If you help him at all, you do it at your own peril."

He certainly looks the part with his bloody penis hanging out of his pants.

I leave his mouth taped, his hands cuffed behind him, and push him into the cage.

Then I go back over to the cabinet and pull out a second set of steel stakes with cuffs for wrists and ankles. I set them into four more pre-set holes in the concrete.

Two down, one to go.

CHAPTER 31

LANA LISTENS INTENSELY TO the phone and follows the directions scrupulously. She has little doubt that Emma is nearby. Hayden Lake makes so much sense. Although the original, infamous group of neo-Nazis was bankrupted and forced to sell its compound, the region's reputation had been well established and continued to attract like-minded zealots.

The phone's voice draws her closer and closer to the town. Cairo, in the passenger seat next to her, senses her tension. The Malinois watches everything, even looking behind them. He's shifting his weight, as if he's getting ready to spring out of the old Toyota 4x4 van. He's got the heart, but the legs? At his age?

The phone never leads her into the town proper. Instead, it directs her to country roads, flanked by trees that crowd the land all the way to the lakeshore. Lana notices a compass hanging from the dash like a pocket watch. She's heading northeast, passing large properties hidden by stone walls, steel gates, and nature's beauty, though pine beetles have been sowing the death of the forest that veils them from public view.

The phone tells her to turn "at your next right," but doesn't offer a street name. The voice sounds different. Lana can't put her finger on why. Not a change in tone. Maybe cadence.

She drives onto a single-lane road. But it's not leading her to a house, not immediately in any case. It's taking her deeper into thick woods with dark shadows. The branches look stark, skeletal, and scratch against the van, making harsh sounds, as if they're reaching out to grab her.

Don't be ridiculous.

But the enveloping trees do look eerie, like woodcuts from a macabre fairy tale.

And now she sees why she was given this ragged old beast of a van: the paved road vanishes. There's nothing ahead or to the sides but trees and bushes and rough, uneven terrain.

"Keep driving east," the voice says.

She must be able to see me, or she's got a locator or tracker. On the phone or van.

Lana moves on, as commanded. She hears forest debris crushed by the tires. The visibility is horrible. She can't see five feet ahead. She slows to a crawl, but still drops the front of the van into a gully.

She tries to drive forward. Can't. Backward. Can't.

"Get out and walk east."

She manages to open the door just enough to squeeze out. Cairo follows her, landing gingerly, but upright.

Lana carries the compass in one hand, the Glock in the other. She feels observed, though she doesn't know how. Maybe from the racket she makes as she forces herself forward.

She smells the freshwater pungency of the lake, the dead fish that wash ashore, but can't see water through all the foliage.

Cairo has his nose in the air. "Good boy," she says softly.

They keep trudging east. The phone has fallen silent. Lana's more scared than she's ever been. Scared for Emma, scared for herself. For having to go it alone—or forgo the life of the one person she'd defy anybody to save.

The quiet around them is unnerving. She wonders what Cairo can hear with ears more sensitive than a human's. The forest darkens, making her feel as if a giant cloak is settling over them. She feels vulnerable to Steel Fist and wants to kill the son-of-a-bitch as soon as she lays eyes on him.

"Freeze!"

She hears feedback on the phone and a different voice, realizing that it comes from both the device and a real person. Someone who must be nearby. And a woman, which surprises Lana most of all.

She looks around, trying not to appear panicky. Then she lifts her gaze and spots a camouflaged deer blind about fifteen feet up in a thickly limbed oak tree. The muzzle of a rifle is trained on her from the elevated platform.

"Kneel on the ground," the unseen woman yells.

"Where's Steel Fist?" Lana asks as she lowers herself. Cairo stands beside her. "Down," she says softly to the dog; she doesn't want him shot. He settles by her side, still staring up at the blind.

"What makes you think I'm not Steel Fist?"

"I profile online subjects. That's what I do. He's a man."

"Good answer, Elkins. I'm not Steel Fist yet. But I will be."

What the hell does that mean?

"Toss your gun and the phone onto that pile of leaves." They're bunched against the base of a tree. "Nowhere else."

They land softly. No accidental discharge. *She's thought of everything.* Lana looks again at the tree. *Maybe not. She has to get down from there.*

But the woman's planned for that, too. A plastic handcuff flies out of the blind and falls in front of Lana.

"Put that around your ankles. Do it tightly. If you don't, I'll shoot out your legs. One way or the other, you're not going to be running away. You choose. I'm watching you through a scope."

Lana pauses, wishing she had a derringer to whip out the moment the woman starts down.

She picks up the cuff, feeling meek. She hates herself for that. She sees the muzzle follow her every moment, a murderous shadow.

She doesn't want to kill you . . . yet.

Trying to find hope when her mind keeps racing away to the worst that can happen.

"Stand and roll up your pants. I want to see that plastic squeezing your skin."

Lana cinches herself.

"Tighter. Don't mess with me."

She hears a metallic click. She pulls the cuff hard enough to hurt. "That dog's trained, right? I saw him obey you."

"Yes."

"Good. I don't want to kill him. I'd much rather kill you, but if you can't back him way off and have him lie down again and stay, I'll shoot him."

Lana hand signals Cairo into the forest. He backs away, as though grudgingly, keeping his eyes on her. "Down," she says.

He drops to the position.

"I want you to kneel again. Hands in the air. Let them drop and I'll belly shoot you."

Lana goes back on her knees and raises her arms, the look of a worshipper.

Here she comes.

The woman lowers herself in a climbing harness, now wielding a handgun with her rifle strapped across her back. Her descent is as smooth as a paratrooper's, the pistol never shifting from her target. She's pretty, too. Her appearance doesn't add up. Has Vinko found a woman to do his dirty work?

She sheds the harness and advances past Lana, pressing a semi-automatic to the back of her head. Lana's skin tingles, her stomach clenching. She's been a total fool. She's on her knees all ready for an execution-style murder.

But before she can beg for her life—and Emma's—the woman tells her to put her hands behind her back.

Lana's relieved, for surely she wouldn't bother to cuff her if she were about to bury a bullet in her brain.

The cuffs tighten on her wrists, then the woman comes around to help her stand. She has flawless skin. Youthful. She looks familiar. "I know you," Lana says. "Where do I know you from?"

"It'll come to you," she replies. "Don't move."

She gets behind Lana and cuts off the ankle cuffs. "Walk in front of me. Don't do anything stupid. And if that dog breaks your command, he's dead."

Lana walks through the forest, trying to see everything around her, to remember trees that have fallen or tilt precariously so she can find her way back to the van, if she can escape with Emma. She searches so intently she spots tiny cameras mounted in the trees. A dozen of them at least.

"Are you going live with this?"

"Not yet. But I'm documenting everything so the world will see exactly what happens here."

"Isn't that stupid? Documenting your own crimes?" Wanting to get a rise out of her, some hint of who she is.

"Not in the world I come from."

The world I come from? Lana's heard those very words before. *Who is she? What world would celebrate this?*

Islamist radicals, yes. Russian oligarchs, indeed. North Koreans, them, too. Lana could go on with her list of people who want her dead. The successes she's known, both in cyberspace and in ferocious combat, have created enemies around the world. And to think some stupid neo-Nazi and his gal Friday, or whoever she is, have caught up with her.

They find your weak spot, the way you love your kid, and they control you.

The woman nudges her with the gun, accelerating their pace. Within minutes they come to a bungalow. Lana still can't see the lake. The woman opens the back door and tells her to go down to the basement. It's lit, and the moment she descends Emma yells, "Mom!"

Her daughter stands clinging to the bars of a cage, naked. A man whose hands are cuffed behind his back and whose mouth is duct taped looks over, too.

Oh, God. His bloodied penis hangs from his fly.

Lana has never seen this much fear on her child's face. Her mother has come not in rescue but as a prisoner, too. The woman opens the cage, telling Emma to stay back. The man simply stares. If possible, he's even more frightened than Em.

Lana notices metal posts sunk into the floor with snap clamps attacked to each one. The next second brings an even more wrenching sight: chainsaw.

Pushed from behind, Lana stumbles into the cage. Emma, who remains unbound, catches her. She holds her mother, hugging her fiercely, crying loudly.

"That's the great Steel Fist," the woman says over Emma's sobs. "His name is Vinko Horvat. Okay, Stinko, you're coming out."

He backs up.

She picks up small pruning shears. "I will come in and cut it off completely if you don't come out of there."

Vinko Horvat, looking wretched, steps out of the cage.

She grabs his penis with her free hand. He twists away, which only stretches his organ, making it an easier target.

"I really don't want your dick, Stinko. Just do what I say and you'll get to keep it the rest of your life."

Lana doubts that will be more than a few more minutes. She's just spotted three more cameras in the cellar above the metal posts.

As ordered, Horvat lies on his back, the look of terror deepening in his eyes.

Always holding the gun on him, the woman clamps his hands with two quick snaps, then one leg as efficiently as before Horvat explodes in panic.

He rears back with his free leg, kicking her hard enough to spill her across the floor. Rolling to his side, Horvat pounds the post holding his other leg with his foot. It doesn't budge.

The woman stands and watches him exhaust himself, then seizes his leg and clamps it with practiced ease.

When he turns his horrified gaze on her, she leans forward, smiles, and shoots him in the crotch.

His muffled agony sounds like an earthquake is ripping him apart from the inside out. Gouts of blood spill onto the floor. He twists and yanks on the metal clamps, bloodying his hands and ankles down to the bone.

An Obama mask covers her face and hair. Waving away gun smoke, she ties on a full-length white splatter apron, then opens a wall console with a computer and works the keyboard. She stares at the screen for a few seconds before pulling on thick black rubber gloves. She looks Felliniesque, but for the chainsaw she quickly hoists. She jerks the starter rope. The saw's roar fills the cellar, obliterating Horvat's tortured moans.

She walks toward him, blade screaming, as though she's committed this horror a hundred times before. She points the saw at the camera above him, then nods to Lana and yells, "*Now* we're going live."

CHAPTER 32

DON'S FRANTIC. HE HASN'T heard from Lana since yesterday. Can't reach her. He's tried over and over. Not a word from Emma, either. Wife and daughter have vanished.

He paces the kitchen, pulling out his phone—*again*—this time to call Jeff Jensen.

"Is she in Idaho?" Don demands.

"Idaho?"

"Don't get coy with me," Don says. "She texted me last night saying she was going after Emma out there. Has she found her? Are they okay?"

There's a pause. In Don's experience, that's never a good thing.

Jensen clears his throat. "She's in Idaho. We can't say where right now."

"Can't or won't? And don't dance around this. We're talking about my wife and kid."

"Can't. We're waiting to hear from her."

"I'm not hearing from her, either." Don feels like putting his fist through a wall.

Sufyan rushes into the kitchen, holding his own phone, shaking his head and mouthing, "Nothing." He's been trying to reach Emma.

Jensen, a Mormon, swears, startling Don.

"What is it?" Don shouts.

"Something's just come up on a website we're monitoring."

"Which one?" Don stops pacing at the cooking island and flips open a laptop.

"Steel Fist," Jensen replies.

Don squeezes the edge of the island, then starts typing.

"Oh, Jesus Christ," Jensen says.

Hearing Jensen this upset freaks Don out in a serious way. Lana always said he was the coolest cucumber in the garden, no matter how hot it got.

"Shit-shit-*shit!*" Don's staring at a live feed from the neo-Nazi's website. Now he understands Jensen's reaction. He looks away from the screen almost as fast as he glanced at it.

Sufyan is at his shoulder. They hear a woman screaming.

"That's Emma!" Sufyan shouts.

"*Is* that your daughter?" Jensen asks Don.

"Absolutely." Don forces himself to look once more. He can't see her, but Em's clearly out of her mind with pain or fear—and for good reason: a decapitated body lies in a blanket-size pool of blood on the floor of a shadowy room. Male? Female? Don can't tell. God, he hopes to Christ it isn't Lana, which would explain Emma's hysteria. There's blood everywhere. All over the victim's clothing.

With Emma still screaming, Don can't help believing his wife is dead or dying. He looks up, dizzy, as Sufyan darts away, racing into the half-bath off the kitchen. Don hears him vomit. He can't look at the screen anymore himself. This is sheer butchery. And whomever's wielding the chainsaw is about to start again. No horror he's ever seen rivals this. But he has to know if he's staring at the remains of his wife, so he looks back. That's when he sees some poor guy's head sitting like a stump to the side.

Sufyan walks out of the bathroom, face wet from rinsing. His eyes are damp, too. "Is she going to be okay?"

Don can't speak. Not a word in the world can make this better.

• • •

Cairo remains on the ground in the forest. But his head turns back, though not as far as it used to; he has arthritis in his cervical spine. He sees a border collie running toward him.

The elderly Malinois soldier stands, as if to say, *"Enough's enough."* The border collie is not alone. A stately blonde in camouflage pants and jacket with a short-barreled .357 Ruger is close behind. She stares at Cairo, who's exchanging sniffs with the gray and white dog.

The border collie moves on, leading the woman to where his herding instincts may be telling him his master has gone. A scent seems to have him excited.

The Malinois trots along, not as fast as the smaller dog, but quicker than the woman, who ignores him. She has eyes only for the border collie.

Vinko Horvat told the woman to come back when her husband Bones Jackson died. He said he'd show her a good time. She's determined to take him up on his offer—on her own terms.

And she has Horvat's gun to return.

On her own terms.

• • •

With her hands cuffed behind her back, Lana can't hold Emma. But she keeps warning her daughter not to look. Em's eyes are buried in her mother's shoulder, though they both hear the woman revving the chainsaw as she cuts off Horvat's right arm, the last of his limbs. The body shows no signs of life.

The woman shuts off the saw and grabs his head from a rising pool of blood. When she sets it down on dry concrete, it makes a nauseating *splat.*

She walks to the console and speaks into the computer: "You have just watched me torture and kill the Nazi-lover and *kafir* Steel Fist.

"I openly declare war on the United States of America on behalf of all ISIS and Al Qaeda fighters who have joined together and authorized me to speak on their behalf today. Allah Himself has moved these great forces. Now we fight side by side against infidels and apostates and will soon declare victory over all non-believers. The caliphate must spread across all oceans."

Lana startles. The woman is announcing precisely the nightmare the intelligence community has feared for so long: that the two Sunni factions would recognize they have far more in common than the differences that have kept them apart. For more than a year, Al Qaeda's top leadership has been publicly extending an olive branch to the upstarts in ISIS, urging all jihadists to act together against their common enemy. Now they are, and the results, as Lana can see at a glance, are terrifying.

The ceiling cameras rotate from the vivisected body to the cage, a chilling sign of shifting interest, as the woman continues:

"I have captured Lana Elkins, one of our greatest enemies. The young woman holding onto her is her daughter, Emma. They, too, must die to advance the caliphate and stop the cyberattacks on our noble fighters."

Lana realizes in a horrifying flash that the woman wants to incite neo-Nazis to attack and murder American Muslims to drive them into the arms of extremists. That was the same strategy jihadists, regardless of affiliation, used to bait the United States into launching wars in the Middle East and Central Asia, invasions that destroyed much of those regions and radicalized millions of Muslims. If the radical Islamists' vicious strategy succeeds here at home, Lana knows it could spell the same kind of disaster for her own country.

If what the woman said were true.

• • •

It's true.

On a hilltop less than a mile away, Tahir Hijazi looks up from his phone at twenty bearded men who have rendezvoused with him. They are ISIS's and Al Qaeda's top lieutenants, each carefully vetted for this mission by their commanders in Iraq and Syria and the U.S. They form the martial heart of their reconciliation movement.

Golden Voice has their admiration. Using her extraordinary hacking skills she's made possible the final steps leading to the imminent slaughter of the Elkinses, a momentous victory struck in the very heart of satanic America. History is replete with examples of single, spirited actions triggering widespread revolt. In joining their forces together, the twenty know they are establishing a new and powerful fighting paradigm for the Americas, the Middle East, Europe, Africa, and Asia. This has been approved by the highest councils of the two factions. Now the twenty know it's their job to demonstrate the inability of America's corrupt and failing government to protect Lana Elkins and her daughter. Torturing and murdering them will symbolize the pervasive weakness that lies at the fallow heart of the United States. Sleeper cells in cities across the land are waiting to witness this victory: then they will rise as well.

"I know this country," Tahir assures them as they look at a bungalow in the distance. "Every drop of blood we spill will bring backlash, and that will drive millions of our weaker brothers into our ranks."

The men on this hilltop have ample reason to believe this, for those dynamics have come into play time and again throughout the Middle East, where the middle ground was squeezed to death in every sense.

They look to Tahir Hijazi, who has performed well. For years now, he's been insinuating himself into the darkest realms of Washington power on their behalf. He's a legendary mujahid.

"Golden Voice has taken our first step," Tahir says to the men around him.

"And we are the second," an ISIS commander says.

Nods follow all around.

"But we must *win* here," Tahir emphasizes.

Not a man of easy geniality, he offers a broad smile now. A great war for him is almost over. He keys in a required code.

They move out.

• • •

"You've got to say you're Muslim," Lana whispers to Emma as the woman wipes down the chainsaw. "You've got to tell her about Sufyan and Tahir and your daily prayers. You can claim conversion. Horvat ran photos of you and Sufyan. He threatened to kill you because you were with him. Throw it back at her, get it out there for the world to hear and you might survive. You've got to do it, Em, now while she's going live. Scream it. Put her in a position where's she's *got* to let you live." *Maybe*, Lana says to herself.

But Emma won't let go of Lana, much less stand up to the woman. Em's trembling horribly and clearly in shock from what she's witnessed. Lana isn't even sure Em heard a word of what she just told her.

"She's going to kill me, Em. Don't let me die without hope for you. Please."

Pleading with all her heart, all her love, which is all Lana has left for her child at this moment—the worst she's ever known.

The woman points her gun at Emma. "Lana Elkins, I will cut her to pieces if you don't come out."

Emma clings fiercely to her mother. Her strength is astonishing.

"I mean it—let me go!" Lana shouts at Em.

When she still holds on, Lana shoves her into the metal bars on the side of the cage. Emma loses her grip and Lana darts to the gate as the woman opens it.

"My daughter is Muslim," Lana shouts to the cameras. "Her boyfriend is a young Muslim who helped convert her." She looks at the killer in the mask.

"Say another word and she dies," the woman says softly, wielding the same gun she used to destroy Horvat's crotch before she cut him slowly to pieces. "I'll shove it right up inside her and pull the trigger."

The threat sickens Lana.

"Lie down."

Lana obeys in the hope Emma will survive. Horvat's blood has run across the concrete. It seeps into the back of her shirt.

First her feet are clamped, then her hands.

"I turned the mikes off," the woman says to her. "Nobody heard a word you said."

She walks over and pulls four more stakes from a cabinet and slides them into slots in the floor next to Lana, right below the third camera.

She was always going to kill us both. Lana tries to think of something she can do, then tries to imagine what she could have done. She fails on both counts.

The woman picks up the blood-streaked chainsaw and starts it, sending a warm red mist into the air that settles on Lana's face.

When she walks to the cage, Emma backs away.

"Do you remember how close I came to cutting off your foot?"

Em doesn't reply. Her eyes are fixed on the whirling teeth of the saw.

"I'm not playing games, Emma. If you don't come out right now, this time I'll throw your mother's foot in there, then her hands. I'll throw her head in, if I have to. I promised her you'd live if she came out. I keep my promises."

"Come out, Emma." Lana finds herself praying softly for Emma's survival. As a confirmed non-believer, she'd never do that for herself. But as a mother, those words come swiftly and with the most desperate hope.

Emma steps out, lies next to her mother. In seconds she's fully clamped.

The woman lets the chainsaw idle while she pauses by Lana's side. "You don't remember me yet, do you?"

Lana shakes her head.

The woman leans over her, the back of her head to the camera above them. She peels up Obama's features. "Flowers had me thrown out of the agency after 9/11. She said I couldn't be trusted. Not just me, but other Muslims, too."

Lana winces in recognition. "Fayah Kouri. I remember you now."

Fayah nods, keeps the mask up. "Fay, that's what Flowers called me. She wouldn't even use my real name. She had to Americanize it. You didn't do that, Lana. You tried to keep so many of the 'questionables' in the agency. Did you know that's what Flowers called us?"

"Yes. It was despicable."

"Here's the irony: If you'd succeeded in keeping us around, I would've stayed by your side the whole time. But you didn't. We were forced out with lies and smears."

"It was wrong. I wasn't party to that. You know it."

"But you were party to it. You didn't resign. You didn't speak out. You did what you were told. You were a good little moderate."

"I *did* try to stop it."

"You risked *nothing*. I risked my life to help the U.S. in Afghanistan and Iraq. I lost a brother, a sister and my mother when they were accused of being traitors because of me. But I *still* believed in America. I believed you would help my homeland. I even came here to work for the NSA. They milked every last drop of information I could give them, every last hacking technique I'd ever developed and used over there, and then they put me on a plane back to Baghdad where monsters were waiting to torture and kill me."

She puts aside the idling chainsaw and opens her shirt, revealing her bare chest. The mutilation is breathtaking.

"That's right, they're gone." Fayah's nipples. "And they used acid for the burns. They didn't stop there. I'll never have children."

"How did you survive?" Lana wants to keep her talking, wants to remind Fayah that she'd never joined the agency's pack of xenophobic jackals.

"Men who knew I'd worked for U.S. intelligence bought my freedom. They knew I could be useful. I've been happy to pay them back *and* the U.S. Once, I was for the same things you wanted. I was a moderate. I was for freedom. I believed all the lies. And what did your country do? It supported the worst people our countries could produce, tyrants who terrorized men, women, and children. They forced millions into the arms of the faithful, the believers who could make sense of a crazy world. And now we're here, Lana. All of us. The chickens have come home to roost."

She pulls the mask back down.

"Flowers is *still* horrible. Go after *her.*" *Not me. Not my kid.*

Fayah stands. "First, I'm going to cut your daughter right up the middle for all the world to see."

"But you promised—"

"You Americans say an eye for an eye. This is a lie for a lie. But I will only kill *her.*" She looks at Emma, then her watch. "In minutes the martyrs will be here, and then we'll all take a piece of you."

Emma is seized by spasms, shrieking "No-no-no-no. . ." Her arms and legs, head, torso, all drum the floor with fear.

Fayah revs the chainsaw and steps between Emma's spread legs. The young woman lies naked below her, shaking uncontrollably. Lana screams, "No, take me. Take me!"

Fayah ignores her.

Emma's cries and the saw are so loud Lana can't hear the gunshot that strikes Fayah, but she sees her arm jerk when it's hit and the saw fall from her hands. The tip hits the concrete inches from Emma's torso and kicks back so fast it's only a flash as the roaring blade rips into Fayah's upper body, chewing through her sternum in a blink.

Fayah falls backward onto the floor as the buried blade stops moving and the engine dies.

A woman on the stairs jumps down. She's blond, full camo, and armed with a short-barreled handgun.

Only then does Lana notice a border collie at the bottom of the stairs. Cairo follows gingerly, then heads straight for Lana. He sniffs her, then tries to open the clamp on her right hand with his teeth and claws.

"Who are you?" Lana asks.

"No, who are you?" the woman demands in a Russian accent.

"My name's Lana. That's my daughter Emma."

Em's eyes are closed, face awash in tears.

The Russian woman eyes the body on the floor.

"Is Vinko Horvat?"

Lana doesn't know what to say, horribly afraid the answer will enrage another armed woman.

"Please let me go and I can tell you."

"You tell me now. Maybe live later."

Lana nods and points to the head, realizing when she moves her hand that Cairo has just freed it. The dog rushes to her feet.

"Vinko die like that?" The Russian's eyes move back and forth between Vinko's remains and Fayah's motionless body.

"Yes," Lana says as neutrally as possible.

"Good. Horrible man."

Cairo opens the clamp on Lana's foot. She frees her left hand. She stands moments later and unclamps Emma.

"You son-of-bitch," the woman sneers at the head.

"He was that," Lana says. "Her, too."

"That I see," the Russian replies. "Do that to young girl." She shakes her head. "Get clothes."

Lana and Emma rush upstairs and find Fayah's bureau and walk-in closet. They dress quickly. Then Lana searches for guns, weapons of any kind. ISIS and Al Qaeda, the "martyrs," would be there in minutes.

She fails to find any firepower until she notices a wood-trimmed opening in the closet ceiling. She pulls on the handle, unfolding a sectional ladder.

"Em, can you help me?"

Her daughter looks like she's in shock. Numbly, she comes over. Lana hands down three M16s, rounds of ammunition, and three Glock pistols with extra magazines, then leads Emma from the bedroom.

Seconds later, she hears a barrage of bullets outside the house and knows it's only beginning.

CHAPTER 33

BULLETS RIP THROUGH THE front walls of Fayah's house, shattering windows and shredding sheetrock. Spirals of white dust swirl in the air above Lana and Emma as they dive to the entryway floor.

Cairo drops beside them, as though trained to belly down when the ammo starts to fly.

The shooting stops abruptly after tearing a line of holes across ten feet of wall and windows.

Lana springs to her feet with one of the M16s she grabbed from upstairs. "Stay down," she orders her daughter and dog, peering through one of three small squares of glass in the upper part of the door.

She sees nothing but trees and thick brush. Lana has no doubt that Fayah's allies want to reclaim the house and their reputation as fighters: the ceiling cams showed a woman thwart their gruesome plan to chainsaw Emma and Lana to death.

The Russian woman and the border collie scale the stairs. So much has transpired in so few seconds. She sees Fayah's armory of rifles and Glocks.

"Who are you?" Lana asks, keeping her eyes on the area in front of the house.

"Ludmila Migunov." She grabs an M16.

"You know how to use that?" Lana asks.

"Russian army five years. Private security U.S., pro football. Do you?" she asks, checking her magazine.

Before Lana can respond, she spots two men sprinting toward the door. She smashes a pane with the butt of her rifle and cuts them down as they barrel within twenty feet of it.

"Answer is yes," Ludmila says, patting Lana's shoulder.

Lana keeps looking for the enemy, wondering how many more are out there. Without looking back, she asks Ludmila why she's there.

But the Russian's already sprinting with the M16 and her dog to the far side of the great room that runs the length of the house and opens to the kitchen. The vantage point gives her views of the side and back of the bungalow.

"Husband Bones Jackson," she calls out. "Met on goodwill tour, Russia. Horvat bastard to him. I come back to kill him. Day late, dollar short. But hate these bastards, too. Kill father in Kabul. Who they killing now?" she asks as shooting resumes, but farther from the house. She looks out a window and answers her own question: "Helicopter."

Lana sees the chopper now. No, *two* choppers. They're taking fire from the woods about one hundred feet away. The birds fly almost directly overhead. The house shudders from the backwash and loud *whup-whup-whup* of the rotors.

"Killer Egg. Delta Force," Ludmila calls out.

"Killer what?" The choppers wheel toward the lake.

"MH-6 helicopter. Good news."

It appears to be stupendously good news to Lana—on both birds heavily armed soldiers sit on platforms on each side of the cabin.

What a relief.

Or would have been if a heat-seeking missile didn't rip out of the woods that very second and blow up the one in the lead, incinerating it in a microsecond. The other chopper starts evasive maneuvers. Too late. A second missile takes it out. Two fireballs drop below trees far from the house.

Lana hopes they fell into the lake, which might spare lives.

She nudges Emma with her foot. "I want you in the basement. They've got missiles. It's all concrete down there. Take a gun."

"I don't know how to use that kind," Em says, standing slowly.

She's fired revolvers at a gun range with her mother, but not semi-automatics. They were next in her weapons training, which had been upended by the swiftly escalating violence of recent events.

Lana glances, sees it's clear, and grabs a Glock. She racks it, inserting a round into the chamber, and hands it to her daughter. "It's all ready. Remember, two hands, point and shoot. Go!"

Emma scampers toward the cellar door, watched closely by Cairo. Lana hopes Em can handle being around the remains of the bloodbath down there. *Better than dying up here.*

• • •

Em freezes at the sight of Fayah's chainsawed chest. The blade is still buried in her body. She hears more shooting and forces herself to go down the last few steps.

The door slams behind her. She figures that's her mother's doing. All Em's really worried about is the woman who tried to cut her in half for all the world to see.

She looks down at her captor again.

What if she's still alive?

Em tells herself that's not possible. Rationally, she knows this is true, but her skin feels like it's crinkling from her groin to her upper back, as if she's made of tinfoil. The brute fear also shallows her breath.

She tries to step around the blood. That's hard, it's everywhere. And then it's impossible—because the lights go out.

• • •

Ludmila tosses Lana a phone as shots tear into the house again. Cairo flattens on the floor. Glass shatters in the kitchen. Lana looks up, drops the device and fires toward the back door three times. A bearded body crashes into a counter and onto the floor.

Lana sprints forward and looks over a half-wall divide into the kitchen. The man's hand grasps his abdomen. She sees a wire and shoots him twice in the head, yelling to Ludmila, "Suicide vests."

Black smoke billows into the sky more than 150 yards away from the crash of one of the choppers; the other must have fallen into the lake. She retrieves the phone and backs up till she can keep an eye on the front of the house. Then she keys in a code for a Department of Defense command center. It's so secret she's never known where it's located or even if it's ground-based.

"Identify yourself," a man says.

Lana reels off a digital code, then a series of letters in Alpha-Bravo-Charley style before reporting the Delta Force choppers down at Hayden Lake. "Heat-seekers hit them."

"We have it on satellite."

"We need help. We've got two adults and a seventeen-year-old. We don't know how many we're facing."

"Our count is eighteen. You have some dead inside, correct?"

"Yes. But eighteen more? Can't you get us help? We're way outgunned. One of them had a vest." Shots ring out in front of the house and behind it. "You hear that?" Lana yells as Ludmila takes cover behind a blue enamel wood stove and forces the border collie into the down position.

"We've alerted the county sheriff and local police. The chief is on his way."

"Please tell me you're deploying forces from Fairchild Air Force Base." Lana recalls her planned testimony before the Senate Select Committee on Intelligence about the mistake of relying too heavily on local law enforcement during national emergencies. Then a national emergency—a terrorist attack on the Capitol—claimed scores of lives and shut down the hearing.

"Negative. We sent you everything we have . . ."

Which isn't much these days.

". . . and now we need you to deploy at the first opportunity to see if there are any survivors on those MH-6s."

"Seriously? You want us to go out there? They were coming to rescue us."

"And they were downed by enemy fire. Ms. Elkins, you've had more combat experience in the past two years than anyone I could possibly send your way. I repeat, can you deploy for any survivors? We have no one else available."

"We'll see." Lana ends the call. Ludmila's staring at her.

"They're sending the local police chief and Deputy Dawg." The cartoon reference means nothing to the Russian. "And they want us to see if there are any survivors."

The back door flies open. Ludmila is targeted by at least two more men bursting into the house. Maybe three. It's hard for Lana to keep count as she upends a coffee table, using it to shield her advance.

Ludmila hits one man, who pitches forward as Lana wings a second. He drops his AK-47. She abandons the table and runs to the short wall once more. Peering over the top, she sees him grabbing his shot-up arm and nails him twice with the Glock.

"Just two?" she shouts to Ludmila, who shrugs and shakes her head.

We gotta know. But Ludmila's view has been hampered by the stove she's keeping between her and the men trying to take back the house.

An explosive blows open the front door about fifteen feet behind Lana. She pivots and sees a rifle poke through the smoke and dust. Before Lana can shoot, the Russian delivers a burst from her M16 that knocks the attacker back out the opening. The border collie cowers behind her.

Six down, fifteen more to go. But Lana knows a single heat-seeker could blow up the whole place.

She hears a siren growing louder and races to the gap where the door stood until seconds ago. She spots a Hayden Lake Police SUV and two pickup trucks with heavily armed men in the beds covering their flanks. The three vehicles brake about a hundred feet away, no doubt to give the chief a chance to assess the situation before drawing his men any closer. But blasts of gunfire behind the vehicles force all of them to speed toward the house.

The SUV's rear window explodes and a bullet exits the center of the windshield, narrowly missing Lana's arm.

She throws herself behind the doorframe as the vehicles skid to a stop feet away. The armed men jump over the body of the jihadi Ludmila just killed and dash inside. Using the doorframe for cover, the chief pumps a shotgun and fires at the first hostile who's foolish enough to pursue them at close range. The man falls to the gravel drive with a gaping stomach wound.

With his eyes now scanning the front area, the short, barrel-chested chief asks, "Why didn't you answer my call? We almost got killed out there."

"I didn't get any call. Been a little busy here."

"They out back, too?" he asks, looking at her for the first time.

"All over," she replies. "They took down two choppers. Fourteen of them left, we think. Is the county sheriff coming?"

"He's thirty minutes out. We've got my posse here." He eyes the men.

So does Lana. Some have got to be in their sixties. "Do you guys have any experience? This is war."

The chief points to the older gents. "They're Vietnam combat vets. Those guys," he indicates the other five, "are from Operation Iraqi Freedom. They've got more medals for bravery than you've got bullets, so maybe some gratitude's in order."

"Sorry, I didn't realize that."

"Who's she?" the chief asks, glancing at Ludmila.

"Russian army vet. She's real good." Ludmila nods at him. "Command wants us to go out and look for Delta Force survivors."

"I know. They briefed me. And ISIS and Al Qaeda want this house back for a webcast so they can slaughter you guys online, right?"

"Exactly."

"These guys are gonna be some mighty disappointed monsters. Can you handle that search and rescue?"

"I've got my daughter hiding downstairs. I'm not leaving her."

"We can hold this place," the chief says. "Guaranteed. If you and the Russian are willing to go after the downed soldiers, Will here can go with you." He glances at a tall, light-haired man. "He knows these woods like the back of his hand."

Lana studies the men before her. They look loaded for bear. Not weekend warriors. Real protection for Emma, thank God.

"You up for this?" Lana asks Will.

"I'm ready," the younger man replies.

"I'll leave one of my guys with your kid," the chief says. "And the rest of us will set up a perimeter here. They're not taking this place or your daughter. This is America. This ain't Mosul."

Lana hates to leave Emma, but the chief's posse is already fanning out like a steel curtain around the house. And if any of the soldiers or pilots on those choppers survived ... well, she knows what it's like to be taken captive—and two years ago she also knew what it meant to be saved by heroes in helicopters.

It's payback time, she tells herself.

In so many ways.

• • •

Minutes ago, during the most recent spate of shooting, Emma heard heavy footsteps overhead. She hears more now and someone pounding into the house. Then, almost as quickly, there are other footfalls and a grotesque moan that makes her stiffen. Somebody falls to the floor right above her.

In seconds, a jihadi with a gun and bloody knife slips through the cellar door, spilling enough daylight to let her to know she's facing a killer all on her own.

Was it also long enough for him to notice her crouched in the corner? She doesn't think so. Emma definitely can't see him in the dark. She can't even hear him. Since he came down the stairs he hasn't made a sound. She's trying to be super quiet, too, but worries even breathing will give her away. She starts taking short breaths, but can't stop shaking as she holds the gun. *Maybe he can hear that. Maybe he's right there.* She stares at the darkness in front and to the sides of her.

"I see you," he says softly.

How?

But she doesn't doubt him. And he sounds close.

You've got a gun, she reminds herself over and over. But he's moving closer. He just took a step and made a squishy sound. *Blood. Gotta be.* She tenses. She's wildly tempted to shoot, but holds her fire. If he doesn't know where she is, she'd be giving herself away.

There ... she hears him again.

Oh, God. Does she ever.
He's coming closer.

• • •

Lana, Ludmila, and Will run to the woodpile. Pine scents riddle the air. So does smoke. The drought-stricken forest is burning up ahead. At least one of those fiery choppers must have crashed into the trees.

Will peers over the thick stack. "There's a deer trail over to the right," he says. "We might even get around most of the smoke heading that way. We got us a little onshore breeze that comes up in the afternoons around here. It's going to push the smoke and fire this way. Away from wherever those birds crashed."

Lana looks around. Smoke's plenty thick where they are. Up ahead it's so dense it looks clotted.

Will leads them to the trail. Lana has to choke down the urge to cough. Ludmila's doing the same. But the smoke also gives them cover. Taking the good with the bad.

They draw closer to the fire as they move along the meandering trail, and hear the eerie crackle of flames shooting up towering firs fast as squirrels. The boughs are brilliantly red, spilling cones that look like splashes of fire as they fall. On the ground, they spark the brittle underbrush. Heat wafts over them.

Lana can't see how any of the Delta Force operators could have possibly survived. First, both of those choppers were blasted into fireballs. Second, they crashed. Third, the jihadis would have been on them like hyenas.

Skirting the fire line, they spot the first helicopter's roasting carcass and take cover behind a closely knit stand of trees. Lana guesses the second incinerated bird went down over the lake. She's about to tell Ludmila and Will her three reasons for turning around when they spot a soldier with blackened skin, shirt all but burned off his back. He's stumbling in their general direction, his eyes on the ground.

What Lana and her cohorts don't see are the eyes looking down on the soldier, staring from a camouflaged deer blind in an ancient oak.

Tahir Hijazi commands the coalition of ISIS and Al Qaeda jihadis from the tree's thick limbs. He ordered a small tactical squad to try to take back the house quickly. They failed. Now Tahir guides the rest methodically. He advances them with the cold calculating precision of a man deeply versed in killing, much as he's orchestrated this entire operation, with help from Fayah, for many months now.

He watches the badly scorched American soldier stumble away. *He'll die*, Tahir thinks, either from the burns or the bullets of the jihadis, and will never know the real nature of the historic ISIS and Al Qaeda reconciliation that will soon become known to everyone. Its shocking culmination will be on full display here in the heart of America. Undercover for more than twenty years, he's been providing information and disinformation, depending on the time, place, and people. He's been playing the perilous role of a double agent, always looking for threats from every conceivable direction. But also delivering deadly blows when others least expect them.

That was what he expected to do today, because Tahir has played the game consummately well. He's carefully enticed the world's top jihadi operatives into a grand ambush by the Americans. A deadly sting operation worthy of his long career.

A few years ago he accepted that he couldn't keep playing the double agent forever. His CIA handler insisted he'd be killed if he didn't relocate to the U.S. So precisely when the cyberwars began in earnest, Tahir arrived in Bethesda—a suburb home to so many spies and government officials. Both he and his handler believed having him in the town would play well with the men Tahir was duping in Al Qaeda and then ISIS. And it had.

Tahir hatched a plan to cripple the monstrous forces heaping shame on Islam with their ceaseless slaughter of innocents: He would lure them to America with the promise of chainsawing to death Lana Elkins, the U.S.'s most celebrated cyberwarrior, along with her daughter. They leapt at the opportunity, knowing Steel Fist's execution would trigger a violent backlash against American Muslims that could drive many into the ranks of radical Islamists. Moreover, every move would be captured on camera to inspire jihadis worldwide.

How could they resist such powerful bait from a trusted confidante and proven killer?

He planned each step down to Emma's abduction by Fayah, an old comrade.

But the Americans underestimated the firepower and skill of jihadists, as they had so many times before. As soon as the choppers were shot out of the sky, Tahir knew his own plans had also gone down in flames and that nothing could stop the jihadis he'd cultivated for so long. The forces that were to ambush his presumed allies were dead.

Now, against his every wish, he must command a military operation to murder the very people he wanted to save. The irony is as horrid as it is unavoidable—if he is to continue working as the U.S.'s most valuable agent in the radical Islamist underground. Only his CIA handler, the director of the agency, the President, and the very highest echelon of the intelligence community have ever been aware of the role he's played, or how critically positioned he's been for so many years. "Need to know" hasn't been applied so strictly to anyone since the height of the Cold War.

He looks down from the deer blind in disgust, watching a fighter from Jordan level his rifle on the soldier. But the Jordanian lifts his eyes from his rifle sight. Tahir sees why: two women and a man are rushing to aid the wounded American. The jihadi is doing what Tahir has done many times: waiting until the four come together so he can gun them down all at once.

The smoke forces Tahir to use binoculars. A dark-haired woman is in the lead. She's now less than twenty feet from the burned man. Tahir focuses on her. Lana Elkins ... just as he suspected.

She's a gutsy woman. He's disappointed she'll have to die. But he hasn't survived by making decisions based on sentiment. He'll have to remain a double agent until he can set up ISIS and Al Qaeda again. He has no choice, not if the U.S. is to prevail in the long run.

He watches as Lana's death begins to play out. He thinks of Emma and Sufyan, knowing his nephew will suffer terribly for the killings. They'll kill Emma as they planned, and at some point Sufyan will see her execution by chainsaw.

Tahir tells himself to be resolute. *This is war.*

But he has seen Sufyan's love for Emma. The boy spoke of it in Lana's living room. He remembers Emma's tears when she professed her deep feelings for his nephew. And he remembers his own words to them: "If you are ready to die for love, then you must be ready to kill for it."

The Jordanian is sighting Lana and the others that very second. Three more jihadis come up behind him. They raise their rifles, too. They are silent predators, as quiet as the death the four rescuers will soon know.

Elkins reaches for the soldier. Her companions step behind her. The four are now close together.

Four shots ring out in fast succession. The lethality is devastatingly effective. All the bodies crumple to the ground. Whatever they found noble in their mission dies as Tahir watches, cheek still pressed to the stock of his rifle.

He's shot the Jordanian and the three jihadis by the man's side. A fifth now appears, staring at Tahir, eyes wide at what his commander has done. He's already on his phone, surely alerting the others. Tahir has known this Al Qaeda fighter since they fled Afghanistan together. As the man darts toward a tree, Tahir shoots him, too, declaring his ultimate allegiance.

Tahir has killed for Sufyan, for the boy's future. He has killed for love.

He sees Lana staring at him. She looks shocked. She staggers, like she's dizzy for a second or two. But maybe she also sees that the deaths he's delivered will not be enough. At best Lana and her cohorts have only the slightest chance of succeeding, as Tahir judges it highly unlikely the jihadis can be defeated by two women, two men, and a soldier who looks like he's dying.

But Tahir knows nothing of the veterans who've established a perimeter around the house. What he would recognize now, if he could see them in their ball caps and hunters' camo, is a fierceness he knows well: the strength that comes from making a firm and final decision to defend decency.

• • •

Lana watches Tahir race toward them, tells her companions to hold their fire as she kneels by the soldier, who's collapsed to the ground.

"Pull him out of sight," Tahir orders. "We can't take him. We are outnumbered two to one."

"No we're not," Will says. "I don't know who you are—"

"He's with us," Lana interrupts.

"—but we've got six combat vets securing the house."

"Not enough," Tahir says. "It will be guerilla war in this forest."

"Which is burning down," Will responds. "We can drive them like animals right into the arms of my buddies out there."

"The jihadis are all headed to the house, right?" Lana says to Tahir.

"That is correct."

"Then we just have to make sure they can't retreat. And they won't know we're behind them."

Tahir nods, but Lana senses his uneasiness. She has worries of her own. "What about the heat-seekers? Will they use them on that place?"

"No, they want the victory on camera. They will die before giving that up."

"That's what I figured." Web propaganda savvy, as always.

Will calls in the plan to the chief, who tells him they'll be ready.

Lana and Tahir carry the soldier to the base of the tree with the deer blind.

She, Ludmila, Will, and Tahir circle back, making sure they're well behind the invaders. Much of the forest is burning, but they glimpse men up ahead advancing along both edges of the fire line.

Lana and Ludmila trail the men on the right, keeping a good couple hundred feet between themselves and the jihadis. Will and Tahir track the men skirting the flames on the left. With all the fire and smoke, it looks like the gates of hell.

• • •

Emma hears shooting farther from the house. She feels horribly abandoned and scared out of her mind, but she can't make a sound because the man is still down there with her in the dark.

Somewhere.

Minutes pass. An eternity for the terror she feels. She can't hold the gun out any longer. Her arms throb from the weight, her stomach from fear.

She tries mightily to make her ears hear more than they've ever heard before. But of course they can't. Neither can she understand how he can possibly move without giving himself away. Then she startles when she hears him only a couple of feet to the side. She fires impulsively before realizing he's tricked her by tossing a tool or . . .

Or a what, Em? she says to herself. *A head?*

She feels sick. Now he knows exactly where she is.

He throws something else. It lands right in front of her. She doesn't fall for that stunt again. But this time it's no trick. He grabs the gun and twists it away from her.

"I've got you," he says merrily with an American accent. One of the country's homegrown horrors. "I had to kill some old creep up there to get to you, and now it's your turn."

He forces her to the concrete, jamming his knee into her chest until her ribs feel like they'll crack. Then he pulls out a penlight and points it at her face, blinding her. "Let's finish what Golden Voice started."

He drags Emma across the floor and begins cuffing her to the posts. She screams herself hoarse and tries to fight him off. He pistol-whips her so fast she's paralyzed with pain and, bereft of hope, gives up because they really are alone in the house. Em's sure of it now. Her mother would have saved her somehow.

Now that she's spread-eagled on the floor, he pulls the chainsaw out of Fayah's chest and starts it. "Still works." He waves it in front of Emma's face before letting it idle. "But first, I'm checking the breaker box. Gotta get those cameras working."

She watches him rest the chainsaw inches from her head and rush up the stairs, where he pauses to look out. Before disappearing from view, he calls out to her, "It's just you and me."

Not quite.

A moment later Cairo stands at the top of the stairs. Emma sees him backlit, his nose in the air, sniffing.

"Come, please come," she calls to him.

The old dog descends slowly and ambles over to her. He sniffs her cuffs, as he had her Mom's. "Yes, do it," Em says to him, having no idea what kind of command makes a dog free you. Maybe no command. Maybe instinct for his master.

Em would never learn the answer because the jihadi returns, throwing on the lights. The camera directly above her responds to movement, pointing down at Emma. She tells Cairo to sit. The dog settles on his haunches.

As the young man approaches, she begs him not to hurt Cairo. "He's my dog. He's really old. Just leave him alone, please." Her plea is genuine, and she doesn't have to force the tears, but she's trying to pull off a trick of her own.

"Your pet, huh?" he says, smiling.

"Yes," she sobs. "He's old and sick. Just leave him alone."

The guy walks closer. Cairo glances at him, but remains sitting as commanded.

"Good dog, eh?" He smiles, petting Cairo's head.

The dog remains still.

"So you won't hurt him, then?" Em says, crying.

"No, why would I do that?"

The man crouches down, one hand on Emma's breast, the other resting on Cairo's shoulder. He's petting both. "Matter of fact, I'll give him a new home 'cause he's gonna need one, right, boy?" His hand moves back to Cairo's head, which he strokes affectionately.

"Don't ever hurt him, whatever you do."

"Of course not, but I'm gonna have to hurt you. You've got it coming. Him, never," he adds with a glance at Cairo.

Em's trying desperately to remember the command for attack. *Kill*? *Get him*? She and her dad learned all that with the trainer when they brought Jojo home. She thought it would be the same with Cairo but she can't remember.

Em's about to try "Kill!" when the man pulls Cairo close to cuddle.

With a grisly growl, the old Malinois rips into his face, tearing off beard and cheek down to his jaw, then seizes the bastard's neck and pins him to the floor.

Cairo has one of his own commands: *never ever try to cuddle with me.*

He's growling with a mouthful of neck, fangs deep in the man's flesh. He shakes his prey as he might a big fat rat, and looks at Emma, who sees the man reaching for his gun.

"Kill him!" she screams.

A second later, certainly no more, there is only a gaping red hole where the man's throat was.

Jugular severed, he bleeds out quickly.

Cairo starts to work on one of Emma's wrist cuffs.

• • •

Lana moves as quietly as she can to the right of the charred, smoldering forest. Ludmila is by her side. The flames move forward on the strength of the onshore breeze.

She and Ludmila have one objective: keep the jihadis in front of them so the chief and his posse can ambush every last one of them.

Each step Lana takes in the brittle undergrowth sounds like a thunderclap to her, even though the sharp crackle of burning trees and bushes overwhelms their footfalls.

There are at least six killers up ahead on their side of the fire.

Lana knows she'll do anything to stop those madmen from slaughtering the vets and getting into that house. *That cellar.* Emma always foremost in mind.

Looking left, she glimpses Tahir and Will, the one so dark, the other fair. She remembers meeting Tahir for the first time, the anger she felt from him as palpable as molt. But Tahir's love for Sufyan, and his nephew's love for Emma, had turned the former jihadist around. The irony of love's role in bringing them to this blood-ridden battleground is not lost on Lana.

Ahead of her, through shifting veils of smoke, she sees jihadis nearing Fayah's backyard.

Ludmila, as tall as Lana, settles next to her and motions for her to kneel in the sparse cover. They both watch as the bearded men venture into the open.

When the posse's first shots ring out, she and the Russian duck deeper into the unburned forest to their right, seeking shelter from the potential friendly fire.

Two jihadis are hit instantly. Four others race forward shooting and are also cut down. But the rearmost fighter retreats, running hard from the posse's small-arms barrage. He barrels into the forest and hunkers down.

Lana and Ludmila watch him. They creep forward, staying low.

One of the men in the yard looks back at the sound of their shooting, but the next instant is killed himself.

Lana hears distant shots and sees that Tahir and Will on the far side of the fire are also cutting down jihadis. One of the men in front of them barrels toward the woodpile before detonating his suicide bomb. His cohorts, Lana guesses, must already have been hit. The woodpile, eight feet deep and six feet high, is singed and shakes violently. Most of it, though, remains standing.

The shooting stops, but Lana feels the tension still building. Who among the jihadis is simply wounded and now waiting with his hand on a button? And there's the man hiding ahead of them in the trees.

They continue moving toward him, wary of another suicide vest, when he rises up with the rocket launcher, which must have been stashed behind a tree. Lana realizes the missile is the jihadis' last resort. She and Ludmila open fire, cutting him down.

After moving closer, Ludmila shoots him in the head, taking no chances. The pair enter the clearing with extreme caution, every step feeling like a passage through a minefield, not of munitions but of men.

Ludmila puts a bullet into the brains of all six bodies. Lana didn't have the stomach for systematically executing men who might be wounded, but she can't deny that she's grateful for Ludmila's actions.

The posse has yet to step from behind the woodpile, but the police chief calls out to them: "Thirteen accounted for here, plus the seven back at the house. There's still one out there."

"No, he's in here," Emma calls from the house.

Lana can't see her daughter, but warns her to stay inside.

"Cairo killed him," Em goes on.

"Then that's twenty-one, all of 'em," the chief yells.

But it's not over.

At that moment, Lana realizes the posse doesn't know about Tahir.

They'll mistake him for—

"We have an African man with us now," she yells, interrupting her own thoughts. "He's one of us."

Her shouts issue just as Tahir steps from the brush and smoke to join Will, who's keeping his distance from the fallen, but eyeing them carefully.

Tahir, like Ludmila, spares no sentiment. He shoots six of the enemy in the head, veering left for the seventh, a man lying crumpled on the ground. Tahir raises his rifle for the last time when the jihadi detonates his suicide vest.

Will, Ludmila, and Lana dive for the ground as a roaring pressure wave expands the air around them. She hears burning fragments whistle by her, every one of which can kill or maim.

"Ludmila?" she says the second she knows that she herself has been spared.

"Fine," the Russian replies.

So is Will. But Tahir is not.

Lana runs to the bloodshed, hoping for a miracle. There is none. She freezes at the sight, eyes squeezing shut. All she can think about is the life-saving choice the Sudanese made minutes ago up in the deer blind. He didn't have to kill the four jihadis. He could have let her die along with Will, Ludmila, and the soldier. But he bet that after so many years of his double life, he could take a final stand and try to give his family a stable future.

And perhaps he had.

EPILOGUE

THE BRIDE STOOD WITH her father at the end of an aisle, flanked on both sides by rows of crisply attired guests on folding chairs. She glowed in the brilliant sun-cast rays streaking her white gown. The park setting was as lush as the orchids and magnolias adorning the bridal arch, where the pastor, groom, and best man waited.

A harpist struck the familiar first notes. About a hundred people rose to watch the young woman stroll past.

Don stood to Lana's left on the aisle proper, Emma beside her with Sufyan. Lana glanced at the young man, knowing how empty his home felt since the loss of his uncle. He had grieved for months, but smiled now as Em took his hand. At least his uncle had long ago seen to their well-being.

Lana also took some comfort in the fact that while Fayah Kouri's indoor and outdoor cameras had captured most of the violence in Hayden Lake, smoke had obscured the gruesome killing of Tahir by a suicide bomber. Sufyan would never have to endure the sight of that explosion.

More than one billion viewers had so far clicked onto the videos of the battles at Fayah's house. The decisive defeat of ISIS and Al Qaeda's first major act of joint terrorism had led to the exchange of vicious recriminations on social media from partisans of each radical Islamist group.

Divide and conquer.
Maybe.

Emma took her mother's hand. Lana noticed that she still held Sufyan's, and wondered whether they'd marry. She hoped that decision remained a few years away, although they had both decided to attend the University of Maryland at College Park to study computer science. Emma planned to minor in criminal justice with an eye on eventually joining the FBI Academy in Quantico, Virginia. Sufyan joked that he planned to minor in basketball—a small miracle that he could laugh at all so soon.

Now the ring-bearer started up the aisle. The pastor needed but one small hand signal to bring the border collie—now named Good Boy—to the arch. Soft-gripped in his mouth, the dog held the handle of a small wicker basket carrying the wedding bands. When he heeled by the couple, Lana would have sworn the dog was smiling. His new master certainly was.

Lana's own dog, Jojo, was back on his feet after more than a month of drug-induced immobility. When he rose for the first time at the veterinarian's office, his legs were shaky as a newborn calf's. But as soon as he steadied, he walked over to Emma. It was as if he sensed that she, more than anyone, needed to feel extra-protected. Jojo went almost everywhere with Em now, as much an emotional support dog as a guard.

Cairo was back in retirement at the kennel owned by Deputy Director Holmes's son. The old Malinois and Bob were both in pretty good shape, considering all they'd been through. Holmes's first act upon reassuming his duties was to force Marigold Winters to resign. She promptly took a position with a Washington think tank that shared her xenophobic beliefs.

Fortunately, she hadn't had much to seize upon of late. For more than five months, the country had experienced a respite from radical Islamist violence, but Lana had not let down her guard. She knew the invisible invaders hadn't disappeared. From her own cybersleuthing she'd gleaned that those men and women remained as determined as ever to defeat the U.S. and, like their kinetic counterparts, were doing all they could to learn from their failures so their successes could prove more deadly in the near future.

The other invisible invader was smallpox, but those outbreaks had become rarer and more tightly contained.

The pastor cleared his throat and the ceremony began. The bride and groom exchanged vows and rings and then kissed at the pastor's invitation.

Lana marveled over the lovely couple. *Who would have thought?*
She looked around, spotting a few smallpox survivors. They would always bear their scars, but some were luckier than others. Among the latter was Matt Lauer, leading the applause as the couple walked down the aisle together. Without him, Jimmy McMasters and Ludmila Migunov might never have met.

The Today Show had dedicated an hour to the pair's "spectacular bravery," as Lauer called it, introducing them a couple of weeks after Hayden Lake and Jimmy's long-odds heroics in the Gulf.

The boat racer had been brought on set first, appearing with his hands up and saying, "Don't worry, Matt. No hugs today, I promise."

Lauer had laughed and pulled Jimmy close for a squeeze. Ludmila, appearing seconds later, received a warm embrace as well.

Tasteful videos of Jimmy's shootout on the oil rig—and quick thinking on the speed boat—earned the admiration of millions of viewers, as did Ludmila's daring marksmanship in the basement that Fayah Kouri had turned into a torture chamber.

But the real excitement on set had taken place between the two heroes, who might have been on a dating show for all the chemistry that sparked during those sixty minutes.

By the show's end, Lauer jokingly asked if a wedding would soon be in the works.

Indeed.

Ludmila had invited Lana and her family. For her part, Lana had been honored, but she also realized the wedding would make a likely target for terrorists. What better way to take revenge than by striking back at America's newly crowned heroes?

So Lana's Sig Sauer hid in her clutch, and ample agents had stationed themselves around the perimeter. Even a chopper had swept over the Oysterton park moments before the ceremony began.

But for now there were only best wishes for the couple and the country.

ACKNOWLEDGMENTS

I'd like to thank my literary agent, Howard Morhaim, and his assistant, Kim-Mei Kirtland.

Most of all, I thank my readers for their encouragement and their word-of-mouth support.

A number of people were particularly helpful to me in researching and writing this novel. For details on technology and cybersecurity, I thank Ben Johnson, co-founder and Chief Security Strategist at the cybersecurity company Carbon Black. For insights into cell phone technology, I thank Quinn Mahoney, Security Researcher at the cybersolutions company Kyrus.

Any factual mistakes in this novel are mine.

ABOUT THE AUTHOR

Thomas Waite's critically praised debut novel, *Terminal Value*, reached #1 at Amazon. His bestselling thrillers *Lethal Code* and *Trident Code* were also widely acclaimed by readers and critics alike.

Waite is a board director of, and an advisor to, a number of technology companies. His nonfiction work has been published in such publications as *The New York Times*, the *Harvard Business Review*, *The Boston Globe*, and *The Daily Beast*.

Unholy Code is Waite's third Lana Elkins thriller.

Made in the USA
San Bernardino, CA
11 December 2016